Children of the White Star

Children of the
White Star

Linda Thackeray

Dedication

This book is dedicated to my parents and friends who've had to put up with my craziness.

Contents

Exodus

We are the lucky ones.

We survived the exodus to reach the new world, unlike many of our people. We are here because fate allowed us to survive the odds while the rest did not. It is chilling to think the Weavers can be so random when choosing who lives or dies.

From our ship's logs, the journey of House Brysdyn to our new home took place without incident. Thirty ships left our star system, carrying no fewer than five hundred thousand passengers in stasis. However, when the computers installed in our Worldships woke us on our approach to this world, we learned only two ships remained.

Any chance of rebuilding the empire died with the others.

The loss of so many affected us as profoundly as facing the reality of our white star's impending supernova. It is a sobering thing for any race to accept it would outlive the planet of its origin. The White

Star civilisation, representing everything we knew, was coming to an end.

For years, many tried to deny the truth, dismiss it as doomsday hysteria, but the science of the cosmos proved without doubt the dwarf star in the centre of our solar system was dying. Our existence came about through an evolutionary fluke. Life should never have formed here, but through a one-in-a-billion chance it did, and our civilisation came into being.

In the end, it mattered little, because our sun was still decaying.

After the initial shock and dismay wore off and we accepted the situation, speedy action was needed to deal with the threat. It may seem a long time, but fifty years to move an entire civilisation to another system capable of supporting life was not enough time to get the deed done. The Worldships were commissioned by the Grand Council and construction began soon after. For the next five decades, the business of the empire became shipbuilding.

Many deluded themselves until the bitter end. When they time came, they refused to go, unable to face the idea of starting again without the comforts that had always been so much a part of their lives. We tried not to think of those who remained behind, tried not think about their senseless death in the face of their stubborn ignorance when the sun burned its last.

Their deaths added to the tally of the lost since leaving the white star.

The computers recorded as much as possible in their memory banks, storing the information for when we woke up. Thanks to them, we possessed some knowledge of what happened to the rest of the fleet. Most vessels suffered mechanical malfunction, due to our prolonged journey. With no real grasp of how long we would be travelling, we prepared for every contingency, but still too many things remained out of our hands.

The ship arrived on the new world almost ready to fall apart. Considering the effects of the extended voyage on our worldship by the time we set down, it is not difficult to imagine other ships buckling even earlier in the journey. We survived because of good engineering or luck.

Not all victims fell to mechanical failure. Numerous perils exist when travelling through uncharted space: black holes, cosmic strings, meteor showers and supernova. Any of these phenomena were capable of tearing our worldships apart like paper.

The absence of the others proved that no amount of preparation was adequate.

Fortunately, not all ships were destroyed. One vessel discovered an ideal world much earlier than we did. House Jyne chose a world for themselves on the far side of the quadrant. During the ten further years it took us to reach our paradise, they began colonisation of their new home. News of their survival gave us hope. Perhaps scattering our people among the stars would not mean an automatic doom. Even in their damaged state, they reached worlds they could call home.

In some distant future, time might reunite the children of the white star.

We might even see each other as friends.

I

Dreams

He was back.

The same hot, dry wind blew across his cheeks as he blinked and renewed his acquaintance with this familiar dream. Everything here always appeared new, no matter how many times he visited. Perhaps it was because the terrain appeared so alien, with new things to discover.

The blue sky was always the first thing that caught his attention.

For most of his life, he had woken up to an amber sky being warmed by the glow of a dark orange sun around which Brysdyn orbited. The stark brilliance of it took his breath away. Blue seemed like such an unnatural colour. Throughout his military career, he'd never seen another world like this.

Blue was for oceans and frozen icescapes, not for a sky.

Still, this was one of the many enigmas about this place. The golden fields sweeping across the landscape, with the occasional patch of green, was another. He always thought gold or brown in a plant meant vegetation dying, baked in the heat of a warm climate. Yet as he looked at the land before him, he knew these were healthy. The stalks stood majestically in the sunlight, proud and defiant against the wind that gently coaxed them to bend.

They gave off a peculiar odour, unfamiliar but strangely soothing. An ember of recognition sparked in his mind, but its light was so faint and the fragments disappeared before he had sense enough to put them together. Tiny grains of pollen, carried by the breeze, danced in the air. He heard rowdy chatter of strange white birds wearing yellow crests sailing through the sky, chirping with almost human-sounding voices.

How had this world come to be in his head? Was this an amalgamation of places conjured up his psyche? Was everything here a symbolic piece of an unrealised puzzle in his subconscious?

There was a visible shift in a sudden drop of temperature. The trouble with a blue sky, he decided, was that when it grew cold, it seemed darker. Overhead, the white clouds turned an ominous grey, reminding him of smoke. The wind became a gale, stirring the pollen dancers violently from their graceful performance to scatter frantically.

He knew what was coming. The momentary calm always made him forget, but when the tempest swept across the land like a vengeful god, he remembered what came next.

What this represented, he desperately wished to know. Since the beginning, it had provoked a fear so intense it was unlike anything he ever experienced in his life. Not a coward or a stranger to the meaner things in life, Garryn was more than capable of standing up to his fear, but when the explosions began, he wished he could run and hide under a rock.

The initial explosion forced him to his knees. Even in a dream, years of soldiering sliced through the terror and took charge. Above him, he saw them come, dark, evil shapes, like birds of prey, swooping in for another pass. The shape made another strafing run, but he knew he wasn't the target.

It wanted something else here, something hidden.

He never learned what they sought, only that they would set the golden field ablaze and ignite the sky to find it. The beautiful white birds tumbled to the charred ground, their pristine white feathers blackened by soot and dirt. His eyes began to water and his lungs burned as the smoke starved the fresh air and the heat pricked across his skin.

He wanted to wake up and be away before this serene place disintegrated further, but something always held him back. No, not something, he realised. Someone.

The instant he thought about her, she appeared.

It seemed as if he needed to conjure her up in his mind before she made an appearance. The young woman had hair of such light gold it was almost white. Sunlight bounced off it, despite the destruction around her. Her skin was bronzed and, as she ran across the burning plains, she resembled some untamed fire sprite. He never woke before her arrival.

Her blue eyes scanned the fields, always searching while filled with fear, not in terror at the flying things raining death from above, but of something else. Something fuelled her determination to go on, despite her anxiety. It was a futile search in this chaos of fire and smoke. Even he realised it. But she forged ahead, adamant in her refusal to yield. She was driven by something greater than the preservation of her life.

She cried out a name, but he could never hear it. He saw the desperation in her eyes, riding the coat tails of panic when she began to realise she might not find what she was looking for. Tears streamed down her cheeks, creating trails across her sooty skin. He wanted to help, but like on so many occasions before this, he could not reach her in time.

Barefoot and still in his bedclothes, he ran towards her, trying to get to her before the inevitable claimed them both.

It came in the form of an all too familiar final explosion. It detonated inside his skull as all the noise and colour from the attack overloaded his senses. A short scream followed, the only sound she ever see to make in this place.

Out of breath, he reached her at the place he always seemed to find her. Like those countless other times, nothing changed as he approached her. The flames from the burning field towered over them and the smoky cloud so thick it became difficult to see the *sky. The world turned into a haze of bilious smoke and encroaching heat.*

A sluggish vein of reddish ooze trickled towards his bare feet, its warmth staining his soles. He did not recoil or turn away. This was necessary to the ritual, a trial to be endured until nightmare would release him. Maybe all he needed to leave, to wake up, was to see her first.

Her vacant blue eyes stared into nothingness as her golden hair matted with blood. Crimson streaks ran across her cheeks, intermingling with dirt and drying tears. Her face wore an expression of annoyance, as if Death was an early dinner guest. Her chest bore the killing wound. Her charred flesh continued to sizzle, the energy yet to fully dissipate from the blast she had taken.

The swell of grief and anguish rising from inside him was like a tidal wave of unyielding force and he cried out.

He screamed the one word he could never remember when he woke up.

* * *

Garryn sat up in his bed.

For a moment, he half expected to be surrounded by the flames and smoke from his dream. As always, once he attempted to remember the substance of it, the memory fled from his mind. By the time he realised he was awake, it left him with his pulse racing as he struggled to recall why.

Taking a deep breath, he ran his fingers through his hair, shaking away the residual effects of the nightmare. Despite the cool night, his sheets remained plastered to his skin. For a long while, a sensation of being lost and uncertain gripped him, before it evolved into frustration. This was the same dream from almost every night since his return home and, if the pattern held, he would not be sleeping the rest of the night.

After a futile effort attempting to defy the odds and try anyway, he decided to get out of bed. It was still dark outside. The chrono on the wall told him dawn was not far away. It was years since he'd watched the sunrise in Brysdyn and even longer since he was home to appreciate it.

"Lights."

"Lights activated."

The computerised environmental controls responded in a calm and feminine voice, flooding the room with soft, ambient light.

The sight of this room still jarred him.

He would have preferred to move back into his own, but the choice was no longer his. The room was a suite and it adjoined a balcony overlooking the courtyard below. It housed antiques and priceless art from a dozen worlds and boasted fabrics both luxurious and elegant. Garryn felt like the final piece in a museum display.

He climbed off his bed and wrapped a robe around himself before stepping out on the balcony. He needed to breathe the night air in his lungs and escape the rising panic in his gut. Deciding to take up the official residence of the Prime had never felt more claustrophobic.

Garryn leaned against the marble palisade and took in the view of the glorious dawn. It was still dark, but the deep amber sky revealed a warm day ahead. The suite belonging to the Prime was situated on the higher floors of the Domicile and provided a panoramic vista of the city.

Paralyte slept below him, making him envious of its ability to sleep. The capital reminded him of an ancient dowager who sat at the centre of the Brysdynian Empire. Home to the Imperator and the Prime, his heir apparent, it had been immortalised in prose, plays and art since the earliest days of the Empire. The first colonists, emerging from the Exodus, had chosen this site as the place to build their new settlement, after reaching this part of the galaxy.

The Empire had begun from this city.

Now, the jewel was a blanket of darkness, its life revealed only by the twinkle of lights across skyscrapers throughout the sky. Garryn loved Paralyte. He enjoyed wandering through its pavilions, promenades, museums and its parks. One could make a day of riding a hover train from one end of the metropolis to the other, stepping off only when something of interest happened to be along the route.

His mother loved the bazaars and she made him love them too. He relished walking through the stalls, taking in the aroma of spices from exotic places. One could listen to the merchants for hours, haggling as they sold their wares to wily customers who came from all corners of the Empire. When they were children, Aisha had brought him and his sister to explore the markets. They would conduct these trips in anonymity, because she thought the best bargains were made when the pedlars did not know she was the Imperator's wife.

She was gone now and Garryn still missed her. Being home again without his mother waiting to greet him was almost as disconcerting as sleeping in a room opulent enough to be a museum. He was a fool to believe life could ever be the same, given the approach of the Ceremony of Ascendancy. His being in this ridiculously lavish room was proof of it.

For the last decade of his life, Garryn had played the part of soldier. Joining the ranks as just another recruit, his comrades had no idea of his real identity and he preferred it, to avoid any special treatment. He enjoyed soldiering and would have been content to remain one, if not for the responsibilities of his station.

He was always proud to be the son of the Imperator. Not because his father was the ruler of Brysdyn, but because he was a good man and a better father. He'd led them through its most turbulent years and won the undying devotion of his people in the process. It was hard for his family to not share it. After the nightmare of the Scourge, family became the singular concern of every Brysdynian and Iran was no different. He treasured his own as a precious gift.

Even though Garryn was a New Citizen, he was expected to become Imperator one day. The ceremony was only the first step. He wondered if hesitation in taking up the mantle was due to being an adopted child. Perhaps royal blood was necessary to be the Imperator. He was the same as any other New Citizen brought to Brysdyn after the Scourge.

What made him special enough for the Imperator to choose him as the next ruler?

Nothing, except he loves you, Garryn told himself. Because, adopted or not, you're his son.

Garryn discharged himself from military service to return home for the Ceremony, which was only a month away. Once he became Prime, he would fall under the direct tutelage of his father and learn the intricacies of running the empire. Even if the responsibility was daunting, Garryn knew he would do the best he could, because the only thing worse than failing the Imperator was disappointing his father.

Now, if he could only get a good night's sleep, things would be fine.

The number of times he was waking up in a cold sweat was growing. The nightmares had started months ago, but he was at a loss to understand what had triggered them. True, he recently returned from Erebo. The military was sent to suppress a violent uprising on the colony world and, while war burdened a man's conscience, he was a pilot, not a front line combat soldier. Aerial attacks spared him the ordeal of seeing the devastation of his missions up close.

If Garryn dreamed about war, it was one not familiar to him.

Perhaps he should take Elisha's advice.

His sister, the Princess Royal, was two years his junior and very much her mother's daughter. Breaking the stereotype of the vain, frivolous aristocrat, Elisha was no dilettante. Aisha, a child of the Jyne Delegation, raised her children to value tolerance and knowledge. Thanks to their mother, she grew up to be a conscientious young woman whose first loves were her causes and her books.

Spoiled scandalously by their father, Garryn dreaded to imagine what monsters they could have grown up to be, if not for Aisha's discipline. Since her passing, Iran was free to indulge Elisha's fancies, including allowing her to choose her own husband. The majority of Brysdynian aristocracy frowned upon the decision, of course, but Garryn knew his father did not care. Elisha was his little girl and he would never force a political marriage on her.

He was grateful for this. When they were children, they were confidantes; as adults, best friends. It was Elisha who knew the right things to say when he had doubts and it was only natural he would confess his nightmares to her.

Like all soldiers, he distrusted men of medicine, even if he recognised their contribution to society. Elisha suggested he consult a mentalist for his problem. At first, he baulked at the notion. If Healers were bad, mentalists were worse. These physicians, who claimed to study the psyche, saw no sacrilege in demanding access to one's most intimate memories. Garryn neither liked the idea, nor wanted to submit to such treatment.

Still, he couldn't afford to be mentally unbalanced at this time. Not when he was only weeks away from being crowned the Prime. There was also a nagging fear in the back of his mind that he might truly need help. If so, he not only owed it to himself to correct the situation, but to the Imperator, who would need his Prime in the best of health.

So, for his father's sake as well as his own, he had no choice but to see a mentalist, no matter how loathsome it might be.

II

Imperator

"We are the children of the White Star, warriors of House Brysdyn. Are we to give up the warrior instincts that helped us build our empire? When did we become a gaggle of cowards choosing to hide behind a book of law! Peace, my friends, is a word we are using to become a nation of old women. When will these alien ideas cease to influence our society? We must defend our heritage before it collapses from our indulgences!"

Garryn stared in amazement. General Edwen had always disliked his father's policies, but listening to the man voice his opinion before the whole Quorum was unnerving. The commander of the Security Elite stood proud and defiant, staring hard at the Imperator, daring him to respond, but he lacked the authority and charisma Iran commanded in the Quorum. Still, Edwen's nondescript and disarming features bore a quality that often tricked people into underestimating him.

Garryn did not.

Being a member of the royal household had taught him how to distinguish friend from foe. Years before, Garryn knew which camp Edwen belonged. He wondered how Iran intended to deal with Edwen's anti-Jyne sentiments voiced so publicly. This was years in the making and did not surprise Garryn at all. Aisha had made Garryn aware of Edwen's rising discontent with the Jyne years ago.

Her father was Elvan, Chancellor of the Jynes' Delegation. The match took place during a visit by Iran, then Prime, to Jyne, where he met Aisha at a state ball. Neither Elvan nor Darian, the Imperator at the time, intended a wedding to come out of the trip. The Jyne did not believe in political marriages and Brysdyn found the Jynes' diplomatic approach to everything tiresome.

Nevertheless, the two different young people fell in love, to the complete surprise of both fathers. Their relationship produced the unexpected possibility of a new White Alliance, in the manner of their ancestors of ages past. Many welcomed the union as the merger of two powerful nations, while others, such as Edwen, supposed evil from the start.

Until the Scourge, the marriage and the impending alliance became a constant source of debate on the Quorum floor, leaving Aisha with the guilt of causing so much enmity.

Garryn never forgave the slight against his mother.

Today, the old argument had resurfaced in force and Garryn was grateful Aisha was absent for Edwen's vitriolic speech.

Not yet the Prime, Garryn could only view the proceedings from the visitor's gallery. How would the Imperator react to the General's challenge? No matter what the context, this wasn't just a challenge to Iran's favouring of a non-aggression treaty with Jynes, it was also an insult to his wife.

In announcing his opposition, Edwen denounced both.

The members of the Quorum, the elected body representing the regional districts of Brysdyn, held their breaths as two titans waged their cold war across the floor. General Edwen had fired the first volley and they awaited the Imperator's response with anticipation.

After a lengthy pause, he spoke.

"General, if I may be allowed rebuttal."

Iran the First stood up from his seat and descended the steps leading to the Speaker's podium. Edwen, a tall thin man, who sometimes appeared ghoulish, vacated the position and returned to his own place in the Quorum Hall.

As he prepared to address them, Iran reminded Garryn once again how impressive his father could be. His father matched Garryn's tall height and bore the same dark hair. They both shared blue eyes and were often mistaken for flesh and blood, even if any similarity between them was coincidental. In Iran flowed the bloodline of a thousand generations of

House Brysdyn, something Garryn would never possess.

When he reached the podium, Iran did not glance at Edwen before he started speaking.

"My friends, throughout our recorded history we have been a race of conquerors. We defined our culture by expansion and the subjugating of less aggressive races. For us, there was no other way to live. Our empire is proof of everything we achieved, but the Scourge forced us to change."

A ripple of acknowledgement moved through the assembly and Garryn witnessed the effect of mentioning the Scourge. No matter what argument Edwen made against Brysdyn losing its identity, nothing withstood the reality of the Empire's darkest time.

"Many of our children are only now thinking about having their own," Iran continued. "The Scourge is only a quarter of a century behind us and our lack of a sizeable new generation cannot be ignored. Years ago, our dedication to war stymied our advancement in every other field. Perhaps if we had devoted more of our resources to more scientific pursuits, such as medicine, we could have escaped being neutered by the Scourge."

Nothing he said warranted cheer or applause, only a sad acknowledgement. Their condition could not be denied, Garryn thought with a tinge of pity for those who lived with intimate knowledge of what the Imperator meant. Not even Edwen appeared unaffected by the same sadness affecting every Brysdynian man born before the Scourge.

"The Weavers gave us a second chance with our New Citizens. Our hope is renewed because we were given children, strong and healthy. They are our future and I want to see them live long enough to succeed us. I do not want another war where they'll die as senselessly as our unborn did in the Scourge! Our empire was saved from extinction. Let us not squander our next generation by forgetting how precious they are.

In regards to this Alliance, let me remind you all the Jyne were the only ones willing to help us during the Scourge. Remember when the others turned away and refused to even listen to our pleas, the Jynes did not. They didn't exploit our weakness to their advantage, nor did they try to invade us when we were at our most vulnerable. Instead, they helped us try to find a cure. House Brysdyn, like House Jyne, departed the White Star together. Our ancestors meant us to find a new home together and live in peace. We were always meant to be united, if not in territory then at least in friendship."

After the summation, deafening applause erupted, although Garryn expected nothing less. His father was a charismatic leader with the ability to speak and reach his audience. The enthusiastic response allowed General Edwen to make a discreet exit. The challenge was met and answered, for now, but Garryn suspected this matter was far from over.

Still, he felt some satisfaction at seeing Edwen disappear out the rear door with his tail between his legs.

* * *

When the Quorum council chose to break up for day, Garryn waited until the last of its members finished with the Imperator before he went to meet his father. Making his way into the restricted entrance, Garryn was allowed passage by the guard on duty.

His father, flanked by his guards, was on his way out when they met halfway down the hallway. Falling into stride with Iran, his protectors stepped aside and increased their flank to allow father and son some privacy.

"Edwen showed his hand," Garryn remarked.

"I was not surprised," Iran shrugged. "He was never thrilled at the idea of an Alliance and I expected him to voice his opposition at some point. I gather you weren't either."

"Mother taught me well."

His father's expression saddened and a flicker of a private pain surfaced in his eyes. Garryn suspected Aisha's death was still raw for him, making him squeeze Iran's shoulder in comfort.

"Yes, she always was so clear on such things. I still miss her."

"You were married for thirty-five years, father. Letting her go can't be easy. She was my mother and when I go past her favourite garden, I still hope she might be there at her bench, reading. I can't imagine the pain you must feel."

Iran gave his son a grateful smile at his understanding before they both lapsed into a silence as they walked through the halls of the Panopticon, where the Quorum conducted its meetings.

"Edwen bears watching now."

"No, I don't think so." The Imperator stated, but did not care to explain as they reached a set of doors at the end of the hallway.

They hissed open and both men stepped into the Panopticon Bay. While not as large as commercial ports in Paralyte, the bay was adequate in size to accommodate the transports belonging to the Quorum leaders. It also housed mechanics and the equipment necessary to service the vehicles.

Most of the Imperator's protectors were waiting for him in their escort vehicles. A guard took his customary seat up front with the driver and the skimmer began to move after Iran and Garryn climbed into the back seat. Upon approaching the exit, a computer voice declared its deactivation of the security grid, allowing the motorcade passage out of the Panopticon.

Outside, the day was warm. Paralyte was full of activity today. The good weather brought everyone out and the bazaars and pedlars were out in force across the city. With tourist season here, visitors from all over the Empire and beyond were moving through the streets in an exotic assortment. Some paused to gawk at the Imperator, snapping holo shots as his convoy passed them by.

"I wish I could enter into Paralyte unnoticed like you do. Your mother had the right idea about using disguises."

"She did," Garryn agreed, but was not about to be deterred regarding Edwen. "So what are you going to do about the General?"

With his gaze still fixed on the sights as they drove past, Iran answered without looking back at his son. "I am going to do nothing at all, Garryn. Edwen is a voice and voices are allowed to say whatever they wish."

"He has support. His Security Elite are still very loyal to him. I wonder whether we are wise to allow him a forum with the people he has at his disposal."

"True," Iran conceded the point before turning to Garryn. "But the numbers of raw recruits joining them are small. Erebo left a bad taste in people's mouths and the Security Elite was in some part responsible for what happened there. Edwen may be a formidable speaker, and I do not doubt he has supporters in the civilian sector, but it's not enough to overcome Erebo."

"I have to agree with you."

He was lucky to have been only a pilot during the uprising. The surface troops who landed on the moon endured the real hardship. No good soldier enjoyed shooting down civilians, let alone a poorly armed, untrained group of civilians. For months, the settlers of Erebo fought desperately to keep alive the dream of a new nation, even if it never had the slightest chance of becoming reality.

Iran did not miss the shadowy expression on Garryn's face.

"They gave us no other choice, Gar. We offered them full pardons to lay down their weapons and go back to work or to come home if they wished. They declined and we will never understand what they were thinking when they chose to suicide by igniting the ore. Perhaps, for them, dying was better than to face defeat."

"They shouldn't have been driven to such a position at all. The soldiers who came back from Erebor after the clean up was done were haunted. I don't think I'll ever forget the horrors on their faces and it won't be dispelled from their minds for a long time."

"I share their torment," Iran sighed and Garryn guessed he was thinking about something other than Erebo. The grave expression passed from his face and, a moment later, he regarded Garryn again. "Are you now convinced Edwen is no longer a threat?"

"I don't know. I still think he should be watched," Garry admitted.

"But we would be no better than his Security Elite, would we?"

Garryn had no argument to offer.

III

The Mentalist

"Jon, you are not going to believe this!"

Jonen gaped at his normally efficient and composed assistant after she burst into his office out of breath and excited. Always perfectly coiffed and never prone to making unnecessary displays of emotion, Mira was a monument to restraint. Except when she was standing at his desk, staring at him like a wide-eyed teenager.

"Mira, please, pull yourself together." He couldn't resist teasing her.

He never had the opportunity to turn the tables on her. It was always Mira telling him to calm down when some matter made him raise his fists to the universe in protest. Small as this victory might be, he relished the chance at vindication. Mira had managed his practice since its first day and over the years they had enjoyed a comfortable relationship that allowed for playful ribbing.

Eyes narrowing, Mira Giving straightened up immediately and adopted her cool demeanour once more.

"Garryn is here," she stated, her voice devoid of its earlier enthusiasm.

Jonen did not immediately understand the significance.

"Garryn?" He stared back at her bewildered.

Mira rolled her eyes in sarcasm. "Garryn, the one who is going to be crowned Prime in a matter of weeks, *that* Garryn."

Watching the shock descend across his face, Mira took some pleasure in his reaction and held back any further information until his impatience grew intolerable.

"*And*?"

A smug smile stole across her face at making the winning move in their bout of verbal chess.

"He is in the waiting room outside."

"The heir apparent needs a mentalist?" Jonen blinked, still grappling with his surprise.

He was used to seeing patients of importance in his practice, but unprepared for royalty. Technically, Imperators were not meant to be considered such, but to a common Brysdynian they were near enough. Even if his reputation as one of the Empire's most notable mentalists was deserved, receiving a visitor of this calibre was still a coup.

Did Garryn need his services?

Other questions emerged during the short seconds before he gave Mira further instructions. Why would

Garryn come all the way here to consult him otherwise? His office was located in the heart of the respectable Rura District in Paralyte. Someone of Garryn's stature could afford to summon a mentalist to him without any difficulty.

"Shall I show him in? We can't leave him outside to wait. He is, after all, going to be our next Imperator." Sarcasm dripping from every word.

"Yes, of course!" He made a face at her unabashed triumph.

She left the room smirking.

Watching her go, a sudden burst of affection filled his chest and Jonen wondered what he would ever do without her.

Once she disappeared out the door, Jonen tidied his desk of any work conducted prior to Mira's unexpected announcement. He got to his feet and smoothed the material of his light-coloured suit, hoping he was in the state to receive such an auspicious visitor. Cursing himself for not trimming his greying beard when he had the chance this morning, he grimaced as he ran his hand over his chin.

Despite a receding hairline, he kept his once dark hair neat and that made grey streaks seem distinguished. Standing at an average height with a slight paunch at the belly, he projected the image of a man who took care of himself without being vain. At least he no longer dressed like a rumpled academic, even if he still felt like one.

Mira returned a few seconds later with the young man following behind. He appeared younger than the media footage Jonen viewed on the Transbands. Of course, those programs were never reliable and it was a well-known fact the Imperator did not like his children in the public eye. It was only recently that Garryn had finally been captured on holo-vid as an adult.

Garryn was a New Citizen, although one could be forgiven for mistaking Garryn as the Imperator's biological offspring. They resembled each other closely. Still, he did not present himself like royalty when he stood in Jonen's office. He wore the clothes of any young men Jonen might encounter in the city, clean-shaven, but his eyes belied his youthful features. They appeared older than his years.

Jonen stepped out from behind his desk to greet him.

"Garryn Prime, I am honoured." Jonen extended a hand and, to his pleasure, the heir apparent returned the handshake with warmth.

"Oh please, just call me Garryn." The distaste at the title crossed his face in a slight wince.

"Then I am pleased to meet you, Garryn."

This put Jonen at ease and dispelled his anxiousness at having such an important visitor. In that one sentence, Jonen gained an insight into how Garryn wished to be treated.

"Please sit down," Jonen guided him to the soft leather armchair in front of his large desk.

Jonen returned to his chair and noticed the young man shifting in his seat, trying not to appear self-conscious.

He doesn't want to be here.

This was not unusual. Most of his patients had difficulty with the first consult.

"Now, Garryn, how can I help you?"

Garryn let out a sigh and swept his gaze across the room. He studied the plaques on the wall, the pictures of family and even the paintings. He took a moment to study the park beneath the window and realised he trying to avoid the mentalist's question.

"I guess you can tell I don't want to be here."

"It's not an uncommon reaction," Jonen assured him. "Please don't be uncomfortable by your hesitation. Many of my patients begin the same way. As Brysdynians, we possess a natural aversion to calling attention to our mental health. Why don't you tell me what brought you here and I'll be able to tell you if I can be of help?"

Despite his ambivalence, Garryn confessed the mentalist was nothing like what he expected. Elisha had recommended him after reading the various papers written by the man in the science journals she was so fond of perusing. His own view of mentalists was not flattering, but the physician appeared be honest and direct and this inspired confidence.

"I still have my reservations about all this. My sister thinks I need help. The trouble with being a soldier is you become used to dealing with mental issues by not dealing with them at all."

"A soldier?" Jonen exclaimed with some surprise.

The last two decades of Garryn's life was not in the public eye. He appeared from time to time with the family during holidays and national celebrations, but remained out of sight for the most part. Now Jonen started to realise that it might be for a greater purpose than just their safety.

"Yes," Garryn answered, understanding the man's confusion. "I have been a Fleet pilot since my eighteenth year. I enlisted under an assumed name to avoid complications. I only recently left the Corps, because its time for me to assume my duties as Prime."

"And soldiering was your choice?" Jonen asked, fascinated.

"Yes. Believe me, this is a long-standing tradition. I think one Imperator studied and became a Healer, while another sculpted under an assumed name. In my case, I didn't believe I could lead an empire if I didn't understand how it works."

This impressed Jonen. Aristocratic children with exalted lifestyles often grew up to be arrogant adults, but the Imperators avoided this by allowing their children their own paths. It made them become more than just political tools and allowed them to escape indulgent upbringings to become better rulers.

"I must say, I'm rather impressed," Jonen admitted. "Is your reason for being here related to your experiences in the recent engagements on Erebo?"

Following the uprising, a few of his patients were soldiers suffering from the effects of the war. It would make sense for Garryn to be similarly afflicted if he was in active combat.

"I don't know," Garryn admitted and he started to relax the more he spoke to this mentalist. "The truth is I have bad dreams."

Jonen tried to hide his shock and give away nothing as he bade the Prime to resume his tale. He activated the recorder on the side of his desk as part of the standard procedure for a consultation.

"Please continue."

"They began when I went to Theran. The Uprising was in its third month and my squadron and I lent air support to the ground forces. The dreams started not long after I arrived in the system. While I was stationed on the orbital above Erebor, they came almost every night. At first, I thought it might be the stress, because of the civilian targets. Except I was dreaming them even before I flew my first mission, so I'm at a loss to explain what they mean or why I'm having them."

"Describe them."

The idea of describing what he had been living with these past few months was difficult, but Garryn knew if he wanted this mentalist's help, he would have to share his dreams.

"They begin peacefully. I am on an alien planet, one with a star not quite as amber as ours. The sky is blue. Can you imagine it, a blue sky?"

He expected Jonen to stare back at him with incredulity, but the mentalist only leaned forward in interest.

"I remember the place so clearly sometimes. The trees have ash-coloured bark and the birds are snow white, with enormous yellow feathers cresting the top of their heads. I'm surrounded by some kind of wheat, but it's nothing I recognise. The aroma of them is rich and they're the colour of gold. I'm standing in a field of them and it's beautiful. Everything is so primitive. I can feel raw soil under my feet and how loamy the dirt feels between my toes."

"It sounds like a most pleasant place to be," Jonen remarked, stroking his beard. "What happens next?"

Garryn's darkening expression did not surprise Jonen.

His chest tightened as he steeled himself to tell the mentalist the rest. When he was in combat, experiencing dangers capable of killing him easily, he was never as frightened as he was when revealing what came next in his dream.

"The scene turns bad, nightmarish. I can't describe it all, but I remember the smoke and fire. I wake up sometimes and still smell the cinders from the flames. It's like the death follows me into the waking world. The nightmare only lets me go when everything around me is dead."

Sweat trickled down his brow, even though the room was cool. A part of him was surprised by how distastefully describing the dreams could be. When he told Elisha, he felt some vulnerability in exposing his nocturnal troubles, but he never revealed them to this detail.

The nausea gripped him like bile creeping up his throat. He'd hoped telling this stranger would help him, but instead he felt worse. Embarrassed, he hesitated meeting Jonen's gaze until he saw the mentalist pouring him a glass of water from a pitcher on his table.

"Take a moment. Catch your breath. Everything is all right."

Garryn nodded and took the cup, swallowing several gulps. His throat still felt dry and a minute lapsed before he was able to speak again. "I didn't realise I would have so much trouble talking about this."

"No one finds it's easy to confide something so private to a stranger. How often are you having these dreams, now you're home?"

"Since my return from Theran, three or four times a week. On those nights, I get two or three hours sleep at the most."

Even if nothing in the way of treatment took place today, Garryn did not regret taking Elisha's advice and consulting Jonen. A weight was lifted off him just talking about it. Perhaps keeping the images to himself was as damaging as the dreams themselves.

"Am I going crazy? Am I suffering battlefield stress? I know it happens."

"You are not crazy," Jonen insisted, because many patients feared not being found out they were ill, but rather being branded with the stigma of madness. In this day and age, people still had trouble telling the difference.

"No doubt something is going on in your head. Dreams are the mind's way of coping with stressful situations and the subconscious vents what the conscious is not ready to reveal. Our goal is to try and interpret these messages, to learn what your subconscious is trying to tell you. Once we discover what the message is, they will go away."

"That is good to hear," Garryn retorted, although he thought this could not happen soon enough.

"Now I need to ask you some routine questions," Jonen asked. "I assume you are a New Citizen?"

"Yes."

"How old were you when you were adopted?" Jonen asked, entering Garryn's answers into a console in front of him.

"According to my mother, three years old. Elisha is not my natural sister. I believe she was only six months old."

"Any memories before your adoption?"

This was the question to which Jonen wanted an answer most of all. This would determine everything.

Garryn tried to recall his first lucid memory.

* * *

He cried a lot until she came and wrapped her arms around him, telling him nothing would hurt him again.

"You're safe now, little one." Her voice was like a song and her scent familiar like flowers. The scent reminded him of someone…

The memory remained elusive, but it was enough to make him cling to her. He would call her mother soon enough, but during the first year, she was the flower lady.

Before her, he remembered nothing.

* * *

"No memories."

* * *

Hours later, Jonen pondered the days' events while
sitting in his chair and staring into the sunset. Garryn's first session lasted more than two hours. Jonen
should have kept the session short, as preliminary
sessions ought to be, but this case was too important to treat as routine. Mira was undoubtedly livid
at all the appointments she was forced to cancel, but
it was worth the inconvenience.

The young man needed treatment, but feared exposing his condition to the Empire. Even though to
Jonen it seemed a minor consideration, Garryn insisted on the need for discretion. As the next Prime
and some day Imperator, his mental state needed to
be above reproach. This was why he came to Jonen
instead of summoning the mentalist to the Domicile.

Jonen had spent the rest of the session listening to
Garryn, making certain his suspicions were founded.
If correct in his assumptions, it would be in Garryn's
best interest to attend his next appointment. What
Jonen had to tell him might trouble the young man,
but in the end would prove satisfying.

"I've rescheduled all the appointments you can-
celled today." Mira announced, making her entrance
into the room. With office hours over for the day, she
closed the office to the public.

Jonen swung around in his chair and faced her. He had known her long enough to recognise her tone of voice. "Do I sense a rebuke?"

"No, only a reminder that one important patient should not be treated at the expense of others."

"Sit down, Mira," Jonen gestured to the chair.

Mira raised a brow at the suggestion. Her dark brown eyes narrowed with puzzlement as she realised something was going on. She sat with her usual elegance. Her hands resting on her lap as she waited for him to tell all.

"We've got another one," he declared.

She did not need to ask what he meant. It was common practice for mentalists to share their assistant's confidence. He discussed his cases with her on the understanding she was bound to the same rules of confidentiality. Jonen found Mira's intellect to be formidable, because she was unencumbered by popular theory or academic fact.

Mira said what she thought and it was often precise and unique.

"The Prime?" She was shocked, but recovered soon enough.

"Yes," Jonen nodded. "With Garryn, the number is now fourteen in Paralyte. I spoke to mentalist Darix an hour ago and he's reported another two cases. That brings its up to nine at Tesalone. Alwi at Rainab says she has seventeen patients now. This may be the first psychological epidemic we've ever seen."

"We have to tell someone!" she exclaimed.

"I would like to, but for now I agree with Darix and Alwi. We still need more information. If this is a virus, it is the most specific one I have ever seen. It does nothing to deteriorate the physical body and only manifests when the subject is dreaming. It also operates in a very particular age group. I doubt the Healers Circle are going to take it seriously."

"But something must be wrong. How can this condition affect only New Citizens? Despite the small number of people unaffected by the Scourge, children were still being born when the New arrived. How can they be susceptible but not our indigenous population?"

"Well, those children were born in the Empire. The New Citizens are not," Jonen reminded her. "We brought them from Cathomira when there was nothing left of their planet. None of the rescue teams dared to remain long enough on the surface to gather anything but survivors. The Fleet had enough time to get them out, not go digging for medical texts about the nature of Cathomira's biological war."

"And the dreams?"

Jonen had no answer. The dreams were the most enigmatic thing about the condition. They seemed so similar. In every case, they had all mentioned a blue sky. What was it about a blue sky? Some had never been off planet. Those who did travel never came across a place like the one described in their sleep.

It couldn't be Cathomira. Once Jonen had learned all his patients were New Citizens, he'd read everything he could about the doomed world. The planet orbited a red giant. Prior to receiving the distress call, no one believed in the existence of any habitable planets in its system.

"The dreams are odd. The pattern is the same, but the description is different. They all start off pleasantly, but descend into violence. It's always on this alien world. I keep thinking it is Cathomira, even if the descriptions are inaccurate. There isn't much information on the place, other than the mission reports when the rescue team landed. What pictures there are described a world that appears nothing like the one people are seeing."

"A memory, perhaps?"

"I considered the idea. The destruction of their home world is quite a traumatic thing. Many have no memories before arriving on Brysdyn, which does lend credibility to the theory of a shared experience. It could suggest repressed memories due to extreme trauma. Children do block what is too distressful to cope with."

"That must be it then," Mira said confidently.

IV

The Dreaming

Justin!

Where are you, Justin?

Surrounded by the fiery remains of golden stalks, she called out once more, but no answer came, only the braying of dying animals over the crackle of fire. Tears ran down her cheeks, either from smoke or anguish. Frantic, she continued to run like a rat caught in a maze with no exit.

What are you looking for? He wanted to ask her, but he was only a phantom in this dreamscape. Despite numerous visits to this place, he'd never found anyone but her. She was alone in this field, with only the exotic creatures around her for company. White birds, herds of large docile bovines and ludicrous animals that bounced across the landscape on powerful hind legs.

Justin!

She cried out again. She slipped past the edges of panic and ran headlong into hysteria. Terror gripped her, although he suspected she did not fear for herself. Whatever she sought with such desperation made any thoughts of self-preservation secondary. Even when the smoke overwhelmed her, she stumbled forward doggedly, determine to keep searching.

Once she crested the hilltop, she paused to catch her breath and wiped the sweat from her brow. Surveying the terrain, she glimpsed something that made her eyes widen and her expression flood with relief.

Justin, stay where you are!

Justin. The word exploded within his skull almost as loudly as the explosions from the assault above.

To his shock, he realised he understood her. For the first time, he knew what she was saying!

She sprinted quickly down the incline towards him. A reservoir of hidden strength surfaced inside her, now that she had reason to hope. She bolted forward like some powerful preternatural creature emerging from the fires of the world. She had never appeared more magnificent.

The explosion came with a deafening roar.

Once more, time froze in a terrible instant. The blast lifted her off her feet and flung her backwards, like a marionette being dragged off the stage. She hit the ground hard. The weight of her body made a sickening crunch as it landed. Her torso became a charred mess of sizzling bone and cooked flesh while her eyes stared vacantly into the sky, seeing nothing. A trickle of blood traced a thin crimson line from the corner of her lip.

The pregnant drop disappeared into the ash-crusted grass.

Once again, he was too late.

The shock at seeing her this way was more than he could stand. As a soldier in war, he'd witnessed the dead bodies after a battle and sometimes during it. They lay across the plains like uncovered graves, even more horrific than this. Why did this woman mean so much to him? Garryn reached for her hand, felt its warmth draining into his palm.

In anguish, he opened his mouth and screamed.

"M...!"

* * *

"Gar! Wake up!"

The voice reached into his brain and dragged him back into the waking world.

He sat up as light flooded his eyes. For a moment, he lay trapped between pain and confusion, until the cry repeated and gave him focus. As awareness returned, Garryn found himself looking into the frightened face of his younger sister shaking him hard. Elisha's eyes filled with concern as she leaned over him dressed in her bedclothes.

"What are you doing in my room?" he managed to ask, still somewhat dazed. Sweat beaded down his brow and along his back as he sat up and ran his fingers through his hair.

Elisha released him and sat back, her shoulders relaxing...

"One of the servers heard you screaming when he walked past your room. He asked if you needed help,

41

but when you didn't answer he woke me instead. He didn't want to invade your private quarters."

She tightened the sash around her nightgown and shifted to the edge of his bed, still looking worried. The extent of her alarm showed in her brown eyes and her dishevelled appearance told him of her haste to reach him.

"I am sorry," he replied, mortified by the display, and glanced over Elisha's shoulder to glimpse the server standing at the door, withdrawing now that things were back to normal. Garryn made a mental note to thank him later. "I didn't mean to be so much trouble."

"Don't be stupid. You're my brother!" she snapped impatiently, as if she could do anything else when he was this distressed.

Despite his embarrassment, his heart warmed at her irate expression, at this intelligent young woman who would always be his baby sister. Not that much of a baby anymore, he realised.

"Thanks, Ellie." He leaned forward and kissed her on the forehead.

"Are you okay, really?"

He couldn't answer her and evaded the question by climbing out of bed. The sheets stuck to his damp skin as he rose, plastered by sweat and heat. He neared the door to his suite and peered into the hallway, grateful he'd awakened no one else. He closed his door.

"Did you see the mentalist?" Elisha moved from his bed to the nearby sofa.

"I met with him yesterday," Garryn replied as he went to get himself a glass of water from the food unit in the corner of the room.

"What did he say?"

"Not much. He only listened, but explained this is standard in a preliminary session. I have another appointment in a few days, so I'll learn more then."

He took a long sip of water and was soothed by the coolness against his raw throat. He still had trouble believing he'd screamed aloud.

"Good." Elisha rose to her feet and rubbed her eyes. Assured of Garryn's well-being for now, the need for sleep returned. She came towards him and placed a comforting hand on his shoulder. "Do you want me to stay for a bit? You still seem a little shaken."

"I am." He wouldn't lie to her. "But I'll be fine. It was just a dream."

"No, Gar," she shook her head and Garryn noticed something else in her eyes he had not noticed before. Fear. His outburst frightened her. "I've never heard you scream like that before. I don't think I *ever* want to hear you like that again."

"I'm sorry I scared you," he apologised, realising how worried she had to be to react this way. She didn't scare easily.

Despite being the Princess Royal, Elisha was raised without the frivolity common to aristocrats. If she desired, any one of the young men in Brysdyn's noble families could be hers for the asking. She was a beautiful young woman, confident and intelligent. Like their mother, Elisha's black hair grew wild, with corkscrew curls against her tawny and exotic, bronzed skin. Unfortunately, she remained uninterested in marriage or a life at court.

Why should she be? Elisha was her mother's daughter, taught to use her mind and possessed of a social conscience.

"Was it very bad this time?"

Garryn didn't want to go into it or decipher what any of the dream meant until his next session with Jonen. However, one thing was clear: *something* had changed. Perhaps talking to the mentalist provided him with clarity that he did not possess before. Instead of fragments, this time he retained a memory.

"Justin," he whispered under his breath, "she was looking for Justin."

* * *

Jonen wished the decor in this room were better.

Each time he stepped into the room with a patient, the cold and impersonal atmosphere of the place struck him. The requirements of the room did not allow for windows, but the tiles with the harsh lights above did nothing to put his patients at ease. When he'd first established his practice, he'd fitted the Neural Analysis Room to the recommended specifications. After gaining more experience over the years, he'd realised specs did little to consider the human element.

Garryn lay against the cushioned table in the centre of the room, surrounded by intimidating machines, trying to hide his discomfort. Jonen didn't blame him and resolved to change the design of the place at first opportunity.

Garryn tried to avoid the glare of the lights overhead with little success. They made the instruments seem more ominous, even if no surgery took place here, only complex mental scans. The machinery broke down thought to its raw components and deciphered the chemical and synaptic functions of the brain.

All of which translated into the ability to read dreams.

Since encountering patients like Garryn, Jonen had begun devising a series of tests that would allow him to study each dream and solve the riddle of what it represented. After his last session with the Prime, and in consultation with his colleagues, Darix and Alwi, he'd bestowed the condition with a simple and accurate name. The Dreaming.

The initial meeting with Garryn had allowed him to establish the Prime as a potential Dreamer. Now he needed to conduct a more thorough neural analysis.

"Is this going to hurt?"

"No, the procedure is painless. I'll put you under with a mild sedative and activate the analyser," Jonen explained, readying the infuser with a tranquiliser.

"Does this mean I can't wake up?" Garryn didn't like the idea of being trapped in his subconscious, when his dreams had a tendency to turn from pleasant to nightmarish with little warning.

"Yes, it does, but we need to see everything your mind is trying to tell you by letting the dream play itself out in your head. It will also open up your neural pathways so that, eventually, these buried memories may surface outside of the dream state."

A flicker of fear ran across the Prime's face, but the mentalist gave him the dignity of not noticing. Instead, he tried to allay Garryn's fears, because the procedure worked better when the patient wasn't fighting the analyser.

"I'll monitor your life signs the entire time. If there's even the slightest hint of concern, I'll revive you. Trust me, Garryn, I won't allow anything to harm you."

"Thank you," Garry said with appreciation and rested his head back down again, closing his eyes to avoid staring into the lights overhead. "Let's do this."

Jonen nodded before administering the drug through his right arm. The reaction was almost instantaneous and Garryn's eyelids began to flutter. Within thirty seconds, he was sound asleep.

Once he was under, Jonen went to work.

Once he'd attached the relay probes on either side of Garryn's forehead, he activated the analyser and initiated the REM analysis program. The activation lights across the machine flared in random order as the relays connected to Garryn's synapses began searching for data. Jonen retrieved the remote interface and sat down on a stool next to Garryn.

"Search for translatable dream patterns."

"Searching..." a simulated female voice replied.

For the first fifty minutes, the patterns revealed nothing out of the ordinary. The images, projected as a holographic display above Garryn's bed, showed quick flashes of the Prime's daily life. There was every possibility the recurring nightmare plaguing Garryn might not appear at all, but this too was expected. Dreams did not have a master. They came and went as they wished.

After years of psychoanalysis, this was the only fact he could claim with confidence.

Only upon entering the second hour did Jonen's patience pay off. At first, he was not certain what he was seeing. The interface was accurate, but not infallible. The analyser translated the pattern of synaptic pulses within an accuracy of ninety-seven percent. Even a three percent variance might affect the result. Still, as the patterns steadied, Jonen was able to define much.

As described by Garryn, the dream started out pleasantly. He recognised the golden stalks described in the initial session. The setting was idyllic and beautiful. He admired the gold shimmer across the sunburnt field as the stalks swayed in unison with the wind. Garryn walked through the dreamscape with a child's wonder, staring up at a brilliant blue sky.

What was it about the Dreaming that caused all its sufferers to see the same amazing blue sky?

The colour was vibrant and drew the eye to it. Unusual white birds sailed beneath equally pristine clouds, while large bovine animals grazed lazily in the surrounding paddocks. None of his other patients described a place matching this one in beauty, even though other similarities were present, such as the blue sky and the crescent-shaped moon fading by the radiance of the neighbouring sun.

A yellow sun.

He'd never identified a star in the dreams of the others, let alone one that was yellow.

There was little opportunity to savour this discovery. because suddenly the scene shifted and the vibrant blue sky was demonised with grey.

Things were about to become unpleasant, Jonen predicted.

Mesmerized by the projection as the peaceful setting was replaced by chaos, he spied Garryn trapped by walls of fire and clouds of smoke. Something was raining death from above, but Jonen was unable to identify it. In Garryn's mind, this was the only way his brain could articulate the dark shapes, full of menace. As he witnessed the ensuing carnage, the Prime's terror was reflected in his body twitching and jerking about against the table.

Then the woman appeared.

Glancing at Garryn, Jonen saw the twitching escalating into incomprehensible mutters and moans. Ignoring his reactions for now, he studied the images again and followed Garryn as the Prime ran towards the woman, desperate to reach her.

When she died, Jonen paid closer attention.

This was a focal point, because Garryn never moved past this moment in his dream. The anguish became too much. Indeed, even as the thought crossed Jonen's mind, Garryn was on his knees, crying words the translator could not decipher.

The drugs that kept Garryn from waking up revealed what came next. He had now fallen silent, both in the dream and on the table. He was gaping at the sky with confusion and fear. A strong gale rushed over the landscape, extinguishing the fires and blowing ash and dirt in all directions. Garryn squinted, holding his hands up to shield his eyes from the swirling vortex of dirt and cinder.

The vortex dissolved the world around him into a dark, soothing blanket of stars.

Garryn was no longer in sight and Jonen guessed he was now witnessing events from Garryn's perspective. Flying through space at incredible speed, they raced past the silvery, cratered moon where, in the distance, the yellow star burned. Was he dreaming of his departure from Cathomira?

No, it wasn't possible, because Cathomira's sun was red.

V

The Scourge

The dreams were pieces of a puzzle.

Each Dreamer carried a piece in their minds. To learn what happened to them, the mentalist needed to put each fragment together and create the picture scattered by years of repressed memory. The session with Garryn resulted in the revelation of a significant piece of the mystery.

Garryn's dream created a host of new questions. After Garryn's dream, the source of the Dreamers' nightmare seemed impossible. All this time, Jonen had assumed the war waged on Cathomira, home of the New Citizens, was the place depicted in all the dreams of all his patients.

Until he saw Garryn's yellow star appear, that is.

Jonen considered the possibility of Garryn being an aberration. Perhaps he wasn't a Dreamer after all. He could be experiencing similar symptoms without actually suffering the condition. Even as the thought crossed Jonen's mind, he knew he was rationalising. Too many elements of Garryn's dreams shared common ground with the Dreamers. Of course, in reaching that conclusion, Jonen faced some uncomfortable truths. If Garryn's dream accurately depicted his memories, then the blue world with yellow star and the sliver moon could not be Cathomira.

Regression therapy might be the answer, but Jonen was reluctant to employ it. While other mentalists claimed regression caused no more harm than dream interpretation, Jonen disagreed. Unlike regression, the analyser did not fill in the blanks when unable to interpret the synaptic response, choosing instead to skip over the undecipherable data, which accounted for some dreams appearing in flashes on the display.

Regression required navigating through the mind's barriers and the obstructions could be formidable, especially if they were created for protection against some trauma. Unleashing those memories without understanding them could endanger the patient, but how else could he prove the existence of the yellow star, other than one man's dream?

Before the arrival of the New Citizens, stellar cartographers had deemed the Cathomiran system uninhabitable. No one believed the baked planets orbiting the red giant on the galactic perimeter were capable of supporting life let alone a semi-advanced civilisation. Even now, years later, the debate still continued about how life evolved there. Still, if life could flourish on a world orbiting a white dwarf star, why could it not appear on a planet in proximity to a red giant?

In the end, the how did not matter; only the reality that Cathomira saved Brysdyn and the Empire.

* * *

The Scourge took the Empire by surprise.

No one knew from where the disease originated, but after everyone knew, it no longer mattered.

Perhaps the sickness originated with a pilot or a cargo hand on a space cruiser returning from the Rim. Suffering symptoms not unlike Tulisian Influenza, the virus' symptoms of an irritated throat and inflammation of the lungs caused irritation but not worry. Unfortunately, the virus adapted quickly to Brysdyn's lush climate and become airborne.

The first death raised no alarms. Exotic illness appeared from time to time in a space-faring society. The Healers Circle usually traced the sickness to the planet of origin, where a local cure existed. This time, the origins of the virus remained a mystery despite their efforts. Reaching out to the Science Council on the Jyne home world for assistance yielded no results. The Jynes' scientists, with their vast medical databases, were no more capable of identifying the disease than they.

After a time, the Healer's Circle concluded the virus was a freak mutation in a previously harmless strain. Synthesizing a cure would only be a matter of time. They had encountered worse. Or so they thought.

The real panic began when more patients fell sick at the facility diagnosing the first victim. The healers coming into contact with the first victim carried the virus out of the facility and infected family and loved ones who, in turn, exposed others. The high communicability of the disease ensured the contamination spread rapidly throughout Paralyte.

By the time the Healer's Circle realised the magnitude of the problem, it was already too late.

The disease became an epidemic in less than ten days. Cases flared up everywhere and not just on Brysdyn. Travellers leaving Paralyte unwittingly carried the virus to the rest of the Empire. The wealthy began to flee off world until the Imperator placed the entire planet under quarantine to halt the spread to the rest of the Empire, but it was a vain effort.

The quarantine expanded beyond the planet to restrict travel within the system and, before long, no one was able to leave the Empire. Neighbouring governments, fearful of the threat to their borders, enforced the decision and created a blockade preventing all ships from breaking the quarantine zone. Those attempting to escape were shot down.

Only the Jynes maintained any ties with the stricken Empire and their scientists worked to find a cure while their Legion fleet became the couriers of much needed medicines and supplies.

The Scourge ravaged the Empire for five years.

Millions died. The mechanism of government within the Empire ground to a slow halt. Ships were permanently marooned at space ports once there was nowhere left to run. No travellers went abroad. Fear of the virus turned people paranoid and they barricaded themselves indoors, as if under siege by their neighbours. Others devolved and resorted to looting to survive.

Despite the best efforts of the authorities, nothing could stop the slow descent into anarchy. Society collapsed with the growing ineffectiveness of law and order. With the Scourge devastating the numbers of the local constabulary, the Security Elite and the Imperial Army, crime skyrocketed. The Imperator did what he could to instil hope in the population, but each new morning saw more corpses of violence. They lay in the streets or floated by the waters of the increasingly fetid Paralyte River.

In the midst of everything, an unexpected social upheaval was taking place in Brysdyn. For as long as the Empire had existed, its children had aspired to become warriors. A military career was the pinnacle of success that originated from Brysdyn's earliest days. The arrival of the Scourge brought home to its people that a strong empire didn't need just need soldiers; men of science were just as vital.

Throughout its history, the Empire had done little to encourage its best minds in such pursuits. Yet, for the small collective of scientists on Brysdyn, the Scourge was their finest hour. Despite their ranks being decimated by the illness, the small community of scientists rose to the occasion, proving their worth to the masses as they searched tirelessly for a cure.

Five years after the death of the first victim, they succeeded.

The groundswell of elation following the announcement ensured its speedy distribution throughout the Empire, without proper precautions taken due to the urgency of the situation. No time was allocated to observe the long-term effects because the high mortality rate of the Scourge demanded immediate action. Desperation forced the Healer's Circle to ignore the strict protocols necessary to determine the safety of the drug before administering treatment to the masses.

The terrible price for this haste would become clear soon enough. Six months after the first treatment, it was discovered the drug caused sterility, impairing the ability of the haploid/diploid genomes to replicate. Horrified Healers revealed the awful truth. Everyone treated would be incapable of producing offspring. Instead of saving the Empire, the drug that would only ever be referred to as the Cure merely delayed its end by some decades.

The psychological effect on the population was almost as devastating as the Scourge itself. Suicides rates rose steeply as despair swept throughout the Empire. More violence and riots followed but, unlike the Scourge, this lasted only briefly. Eventually, the shock of what had happened gave way to acceptance and the population resigned themselves to their fate. Some even picked up the pieces and tried to move on.

The slow process of rebuilding what remained of society occupied their attention. Adoptions from outside the Empire were an alternative, although most wanted offspring from human stock. Life returned to normal, even if everyone knew the Empire's day was done. No new generation would follow those who died and what children were born to those who escaped the Scourge and the Cure were too few to sustain the Empire.

Until, from across the stars, a cry for help became their salvation.

Once the debate over the scientific validity of the signal exhausted itself, the impossible truth remained. A signal was being transmitted in real time from one of the outermost planets of Cathomira, indicating a civilisation of some sophistication. The message, however, was one of desperate need.

Brysdyn, who knew all too well what it was to be isolated and helpless, answered the call for help by dispatching ships in response. The message spoke of a world devastated by biological warfare. Centuries of war had resulted in one faction unleashing a deadly toxin that would end the conflict decisively. Unfortunately, as always with biological weapons, the toxin exceeded expectations and spread beyond enemy territory to the rest of the globe.

Despite delivering a swift and painless death to all the infected, the toxin spared those yet to reach puberty. Only Cathomira's children remained when the carnage ended.

They numbered in the hundred thousands, wandering ruined cities and abandoned countryside, terrified and hungry. By the time the Empire arrived, malnourishment had taken many, while others became prey to the wildlife reclaiming the planet. Infants and toddlers incapable of fending for themselves bore the worst of it. Some older children made an effort to keep them alive, eking out a grim existence in a world of rotting corpses.

When the first rescuers arrived from Brysdyn, they found something they never expected—another White Star world.

The children, bewildered and traumatised by their ordeal, were human.

While they did not know how to regard the strangers who suddenly appeared from the sky, there was no denying their origins. The ancestors of Cathomira were children of the White Star. The rescuers were convinced this was fate. In the midst of so much death, these starving waifs had become the salvation of the Empire.

With the arrival of the New Citizens, the people of Brysdyn felt as if they had been granted a second chance and were determined not to squander it.

The future lay before them and, this time, they would get it right.

* * *

It was almost evening when Jonen left his skimmer by the main street and took the path leading to the Census Registry Building. An amber glow settled over the area, with cracks of sunlight streaming through the branches of trees as he approached the structure.

The Registry resided in the Kleist District. The area was known to the natives as the Domain and was the heart of Imperial government on Brysdyn. From where he stood, he could see the Imperator's Domicile standing on the hill in the distance, overlooking the Quorum Hall. On the other side of the hill was the Enclave, home of the Security Elite.

He knew he should have been here earlier, but Mira would have rebuked him for neglecting his other patients for the sake of one case. The offices closed for the day in an hour and the ever-lengthening shadows along the tree-lined path prompted him to move faster along the paved road.

Like all government buildings, the Registry was an impressive building repurposed for modern use. Constructed in white marble with wide stone steps, a colonnade ran along the front face of the building. The main entrance was sealed with a set of ornately carved wooden doors that swung open when a visitor approached. It was guarded on either side by statues of sombre-faced orators of the past.

Entering the building, he found the lobby of the building almost deserted, as expected during this time of day. Jonen went to the computer terminal in the centre of the wide floor to bring up the listing of various departments. Scrolling through the list of departments, he found the one he wanted and headed out the elevator that would take him there.

While the foyer maintained some of its historical grandeur, the converted office seemed rather dull and uninspiring. Beige walls, dark carpet and too few windows made the place feel cold, even if the temperature was regulated. Jonen made his way to the department of citizenship records, hoping this wasn't a waste of time.

Mira had given him the idea to come here. While complaining about yet another argument with her sister Teela, Mira had accused Teela of being spoilt as a child. Mira's younger sibling denied this most vehemently, of course.

"How would she know?"Mira snorted. "She was too young to remember."

Inspiration struck. If the younger New Citizens could not remember the planet with the blue sky, perhaps the older ones could? Interestingly enough, only the very young New Citizens appeared to suffer the Dreaming. Perhaps older children did not because their memories of the past were complete, while the others only saw fragments in their dreams.

It was a question worth pursuing.

* * *

The Department of Citizenship Affairs occupied the entire space of the floor Jonen stepped into when he emerged from the elevator. The size of the place was not surprising, since the records archived here predated the colonisation of Brysdyn. Genealogy information preserved in their worldship during the Exodus now resided in carbon crystal data banks on the premises. After the Empire expanded, the name of every family on every annexed world conquered was also recorded and stored. Every citizen of the Empire could trace their lineage through the information stored within these halls.

If he wanted to find the New Citizens, this would be the place to do so.

Entering the foyer, he saw that he was not alone in trying to reach the offices before the end of the day. There were an assortment of humans and nonhumans waiting in line, either applying for citizenship or updating their records. Taking his place at the end of the queue, he waited patiently as it moved along.

"How can I help you, Sir?" A woman not much older than he inquired when he reached the counter.

"Yes, good afternoon. I'm looking for any information regarding New Citizens, particularly those sent off world. I would like to locate any one of them who might have relocated back to Brysdyn."

The woman raised a brow at his request. Her severe features made Jonen think of a headmistress at a school. Dark eyes studied him as her lips pursed into a thin line, making her appear more intimidating than helpful.

"Are you a media collator of some kind?"

"No, I'm a mentalist. I'm conducting some research and I would like to speak to some of them. Are you able to help me?"

The question puzzled him. Even he knew he appeared too bookish to be mistaken for someone who made their living on the Transband. His psychoanalytical mind started studying her like a patient. Even though she maintained a professional demeanour, something about her manner implied his question had unsettled. This cannot be the first time someone inquired about New Citizens?

As if reading his mind, she responded promptly, relaxing visibly.

"We don't get many requests like this. Are you looking for anyone in particular?"

"Well, I'm searching for any of the older children brought here from Cathomira. I'm trying to get some information about their experiences of their home world."

"I see," she gestured at him to follow her. She moved to the terminal at the far corner of the counter, allowing the line behind him to progress. On her departure, someone else stepped into her place to attend to their inquiries.

Jonen followed her, feeling self-conscious at being singled out from the crowd. It made sense, of course. His request was unusual and might require more time than normal to deal with. The woman projected nothing but professionalism, but he couldn't shake the memory of the uneasiness he'd seen in her face earlier.

As she tapped on the keyboard at the terminal, Jonen distracted himself by surveying the room and studying the people in line.

"I'm sorry. That information is code locked."

"Code locked? What does that mean?" He stared at her.

"It means you need authorisation to access these files."

"I thought this kind of information is public access," he countered, disappointed he wouldn't get what he needed today.

"Not according to the computer." She studied the screen in front of her and then shifted her gaze to him again. "I cannot give you the reason why it's locked, but it's most likely to protect their privacy."

"Where do I get authorisation?" Jonen remembered how much he despised bureaucracy and the endless red tape it seemed to spawn. No matter how simple the situation, you could always count on the Civil Service to complicate it.

"You will need to fill out this application," she handed him a data pad with the assumption he would like to pursue the matter.

Taking the datapad begrudgingly, Jonen studied the screen and saw the application required his personal details and the reason for the request. With little choice but to comply if he wanted the names, Jonen surrendered to the demands of process.

"Who gives the authorisation?" Jonen handed her back the pad.

"I couldn't tell you," she shrugged as if she were in the dark as much as he.

And right away, Jonen knew she was lying.

* * *

Elsewhere, a short time later, a com unit beeped insistently.

The shrill sound continued for the next few minutes, until its owner wondered what crisis warranted such persistence. The man hurried into his office, annoyed at the absence of the aide who had left for the day a short time ago.

Activating the device, a face appeared on the display screen above the main panel. Recognition rose within him like the slow-moving steam from a hot cup of brew. It was a face from the past.

"It's been a long time," he hid his uneasiness at seeing her. "What can I do for you?"

"There may be a problem, Sir."

Contacting him after so many years meant this must be a credible threat. She would contact him for nothing less.

"How so, Agent?"

"As you know, I have been assigned to the Department of Citizenship for the past thirteen years," she explained. While he might remember her, she suspected he might not remember her assignment.

He was grateful for the reminder because he hadn't remembered even if he knew her. "I am a busy man, Agent. What is the problem?"

"I am sorry, Sir," she stammered, uncertainty in her voice. "Someone is inquiring about the New Citizens we sent off planet."

Her words escaped like the dank, fetid air of an unsealed grave. For a moment, he did not react, although the announcement shook him to the core. No, not a false alarm at all, he thought silently. Being the consummate professional, he hid his surprise from her and resumed the conversation.

"Who?"

"A mentalist, he claims. His name is Jonen. He owns a practice in the Rura District. He claims he's doing research."

"A mentalist?" the harsh edge of his voice softened with genuine surprise. "How interesting."

"What should I do, Sir? I think I managed to put him off for a few days, but he looks quite determined. I'm certain he will be back."

He stared out the window and watched the sun continuing to set for a few seconds as he decided what ought to be done. Fate was a patient predator, he thought. When this began, he remembered the tight knot in his stomach following him for days. Knowing what he did exhilarated him and terrified him at the same time. He consoled himself with the knowledge that what was done was worth the price, but his actions still made him break into a sweat and sent fear running down his spine like ice.

Until this moment, he had believed the truth would stay buried. Perhaps age made him complacent and blunted the edge of his sharp, analytical mind into being so presumptuous. Whatever the reason, the situation needed to be dealt with immediately.

"Send me all the details and I'll take care of it."

"Yes, Sir."

Without another word, General Edwen, Commander of Security Elite, terminated the line.

VI

Accident

There were few things in Jonen's life he could rely upon without any question. One of them was his love for his work, the belief that most people were good and that Mira would always be at the office before he arrived each morning. The last was probably more unshakeable than the first two. For all the years Mira had worked for him, Jonen could not remember a time when he arrived at the office before she did.

Mira's dedication to her work and, to some degree, him, was a constant in his life, one he could not imagine being without. Their relationship was more than professional, but less than sexual. There was no doubt they shared intimacy, but it was not of the flesh and, in Jonen's opinion, was far more meaningful.

So it was disconcerting to find Mira absent when he stepped through the doors of his office.

It was her habit to open up the premises, review his appointments and make amendments if necessary, then have a hot cup of brew waiting at his desk when he arrived. Today, he found the office locked and was mildly irritated at having to remember the security code to the door. It took him almost five minutes to key in the possible permutations, because he so seldom used it.

Her absence concerned him. Even though she disliked doing it, Mira knew she was free to contact him at home if an emergency arose. On the few occasions she was forced to come in late, she always managed to let him know the day before. Mira was a creature of habit and was far too meticulous to have simply forgotten.

As he walked into the waiting room where her desk held court to a number of comfortable waiting chairs, it was odd not seeing her there. The office, painted in warm colours and furnished to look comfortable, felt gloomy without her. Of course, he knew the décor was meant to lift the spirits of his patients. It just felt gloomy because she wasn't there.

Shaking his head to dispel his sentimental musings, Jonen continued to carry out the tasks Mira made her own at this time of the day. How surprised she would be when she came in and saw he'd done it all. He was convinced she thought him incapable of fending for himself without her.

It did not take him long to open up the office, make the cider and go through her appointment tablet to see his schedule for the day. His first appointment was due in about half an hour and he grumbled, not looking forward to it. The patient was a dowager from an aristocratic family who felt she ought to be treated like a Raisan empress. Mira had scheduled her early so he could feign the arrival of another patient if she chose to go over her time.

Cringing, he still remembered when he was treated to the prestigious history of her family because she knew he had no other patients after her. It was the only time he ever considered getting out of the business.

After opening up the office, he reviewed patient files behind his desk, still unconcerned about Mira, until he glanced at the chronometer on the wall. It was getting late with still no word from Mira. While genuine alarm was starting to fill him, he was also debating whether or not he was working himself up for no good reason. He was just beginning to feel the temptation to contact her at home when the com unit on his desk trilled noisily.

Ah, that would be Mira.

Her excuse for being absent from work, like the rest of her, would be impeccable. Mira never missed work unless she had a very good reason. Her devotion to him made such occasions rare. Pressing a button on the device, he saw the image struggling to appear through a glitch of static.

Only it was not Mira's face.

It took him a moment to realise he was staring at Mira's sister, Teela. It took a further second to realise something was wrong. Teela was a much younger woman than Mira. There was a ten-year age difference between the sisters, but right now it appeared as if she'd aged a decade overnight. Her eyes were puffed and red, her expression desolate, and it was obvious she was extremely distressed.

Immediately, Jonen felt his throat tighten and his insides twisting into knots.

"What has happened?" His voice was a whisper.

"Mira's dead, Jon!" Teela gushed, making no effort to contain her anguish. She descended into fresh sobs, unashamed and aware he was sharing her grief. Over the years, through her sister, he had come to know her well. Teela considered him a family friend and perhaps the closest thing Mira would ever come to finding a husband.

Jonen felt his head swim. The need to understand how such a thing could happen suddenly eclipsed the pain tearing away at him.

"How?" His jaw ticked as he fought the tide of grief threatening to overwhelm him.

"It was an accident. A CP called me about an hour ago and told me. He said Mira was involved in an accident with a skimmer. It hit her when she was crossing the street from her house. The animals didn't even stop to see what they'd done!"

"Thank you for telling me, Teela," he said in a soft, strained voice, no longer seeing her as he switched off the com unit without giving her the chance to respond.

For a long time, he merely sat there, numb.

It seemed unreal to think about the world without Mira being in it, that she could be taken from him in such a senseless way. Traffic accidents happened to other people, not his Mira. He wanted to scream and cry, but the strength in him was gone. His training was telling him he should let his grief escape, but he couldn't do anything.

Finally, he leaned forward and buried his face in his hands. With a loud sob, Jonen released the torrent of grief sweeping him into a greyer world.

* * *

The Enclave was busy today.

Major Danten, Deputy Commander of Security Elite, observed this as he marched through the organisation's central command. Danten was well into his forties, a man with tawny-coloured hair beginning to streak with grey and intelligent grey eyes that missed nothing. Under his uniform was a well-muscled physique, worked to perfection through years of discipline. He wore his stature with an authoritative presence, revealing he was a man to be reckoned with.

Today Danten felt nostalgic.

Walking through the halls of the Enclave, he saw fewer and fewer youthful faces and too many like his own, men who were past their prime. The lack of youth meant declining enlistment and, despite the activity in the halls at present, the Elite was still understaffed. It was sad to see that, among all those uniforms, only half belonged to field officers, while the rest were mainly administrative staff.

More and more, he found himself wishing for better days. Danten had enlisted in the Elite two years before the first Scourge victim died. There was nothing grander than to serve in the Imperator's Security Elite. The Elite maintained the security of the empire. Wearing the sleek black uniform was something to be proud of. People looked up to them, as if they were invincible, and Danten remembered feeling the same as well.

Nowadays, there was no such respect. The Elite was largely regarded as obsolete. It was a crumbling institution with a draconian past, no longer useful in this age of peace and treaties. Much of the Elite's power had diminished as the Imperator gave way to the Jyne idea of peaceful coexistence. Danten sometimes wondered if the Imperator wasn't a little embarrassed by the Elite.

The Imperator and the Quorum had neutered the Elite, making it as sterile as the rest of Brysdyn. Oh, there was still power in the walls of the Enclave, but it would die with those strong enough to wield it. Like most of the senior officers in the Security Elite, he disliked the notion of an alliance with the Jyne, no matter how utopian it sounded. Peace, pacifism and enlightened ideals, like the one the Imperator believed in so passionately, were the breeding ground of subjugation.

Why were the Elite the only ones who could see it?

Fortunately, the Elite still had the General to fight for them. He embodied all the warrior strength that had made Brysdyn what it was. With confidence,

Danten knew the Elite would not die without a fight, not if the General had anything to do with it. The Elite was born from his love of Brysdyn and the General was never afraid to do the things necessary to save it. They saw him as their voice in the Quorum and their loyalty for him almost superseded their devotion to the Imperator.

These days, General Edwen was the only true warrior left. All else were pretenders.

Rounding the corner, the number of people walking down the corridor thinned out significantly. Danten entered the short corridor restricted to everyone except the highest echelon of Security Elite. It veered away from the main corridors, almost like an untrodden path in a country road, and was guarded by sentries. It led to Central Command where the General ruled.

None of the guards asked him for identification as he walked past. They knew him well enough.

The corridor emptied into a large foyer where Edwen's executive aid was currently posted at her desk. Peering up from her terminal, Nalia reached for the com unit even as she offered him a nod of acknowledgement. By the time Danten reached her, his presence was already announce to the General.

Nalia rose to her feet to greet him. She was a slender, statuesque beauty whose gold hair was slicked back over her shoulders. Her face, as always, wore no expression whatsoever. Nalia's efficiency was seconded only by her glacial personality and she intimidated almost everyone with her icy stare.

"The General is expecting you. Please go right in, Major."

"Thank you."

Leaving her behind, he strode towards the polished red calsa wood doors preceding Edwen's familiar office. In the past twenty years five years nothing had ever changed. Everything had its traditional place, the same ornate rugs, the same furniture and artwork. The artwork collected by the General was neither priceless nor famous. Edwen collected them because he enjoyed the work.

"Good morning, General."

Edwen did not rise from his chair at the younger man's arrival. Instead, the General acknowledged him with a single nod. His eyes and attention remained affixed on the data tablet before him. This did not surprise or offend Danten, who was used to the General's habits and manners.

"Good morning, Major," Edwen greeted, his eyes still studying the pad.

Danten's reacted with a slight bow that was more effective than a salute.

"I would like to submit my report, Sir."

Even though the General was waiting for it, Danten knew Edwen bore a weakness for dramatics and pomp. This was why Danten never met the older man's eyes until he was being addressed directly.

Today, the General was in no mood for such games.

"Sit down, Danten."

There was a hint of surprise in the major's face, but it went no further than that and he sat down obediently, his back straight against the chair facing Edwen's desk.

"Proceed."

"I did as ordered, Sir," Danten began. "I performed an extensive background check on the mentalist. He is a notable name in the field of mental health and is highly regarded by the Healers Circle. He has, as our agent in the Department of Citizenship already disclosed, a practice in the Rura District. Most of his patients come from Brysdyn's best families. He has two sisters, one who lives in Girawon Province and the other who died during the Scourge. He hasn't seen the surviving sister in a decade, however."

The information was interesting, but did nothing to explain why a mentalist would want to know about New Citizens off world.

"Then they aren't close. Girawon is on the home world, hardly a difficult journey to make to see family." After a moment, he looked up at Danten, who paused when he spoke. "Continue."

"There isn't much beyond that, Sir," Danten admitted reluctantly. "We know that he has been in frequent contact with mentalists from other cities. Darix from Tesalone and Alwi from Rainab."

Edwen took the information in and mulled over it for a moment. "Do we have any idea why he is so insistent on finding out about off world New Citizens?"

"Research perhaps?" the Major suggested.

Danten, too, was at a loss to see why a mentalist would be probing into something they thought they had buried long ago. Like Edwen, Danten was just as surprised to hear agents report the night before.

"It's possible, but unlikely."

General Edwen was a man who trusted his instincts and right now his instincts told him the mentalist's inquiries had little to do with a research paper destined for some obscure medical journal. Great storms often announced themselves with the coming of a gentle breeze and Edwen suspected mentalist Jonen was a just such a breeze.

"Have you distracted him for the time being?" At least that was something they could control.

Yes, our informant suggested some intimacy between the woman and Jonen. We've taken the appropriate steps."

"By that you mean she's dead." The General retorted, disliking Danten's sanitation of what was standard procedure in situations like this. Edwen was not ashamed of the dirtier aspects of his work. Unpleasant things were necessary when the cause was right.

"Yes, Sir," he replied, choosing to speak directly if that was what the General wished. "I had one of our special operatives take care of it. As far as Central Police are concerned, it was just a traffic accident."

"Good. That will buy us some time. Give our agent her instructions and make the necessary preparations."

Danten's response was another short bow as Edwen returned to his data tablet again, signalling their meeting was concluded.

"Sir, forgive me but why don't we just eliminate him? We have the capability to do it without raising questions."

It was an honest question, Edwen decided, as he looked up at the younger man. In their time, the Security Elite had carried out assassinations, incited riots and even silenced voices threatening the security of the Empire. Edwen understood Danten's puzzlement at why the mentalist was the exception.

"Because we don't know why he wants the information and that makes me uneasy."

It shocked Danten to even think the General could be caught unawares about anything. For the last twenty-five years of his service to the General, Danten had never seen the man caught unawares. Their confidence in him stemmed from Edwen's ability to adapt to any situation, no matter how adverse. It was unsettling to see the General at a loss like everyone else.

Danten's surprise made Edwen smile faintly.

"Yes, Danten, I am human too. Sometimes I even have a conscience."

It was a privilege for Danten to see the man behind the uniform. Edwen even felt good allowing it.

"Until we know more about mentalist Jonen and why he requires the information, we will not harm him unless we absolutely have to."

VII

Kalistar

To Garryn's surprise, he missed his sessions with Jonen.

This was understandable, of course. During their last conversation, the extent of the man's grief was plain to see. Mira meant a great deal to Jonen and Garryn's obligatory condolences seemed trite and meaningless. Garryn imagined words would do little to comfort him if he were to lose someone he cared for. Jonen bore his grief with dignity, maintaining his composure when he spoke to Garryn. It wasn't difficult for Garryn to see through the facade when the man stated his need for an off world sabbatical for a few weeks.

Although he disliked the idea of Jonen being gone, even for a little while, Garryn understood the man's need for it. He couldn't begrudge the man some time away, since his consultations with the mentalist resulted in his being able to sleep better. Having an outlet to confide his dreams seemed to have the effect of letting him sleep some nights without incident.

Fortunately, his days were kept busy in the Quorum, watching his father conduct the affairs of state. He enjoyed that aspect of it, learning from the man he respected and loved most in the world. As Prime, he needed to understand his role as the next ruler of Brysdyn. The Imperator governed the people through the Quorum and, in times of extraordinary circumstances, had the power to make decisions without them.

It was a fine line to walk, because lesser men could take advantage of such power and risk civil war. The role of the Imperator was to maintain the sovereignty of Brysdyn and, if the Quorum put its safety at risk, he could restore order. Of course, it also meant if he abused his authority, the Quorum possessed the authority to remove him, with the Prime succeeding in his place.

It was a source of pride to his father that, since the Exodus, no Imperator was ever removed in such a manner.

Unfortunately, Garryn's education in politics was not limited to managing the Quorum. The Imperator was the head of Brysdynian society, which required him to deal with the noble houses. For this aspect of being Prime, Garryn found himself under the instruction of the Chief Courtier, an annoying little cretin called Feroz.

Feroz was constantly arranging his attendance at the endless engagements set up by Brysdyn's social elite. When his mother was alive, she protected him and Elisha from the insipidness of court life, showing them what snobbery really meant in the scheme of things. His mother was a Jyne who saw little value in aristocratic blood. Unfortunately, it still mattered on Brysdyn and it was Feroz's job to ensure the Imperator and Prime were always accessible to the minor houses.

Feroz's designation during this time was Chief Courtier to the Prime in Waiting. It was a pompous title, given to someone whose aim in life was to make Garryn utterly miserable, and he succeeded brilliantly. Feroz was in charge of his daily itinerary, the clothes he wore and the appointments he kept. The man seemed to have little regard for what Garryn wanted, satisfied only in ensuring Garryn was the paragon of culture and nobility.

It did not surprise Garryn to learn that Feroz himself was from one of the families. Ristalia, if he remembered correctly. The Ristalia were aristocratic all right, but possessed little or no fortune, explaining why Feroz was here making his life hell. A short, unimpressive man, he seemed like a caricature, dressed in the best clothes and carrying himself like the Emperor of the known universe. His face was made up, exaggerating looks he did not have, and his hair was styled more like a woman's.

If Garryn had still been in the military, they would have used him for target practice.

Still, the man was sneaky and Garryn could sense a reason for all the engagements he was forced to attend. If he had learned anything about the aristocracy, it was their ability to maintain the status quo with the skill of military tacticians. They planned their appearances like generals preparing for an invasion. The invitations and the introductions were the opening volley in a larger offensive. They were jockeying to become in-laws to the next Imperator of the Empire.

In other words, his father and the court planned to see him married.

He couldn't even begin to remember the exact number of women foisted on him during the last few weeks. Garryn was almost tempted to scandalize Feroz with the revelation that the last woman he'd been with, he'd paid for. Of course, the lady thought she was just servicing another pilot on leave, not the future Prime.

In any case, none of the socialites presented impressed him and, while these were definitely beautiful women, there was little else beneath the glitter. Being a soldier, he'd met interesting women during his time in the service, women who fought beside him, sometimes outranked him and some whom he considered his friends. He knew he would have to marry. The position he was in gave him no out. But he wasn't going to marry just anyone. A lifetime was a long time if you were married to the wrong person.

Sometimes, he wished he could have Elisha's freedom, being able to choose whom he would marry and in his good time. Being the eldest child effectively eliminated any such possibility. After the Scourge, it was more necessary than ever to perpetuate the line. As the eldest, whose offspring would be future Imperators, he was not afforded the luxuries Elisha took for granted.

For the future, he had to marry.

* * *

Returning to the Domicile after a day out, he knew he was late.

Feroz would be nearly hysterical by now. One of the houses, Garryn couldn't remember which one, was throwing him a ball. Why couldn't it ever be drinks down at a local tavern? Why did it have to be a ball? These royal houses, Tesalia, Grigor and Myzyne, just to name a few, were all trying to outdo each other. What was the point? In truth, they were about as royal as he was, which was not very royal at all.

There was only one genuine White Star aristocrat on Brysdyn: his father. Iran was the head of what was once House Brysdyn. During the Exodus, the world-ships were assigned according to the Royal Houses of the White Star Alliance. Brysdyn and Jyne were one of these. The others were lost during the voyage. The modern aristocrats of Brysdyn, other than House Brysdyn itself, were descendants of minor houses with little importance.

Garryn reached the door to his chambers just in time to hear a familiar voice squeal in consternation.

"Your Excellency! Where have you been? Have you forgotten the Myzyne have thrown a ball in your honour? You are expected there in an hour!"

Garryn released a silent groan of frustration before the man could finish squealing his string of words. Who could forget that? Feroz had reminded him all week about it. It should not surprise him the man would be waiting to pounce as soon as he passed through the doors.

"I didn't forget, Feroz. An hour is plenty of time for me to be preened like a prize bull at Kirkaris."

"An hour is never enough time to look like a gentleman," Feroz snorted, raising his bulbous nose in that annoying self-important manner. "Your father expects you promptly."

Garryn ignored the remark and opened the door. Upon entering, he saw his clothes were already laid out on the bed. He felt relieved, seeing it was his dress uniform Feroz expected him to wear. Feroz preferred him to wear some expensive ensemble from the fashion pages that made him look like a well-dressed fop.

"Your clothes, as you can see, are ready. I suggest you take a bath while I summon your groom."

"Fine," Garryn conceded, expecting Feroz to leave, but the man remained where he was for a moment.

"Sire, I know we have discussed this, but if you insist on wearing your uniform," his nose curled up as if the word was distasteful. Of course, it would, Garryn thought. Feroz had no idea what it was like to be a soldier or what a uniform meant. "You might at least allow me to adorn it with the proper appellations."

Garryn, who was in the process of undoing a button on his shirt, looked up sharply. In truth, this was an old argument, but hearing it again did not lessen his annoyance. "I'm not wearing a bunch of medals I didn't earn, Feroz. Just get over it."

"It is not an embarrassment to wear the medals of your forebears. Your father wishes you to wear them!"

That was an outright lie, but Garryn was not going to debate it with the man.

"My father will understand. They were his medals. He fought the wars, he deserves them. I am not wearing anything on my chest I didn't earn myself. Now get out if you want me dressed in time."

He was not undressing in front of a man trying to be *that* pretty.

Feroz threw up his hands in surrender and hurried out of the room. Garryn walked to the door after he had gone and slammed the door shut. He could hear the weasel's footsteps diminish as he scampered away. For a moment, a thought flashed in Garryn's mind. What if he left Brysdyn? Simply jump on a ship and get out of the Empire, perhaps visit Jyne for the first time?

No, I can't do that. He sighed inwardly before the thought could become entrenched inside him. *This is my life and that's all there is to it.*

Garryn stepped away from the door and walked towards the bureau at the far end of the room. All thoughts of the pending occasion disappeared from his mind as he pulled out a drawer and rifled through the belongings within. After a moment, his hand reappeared, clutching something that glittered in the evening light.

The fine links of gold made up a chain he'd out-grown almost two decades ago. Hanging off the chain was a circular pendant inscribed with a dead lan-guage. This was all he had to remind him he was once from another world. It was the reminder of a world devastated and a life lost forever. It was some-thing uniquely his own, having nothing to do with the Imperators. Holding it always made him feel bet-ter. According to his mother, he was wearing it the first time she set eyes on him.

More than anything, it served to remind him he was not supposed to find everything about being the Prime or the Imperator easy. He was not born to it like his father. There was no blood in him that could be traced to the White Star. His ancestors crossed no great distance to chart a new galaxy. He became a child of House Brysdyn because Iran and Aisha chose him to be their son and because of that, he would do this.

Garryn needed to remember none of this was sup-posed to be easy. He was not born to be Imperator. He was chosen out of love and, because of that same love, he would accept it.

* * *

"You are not enjoying yourself, Garryn."

Garryn broke off his vacant gaze across the ballroom floor and turned to his father.

"Should I be?" He tried to hide his boredom.

"There are many lovely young women here." Iran gestured towards the sprawling room.

Garryn looked up and swept his gaze across ballroom. Gold draperies hung from large windows, while crystal chandeliers were suspended across the ceiling. The mirrored walls seemed to make the room larger than it was and the floor was polished so well it gleamed and bounced back reflections. There was music from a ten-piece orchestra in the corner, while servers patrolled the room, carrying silver trays with flutes of sparkling alcohol.

Men and women from the best families paraded across the floor. Some were engaged in small talk. The others chose to dance. Men his age kept their distance while perusing the debutantes in dresses whose value would feed a family for a month. Older men sat on delicate-looking divans smoking their pipes, while dowagers picked to pieces anyone who did not have noble blood in their veins.

"You might think about getting a wife for yourself," Garryn teased, knowing what his father was driving towards.

Iran let out a sigh, knowing that his son was in a testy mood tonight, despite his attempts at humour. Through the facade of his impeccable manners to the hosts of this event, it was obvious to Iran that Garryn wanted to be anywhere but here. Garryn was a soldier, accustomed to doing more than playing court to a room of aristocrats who would never presume to soil their hands in battle.

It wasn't any easier for him when he was the Prime, Iran thought.

Studying the guests, he realised he shared Garryn's distaste for these people. Being Imperator had its unique benefits. It allowed him to deal with people from every corner of the galaxy, no matter what shape or form. The secular world of the aristocrats was prejudiced and tiresome.

From the corner of the room, Iran saw General Edwen appearing through the crowd. Since Edwen's speech in the Quorum, they'd hardly spoken. Even though he said nothing to reveal his disappointment at Edwen's political stance, Iran tried not to make eye contact with the General. Iran sensed that it was best they kept their distance. They were friends, but their relationship was now on tenuous ground.

Still, Iran was surprised Edwen would make his court re-emergence here. Even though he was the absolute master of Security Elite and one of the most powerful men in the realm, he was still considered an outsider. Edwen's crime was not having any noble blood, something the aristocracy never allowed him to forget. None of them would dare to snub him openly, because it was never wise to make an enemy of the Security Elite.

Tonight, Edwen was not alone, however. Hanging on his arm was a young woman of exquisite beauty and one Iran did not recognise. Since Garryn had come home, Iran had been introduced to every young woman at court who might be a potential mate for his son. The young woman with Edwen was one he did not recognise. She was extraordinary beautiful, with dark auburn hair and deep green eyes.

The duo crossed the ballroom floor and approached them. Iran was conscious of the fact the scene was being observed with interest. After all, the souring of relations between Edwen and the Imperator was common gossip these days. As the man approached, Iran realized he had no wish for their friendship to end merely because of a difference of opinion.

If he meant what he told Garryn about Edwen having a right to his opinions, then what he said in the Quorum shouldn't matter.

Edwen reached Garryn and Iran, who were seated at the head of the room, like kings receiving their subjects. Neither man liked the positioning, but the Myzyne were traditionalists. Even though Iran always insisted the title of Imperator was not king, the aristocracy thought otherwise.

"Imperator," Edwen bowed slightly upon his arrival and then repeated the same gesture to Garryn. The young woman at his side curtsied accordingly before taking a step behind him. The General was in his black uniform, which appeared even more impressive with the medals pinned on it. At least that was one thing he had in common with Garryn, Iran decided.

Those medals were earned.

"Edwen, it's good to see you. How have you been? You've been absent from the Quorum lately."

It was an honest question and Iran hoped Edwen would be able to tell the difference.

If any offence was taken, Edwen did not show it. Instead he smiled graciously. "I decided to limit my oratories for the time being and deal with some pressing matters at the Enclave."

"Nothing too distressing, I hope."

"The matters of state are always pressing, Iran. This time is no different. I'm only here tonight because this is Kalistar's first ball since her return from school."

Iran faced the young woman again and felt some astonishment. "You're Kalistar? You were playing with dolls the last time I saw you!"

"They weren't dolls, father. They were little water sprites from Nevar." Garryn rose to his feet and bowed gallantly at her. "It's good to see you again, Kal. How long has it been?"

"About ten years," she laughed. "I'm surprised you remember, Prime."

"How could I forget? You and Elisha played together for most of that summer and it was my responsibility to look after you two. I'm glad you're back. Elisha will be happy to see you again."

"Well, since you know each other so well," Iran interrupted, "Garryn, why don't you ask Kalistar to dance? It would be nice if you at least made some attempt to be sociable."

Garryn threw his father a look, knowing what was running through the Imperator's mind. This time, he was not annoyed. He did want to dance with Kalistar.

"Shall we?" He offered her his arm.

"I would be honoured."

* * *

After a short turn on the ballroom floor, Garryn and Kalistar slipped away from the peering eyes, aware the gossiping was already started. By inviting Kalistar to dance, he'd made her the first woman he'd shown the least bit of interest in since his return home. If they did not escape the ballroom, their actions would be under scrutiny all night and Garryn didn't think he could stand that.

Instead, they left the mansion and headed towards the Myzyne's beautifully cared for gardens. Once away from everyone, he relaxed considerably. It felt good to be away from that stifling air of nobility everyone was forced to wear. Outside, the night was sultry. The hot air of the summer day had abated into a balmy breeze. He could smell the sweet fragrance of flowers carried by the wind from the approaching gardens.

It was a change Kalistar noticed immediately. Her memories of him were vivid, thanks to a childhood infatuation of which she was grateful he was unaware. In her memories, he was a proud, swaggering young boy who knew with total confidence he was going to be a soldier. Now, there was none of that arrogance. Instead, there was just that sadness at time having caught up with him.

"You were miserable!" Kalistar teased as they entered the impressive gardens.

"You can joke, but you have no idea what I've been going through since I got home," he laughed, glad to be himself again.

"I can't imagine. Has it really been that bad?"

Garryn could see she was no longer teasing him. "I don't know. Maybe if I was raised the way these people have been, maybe I might be happier."

"Would you have traded your mother for any of them?"

Garryn could not even imagine anyone else other than Aisha being his mother. "Not a chance."

"I didn't think so," Kalistar smirked with triumph. "When we were children, things were so uncomplicated. I was just another playmate for Elisha and you were going to conquer the universe. You used to say so, and stand like this."

She placed her hands on her hips and mimicked a pose that seemed utterly ridiculous and unfortunately familiar.

"Gods, was I really that pompous?" Garryn winced in genuine horror.

"*Worse.*"

"I'm glad you're here. Now never show that to anyone ever again."

Kalistar laughed and put her hand to her breast as if taking a sacred oath. "You have my word, Prime."

Her laughter was infectious and, compared to the people he had consorted with this evening, a breath of fresh air.

"You know, you're probably one of the few normal people I've met since I've been home."

"Why, thank you! I guess it must be difficult readjusting to all this after being a private citizen." She brushed his arm in sympathy.

"You have no idea."

They stepped across the ornate grass threshold that led into the gardens. The blue moonlight shimmered across the manicured lawns, bouncing off the white sculptures that peeked through the flowerbeds and taller plants.

"Does your father know how much you hate it?" she ventured to ask.

"Subconsciously I think he does, but it doesn't really matter. I am his son. I'm not afraid to do my duty. I just hate the rest of it. Marrying some woman simply to ensure the line, dealing with the nobility, those are the things I can't stand."

"Garryn, the Imperator defines his reign by doing things exactly how he chooses. Not because the court tells him to or because society demands some stupid rules are obeyed. Your father brought us through the worst age in our history and allowed us to change because of it. My father may hate it, but on some level he knows it's inevitable. Define the future by what you think is right, not by all the old rules."

Garryn was silent for a moment, absorbing her words. She spoke with such conviction and earnestness it was hard to argue with her, especially when she was right.

"I guess I have been feeling rather sorry for myself," he gave her a long, meaningful look.

"I hope I didn't speak out of turn," she apologised, realising belatedly this wasn't her childhood crush but was, in fact, the next leader of the Empire. "You just really needed to hear that."

"I appreciate it," he said with a little smile. "I think I've been too much in my own head with all this."

Garryn suddenly found he liked her company very much. Far more than the childhood playmate he could remember only vaguely. These days, the number of friends in his life was lacking and Kalistar being able to treat him like a person, not a title, was just what he needed.

"I'm glad my intrusion helped for a change. My father tells me that I should learn how to be more subtle and impassive about what I am feeling."

"Don't change a thing and we'll get along just fine."

VIII

Officer Trayla

For a while, it felt as if going away would ease the pain.

He took refuge at a retreat in Sellust, unable to face being at her funeral, although he did pay his respects in absentia. On that remote world there was little to distract him. He faced his grief and tried to get used to the idea of living without her. It was easier said than done. His memories of her were clouded with regret and he tortured himself with all the things he should have said to her and didn't. All those years wasted, while they danced around their feelings instead of relishing every moment.

In an odd way, Jonen began to empathise with his Dreaming patients, now that he experienced nightmares of his own.

Eventually the pain did subside, even if the void in his heart did not. The days seem to move forward faster and soon an entire month had passed since that terrible call from Teela. The feelings of self-loathing and regret eased. It almost felt as if they belonged to someone else whose life was inexplicably changed. He even believed he might be able to continue without Mira.

Until he returned home and entered his office.

When he saw Mira's replacement seated at her new post, he knew no amount of time would ever heal the wounds he carried. Telling himself resolutely it was time to go on was no match for the reality of seeing a stranger occupying Mira's customary place. For a few minutes, he stood before the woman like a lost child, not knowing what to do until she greeted him.

All he could do was manage a polite response before hurrying to his office where he could hide from her.

She was out there now, doing all the things Mira had done so superbly, making the job her own and contemplating her employer's odd behaviour. With a flash of insight, he knew she would not be in the position long enough for them to get acquainted. None of it was her fault, of course. She simply had the bad luck to be the one who replaced Mira.

He spent most of the morning hidden in his office, dutifully reviewing his case files, contacting his patients to let them know he would be back and their appointments could be scheduled. Keeping busy prevented him from being reminded it was not Mira who was outside taking his calls.

At one point, he became so engrossed in his work he reached for the com unit to ask Mira to bring in some hot brew. Like a splash of cold water, the voice responding to his request belonged to a stranger. Staring at the device in shock, a split second jumped by as Jonen tried to fathom who it was on the other end, until he remembered Mira was gone. Once he realised his mistake, he was overwhelmed with shame and despair.

Closing his eyes, he forced away the tears and swallowed hard, hoping to steady himself. Only when he'd composed himself did he trust himself to address her.

"I shall be going out for an hour."

"Yes, mentalist Jonen," she answered without any surprise or curiosity at the emotion in his voice. How different she was from Mira, he found himself thinking. If it were Mira, she would be asking him what was wrong by now.

Angry at himself, he switched off the com unit and eased back into his chair. He glanced around the room. The space suddenly seemed empty and lifeless. He needed to escape, even if it was only for a little while. As he walked towards the door, he realised his office was his world and that he had taken for granted how much a part of it Mira was. Without her, it felt incomplete.

After giving the young woman, Ana, a plausible excuse for leaving, Jonen hurried out of the building, not caring where he went. Only after he felt the warm sunlight touch his skin and took a breath of fresh air did the knots in his stomach begin to unravel.

For the moment, the demons were at bay.

Outside, it was not quite midday. The stillness of morning broke into the animated pieces of early afternoon. There were not many clouds in the sky and the brilliance of the sun was glaring in contrast to the ambient lighting of his office. For a while, he strolled leisurely down the main walkway of Rura's busy commercial district, not having a specific destination in mind. He wondered whether he would be frivolous if he did not return to the office for a few hours.

By the time it was noon, he had no desire to return to his office, even if his spirits were considerably lifted. Outside, the world went along its business. People moved back and forth out of his view, just as places drifted by. Watching all of it imbued him with the hope of life going on. Someday, he would be one of those carefree people again. For every person who loved, lost and mourned, time's onward march ensured all wounds would eventually become scar tissue.

Since Garryn was his only appointment of the day, Jonen continued on his walk. The Prime was the only one he'd agreed to see today, because he'd sensed some urgency in the young man's manner the last time they spoke. Jonen was well aware not all of Garryn's problems had to do with the Dreaming. Some of it involved the forthcoming Ceremony of Ascension. Despite Jonen's personal problems, he wanted to help Garryn.

As he thought about the Prime and their afternoon session, it rekindled another thought in Jonen's mind: the investigation he was conducting regarding the older New Citizens. Guiltily, he realised there was much he was neglecting of late, even if he had a valid reason. Still a healer's work continued, regardless of his personal tragedies. The people who came to him needed his help.

It would be good if he could have more information for Garryn before their session. Surely by now, authorisation on his request about the New Citizens would have come through. Not even bureaucracy on Quorum Hill could be so inefficient. If he was going to idle half the day away, it ought to be for something constructive. With a sense of purpose, Jonen strode towards the Kleist district.

* * *

Upon entering the Department of Citizenship, the severe harridan who'd served him earlier fixed her hawkish gaze on him. Despite her aloof manner, Jonen saw she was surprised to see him and she followed him as he approached the counter. Jonen glanced at the name plaque at the edge of her desk. Officer Trayla.

Another clerk rose to attend him, but Trayla froze his advance with an icy glare. Instead of coming towards him, the intruder retreated, allowing his older counterpart to take his place. She seemed determined to deal with Jonen and, for the first time, he regarded her with the high-powered scrutiny he reserved for his patients. No longer did she seem ordinary.

Instead, he was certain there was a hidden purpose to her. As he studied her closely, a few key elements surfaced, making Jonen rebuke himself for his prior ignorance. He'd spent enough time around patients with dangerous mentalities to know everything about this woman was intentionally nondescript. For some unknown reason, she was trying hard to appear ordinary.

He doubted if any one of the people around Trayla knew her well, other than the fact she worked at this department. Her desk, from the brief glimpse he had taken earlier, was devoid of personal effects. No holopictures, no little trinkets of any kind, nothing to personalise a long-term workspace. Even Mira, who was as reserved and professional as any woman he had ever met, had something to mark her desk as hers alone.

It did not escape her that he was staring. The realisation forced away some of the haughtiness from her manner. At this time of the day, inquiries to the department were few and Jonen was alone in the line for attendance. Again, it felt as if the plasteel counter between them was a barrier to more than just information.

"I came here some weeks ago. I filled out an application for access to some information regarding the New Citizens. You remember me, don't you?"

It wasn't a question as much as it was an accusation.

The woman appeared unsettled, her manner fuelling his suspicions.

"Of course, Sir, mentalist Jonen wasn't it?"

"I'm impressed. With all the people you must get in here, I am surprised you remembered me specifically."

"It's not often I get such a request," her fingers rumbled over the keys of the console before her. Her eyes were no longer meeting his.

"I'm sure that must be it. So, have I cleared authorisation?"

"I'm afraid not," she responded, neglecting to look up at him. "Your application was turned down."

Slowly, she moved the screen on its pivot, so he could view the results for himself. Jonen saw a very generic application form with no specific query attached to it. It could have been for anything. Still the red letters at the end of the scroll, left no doubt as to its status.

DENIED

He wasn't surprised, but his suspicions about Officer Trayla were leading him down a very dark path. Mira had been killed the day after he requested this information. Was it a coincidence or was something actually going on?

"I'm sorry, but sometimes that's the way bureaucracy works. I don't make the rules," she explained, but Jonen could see that this attempt to sound concerned, even apologetic, was false. For some reason, she felt the need to change her manner towards him. Did she fear his suspicion? If so, why?

"I'll just have to pursue the matter from another avenue. I have associates in the government who will assist me in any further enquires. Thank you for your time."

He did not know why he added those last words. If the truth be known, he knew no one in the government. Most of his associates were academicians like himself. Politics and the healing sciences were kept in two distinctive realms and, until now, he'd never found the need to cross over. Besides, she must hear boasts like that all the time.

"I wish you every success."

And, once again, he knew she was lying.

* * *

Even though he still believed it was his imagination getting the best of him, Jonen was determined to pursue the matter. Why was it so difficult to get such harmless information? Disappointed at his lack of success, Jonen decided to return to his office and began walking back towards the Rura District.

The Kleist district did not have much in the way of residential space, since most of its land was occupied by government buildings. The people he saw on the way out were mainly civil servants from one branch of the government or another. These people did not look as if they had anything to hide, unlike Officer Trayla.

Jonen had meant it when he told Trayla he was going to find another way. The more he thought about it, the more he was at a loss to understand why the information was unavailable. Surely there could be nothing wrong with contacting the older New Citizens who lived on Brysdyn? When the children were brought to Brysdyn, there was a conscious effort not to expunge their heritage in place of a new one. The hope was to create an amalgamation of two cultures who found salvation by aiding each other.

Garryn could help me.

Of course! Why didn't he think of it before? The Prime was the second highest voice in the Empire. No one would dare deny him authorisation. Suddenly, Jonen found a great weight taken off his shoulders, because he had a way to proceed after all. It was the ideal solution, since Garryn needed to have this mystery answered more than he.

Jonen stepped off the kerb onto the road. The sidewalk on the other side of the street ran parallel to a park and would take him all the way back to the Rura district. It was well into the afternoon and the green was busy with people eating their lunches under the warmth of the sun. As he took in the sight of the manicured lawn, the water birds swimming on the shimmering waters of the pond, Jonen decided lunch surrounded by such beauty was not a bad idea.

"WATCH OUT!"

Jonen looked up just in time to see a skimmer rushing towards him at top speed. With no time to think, he jumped out of its path, hoping he'd cleared the distance needed. A jolt of panic gripped him as the vehicle swept past, so close he could feel the rush of air against his back. He landed hard against the paved sidewalk, his shoulder flaring in pain at the same time a loud crash roared in the background. For a moment, he remained on the ground, bruised and shocked by the whole incident.

"Are you all right?" The same voice who had shouted the warning earlier was asking him.

Jonen nodded, dazed, before registering the young woman staring at him with concern. "I'm fine. I'm just a little shaken."

"You were lucky," she helped him to his feet with one hand, while the other dusted him off. "You could have been killed."

"I could have," Jonen nodded numbly.

"The driver of that skimmer was not so lucky."

Jonen followed her gaze to see the two vehicles had collided with each other and were now at rest haphazardly across the road. A small crowd was gathering at the scene, gaping at the wreckage of metal and plasteel in morbid curiosity. At the sight of liquid fuel pooling beneath the vehicle, they retreated to a safe distance. One of the drivers, an older man, stumbled out of the lesser of the damaged skimmers, appearing unhurt but still disoriented.

Jonen pushed his way into the crowd, still clutching his shoulder, to see if he could provide any assistance.

"I'm a healer!" he announced and the crowd let him pass. While he was not a practicing physician, he still retained enough of his medical training to be capable of offering assistance. Besides, he could hear the sirens of approaching CP vehicles.

Approaching the skimmer that had almost run him down, he winced at the sight of the vehicle's condition. The front end was demolished on impact. The smooth metal surface was torn apart and forced into an impossible tangle of iron and smouldering plasteel. Incredibly, one of the bystanders managed to crack open the hatch. Jonen arrived just in time to hear the metal creaking open.

The hatch to the cabin slid open halfway before the bloody mess of a human form slumped out through the opening. Cries of horror and shock escaped everyone, as blood splattered across the ground, intermingling with the rising pool of plasma fuel. Swallowing away the lump in his throat, Jonen came forward to determine if the female driver was still alive.

She was not.

Her gold hair was matted and tangled with blood. Her head must have smashed against the plexiglass screen on impact. Her skull was a bloody mess of pulp and bone. With the help of the man who had gotten the door open, they pulled her out of the vehicle and lay her down on the ground. When the Central Police arrived, they would take charge of her. For now, Jonen did what he could.

Brushing the hair gently out of her face, Jonen stopped short when he found himself staring into the lifeless face of Officer Trayla.

IX

Distraction

Taking advantage of the confusion following the accident, Jonen saw the chance to slip away and took it. Until he could think things through, he had no wish to bring himself to the attention of the authorities. By now, he was convinced Officer Trayla had tried to kill him. Two traffic accidents in the space of a month was too much of a coincidence for Jonen to accept. Was Officer Trayla responsible for Mira's death? Had they killed her to distract him and, upon failing to deter him, made an attempt on his life? What had he stumbled onto that was worth killing for?

The imperative to get the information he wanted became even more vital when Garryn arrived for his session that afternoon, and Jonen had no choice but to tell his story.

Frankly, I'm amazed you didn't come out of it worse," Garryn looked up at Jonen from the leather sofa.

"So am I," Jonen confessed from behind his desk.

"This is all because you want to know about older New Citizens?"

It seemed so far-fetched, but Jonen was right. Two accidents in a month defied credibility, especially when they immediately followed a request for information about New Citizens.

"It seems hard to believe, but I can't see what else it could be."

If was hard to argue with the man. The denial of the request should have been the end of the matter, unless asking for it was a danger in itself.

The more Garryn analysed the situation, the more he disliked the conclusion he was reaching. Murderous conspiracies were myths created by the Security Elite for as long as he could remember. Edwen and his kind were always concocting some nonsense about subversive organisations within Brysdynian society. It was always Garryn's belief Edwen made half of this up to validate Security Elite's relevance.

Unfortunately, Jonen's story seemed to indicate such a conspiracy might actually exist.

"In fact, the application I saw on the screen was very generic. I'm wondering if it was just a decoy to show an application did exist, to be submitted and denied. I'm wondering if it was ever submitted for authorisation at all. Trayla became very agitated when I told her I'd pursue the matter through other channels."

Garryn decided to approach the fact methodically and laid out the sequence of events.

"You request the information and, for whatever reason, it's deemed too sensitive for access to be permitted. You apply for authorisation, showing your determination on the matter. To put you off the track, they murder Mira. Let's assume they knew how it would affect you. For a month, they get their wish. You're in mourning and they may even believe you've forgotten about it. Of course you don't, and you go back there today, and Officer Trayla reveals your request was denied. You say you can go through other channels to get the information. She then panics and decides to kill you herself."

"When you put it like that, it sounds chilling," Jonen confessed and he thought about Mira, how her life may have been discarded to hide a secret.

"This is all speculation. We need to find out as much as we can about Officer Trayla. I doubt a civil servant has reason enough to murder for what is really public access information. There should be at least three hundred thousand older New Citizens in the Empire. At least, that's what the history books say. What about them is so damaging? Assuming Trayla is even her name."

"You're right," Jonen exclaimed, seizing on that point. "Everything about her was nondescript. It felt like she took great pains to blend in."

"Exactly. For all we know, she might have been posted there simply to guard the information. To report to her superiors if someone came looking for it."

Garryn rose from his chair and went to the window. He stared outside the window, thinking about what was to be done. After a moment, he faced Jonen again.

"I will find out about the New Citizens and look into Officer Trayla's background. In the meantime, I will have some protection assigned to you."

"I don't think protection will be necessary," Jonen began to protest, but Garryn cut him off before he could say anything further.

"Jon, I think it's very necessary. Someone murdered your Mira and has tried to kill you. Maybe on both counts it was Trayla. Maybe it's just a coincidence and has nothing to do with the New Citizens at all but, right now, I prefer to err on the side of caution."

Jonen could not argue with the Prime. His life revolved around his work and his memories of military service were two decades behind him. Even then, he was fulfilling the Empire's mandatory conscription policy and not because he had any desire to be a soldier. This situation was beyond his ability to cope with, and he submitted to Garryn's counsel on how to proceed.

Now that this matter was resolved for the moment, Jonen had more to tell Garryn that did not involve Officer Trayla or the status of older New Citizens. It was time to tell him about the other Dreamers.

"Garryn, there is more. Please, sit down."

His tone made Garryn turn around immediately and he regarded the mentalist for a moment before returning to the leather seat.

"Part of the reason I was seeking out the information about the New Citizens is because you aren't the only one who is suffering from nightmares."

Garryn blinked. "What do you mean?"

"In the past six months, there have been numerous cases reported throughout Brysdyn. My colleagues in Tessalone and Rainab tell me the same story you know already. Their patients have violent nightmares about an alien place they have never been. Some have nightmares every night. Others are more sporadic, but debilitating enough to warrant attention. At first, we thought it was a previously undiagnosed brain disorder, but there's no evidence of it."

That revelation struck Garryn with the force of an exploding star. All this time, he'd thought he was going crazy, that the stress of war and the impending Ceremony of Ascendancy had driven him mad, but it wasn't just him.

"Tell me more," he managed to say.

"Individually, we were at a loss, until we consulted with each other and realised we had an epidemic on our hands. Once we pooled our resources and compared patient history, we learned a great deal more. We saw patterns beginning to form. All the patients are New Citizens exactly the same age, with a variance of no more than a year. Like you, they have no memory before their arrival on Brysdyn."

Garryn did not speak, letting himself absorb the weight of Jonen's words. It seemed incredible and yet sinister somehow. While he should have been relieved to hear the news of others like him, Garryn also felt a chill run down his spine. It was as if the crypt to something unspeakable had been unsealed. "And you believe that we are all having the same dreams?"

"Yes. While the dreams themselves differ from individual to individual, there are elements in all of them that are too identical to be just coincidence. For instance, all of you seem to be dreaming of a place with a blue sky."

Garryn stood up abruptly. It was just too much to take in all at once. He had always assumed that his dreams were memories of Cathomira, but it was well documented that Cathomira did not have a blue sky. The implications of what Jonen was telling him were taking on a frightening edge.

"I thought it was just me. I thought the pressure of becoming Prime was driving me mad."

"No Garryn. You're not going mad." He stepped away from his desk and joined the man on the sofa, placing a comforting hand on his shoulder. "I have a theory that may be disturbing for you to hear."

"It can't be any worse than what's happening to me," Garryn replied.

Jonen nodded and continued speaking.

"Something happened to all of you when you came here from Cathomira, something none of you seem to remember and that is omitted from all the records. The reason I was trying to contact the older New Citizens was to see if they remembered. It's no coincidence all Dreamers were very young when this happened. Your memories may have been suppressed. These dreams are those memories trying to surface."

"We have to find out what that is. I'll take this to Security Elite. If there is a conspiracy afoot, Edwen will know what to do. I may not like the man, but he is the best there at finding out secrets."

* * *

Garryn didn't waste any time. He headed straight for the Enclave after leaving Jonen's office.

Even as the skimmer weaved through the streets of Rura, Garryn was still reeling from the news he was one of many suffering these terrible dreams. Epidemic was a word no Brysdynian took lightly and even one such as this struck cold fear into his heart.

Were there that many cases of the Dreaming? Garryn's stomach hollowed at the thought there were others out there suffering from nightmares generated by a secret past. Why didn't it affect every one of them? Elisha was younger than him, so why didn't she dream? Were his friends at the Academy and the soldiers he served with also gripped in their private hell, too afraid to speak?

Garry thought about those repressed memories fighting their way to the surface. What did he remember of those days? Who cared for him after that terrible war on Cathomira, after the adults had died? He'd been no more than three years old when he was brought to Brysdyn. His earliest memories were of Aisha, his mother.

She had called him her little Prince.

Before her there was nothing. Each time he tried to remember being on Cathomira, he was confronted with a wall so thick and impregnable that nothing penetrated. For the first time in his life, Garryn wanted to know who he had been before he became Garryn, the next Prime of Brysdyn.

* * *

The trip to the Enclave was faster than he thought and Garryn looked around in interest as he directed his skimmer along the roundabout before the main entrance. In the centre of it was a bronze sculpture of the Security Elite emblem embedded into the grass. The Enclave was hidden within a fence of high walls, laser security systems and formidable-looking guards patrolling the grounds.

The Enclave building was a place of high, imposing, grey stone walls and polished marble columns. Grim figures were carved into its masonry, figures whose presence gave the place a feeling of finality. Edwen wanted the centre of Security Elite to command authority and to strike its visitors with awe. To that effect, Garryn could attest to its success.

It was the first time in his life Garryn had visited the Enclave and he did not want to feel intimidated by the fearsome appearance of the place. While Garryn felt the Security Elite was an outdated institution, he could not deny its presence in history. When the Scourge was rife, it was Edwen's rigid discipline of his troops that kept them from dissolving to anarchy. Even though their numbers were small, the group maintained order during the worst years of the Scourge.

As Garryn entered the Enclave to find Edwen, he was inundated with salutes and greetings by officers who were delighted by this unexpected visit. He supposed he ought to be used to this reaction by now. Most Brysdynians never got the chance to see the future Prime in person and would have even less opportunity when the title became official. He tried to be gracious even though it made him very uncomfortable.

Fortunately, the commotion of his arrival also saw to it he received speedy assistance in reaching the General. Not long after he reached the front desk to request a meeting, Garryn was approached by Major Danten, who helpfully expedited matters and escorted him to Central Command.

A short time later, he found himself being shown into the General's office.

"Garryn, this is an unexpected surprise," Edwen declared when Garryn walked into the room.

Garryn could only guess what suspicions were running through the man's mind at this visit. Neither man ever hid how he felt about the other's politics and, while Garryn respected Edwen, he did not support him.

"Thank you for seeing me on such short notice, General. I didn't mean to disrupt your day," Garryn said politely as Edwen gestured him to sit on one of the comfortable leather seats reserved for visitors to the office.

"Nonsense," Edwen dismissed the apology with a wave of his hand. "What can I do for you, Prime?"

"Edwen, I know we don't always share the same opinion, but I respect your service to Brysdyn and your abilities to get to the root of a problem." Garryn decided honesty was the best way to start with this man.

"To the point as always," Edwen commented, respecting the effort. "I thank you for your honesty and your compliments. Now, how can I help you?"

Now that the air was cleared, Garryn decided to get down to business. Edwen was watching him closely and Garryn remembered that, despite his age, this was a man not to be trifled with. "I have a favour to ask of someone who is far wiser in the ways of the Empire than I am."

This day was a veritable fountain of surprises, Edwen thought silently to himself. A favour from the next Prime was nothing to take lightly and he knew how difficult it was for Garryn to ask for his help.

"I will do what I can. What do you need?"

"I believe a friend of mine is in danger. In the last month, he has lost a close personal aide to an accident and he himself was almost murdered in the same manner today."

"Really?" Edwen leaned forward in interest. "What were the circumstances of the death?"

"A traffic accident, immediately following an inquiry about New Citizens."

"I see. And an attempt was made on his life, you say?"

"Only a few hours ago," Garryn continued, oblivious to Edwen's inner turmoil. "He was almost run over by a civil servant at the Department of Citizenship. Her name was Officer Trayla."

"Did they manage to apprehend her?" Edwen already knew the answer. If Trayla was in the custody of the Central Police, then he would have been informed long before Garryn's unceremonious visit.

"They didn't need to. She was killed when her skimmer collided with another, but you see the problem."

"Yes I do," Edwen nodded with all the sincerity he could muster. "You were right to come to me about this, Garryn. Please tell me everything you know about this situation and I'll do whatever I can to assist."

* * *

Major Danten was summoned to the General's office immediately after Garryn departed the Enclave. When he entered the room, Danten saw Edwen at his desk, wearing an expression of stone. The major had never seen the General with such a grim disposition. Danten knew something was dreadfully wrong to affect Edwen this way. Edwen made people fear him. He did not feel it himself.

"You sent for me, Sir," Danten said gingerly, still standing close to the door. He was too uncertain to approach any closer. Edwen said nothing, but kept staring at the window with that mask of granite.

"The situation is getting out of hand," Edwen stated suddenly.

"What situation?"

Edwen took a deep breath, dispelling the mood like a cloak. When he swung around in his chair to face Danten, the fear was gone. Instantly, like a gathering thunderstorm, Edwen's mood became dark and icy. Danten was familiar with the look. The General was readying for battle, in whatever shape or form the threat was choosing to take. Suddenly, Danten wanted to know why the Prime had come to the Enclave.

"Garryn is involved in this affair with the mentalist," Edwen replied, devoid of expression.

"How?"

"He claims to be a friend. I think *patient* would be a more accurate description of their relationship."

"The Prime requires a mentalist's treatment?"

"That is not important," Edwen said abruptly. "What is important is Agent 342 tried to murder the man this morning."

That news came as an utter shock to Danten. He'd been responsible for Agent 342's orders since this whole affair resurfaced. Even as Edwen spoke, Danten remembered his instructions to her. Under no circumstances was Jonen himself to be harmed. Not until they knew the nature of the threat he posed.

"Did she succeed?" Danten spoke, almost frightened to ask.

"No, she did not!" Edwen bellowed. "If she were not already dead I would order her terminated for such stupidity! Not only did she get herself killed, but she allowed the mentalist to live! Now he has applied to Garryn for help regarding the information denied to him!"

The magnitude of Edwen's words made Danten weak at the knees. From the onset of this situation, both men had been confident of dealing with the problem. But the inclusion of Garryn into these affairs changed everything. How could they hide anything from the future Imperator of the Empire?

"What do we do, Sir?"

"The mentalist has to die. There is nothing else for it. I will think of a way to accomplish this, but understand the gravity of the situation. This office cannot be suspect for any reason. Garryn dislikes Security Elite; he always has. His mother taught him well. I have no doubts that, when he is Imperator, he will dismantle the Enclave, brick by brick."

"But he'll come looking for the information. Even if the mentalist dies, he's already aware of the conspiracy."

"Fortunately," the General replied rising to his feet, "he came to me for assistance, a coup in itself. It suggests that, despite his feelings, he knows I am the man to trust in matters like these. That gives us time to prepare. If we do this right, not only will we close the book on this ugly affair, but we will have the gratitude of our Prime."

116

Danten nodded, but he was no longer feeling confident about anything.

X

Dreamers

The following day, Garryn found himself at Jonen's home.

As he guided the Skimmer through the front gates, he noticed the presence of the Security Elite guards Edwen had posted for Jonen's protection. The two sentries with their stony eyes and black uniforms assuaged Garryn's worries about the mentalist's safety. Offering him a brief salute as he passed them, Garryn gave them a nod of acknowledgement before entering the grounds of the modest home.

Compared to the grandeur of the aristocratic estates he'd visited since his return home, Jonen's residence was unimpressive. Still, what it lacked in prestige, it made up in warmth. The gardens were cared for by someone who took great pride in the work. Garryn ventured a guess that many of the shrubs and flowerbeds were likely planted by Jonen's own hand.

The house was of a comfortable size, constructed with polished stone, stained white with deep, red, ceramic slats tiling the roof. When he'd been in the service, Garryn had visited friends with homes like this. It was probably why he was so unmoved by the palatial splendour of the aristocrats' mansions. Mansions were there to impress and to promote some false sense of importance. They weren't homes like this one was.

Today was an important day for him even if Garryn was trying his hardest not to become carried away by his expectations. After telling him about a conspiracy the day before, Jonen had arranged a meeting at his home with all his Dreamer patients. The prospect of meeting others who shared his condition excited Garryn to no end. Finally, he didn't feel as if this insanity was his alone.

Jonen emerged from the front door just as the skimmer came to a halt. Instead of wearing his formal work clothes, Jonen wore casual dark pants and a loose-fitting knitted shirt without buttons. Garryn, who still clung to his military wardrobe, in rebellion against Feroz and his courtiers, found this a refreshing change. Everyone he knew in the palace and Quorum wore the best fabrics in the latest fashions. It was good to see not everyone cared about appearances.

"My house is honoured by your visit, Garryn," Jonen greeted with a wide grin. "The others are already here and they are thrilled at the prospect of meeting you."

"Not too thrilled, I hope." Garryn hoped his title wouldn't overshadow the meeting. "I'd like to speak to them as a member of the group, not as the Prime."

"I explained your wishes to them and they understand," Jonen assured him as he led Garryn through the front door.

The inside of Jonen's home was a place of large picture windows and green plants hanging from pivotal but unobtrusive corners of the house. It reminded Garryn of the cabin he was assigned during his service on a ship. It had felt so novel being able to decorate the thing himself because it was uniquely his own. Old books sat on polished wooden shelves with ornamental rugs on the carpeted floor. Jonen was very much an aficionado of ancient Brysdynian art, but none of the pieces in the place were authentic, simply good replicas.

The foyer dropped into a large living room sitting lower than the rest of the house. The walls of this room were mostly glass and the large trees with overhanging tendrils, taking up much of the rear garden, pressed against it. Descending the steps, Garryn observed a group of about a dozen people lounging around in chairs, large cushions, or sitting on the floor crossed-legged. It almost seemed like an academy study group.

"Garryn!" Kalistar stood up, waving from one of the cushions to greet him.

Completely surprised by her presence, Garryn could only manage a stuttered response. "Kal, what are you doing here?"

For a moment he almost didn't recognise her, because she looked nothing like the young woman wearing the lavish gown at the Myzyne ball. Instead, she was wearing a dark body suit and loose shirt, with her hair tied up in a comfortable ponytail.

"Imagine my surprise when I learned you and Kalistar were acquainted, after I made my announcement earlier," Jonen remarked, pleased to see the Prime relaxing at the sight of a familiar face.

"You are a Dreamer too?" Garryn asked her.

"Yes. It's the real reason I came home to Brysdyn. Father has no idea of course. If he did, he would never tell me. You know how he is."

Garryn did know. The older generation had little patience with mentalism as a science or an instrument of healing. To them, ailments of the mind were nothing more than a weakness in spirit. Seeing Kalistar put him at ease, especially when he was surrounded by so many new faces.

"I'm glad you're here."

"Everyone, this is Garryn." Jonen decided to stark making introductions and avoided any reference to Garryn's title because he knew the Prime would hate it.

Garryn regarded the group and nodded at them in friendly greeting. Now he wished he had worn his street clothes instead of this formal uniform.

They were studying him closely, trying to decide how much like them he truly was. He just hoped none of them had any preconceived notion of how a Prime was supposed to behave. With everything else he had to deal with over the next few hours, protocol was not something with which he wanted to grapple.

"Please find yourself a place to sit, Garryn, and we shall begin."

Jonen waded through the bodies to take a central place where he could supervise the session. Even though the gathering was informal, it was necessary to mediate the discussions, because he wanted everyone to have the chance to speak.

Kalistar gave Garryn an encouraging smile as she took his hand and led him to where she had been sitting on the floor. A tall, dusky-skinned man his age stood up to offer them his place on the sofa, introducing himself as Tam.

"Thank you," Garryn shook the man's hand, "but the floor will be fine."

Once seated, Jonen began the session by having everyone introduce themselves. Only two out of the fourteen Dreamers were unable to attend this particular session. Most of them had travelled from every corner of the Empire to be here, united by the strange dreams plaguing their nights.

The session began with each member recounting their dreams as well as they could remember, with Jonen filling the gaps as revealed by the neural analyser. Garryn listened to the stories with rising horror. Some of the dreams were even more violent and disturbing than his own.

Tam's story involved seeing people dying in the street of some alien city. They fell to the ground where they stood, succumbing to a deadly fog, undoubtedly responsible for wiping out the adults of Cathomira. Racial diversity was the norm in Brysdyn, but the city Tam remembered bore no such variance. Everyone looked like him. Garryn supposed it was possible the difference was enough to make the Cathomirans war with each other.

Kalistar's dreams revealed a world of tall, white, mountains, magnificent in their appearance. She spoke of snow and how cool it felt against her skin. There were primitive vehicles moving across ice covered streets and tall coniferous trees of rich emerald colours, sprinkled with snow. This almost pristine setting dissolved into the same violence Garryn experienced.

In her dreams, the white snow was soon splattered with red and soiled to a grey slush. Trickles of water hung tremulously from the tips of frozen icicles to become drops of blood. Terrible birds soared through the air, appearing dark and menacing, raining death on those around her. A man fell down dead in front of her. His blood pooled into a crimson crown around his head. She couldn't explain why his death woke her up screaming.

Another man, a medician from Kaltor Valley called Holaran, described a wall.

It was wall running from one end of the world to the other. It moved like a snake through mountains and rivers, keeping barbarians away. Holaran had no idea why he thought this, only knowing with every fibre of his being it was the truth. Like Tam, Holaran was of a different racial type, with deep yellow skin, dark eyes and a leaner build. In his dreams, he saw his people dying too, running along the wall as the same demon birds lay waste to his world.

Oren, a Central Police officer, revealed a dream of being chased through the tall grass of some unknown place. He never ran alone. There was always someone with him. She was about eight years old and had the same red hair he did. Despite the fear in her eyes, he recognised them as his own.

He is never able to speak to her to ask what they are running from. All he knows is she does not abandon him, even when the footsteps crushing the grass behind them grow louder. When the dark birds descend, he is ripped away from her, spirited into the sky. She screams after him, her hands flaying wildly as she tries to reach him, but she never does. He wakes up when he can no longer hear her.

It went on for most of the day, each one of them recounting their nightmares. As Garryn listened, the emotion welled inside of him, each story affecting him as deeply as his own affected them. After today, there would be no doubt in his mind that something terrible took place on Cathomira and that he was a part of it. Did the adults of Cathomira know what they were doing? Had they known, when they created their weapons of death, how it was going to end for all of them?

The last to speak was a young woman called Nikela. She was younger than all the others and, when it was her turn, it was Jonen who made the introduction first.

"Nikela's dreams are even more difficult to interpret than yours. When she came to me, I put her through the analyser like I did for all of you. Except her dreams were so abstract the analyser was unable to rebuild them."

Garryn observed Nikela closely and realised she could not be any more than twenty-three years old. He was twenty-six now, but he had come to Brysdyn when he was three years old. How old was Nikela when she arrived?

As if in response to Garryn's unspoken question, Jonen continued, "Nikela is also the youngest Dreamer we've encountered. She was less than a month old when she arrived on Brysdyn. She would have been born within days of the Cathomirans' cry for assistance. As a result of being unable to use the analyser, I attempted regression therapy, with better success."

Garryn could well believe Nikela was the youngest among them. Her skin was white, almost like a newborn child. Her brown hair was a glaring contrast to her skin. Except for a tinge of pink, her lips were devoid of colour. She was a willowy young woman who looked like some mythical sprite best left in an enchanted forest somewhere.

Nikela recounted her dreams to them when Jonen was finally done.

She dreamed of darkness, but this did not inspire fear; rather, it inspired comfort. She floated as if wrapped in a blanket of night, all safe and warm. There was neither hunger nor pain, just a sensation of lazy contentment. In the background, a muffled drumbeat continued to sound, rhythmic and oddly soothing.

The peace did not last and soon the drumbeat was eclipsed by the sharp sound of screaming. The shrill, disturbingly close cry of agony shook her entire universe, disrupting the soothing beats in the background. They hastened, gaining in momentum until they became harsh thunderclaps against her ears. Two distinct sounds clashed against each other, culminating in her world being ripped apart by a flood of light.

She felt the warmth of the liquid spill out in thick, viscous splashes. The light stabbed through the black, piercing her eyes, tearing through her consciousness. Her world was devoid of colour, with vague shapes hovering over her. The screaming became the shrieks of a world dying around her. Touching her face, her fingers slid over the slick of blood smeared across her skin.

The dark birds descended, carrying her away from the corpse with the split open belly.

Nikela was sobbing by the time her story was done. It was heartbreaking to see her tears, because she seemed so fragile. Kalistar gathered the young woman in her arms and held her as she broke down and Garryn wondered if the others drew the same conclusion as he did about Nikela's dream.

What in the name of the Creator had happened on Cathomira? Had someone actually slit her mother open like a ripe fruit and stolen her away? Garryn prayed this was a too vivid memory of Nikela's birth through a surgical removal. It was not unheard of for an expectant mother to need help during delivery. Surely this is what Nikela dreamed?

It had to be, Garryn thought.

Anything else was too monstrous to imagine.

* * *

After the session was over, only Garryn and Kalistar remained with Jonen when the other Dreamers left. It had been a long day and the scope of the dreams had become too much for some to bear. Nikela's version was the worst of all and affected Garryn more than he cared to admit. He wondered just how many New Citizens were Dreamers without knowing it.

In the meantime, Kalistar was inducted into the conspiracy resulting in Mira's murder. Garryn saw no harm including her, since it was her own father investigating the matter. Understandably, Kalistar was shocked. Like the others in the session, she attributed the presence of guards to Garryn's presence among them, not Jonen's protection.

"So you went to my father about this?" This surprised Kalistar, since the relationship between the two was never warm.

"You have to admit, if anyone knows how to root out a conspiracy, it's him. I take it he doesn't know you're seeing Jonen?"

"I thought of telling him, but you know the attitude towards mentalists." She shrugged, casting a sheepish glance of apology at Jonen.

"I do," Jonen dismissed her needless apology with a wave of his hand.

The study of mental health was a relatively new science on Brysdyn. The demand had arisen during the Scourge when the population, devastated by the loss of so many loved ones and facing life without children, needed to cope. Since then, the field had grown considerably but, to many of the old guard, it was still viewed as enabling the weak.

"At some point I will have to tell him about this group. I'm sure he suspects that I'm your patient, but to help us, I think he needs to understand the scope of the problem," Garryn explained to Jonen.

"I believe you may be right," Jonen conceded the point, handing Garryn his data table. "Without access to the official records, I've gone as far as I can with my own investigations."

"What have you found so far?" Garryn's fingers flew over the screen to peruse the data Jonen had gathered.

"Well, as far as I can tell, until we actually received the distress signal, there was never any evidence of Cathomira's planets being populated."

"That's right," Kalistar agreed, recalling her studies at school. "Life on Cathomira was a surprise to the scientific community. They were certain the environment was too hostile for human life to evolve there naturally.

"That can't be right," Garryn pointed out. "Look at the diversity of the population. The variances are just like ours. It can't be just one baking dust ball if it produced that much variation."

"Has anyone been to Cathomira since the rescue?" Jonen inquired. As a mentalist, astrophysics and space exploration was not something of which he kept abreast. Until the Dreamers, Jonen had little reason to think about the place at all.

"No," Garryn replied despite the fact the Imperial Fleet was shifting its focus towards exploration, like the Jynes. With peaceful co-existence, the Imperial Fleet was finding new purpose by exploring uncharted areas of space. For the first time, they were expanding the Empire through means other than conquest. "It's not surprising, though. The planet's under quarantine."

"I wish we knew more about this biological weapon they unleashed. Even if it wasn't fatal to you, it could have produced unforseen side effects. Your dreams might be a result of that. Unfortunately, there is no medical data on the Cathomiran virus."

"Why can't we send someone there?" Kalistar asked.

"Now that's an idea. I do have the authority to launch a mission like this."

"I know colleagues who would love the opportunity to examine the Cathomiran virus," Jonen added. "Of course, the Healers Circle would never allow samples of the virus to be brought back to Brysdyn, so we could conduct our research within the system and then destroy the samples before returning home to minimize contamination. There would be no need to put the Empire at risk."

"Perhaps you can study the planet itself as well. There are still a lot of grey areas regarding Cathomira. It would be good to clear them up."

"Do you think you can arrange this?" Kalistar asked.

"I don't see why not. I'm supposed to be the Prime, I might as well see what I can do with the title."

XI

Expedition

Organising an expedition to Cathomira was no small matter.

Garryn quickly learned it took more than a title to navigate the maze of bureaucracy required to make such a thing happen. The more inquiries he made, the more convinced he became he was ill-equipped to handle any of it. In the end, he appealed to his father for help and the Imperator's advice was to get himself an aide familiar with the political terrain of Brysdyn.

For Garryn, there was only one man who would do.

Benaris was the agricultural heart of Brysdyn. It provided the bulk of the planet's sorghum food supplies and existed in vast, neatly sectioned plantations. Most of these were government-owned, although some nobles and wealthier Brysdynians invested in parcels of land for retirement purpose once they were done with life at court. Ashner, whom Garryn was journeying to see, was neither wealthy nor an aristocrat.

Ashner was a Jyne. He was tutor to the young Aisha before her marriage to the Imperator and had joined her in Brysdyn as her aide. When Garryn and Elisha were children, he took on the role of tutor and both the royal children adored him. Until Aisha's death less than two years ago, Ashner was her constant companion and friend. It was Iran who awarded Ashner with an estate in Benaris in gratitude for a lifetime of service and friendship.

The trip from Paralyte took less than an hour in Garryn's private ship. He set out early and was cruising through the warm skies of Benaris by mid-morning. The climate was less humid in comparison to Paralyte, edging closer to a hot savannah. Even though the environmental controls of his ship kept the dry heat out, Garryn felt the drain of moisture from the prickling in his skin.

As he approached *Serafia*, the fanciful name Ashner gave his estate, he had already crossed over hundreds of acres of lusty green fields and rolling hills. *Serafia* was not as lavish as some of the other aristocratic residences in the area, but it had its own elegant charm. There was a moderate sized manor house Ashner had decided to renovate instead of demolish and a good sized lake where Garryn and the old man occasionally fished. The more recent addition to the place was a small flight pad where Ashner's small T25 Runner transport was docked.

"Garryn!"

Garryn had wanted to surprise the man with his visit and hadn't announced himself until the very last moment.

"Hello, old man." Garryn embraced Ashner warmly. "How is life in the provinces?"

"Perfectly quiet," Ashner replied as they both began walking towards the house.

Ashner was well into his seventies now, with a full head of white hair worn close to his scalp and a neatly trimmed beard of the same. He was a tall man once, but the slight stoop in his shoulders made him shorter than Garryn. His clothes were remarkably casual for a man who was once a resident of the Domicile, but Garryn was unsurprised by Ashner going native.

"And you hate it," Garryn retorted.

"Desperately so," Ashner laughed.

They spoke of family and court gossip as they walked to the house. Garryn noticed the gardens had undergone changes since his last visit. Under the occupancy of the previous owners the gardens were sculptured perfection with manicured lawns and fashionable shrubs and flowers. Now most of it was torn out and replaced with farrowed rows of cabbages and other vegetables. There was even livestock roaming the paddocks around the lake, grazing in contentment in the afternoon sun.

Garryn could not help thinking this place was in severe need of children and a family. Not that he voiced that observation. Ashner was no lover of women and his preferences for young men had long since passed. Both men retreated into the house of provincial design and decor. Most of the walls were covered with full bookshelves, as was to be expected of the man Garryn always knew to be a scholar. His library consisted of text from all over the galaxy.

While Ashner's housekeeper, Dian, fetched them something cool to drink, both men settled down to talk in the sunroom. Wide windows and light coloured paint gave the room a feeling of perceptual warmth. It also gave a wonderful view of *Serafia's* pastoral life and its lake. Garryn felt more at ease at this place than he had at any other since returning home.

"So, how does it feel on the eve of becoming Prime?" Ashner asked as he studied Garryn in the opposite armchair.

"I still have *five* days," Garryn countered petulantly.

"Five days or weeks, does it matter? The inauguration is coming. You will soon be Prime."

"A Prime who is in dire need of an aide," Garryn declared, using Ashner's question as the perfect segue into his reason for coming here.

"And here I thought it was your sentimental need to see your old teacher that led you to come all this way to see me."

"That too, but mostly because I need you in the same way my mother did."

"I did teach you well." Ashner smiled with approval at the play on his sentiments. "Hitting the old man where it hurts? Bravo my boy, I couldn't have done better myself."

His playful tone subsided after a moment as his expression saddened. "Your mother was like my child, you know. It gave me so much pleasure to be a part of her life and then, later, a part of yours and your sister's. It wasn't right she should die before me."

"The Scourge's claws were sharp. Father told me she never recovered the way she should have, always pushing herself harder than anyone else."

"Your mother was a remarkable woman and your father adored her. Perhaps to his fault, he could never say it to her."

That was true, Garryn decided. Iran did love her deeply. Many at court could never fathom how two people from such different worlds could have so successful a marriage. Aisha was the daughter of the Jyne Chancellor, and Iran the Imperator of Brysdyn. One cool and civilised, the other fiery and aggressive. They complimented each other and, even now, Garryn could see how incomplete his father felt without her.

Getting back on point, Garryn continued to make his case. "Ashner, I need you even if it's for a while. I have some things I need resolving quickly and I don't have the political experience to weave through the bureaucracy to get it done. I need someone who knows the terrain better than I do."

"I see," the older man's expression hardened into the astute political animal of reputation. "What sort of things?"

"I need to launch a scientific expedition to Cathomira."

Ashner's surprise showed in his eyes. "For what purpose?"

Without hesitation, Garryn revealed the nightmares leading him to the Dreamers and the conspiracy stumbled upon by Jonen. Ashner listened quietly, offering no judgement until Garryn had related the entire story. When he'd finished, Ashner took a deep breath and both men remained quiet for a few minutes.

"Going to Edwen may not be the wisest thing you could have done."

"Excuse me?" Garryn had not expected that.

"Perhaps it is my paranoia," Ashner replied, leaning closer, all trace of mischief in his eyes disappearing for something edged and dark. "I have found over the years dealing with Edwen is like making a pact with the Dark One. I would not be too quick to trust him. He has a tendency to use a situation to meet his own agenda and put you in a vulnerable position."

Garryn's stomach hollowed at the idea he might have compromised himself by involving the Security Elite. "But Edwen agreed to help. He said he would help me find out the truth."

Ashner's scepticism showed. "Perhaps he will do that, but he will also use what he needs to gain the support of the Imperator, to ensure the survival of his Security Elite."

Garryn was aware of Ashner's opinion of Edwen and his Security Elite. Edwen could never stomach the idea of the Imperator's wife being a 'foreigner'. He cared just as little for her aide and anything Jyne. As much as he loved Ashner, Garryn could not ignore the possibility that his teacher's opinion might bear some prejudice, but he could not ignore it either.

"If I don't go to Edwen, then to whom do I go?"

Ashner frowned, seeing Garryn's dilemma. "Does he know his daughter suffers from this Dreaming disease?"

"No, Kalistar didn't dare tell him. You know how the old guard feel about mental illness."

Ashner knew only too well, because he knew Edwen. "It would be advisable if she didn't tell him. You are correct in believing Edwen would be the one to find out if there is a conspiracy afoot, but it may be information he will use to his advantage."

"Edwen has men protecting Jonen. I believe that his eagerness to help me is to save his own skin. He knows how I feel about the Security Elite."

"Perhaps you're right but, remember, the General is no fool. He will not allow any suspicion to fall on his precious institution if the mentalist should die."

"So what do I do? The information about Cathomira is scarce. We don't know whether what's happening to us is an actual brain disorder or a shared experience. You were at court when we were brought to the Empire. Was there anything unusual about it?"

Ashner did not immediately answer, giving the matter some deep thought first. "The existence of life on Cathomira was always a shock to us. We didn't believe it possible. The red sun should have killed any chance of that, but we did receive a distress signal and, after that, it all happened very fast."

"Who received it?" Garryn questioned.

"It came from one of the relay stations on the Imperial perimeter. Tasys, if I remember correctly. By the time the news of the distress signal reached us on home world, the rescue ships were already despatched."

"The Imperial Navy, you mean," Garryn finished.

"No, the navy was fragmentary. You must remember, Garryn, one-third of the Empire died during the Scourge. What remained of the navy protected the main space lanes from bandits and pirates. All our mineral deposits and commodities were vulnerable, because we lacked the manpower to protect them. The Imperial fleet couldn't be spared to make the journey to Cathomira."

"So who came to get us?"

"The Security Elite, of course."

* * *

When Garryn returned to Paralyte, Ashner went with him.

The old tutor made it very clear the appointment was temporary. He would remain long enough to help Garryn solve his current mystery, then return to his provincial life. As much as Ashner hated the quiet, he had also become accustomed to it in his old age.

At first, Garryn thought Ashner's suspicions about Edwen to be the venom of an old man for a hated enemy, but the more he thought about it, the more logical it became. Edwen's power was second only to the Imperator and his house.

Edwen knew more dirty secrets and unexposed scandals than anyone else in the Empire. Throughout the years, he'd fortified the Security Elite with a buffer of protection built on intimidation and fear. Garryn was certain little occurred in the Empire without Edwen's notice. With Garryn's rise to the position of Prime, Edwen would be foolish not to exploit any vulnerability in order to survive.

Ashner returned to the Domicile and set to work immediately, assembling Garryn's expedition without direct involvement of the Imperator or the Elite. In the meantime, Garryn continued his consultation with Edwen and the investigation. As Ashner predicted, the General did not report anything of value. Meanwhile, Garryn continued to see Kalistar, who gave him some insights into the General, even if it did set the court abuzz with rumours of their relationship.

While Garryn found this innuendo irritating, it did serve a purpose. Despite the rumours, he confessed his affections for Kalistar were strong, though he worried he might be doing her an injustice. At a time when his life was about to change irrevocably, she was one of its bright spots. She was a beautiful woman, but there was kindness in her he found comforting. It was also good to have a friend who understood what he was going through with the Dreaming.

"So your new aide managed to secure a science ship from the navy?" she asked during dinner at the Domicile.

"Yes, apparently our scientific community is thrilled at the prospect of going to Cathomira for research."

Garryn explained how amenable the Minister for Scientific Research was to the idea after Ashner spoke to him about it. The scientific world had grown in prominence since the Scourge, but not even its power could overcome the Healers Circle's paranoia at the study of virology. With their very considerable influence, they had always quashed any request to study Cathomira's virus but, this time, with the office of the Prime driving the demand, they were unable to refuse.

"All it took after that was a whisper to the right people of my gratitude for their cooperation."

"So you didn't really promise them anything," Kalistar found it amusing to see how Garryn wielded his newfound power.

"No I didn't," he took a sip of his wine.

"So when do they leave?"

"Shortly after the inauguration. I'd prefer it sooner, but you know what the festivities are going to be like." A grimace stole across his face like an automated reflex. "Nobody wants to miss any of it."

"What does happen?"

"Let's see." He eased back into his chair and gazed at the lights beyond the balcony. For once, Feroz did not object when Garryn suggested their dinner be served here. The view of the balcony from the city was certainly worth the effort. "There's a circus in front of the Quorum in the morning. Everything from fire swallowers to the acrobats of Tayto, complete with performing Sayleen dragons and the Lords only know what else. Some of the vendors at Kirkaris will be moving their stalls to Quorum Hill for the day."

"Where will you be?"

"Hopefully stowed away on a freighter with Borellian stock horses on its way to Jyne."

Garryn was not entirely joking.

"Be serious." Kalistar laughed.

Garryn shrugged in defeat. "I'll be here in this room, watching the whole thing from here, with a very tall glass of something strong. At the appointed hour, I'll make my way to the Quorum Hall with Feroz and an entourage of I'm not sure who and then I'll become Prime."

"What's after that?" She was fascinated by the subject, even though she was aware Garryn hated every minute of it.

"I think the street party will continue." Garryn tried to remember the details as Feroz had explained them. "By then it should spread all the way to the Domicile. Essentially, the entire Hill will be one big party. The Domicile gates will be open and the courtyard will play host to a ball with the entire city in attendance. There will be entertainment, amusing animals and one Prime for all to see."

He didn't mean to sound bitter, but it came out that way nevertheless. Garryn dropped his fork on his plate, suddenly feeling in no mood to eat. "I just wish I could get it over with quickly. I want it done so I can get on with the rest of my life or at least start making the proper adjustments."

"You have too much time on your hands, Garryn," Kalistar said, leaning closer towards him across the table. Reaching for his hand, she gave it a gentle squeeze. "You've spent too much time thinking about how awful being Prime would be. It also hasn't helped they treat you like the temple sacrifice while dragging you from one place to another. Maybe what you need is to do the things you want until then. Forget Feroz and those courtiers, what are they to you?"

"I do know as Prime I have a painful death planned for him. Probably something involving suffocation by cheap clothes."

"That's the spirit. Live for revenge if nothing else will do," she winked.

XII

Secrets

"How do I look father?"

Edwen looked up from the console at his desk as Kalistar glided into his study unannounced, wearing a sweeping blue gown. As he let his eyes run up the length of her, he felt exceptionally old. Was it really a decade since she used to sit on that small table in the corner of his study doing her lessons while he worked?

"Uncommonly civilised," he answered with genuine pride.

"Thank you," she beamed, knowing him well enough to take that as quite a compliment. "I shall be joining Garryn after the ceremony, father. He's a bit overwhelmed by all the attention and I think he could use the company."

Today was the day, wasn't it? Edwen sighed, feeling his age again. Garryn would officially become Prime and successor to the Imperator. Glancing out the window of his home a short distance from Quorum Hill, he saw that the streets were already filling up with people. One could only imagine the crowds clamouring to see the Prime on his historical ascension.

"He will do fine, I am sure. That young man has a streak of granite in him. If I know Garryn, it's the festivities he dislikes, not the title or the power he will be gaining."

"Garryn is not like that, father," she protested, trying to keep the annoyance out of her voice. The remark stung, though she did not know why. "He's given great thought to what he'll do when he becomes Prime, but I don't think he means to shake the halls of the establishment."

"Star," he eased back into his chair and looked at her critically. As much as he loved her, he had to remind himself that she was, after all, female, highly emotional and incapable of thinking clearly when it came to matters of the heart.

"Think what you may like of Garryn when he's your lover or your husband, but never deceive yourself to what he is. He is not Iran's son. He has not inherited Iran's weaknesses. Like me, he is not a man who craves bloodshed or war, but he is a predator. Make no mistake of that. When he has the power, he will use it accordingly. Only the Lords can help those who get in his way."

"I think you are wrong," she declared hotly, letting her feelings get the better of her. "Garryn is a good and kind person. He cares about people. Even now, he's organising a research trip to Cathomira, because he wants to help studies about New Citizens."

Edwen's eyes flashed. "A research trip?"

Kalistar swore inwardly, realising she might have inadvertently revealed some information purposely kept away from her father. While Garryn did not tell her to keep it a secret, she was certain he did not mean for her to tell everyone either. Still, what possible harm could come from telling her father? The expedition was going to happen, whether he liked it or not.

"Yes," she answered, the bluster gone from her voice. "Garryn tells me he's endorsed a trip to Cathomira for scientific research."

"Very admirable." Edwen's face betraying nothing. "Perhaps I was wrong about him."

Her surprise at his concession made Kalistar even more nervous but, like him, she knew how to hide what she thought.

"Maybe you were," she replied softly and retreated from the room.

Even though he'd conceded the point, there was no satisfaction in the victory. The General rarely conceded the point on anything unless it served his purpose and there was something very disturbing about this.

Departing the room, she left her father to contemplate the news she had unwittingly delivered into his hands.

For the hundredth time, Garryn paced the floor of his suite, like a caged cat.

Outside the balcony, the roar of the crowd was deafening and he considered if closing the doors would make any difference. He suspected it wouldn't and so kept them open, because crowds were something he was going to have to get used before the day's end. In the streets below, they were already jockeying for the best view when the ceremony began.

Not for the first time that day, he wished he could escape all this.

A sudden knock against the door to his suite startled him and Garryn regarded it with puzzlement. He didn't think anyone would have time to visit him today. The atmosphere inside the Domicile was utterly frantic today. Everyone was racing to complete the final preparations for the ceremony and the banquet that followed.

It isn't Feroz, Garryn thought with certainty. Feroz was rarely courteous enough to knock. Garryn just hoped it was not another courtier asking him if he needed any help getting dressed. The blessed event was four hours away and no one would be coming to collect him for at least three.

It couldn't be either Elisha or his father either. At the moment, the Imperator was playing host to the Chancellor of Jyne, who was attending the ceremony as further affirmation of their new alliance. His sister, on the other hand, was down in the courtyard, running the household like a general preparing for war. She wanted everything to be perfect for her big brother's day.

When the door opened, Garryn found himself genuinely pleased to see Kalistar standing with Feroz in the corridor.

"Kal!" he exclaimed, grateful to see a friendly face. "What are you doing here?"

"The young lady felt you might need the company, Sire," Feroz spoke before Kalistar could. "Don't worry Prime, I will be happy to see the young lady escorted to the Hall when you leave for the ceremony."

"That would be fine, Feroz," Garryn answered, surprised by the magnanimity of the Head Courtier. "Thank you very much. I truly appreciate it."

"Prime," Feroz said with some genuine feeling, "I know we have not always agreed, but I am most proud today to be honoured as your courtier on this occasion."

His words were so exaggerated it was almost comical, but there was genuine sentiment in the statement. He did not doubt the pride he detected in Feroz's voice and was touched by it.

"The honour is mine, Feroz," Garryn returned graciously. "I apologise for giving you so much trouble."

"Oh," Feroz's eyes lit up by the unexpected apology. "You are no more difficult than your father, Prime. My predecessor was similarly challenged, but thank you. I shall always remember this."

With a slight bow, he turned on his heels and hurried away. Within seconds, Feroz disappeared down the corridor and Garryn looked up at Kalistar, who was smiling at him.

"Please come in," he gestured her into the room.

"Yes," she said sweeping in with her gown. "I am so proud of you! You've made his career, you know."

"Well, I have put him through quite a bit. I've never had much patience for royal protocol and I was never very good at hiding my dislike."

The rumble outside made it difficult to hear him, so Kalistar took it upon herself to shut the balcony doors. Once closed, the roar dropped to a low drone, permitting them to hear each other clearly. She noticed he wore only a robe, even though his full dress uniform was laid out for him on his bed.

"I take it you've been shut up here all day." She took a seat on the sofa.

"Like a hermit." Garryn joined her. "Although I'm not sorry. It sounds crazy out there."

"I know. I had to get through all that."

She did not elaborate that she had arrived in her father's skimmer with its Security Elite designations emblazoned across its hull. Had she tried to gain entrance without it, she would have been turned away by the Domicile guards. Her intention to surprise Garryn with her visit meant he wasn't able to leave word at the sentry stations to permit her entry.

Garryn grimaced at the thought of wading through the crowd before forcing the thought out of his mind. Paying more attention, he noticed her gown for the banquet after the ceremony and had to admire how much it flattered her.

"Not that I'm complaining, but you really didn't have to do this," Garryn said, even though he was glad to see her.

"Well," she reached for his hand, squeezing it gently. "I knew how crazy things would get before the ceremony and that you'd be here all alone. I thought I'd keep you company until you had to go."

"Thank you," he said gratefully.

Meeting her gaze, there was an unfathomable expression in her eyes he couldn't quite read. Then, without giving him any warning, she leaned over and pressed her lips gently against his. Her mouth felt warm and inviting and Garryn felt himself react to her immediately. So far, their relationship had been mildly flirtatious, but Garryn's head had been filled with so many things, he'd never acted on it. Furthermore, as Prime, he no longer had the freedom to be so carefree with his dalliances. Any relationship he began with anyone had lasting implications for both parties.

Despite his reservation, he allowed himself to enjoy the taste of her lips against his. Right now, this was the best distraction to the day ahead, even if he was uncertain how far this was going to go. As she continued to kiss him, baser instincts took over and lust won over sense. He'd been with enough women to know she was urging him to take control and that she was happy to oblige the need she had provoked.

They explored each other tentatively until lust escalated things to the point of no return. With gentle consideration, he slid into her body, enjoying the intimacy. While the pleasure was exquisite, he wondered if there were other lovers before him. He hoped he was not the first. Such an occasion deserved better than a hasty coupling meant to distract him from the day's ordeal.

Nevertheless, their lovemaking was a tender, pleasured affair and they moved like dancers to a sweet song only they could hear. It drowned out the world and for that moment, they were alone in a universe made for two.

When it was over, they lay in each other's embrace, basking in the heat of flesh against flesh and a sense of intimacy that was more than just physical.

"I hope that made you relax a little," she teased.

Garryn smiled, even though he did not look up at her. "It did, but I hope this wasn't just because of that."

"Of course not," she scoffed. "I care about you and if we can't take comfort in each other when we need it, then we're not very good friends."

Was it just friendship she felt? Garryn didn't think so but he didn't press the issue. The truth was, he did care for her a great deal but, in retrospect, he wondered if he shouldn't have tried harder to resist her.

"Kal, I care about you," he spoke, aware he needed to tread carefully. "This was amazing and you're amazing..."

"Garryn," she stopped him from speaking. "I didn't do this because I want to snare a husband or because I took pity on you. I care about you and if this leads to something so be it, and if does not, then we will remain friends. This is a beautiful moment. Don't spoil it by over thinking."

Still uncertain if he was being unfair to her, Garryn nodded and accepted her words, even though he couldn't help but think the moment might have already been spoiled.

XIII

Ascension

The doors to the Avatar would open today.

Iran was seventeen years old the last time any light entered the sacred room. He was escorted by his father and the Master of the Records as they entered the small, seldom visited room inside the Quorum Hall. Twenty-six years ago, Iran was convinced there would never be another Ceremony of Ascension, because of the Scourge.

Yet here he was, about to take the historic walk with his son.

As he thought of Garryn's ascendancy, he felt as if his life had finally come full circle. Today, he had fulfilled the oath made to his people inside these walls. Iran led the Empire through its worst years, married and produced an heir for the next generation of Brysdynians. If he wished, he could make himself ready for retirement. Once Garryn became comfortable with ruling in his place, he might consider it.

Iran knew Garryn had no such expectations. His son was raised to be neither ambitious nor greedy. He would wait until his father was ready to step down.

It warmed Iran to no end knowing Garryn loved him more than he wanted to be Prime.

Adopted or not, he was his mother's son and she left the best of herself in him. She had seen to it that his education was an amalgam of two worlds. Gone was the brute strength and savagery of the old ways. Garryn's education was tempered by logic and compassion. It was an exceptional combination, but then the boy had always stood out.

From the very first.

* * *

The Imperator remembered the day he laid eyes on the child who would be his son.

At the time, there were no exact figures on the number of children being brought back from Cathomira, because not all the ships had returned. Three Security Elite ships conducted the rescue and no one expected them to return with children who would become the hope of the Empire.

The first batches of children were held in quarantine by the Healer's Circle. All manner of tests were conducted on the refugees to ensure the virus responsible for the decimation of Cathomira did not survive the trip to Brysdyn. Only after they were satisfied the children carried no hidden pathogens were potential parents finally allowed to see them.

Iran had thought it was no way to get a child as he walked through the sterile rooms of the building and spied healers tending to frightened young. The process was obscenely clinical.

They adopted Elisha first. She was barely a year old and Aisha took one look at the smiling baby in the cot with her dark curls and bright eyes and was utterly lost. She was named Elisha after Aisha's mother and she enchanted both of them with her first gurgle of a smile.

Finding Garryn was a little more complicated.

After the documentation was processed and they were preparing to return to the Domicile with their new daughter, a little boy ran out in front of them. Somehow, he managed to escape his minders and make his way to the main exit of the building. The Healer in pursuit was unamused. The boy paused in the middle of the white corridor for a moment before turning to run. His three-year-old legs were still quite uncoordinated and he took no more than a few steps before tripping clumsily over his feet, hitting the floor hard.

He didn't cry. If anything, he looked annoyed at the clumsiness allowing the Healer to catch up with him. The expression of complete irritation on his cherubic face made Iran smile. Before he could be wrestled away, he caught sight of the Imperator and his eyes lit up like the sunrise. Before Iran knew it, the boy's arms were outstretched towards him.

The child spoke and, even though Iran did not recognise the word, it transcended language. It was one word, but there was so much behind it Iran was completely won over.

Da.

* * *

Garryn's arrival brought the roar of the crowd to feverish pitch and returned Iran to the present.

As soon as he appeared, cheers and applause broke out and, amidst this furore, some chanted his name. The atmosphere cackled with the electricity of anticipation and a feeling of hope. Iran did not remember his Ascension being so jubilant, but then a great deal had changed for Brysdyn since those carefree times. Twenty-six years ago, the population never thought there would be another Prime to take his place.

Iran shared the feeling of exhilaration with his people and the guests at the podium with him as they watched Garryn ascend the large steps. Garryn's gaze met his before continuing across the rest of the assembled guests, pausing momentarily when he sighted Kalistar seated next to her father, Edwen.

The Imperator was not deaf to the rumours making the rounds at court, although he didn't think the relationship was as passionate as many believed. Not that he minded if it were otherwise. Kalistar was a young lady of good standing and intelligence, a suitable wife for the next Imperator, if Garryn chose her. Aisha would have approved.

Thinking of Aisha, Iran glanced quickly at Chancellor Garin of the Jyne behind him. The older man was beaming in pride at his grandson and namesake. Garryn was his oldest grandchild and the Chancellor had made a special effort to be present today. Aisha was Garin's only daughter in a household full of sons, and his favourite. Her death was just as hard on him as it was for Iran.

Among the guests were the elite of the Brysdynian aristocracy, as well as leaders from numerous aligned worlds. Ashner, Aisha's old tutor and aide, was also present and instrumental in helping Elisha coordinate the festivities for this momentous occasion. While Iran was dubious about the choice—a new Imperator should really have an aide closer to his age, Ashner was still a good man to have at one's disposal.

The Master of the Records appearing behind Iran prompted the crowd's roar to drop to an audible hush. The keeper of Brysdyn's spiritual history emerged from the entrance of the Quorum building, commanding the respect of everyone present. Lord Disciple Salym was the spiritual leader of the Brysdynian people, who spent his days at the Cathedral at Alwi, training acolytes for service to the Lords.

If Salym was nervous on his momentous occasion, he certainly did not show it. His expression was calm and his brown eyes showed little emotion. With the breeze ruffling his hair, he appeared younger than his years, certainly too inexperienced to be Master of the Records.

When Garryn finally reached him, the great horn at the top of the Quorum building was sounded. The horn was a relic of the old White Star Empire, when their civilisation was still in its infancy and men lived in caves. The horn had acted as a way to gather the community together in the days before sophisticated methods of communication. On this occasion, the horn demanded silence from its audience and the crowd was silenced even further.

"Today, the Great Wheel of Ascension turns once more. The old must pave the way for the new and a new dawn to begin. The cycle of the beginning and the end, as taught to us by the Transcendent Lords, has reached full circle and it is time for the Empire to enter a new age."

Salym stood on top of the steps, the red carpet running down from his feet like a river of blood. He motioned father and son to approach and they did. They stood one step beneath him as custom demanded.

"Who has ridden the Great Wheel before this day?" Salym spoke in a loud booming voice.

"I, who was ordained Iran the First – Imperator and ruling son to House Brysdyn."

Salym nodded. "Who is chosen to take his place on the Great Wheel from this day?"

"I, Garryn the First – Prime and heir to the ruling House Brysdyn."

"It is witnessed," Salym continued. "With the grace of the Transcendent Lords and that of the Brysdynian people, let Ascension begin. First born of the Imperator, speak your name and then hear me to repeat my words."

"I am Garryn."

The Imperator's eyes flickered and Garryn guessed the last time his father had heard these words, it was when he was taking the oath.

"Garryn, know your Empire as you know yourself. Do you take upon yourself the mantle of Prime, to be in service to the Empire and House Brysdyn until such time as you become Imperator? Are you ready to take the Oath?"

Trembling, Garryn nodded, but remembered the answer required according to law.

"At the dawn of civilisation, when the heat of the White Star upon us was young, the Imperator stepped forward to protect the people. I speak the words spoken by my forebears, passed from father to son and from mother to daughter. Twenty generations from the beginning of the Exodus, I Garryn, son of Iran, say these words as my bond to the people of Brysdyn and the Empire. I will serve as Prime until such time as I can become Imperator and, when the time comes, I will prepare the way for he who comes after me."

"The Oath has been spoken in accordance with the forms. The age of Garryn the First begins."

* * *

With the conclusion of the ceremony, the crowd broke out into roars of jubilant applause and cheering. With the formalities taken care of, the celebration would now move to the Domicile courtyard as the street festivities began.

It felt appropriate to wear his uniform, since the crowd cheered him like a conquering hero instead of their newly appointed Prime. He wondered if they saw any real difference. There was no chance to talk to Kalistar after Garryn was shuffled back onto his skimmer, so he had to wait until the ceremony at the Domicile before he could see her.

This time, he did not journey alone. His father and Elisha joined him for the return trip to the Domicile. Ashner would follow soon after, escorting their guests to the festivities. The gap gave the family a moment to catch up before the next part of the celebration began.

The roar of the crowd was almost deafening as the skimmer flew past the thousands of people waving and cheering him, young and old alike. There was genuine warmth on their faces as the skimmer moved through the streets at half speed, allowing everyone to catch a glimpse of their new Prime.

Garryn supposed it wasn't just his Ascension they were celebrating, but the last bit of proof that the threat of the Scourge was finally over. After believing there would never be a new generation, the succession of the Prime was proof that the Empire would survive after all.

"Well, how does it feel to be Prime?" Garryn heard his father ask, amazed that he was able to hear through the din.

"I don't know yet," Garryn answered honestly. He did feel proud and happy to take up the role, but it was still too new for Garryn to realise whether he liked or hated it. At the moment, the only emotion he felt was pride at being able to please his father and his people, but he felt overwhelmed as well.

"You will be wonderful, Gar," Elisha declared, beaming. "Once all this is over and you get to work, it will be less terrifying."

After returning to the Domicile, Iran officially opened the celebrations to the masses. Most of the festivities revolved around the Kleist district, but a carnival-like atmosphere descended over the entire city of Paralyte. Fireworks would follow the aerial salute by the Imperial navy and light up the sky like shooting stars.

It was after dark when Garryn finally saw Kalistar.

"Isn't it wonderful?" Kalistar exclaimed as they sat in the courtyard, watching the sleek ships moving across the starry sky. Around them, there was music playing and people dancing.

"It certainly is," Garryn agreed, admiring the aerial stunts being performed, wondering how many of those pilots were former friends and comrades.

"I remember seeing Garryn fly once," Iran declared to everyone at the table with them. "You were very good." He cast a proud gaze at his son. "Don't let being Prime get in the way of your flying talents, my boy. It would be a terrible waste."

"I don't think I'll ever become accustomed to seeing men fly in these tiny fighters," Garin, the Chancellor of Jyne, added. "It's so disconcerting to be trapped in such a small space when there is so much vastness outside."

"That can be true," Garryn remarked, "but it makes you feel very much a part of it all."

For Garryn, there had been nothing quite like soaring through the skies in his ship, seeing the stars rushing beyond the canopy of his small ship. He remembered racing a comet and knew most pilots found such moments difficult to describe to someone who didn't live the life. It made star gazing as intimate an experience as any shared with a lover.

The Jynes did not travel in small, one-man fighters. Instead, their starship design allowed for the manoeuvrability of a smaller craft while possessing the armament and shielding required of any warship. Relying on superior sensor equipment and tiny shuttles for non-combat travel, the Jyne Fleet had abolished the need for small, one-man fighters that were very much a staple of the Brysdynian Navy.

"I guess it will always be a matter of preference with us," Garin replied good-naturedly.

Garryn's grandfather often looked oafish and much too amiable, with his bushy white beard against his dark skin, but Garryn knew from experience that the Chancellor was a superior diplomat. He had been told a number of times that, beneath the disarming façade of the lovable old man, Chancellor Garin was an intellect never to be underestimated.

"Tell me, Grandfather, was it a surprise when Jyne learned about life on Cathormira?"

The question drew the attention at everyone at the table.

"It was a long time ago," Garin was suddenly unable to meet Garryn's eyes. His voice, only a short time ago so filled with humour and warmth, was now taut and sober. "What I remember is inconsequential."

His grandfather's discomfort was obvious and even Iran was shifting in his seat while Edwen stared at Garryn with steely eyes. Only Elisha and Kalistar were oblivious. Ashner cleared his throat, a sign he was about to change the subject, but Garryn pressed on before he could do so.

"I'd be interested to hear what you little you know. Your astrogators and scientists are well ahead of us in stellar cartography."

"That's true, but Cathomira is well within Brysdynian boundaries and we weren't inclined to conduct exploration in other territories."

"Not even after our alliance?"

"Its not good manners, Garryn," the Chancellor replied, and this time his gaze did meet Garryn's. "Such a request would require miles of red tape and it seemed pointless when we could get the data we needed from your researchers. Besides, our requests were always met with denial."

"I wasn't aware you tried to study Cathomira." This time the question came from Iran.

"Some of our astrogators were curious how a red star managed to produce worlds suitable for human inhabitants. We wanted to study the ecosystem from orbit."

It seemed to Garryn the Chancellor knew a great deal about the research attempts. At some point, he must have tried to investigate Cathomira itself and come up against the Healer's Circle. Since the Scourge, the Healer's Circle had extraordinary powers when it came to the health of Brysdyn. Still, what harm could there have been to allow the planet to be studied from orbit?

"You should have come directly to me, Chancellor," Iran declared, appearing disturbed that no request was ever made known to him. "I would have seen to it that you were afforded every courtesy."

"I did not want to impose on our personal relationship, Iran." Garin appeared touched by the offer. "At the time, it seemed more appropriate to go through the correct channels for our requirements."

"If you're still interested in research, I have endorsed a Brysdynian expedition to Cathomira which is due to depart in the next weeks. I'm sure the Chief Investigator would welcome a Jyne science team to accompany them," Garryn suggested.

"You've endorsed a ship to Cathomira?" His grandfather exclaimed with surprise.

"As much as I love Brysdyn and being Brysdynian, I do feel it important that I know something of the world on which I was born. The scientists who are leading the expedition have their own agendas, which I found sound enough to support, and I'm interested to see what they learn."

"Science is its own danger," Edwen spoke for the first time. "Your expedition will be moving into remote space. There is so much we don't know about Cathomira. It may not be safe."

"Safety is the last thing that scientists think of," the Chancellor declared. Edwen's objections heighten the leader's interest. "As for your offer, my boy, I will bring it up to the Science Academy on the home world and let you know."

"At your convenience, Chancellor," Garryn smiled. Edwen said nothing more.

XIV

The Asmoryll

Until Kalistar's revelation to Edwen regarding the research expedition to Cathomira, the General had no idea of its existence.

Once he did know, Edwen admired the simplicity of its secrecy. Nothing was concealed outright. The paperwork and the official sanctioning were there for public record. No attempt was made to conceal it in any legal fashion. To his annoyance, even the Healer's Circle was fully appraised of the situation, leading Edwen to question the effectiveness of his operatives in the organisation. The only unusual thing about Garryn's expedition was Edwen's lack of awareness until the day of the Ascension.

Through the years, Edwen had developed a reliable network of unofficial sources of information. This assured that he was kept abreast of everything taking place in the Empire, no matter how insignificant. Now it appeared Garryn had managed to bypass his entire intelligence network to organise this expedition of his.

At first, he wondered if his informants had been deliberately silent, but he knew better. They were trained espionage agents, most of them, with deep-seeded links to the Security Elite. Edwen made it a point to select his agents with care. In the espionage sector, the criterion was twice as rigid. Not only did he have their sworn allegiance to the Elite, but their oath extended to him personally. Betrayal was not in their vocabulary. Those who did incur his wrath served as a warning to others.

Despite his conjecture at how little he knew, Edwen had to acknowledge one thing – Garryn's actions meant he suspected the Elite.

Normally, this would be of little concern to him. Garryn had always disliked Edwen and the institution. However, this time the young man had manoeuvred things to ensure that Security Elite was kept utterly out of the loop. Ingenious, when one recognised the orchestration of information.

Authorisation for the kind of enterprise Garryn was mounting had to come from the highest level. Most of Edwen's informants were nondescript personnel who did not have access to top-level security. They were effective because they heard and noticed things out of the ordinary, reported their findings, and left it to Edwen to decipher the rest.

Garryn had gone straight to the top and made his requests.

After that, it was simple for Edwen to guess the rest. The young man was the next Imperator of the Empire. Despite their ambivalence to such an enterprise, the powers that be would be unable to ignore the request. Careers were made on favours like this. These tiny backroom bargains and secret handshakes were not uncommon. Edwen's own rise to prominence owed a great deal to the support he'd given an Imperator years ago.

Garryn was no fool, however. He would never promise them anything outright. Most likely, he would seal their transactions with subtle words. Words like 'undying gratitude', 'I will not forget your co-operation', ' maybe I can return the favour'. The nature of politics made these words as priceless as gold.

Yes, Edwen thought, that is almost certainly how it went.

Later, once the deals and favours were made, Garryn would request one small provision. Confidentiality. No paperwork other than what was necessary. All involved would remain silent and carry out the request like another routine function. Nothing to excite the informants working for him. All to make certain that he, General Edwen of Security Elite, did not find out anything. Did it mean Garryn suspected him of complicity in the Cathomiran affair?

Edwen could not be certain, but he still had to act.

"Well, Danten?" Edwen asked of his second in command after the man had been shown into his study a few days after the Ascension.

Danten appeared anxious. This did not bode well for their meeting. The Major did his best to maintain his professionalism, taking his usual rigid stance before the General's desk, as if he was delivering his report at the Enclave. Edwen did nothing to change that perception.

"They leave the Orbital in four days."

Edwen slumped visibly in his chair. "Where did they get the ship?"

"From the Imperial Navy. They're taking the *Asmoryll*."

The *Asmoryll* was a small, Beta class frigate. However, it was fully armoured, capable of matching speeds with their largest destroyers, and had an arsenal to fend off any attack under the command of a good master. Again, Edwen found he had underestimated the young man. Why ever did Iran allow him to languish in the service as a pilot? The boy was a tactician and should have been an officer on a ship of the line.

"He expects trouble. He's selected a ship capable of protecting itself. The *Asmoryll* is Petron's ship, isn't it?" Petron was an able commander, but not an exceptional naval tactician. One of Edwen's better-trained commanders could fly circles around the man.

"Not for this trip," Danten said uncomfortably, guessing what was in the General's mind. "Petron is on his way to Krysta for shore leave, so Admiral Vyndeka is in temporary command."

Another underestimation.

Vyndeka's record was the stuff of legend, commanding loyalties from the Imperial Navy rivalling the Imperator's popularity. Her eminence as commander was no exaggeration. In the years after the Scourge, Vyndeka commanded the fleet sent to deal with the pirates and mercenaries looting the Imperial worlds. The Pirate Wars, as they became known later, made her a heroine in the eyes of every Brysdynian.

Vyndeka's dislike for him and Security Elite was equally well known.

"I wonder how much Garryn has told her. Vyndeka must see a chance to embarrass me to take such a menial task. Ferrying scientists around is hardly the work for a distinguished veteran like her."

"General, what are we going to do?"

For the first time, Danten began to feel real panic. Years ago, their path seemed so clear. Now, Danten wasn't so convinced. Despite their raw wounds from the Scourge, there was no justifying what they had done. Worse yet, with Brysdynians no longer feeling the threat of extinction, could they bear knowing the truth?

"Going after the ship while it is in our space is not an option, whether Vyndeka is in command or not. As I said before, the Elite must be blameless in this situation. Tell the *Warhammer* that she is to leave Cathomiran space immediately. She cannot be in the vicinity when the *Asmoryll* arrives."

"Yes, Sir." Danten nodded, regaining his composure somewhat. "But the *Asmoryll* can't be allowed to transmit what it learns about Cathomira."

"Obviously, but it is a long way to Cathomira and, even then, stars on the verge of nova can be unpredictable; *anything* could happen."

* * *

The *Asmoryll* was a sleek ship, compact in its design.

As Garryn stared at it through the window of the observation deck, he found himself pining for his former military existence. Only a fortnight had passed since the ceremony of Ascension and already Garryn felt trapped by the position. Learning to understand the business of government was a labyrinthine maze, testing his considerable navigation skills. Not for the first time, he longed for skies.

He was Prime and that was all there was to it.

Through the glass, he saw the Admiral giving last minute instructions to an adjutant who scurried off shortly after to carry them out. Admiral Vyndeka was a small woman whose greying brown hair was pulled tightly back in a severe bun. While she appeared glacial with authority, Garryn knew better. During her lifetime, Aisha and Vyndeka had developed a close friendship that was a part of his childhood.

Leaving behind the observation deck, he made his way to the flight deck of the Orbital Station Ashyaen, above Brysdyn, so they could talk before the *Asmoryll* left.

"Prime," she bowed in adherence to protocol, even though he was family in her eyes. "I'm glad to see you here."

"I wish you'd call me Garryn."

"You will always be Garryn to me, even if I call you Prime," she winked.

"I'm glad," he smiled back at her warmly. "I appreciate you doing this, Vyn. I know I'm probably being paranoid, but I just feel we need to take precautions."

"You still think that there is some kind of conspiracy?"

While she was dubious about the whole idea of a conspiracy regarding the New Citizens of Cathomira, Vyndeka did see the reasons for his concern. He'd confided to her about the Dreamers, knowing she could be trusted. Furthermore, Vyndeka had to confess it was troubling the generation Brysdyn was counting on to save the Empire might be subject to some unknown ailment. That alone warranted the investigation.

"I know that there's more to this than meets the eye" he confessed as they began walking towards the embarkation corridor. "If there is something on Cathomira affecting the New Citizens, it can't be ignored. I can appreciate the reason for caution after the Scourge, but something happened to us then that is affecting us now. We need to understand what it is before it gets worse. Although I don't entirely share Ashner's belief that Edwen might have something to do with it."

Vyndeka's expression darkened.

"Never underestimate Edwen, Garryn. There are a handful of people in the Empire capable of keeping everyone from Cathomira, but only one who would dare. That's Edwen. He deals in shadows and dirty little whispers, Garryn. That's why he is still in charge of Security Elite. The only one who isn't afraid of him is your father. If Edwen is involved, the only reason that your mentalist friend is still alive is because of you."

Garry hoped it was not the case, for Kalistar's sake. Garryn cared for her, even if he did not love her, despite the intimacy they'd shared. "I hope you're wrong. Kalistar loves him dearly, even though she is aware of his reputation. For her sake, I hope Edwen is not involved."

* * *

After saying his farewells to Vyndeka, Garryn went to the passenger deck where the science team was gathering before they boarded the ship.

"Prime!"

Garryn heard his name being called and turned to see the mentalist weaving through a collection of scientists to reach him. The academics were checking their equipment and talking amongst themselves as they waited to board. As always, they came with a dizzying array of scientific equipment packed in crates, awaiting loading into the *Asmoryll* by its crew. Jonen would be the only mentalist on board.

"Are you all ready to go?" Garryn asked as Jonen approached him. His enthusiasm for the journey showed on his face and it pleased the Prime that Jonen seemed to be recovering his spirit following Mira's death.

"Yes I am," Jonen lifted one of his arms to show the bag he was carrying. "Although I wished it were possible for you to come with us."

"I don't know whether I want to be stuck on a ship with a gaggle of scientists for several weeks," Garryn lied. He would have loved to make the journey himself.

"Well, don't worry," Jonen assured him, seeing through the lie. "I will try to find some of the answers to our questions."

"You better get going." Jonen's reminder that he was being left behind stung acutely.

"You're right," Jonen agreed when he cast a glance over his shoulder and saw the forming queue of scientists being herded onto the embarkation ramp. "I almost forgot, these are copies of my case notes regarding the Dreamers. There's nothing in there you don't already know, but I thought you might find them interesting reading. Who knows, it could spark a memory."

He handed a clear, multifaceted archive crystal to the Prime.

"Thank you." Garryn was grateful for the copy. At least reading it would make him feel like he was contributing something to this expedition instead of being trapped at the Quorum.

"Thank you for this opportunity, Garryn," Jonen shook Garryn's hand vigorously, "I've always wanted to go to space to conduct some extraordinary research. Thank you for making this possible."

"Find out the truth, Jon, and that will be thanks enough."

"I'll do my best," Jonen said before turning away to follow the procession into the *Asmoryll*.

XV

Core Breach

The life of the Imperator and his family involved so many traditions and rituals, Iran was loath to force any more on them. Dinner was the one exception to the rule.

Following the Scourge, both he and Aisha were so grateful to have a family they swore never to take the experience for granted. Even after her passing, he still insisted on continuing the tradition, even if her empty seat in their private dining room still tugged at his heart. Nearing the twilight of his life, he could not ignore some of his best memories took place at this table and he was reluctant to let go of it, even if both his children were adults.

There was Elisha's declaration at seven of her intent to join the gypsy acrobats of Kree. At thirteen, she decided she would marry a scoundrel in a pirate ship, so they could embark on a life of adventure across the galaxy. Aisha's refusal to let nine-year old

Garryn learn sword swallowing resulted in the boy embarking on a hunger fast lasting as long as it took for desert to be served. Now that would-be sword swallower was his grown up son and Prime.

On this occasion, Kalistar was sharing the meal with them and Iran wondered if the friendship between Garryn and the young lady was much deeper than he'd realised. Not that Iran had any objection to this. Kalistar was a lovely young woman and her relationship to Edwen meant any engagement between the two might help restore the Imperator's and General's fractured friendship.

For the moment, Garryn's intentions remained unclear. They continued with dinner as always, with Kalistar remaining quietly restrained. The colour of her cheeks indicated her anxiety at being present for such a cherished family tradition. Despite her dislike of court and its social gratification, she was unable to ignore the implications of her presence at the table. Dinner in the family room of the Lady Aisha's chambers was an intimate affair for the Imperator's family and not just anyone was invited to join it.

"Lords! Garryn!" Elisha groaned with exasperation as Garryn recounted one of the more embarrassing exploits of her and Kalistar as children to her father. "Do you have to tell *that* story!"

"Oh yes, he does. Your mother never told me that one." The Imperator grinned.

"No wonder," Kalistar declared, her cheeks reddening with embarrassment at the Imperator's amused gaze. "Lady Aisha was extremely restrained, considering Eli and I stole all the desert for her tea with the ladies of the great houses."

"I found them sick to their stomachs," Garryn added helpfully, "their faces blue with bristle berries, on the south balcony. I don't think I ever saw mother that mad."

Iran winced visibly. "She didn't get angry often, but I learned well enough not to get on her bad side. Considering she came from a people capable of managing their emotions, having her yell was enough to make even the bravest Brysdynian warrior flinch."

In the shadowed corners of the room, he could see some of the serving staff also sniggering with amusement and wondered how many of them actually remembered the occasion. It was nice to remember they were almost as much a part of their lives as his family. The laughter reminded him of the days when Aisha was at the table and, even though it wasn't the same with Kalistar sitting by Garryn, the Imperator was nonetheless pleased.

When he heard voices coming from the door, Iran shifted his gaze to see Ashner entering the room after exchanging a few words with the Head Server to gain entry. The servers attending the meal were under strict instructions not to interrupt the family, so this intrusion by Ashner mean there was a good reason for it.

Their lively chatter died immediately when he appeared.

"Ashner," Iran stared at the man hard, "what's the matter?"

"I'm sorry to intrude, Imperator," the older man said with an apologetic bow, glancing quickly to Garryn before turning his gaze to Iran. "But this news could not wait."

The instant Ashner had appeared, Garryn knew something was wrong. His spine became ramrod straight in his chair and he stared at his aide, daring him to give his news. "What's happened?"

Ashner approached the table a little closer, his expression grim. He knew the impact his words would have on the family, Garryn in particular, but there was no way around it. Nothing he said could alter its impact.

"About twenty minutes ago, Ashyaen Station received a message from Outpost Wylo," Ashner began.

Outpost Wylo. Garryn immediately recognised it as one of their outermost space stations.

Ashner drew in another deep breath before forcing the rest of his message past his lips, his eyes now staring at the table and not Garryn. "They have received a distress buoy dispatched from the *Asmoryll*. The buoy reports the destruction of the ship, with all hands lost."

Ashner raised his eyes to their faces then and saw the familiar emotions surfacing with such news. Shock, dismay and horror. They all knew that Admiral Vyndeka was on board with the best scientific minds in the Empire, to say nothing of the *Asmoryll*'s crew, all gone forever.

Garryn's expression was unreadable.

His face was a mask of stone. Ashner saw something flash in his eyes and then vanish just as quickly. It was extinguished with control he'd never imagined Garryn possessed. There was no grief, no anger, no regret, just an impenetrable façade the older man could not read.

"How?" Garryn asked, his voice barely a whisper.

"According to the buoy, a core overload. We're unsure of the cause at this time. Judging by the damage, the distress buoy was launched quickly. There was no time for the Admiral to record a final log."

The buoys were launched when a ship had suffered catastrophic failure and destruction was eminent. It recorded everything about the ship's status until the seconds before launch. Internal and external ship communications, captain's logs, sensor scans and stellar positioning were recorded for engineers to analyse later and determine what had gone wrong.

"An onboard malfunction," Garryn mused slowly, taking it in. Raising his eyes to his aide, everything he needed to say was exchanged in a single glance between them.

Sabotage.

Elisha's and Kalistar's tears sounded a thousand miles away. Garryn could only think about the friends who had left him only weeks ago. Admiral Vyndeka, Vyn, his mother's best friend and newest ally. She'd promised to find him answers, even though he knew she didn't quite believe him about a conspiracy.

And of course Jonen, the idealistic, kind man who'd set out to help him with the best of intentions and paid for it with his life.

It was the mentalist who opened his eyes to something dark and sinister, lying beneath his memories of Cathomira. Not just his memories, but those of countless others across Brysdyn. Jonen who listened to him talk about the most intimate parts of his psyche and told him he was not crazy to feel overwhelmed by being Prime. The man hadn't just treated his condition as a Dreamer, but also listened to him expunge his anxieties about being Prime.

Jonen had become his friend.

"This is a terrible loss." Iran shook his head, seeing the profound effect this was having on his son. "Ashner, please take steps to ensure the families of those on board receive my personal condolences. We must make full restitution for this tragedy."

Garryn left the table before he finished speaking.

* * *

When Kalistar found Garryn, he was staring out into the balcony of his room, looking down on the city below. Even though he reacted at the sound of her approach, he said nothing until she was standing next to him.

"Your father is worried about you, Garryn," Kalistar placed a hand on his shoulder.

He flinched at her touch and flashed her a cold stare, prompting her to immediately remove it. She shuddered at the hatred behind that look, but dismissed it for what it was. He was grieving. "Vyndeka's death has hit Elisha hard. Your father is with her and I told him I'd see how you were."

"There is no need. I'm fine."

"Garryn, there's no shame in admitting your sorrow."

He turned to her slowly and the darkness in his eyes made her uneasy. It was the first time in her life she had seen him this way.

"I am not grieving, Kal. I'm angry. Don't you understand? Don't you see? They were murdered!"

His words hit her like a physical blow. She knew something of the irregularities he and Jonen had discovered, but had believed the answers would present themselves once they reached Cathomira. She'd never considered anything sinister about it, not until now. In fact, until he said the words, the conspiracy didn't seem real, just a vague shadow, like the nightmares they shared.

"How could they be?" she stammered. "You heard Ashner. It was an onboard malfunction…"

"I do not have time for this!"

He brushed past her, entering his room again. Garryn had returned here to think about what he would do next. Everyone who came close to this died. He'd thought having the resources of the Prime would be enough to unravel this mystery and show the faces behind the shadows. Now he knew better. There was no ending to this, unless he finished it himself.

He couldn't do it as Prime.

Kalistar hurried after him and found him packing his belongings into a military issue duffel bag. For a moment, it almost did not register what he was doing, but as he stuffed more clothes into it, the reality dawned on her. He was leaving and he was leaving *tonight*.

"You're going?"

"I am going to find out the truth! I'm going to know why I dream about a planet that looks nothing like Cathomira! I want to know why a mentalist inquiring about Cathomira is murdered along with his secretary. I want to know what secret is worth murdering an entire ship, including the most decorated admiral in the fleet!"

Kalistar was terrified now. Something inside told her if she let him go, there was a chance he might never come back. He was not rational and she could not understand what he thought he could accomplish on his own.

"Garryn, ask your father for help! Ask anyone! Don't run away like this!"

He was almost fully packed now, grabbing the last thing he needed to begin his journey. Garryn walked over to his bureau and reached into one of the drawers. He rummaged for a few minutes, ignoring Kalistar completely, before withdrawing his hand. He regarded the prism glittering in his palm for a few seconds before packing it as well.

"I have to go now," Garryn said, looking up at her.

"Go? Go where?"

"I have to find the truth. I won't let anyone else risk themselves for me. Whatever happens next will happen to me alone. I'm not going to let those people on the *Asmoryll* die for nothing. I will find the truth – not just for me, but for all the Dreamers."

Kalistar did not know when she started crying, but once she did, she couldn't stop.

"Garryn I'll come with you. We'll find the truth together." She tried to reach for him, a desperate attempt to hold him to her, but he backed away. Almost as if he knew what her power would be if she touched him.

"Absolutely not," the hard edge returned to his voice. "Do not think for a moment you or I are safe. If they dare to kill Vyndeka, then we are nothing to them." He was glad he had so far managed to avoid bringing Edwen's name into this.

Until he knew for certain, there was no reason to voice his suspicions regarding her father. "I need to know you're safe. I will leave instructions with Ashner. You'll move your things here and you'll stay here in the Domicile until I get back. I'm sure your father will understand."

"But..."

"I am speaking to you as the Prime. I have given you an order. You will obey me, Kalistar, and you will stay here until I get back. One other thing: I would prefer it if you do not tell your father that I'm gone."

Her eyes wrinkled in confusion at that. "What do you mean?"

"For his safety," Garryn lied before kissing her gently on her lips. For a moment, he felt his resolve falter, aware she was right. He was rushing into this propelled by grief and anger. Yet as he thought it, he knew if he didn't go now he would not have the strength to do it later.

With that decree delivered, he reached for his bag and headed towards the door.

"Garryn!"

He paused at her words, closing his eyes to brace himself for what he had to say. Gazing at her, Garryn felt the first semblance of sorrow since learning his friends on the *Asmoryll* were dead.

"Kal, I can't let this go and I owe it to them to find out the truth, whatever it might be."

At that, he disappeared out the door and Kalistar knew quite absolutely that she had lost him.

XVI

Home Base

Leaving the Domicile, Garryn's destination was Paralyte's civilian spaceport, called Home Base by the pilots who worked out of the facility. Unlike Ashyaen, with its shiny walls, organised routines and its air of predictable military efficiency, Home Base was a monument to civilian disarray.

Home Base operated around the clock. There were shuttles waiting here at its hangars and berths, carrying passengers to large, unseen cruisers orbiting Brysdyn. It was the largest spaceport on Brydsyn and also the main destination of travellers from the colony planets in the rest of the Empire. It was also a popular place for trade to be conducted, though not always legitimately. When he was still serving in the military, Garryn had come to Home Base either to drink or gamble with the local pilots.

The most popular tavern was a place called *Port in a Storm.*

It was the one part of the space station devoid of tourists or sightseers. In the main complex, there were commercial restaurants, with fast food and clean tables to accommodate them, and the seediness of the tavern did little to entice them. Still, the *Port in a Storm* was not merely a tavern where people came to drink exotic liquor. It was a place of business.

Garryn sat next to the bar where a very surly looking Borlian, with big round black eyes showing little expression, held court as the bartender. The Borlian grunted a few words quickly translated into Standard Galactic, demanding Garryn's order. With his large, thick hide and protruding tusks, he took the request for Delurite brandy with a loud snort through his extended proboscis.

After the bartender returned with his order, Garryn surveyed the room while he nursed his drink, though he did not allow his gaze to linger too long on anyone. While some of the patrons came here to drink and gamble, others came to conduct business in anonymity. His scrutiny would not be welcomed and it was the fastest way to ensure no one would do business with him.

The bounty hunters were easy to spot by the arsenal they carried. One of them scowled at him, so Garryn looked away quickly. The bulk of the patrons were freighter pilots. During his time in the service, Garryn had come across them occasionally. While they were not the most reputable people, he gave them credit for their skills as star pilots. Some even surpassed Imperial pilots in ability.

They also knew a thing or two about bending the rules, and asked few questions about their cargo or passengers, if the money was good enough.

In the middle of the dimly lit room, a small crowd had gathered around the two players at the gaming table. A human and Klattonian were playing a game of Silverstar, a popular card game. The human's expression of confidence was in stark contrast to the fidgety anxiousness displayed by the Klattonian. The twitching of the Klattonian's insectoid antennae and his nictating compound eyes were like the lenses of a visual recorder, providing his opponent with an effective tell.

Garryn suppressed a smirk, because the human's nonchalance made his opponent even more nervous than he already was. Klattonians were excitable and twitchy by nature. It didn't take much to provoke a response from them. Considering the number of credits at stake, Garryn could tell this Klattonian was almost at the breaking point.

When the human laid down his cards, a loud gasp of surprise escaped the crowd. Garryn couldn't see the cards, but by the way the Klattonian slumped forward, it was clear the winning hand had just been dealt.

The winner extended a hand towards the Klattonian, who accepted it reluctantly and seemed glad the game was concluded. Getting to his feet, the human left the gaming table and approached the bar. As he did so, Garryn saw the faded insignia on the man's clothes. The jacket he was wearing was worn, but

Garryn recognised the embroidery of a Jyne's Fleet gold insignia against the black material.

The man was about his age, if not a little older. His dark gold hair was unruly and his blue eyes caught a glimpse of Garryn's observation before his lips stretched into a smile.

"Are you lost, Navy?" he asked, approaching Garryn.

"Not at all. I just came to watch you fleece the locals playing Silverstar."

"Fleece?" His expression became one of mock hurt. "That was pure skill. Not my fault if he's too twitchy for his own good."

They had met the same way a few years ago in a bar on the edge of Brysdynian space, when Garryn was on furlough with his comrades. He'd been forced to break up a fight over a game not unlike this one, involving the man standing before him. Flinn Ester.

Flinn was an officer of the Jynes Legion Fleet who had left the military to become a private operator. Despite the violence of their first meeting, they had become friends and shared a drink and a game of cards whenever they ran into each other.

"It's good to see you, Flinn," Garryn smiled as he gestured at the bartender to bring Flinn another round of what he was drinking.

"Nice to see you too, Navy." Flinn Ester took up the stool next to Garryn. "What are you doing out here? I heard you retired. Is this a social call?"

"Yes, I did retire but no, this isn't a social call." Garryn chose not to elaborate further. Despite their friendship, Garryn had never revealed his true identity to Flinn. "I heard you were in town and thought I'd look you up because I need passage out of the system."

Flinn's expression was one of surprise. "I thought you would have gotten yourself a nice ship after retirement."

"I'm afraid not," Garryn shook his head. "I have a dull government position. No more ships for me."

"Really?" Flinn's eyes narrowed a moment before he spoke again, "Well you know me, for the right price I'll fly you anywhere, but let's not talk business here."

He picked up his drink once the bartender delivered it and gestured at Garryn to follow him. Garryn followed him without question, grateful for the suggestion because he wanted secrecy above all else. Involving too many people had doomed Jonen and the crew of the *Asmoryll*. He was not making that mistake again.

"So what's the destination?" Flinn asked, once they were settled in a private booth at the far end of the room, away from the bulk of the activity in the establishment.

"I can't tell you until we are airborne."

"I have to lodge a flight plan," the pilot pointed out promptly.

"You always said you could find a way around those things, Flinn. I can pay you for whatever bribes you need to make it happen."

Flinn eased back into his seat and took a sip of his Aleuthian scotch, eyeing Garryn closely. "What, are you in trouble or something?" Leaving in secrecy always meant someone was interested in your departure.

Garryn did not correct him, because the assumption would do for now. "Something like that. I need to get off the planet immediately. I'll pay extra if you can leave right now."

"I'll need it," Flinn stated. "Alright, thirty thousand should be enough to get us off world and give me a tidy profit even if I am charging you friend's rates."

"Thanks."

Garryn would have paid Flinn whatever asking price the man wanted. This was no small thing he was asking from the pilot and less scrupulous operators could take the money and turn him in anyway.

"We can go to the ship right now if you like, but it will take me a few hours to get her ready and forge flight plans, since you won't tell me where we're going."

"You might say no if you knew where we were going," Garryn remarked with a faint smile.

Those were fighting words to the pilot, because if there was one thing Garryn knew about Flinn, the man loved to take risks. He'd walked away from a career in the Jynes fleet because he longed for the freedom of the skies without answering to anyone. An exceptional pilot, Flinn's inability to play by the rules made him one of the best private operators around.

"I never say no," Flinn snorted in predictable fashion.

"Yeah that's what the boys used to tell me about you."

He ducked when Flinn swung at him.

* * *

Garryn followed Flinn out of the *Port in the Storm*. The deeper they moved into this section of the space station, the more he felt as if he were stepping into a different, seamier world. The walls were not so clean. There was graffiti scrawled on their grey surfaces. This part of the complex seemed forgotten by the custodians of the centre, as well as by those who ran it.

Within moments, they entered the berth housing Flinn's ship. It was dirty and unkempt, minimally serviced. Diagnostic panels and maintenance equipment were in a state of near disrepair and Garryn did not need to see the other berths to know they were all kept in this state. Obviously, private charter was not considered as high priority as the larger, commercial ships.

Flinn Ester's ship was called the *Wayward Son*.

It was an old T25 Runner model whose original design was obliterated to suit the need of the current owner. Whatever purpose the *Wayward Son* was intended to serve was lost under plates of dutronium armoured shielding and multiphasic sensor arrays. She was refitted with an engine belonging to an older

Rapier class frigate, making her incredibly fast. The speed came at the cost of the additional shielding to avoid super-heating. Nevertheless, the modifications made the ship quite formidable.

"What speed does she do now?" Garryn was aware Flinn was constantly making upgrades to the original design.

"Factor 9 in hyperspace," Flinn said proudly, walking towards the ship's extended ramp. "I installed some boosters last year. They're Amarian. You know what those are like."

"Only by reputation," Garryn confessed as he followed Flinn up the ramp. "I know they like building small ships with lots of grunt."

The interior of the *Wayward Son* retained most of its aging décor and was clean and well kept, even if the paintwork and metal finish was faded in places. Flinn lowered himself into one of the seats in the main passenger compartment before gesturing Garryn to do the same.

"Look, we're friends and I respect you. More importantly, I've made you a deal. I will take you wherever you want at the price we've agreed upon, but I want to know where we're going."

"Not until we're airborne," Garryn insisted, not wanting to risk the revelation so soon.

"Then we're not going to be airborne. I gave you my word and it probably doesn't mean a lot to anyone but me, but when I give someone my word I don't take it back. Trust me or don't trust me, but I'm not moving until I know where we're going, *Prime*."

Garry stared at him sharply.

He supposed it was naïve to assume he could return to anonymity simply because he tried to blend in with the masses. During the years of their association, Garryn had to admit the man's powers of observation were quite impressive.

"When did you know?" he asked wearily, seeing no reason to continue the pretext. Perhaps it might make things simpler if Flinn understood what the stakes were.

"Ever since the Ascension, made me spit up my whiskey when I looked at the vid and saw your face there. It made sense why you were always such an entitled ass." He smirked.

"Thanks," Garryn uttered a humourless laugh. "It was my attempt at having a normal life for as long as possible."

Flinn nodded and gave him a look of sympathy. "So, are you going to level with me or not?"

Garryn conceded defeat and prayed the destination would not affect Flinn's promise to help him. "Okay, the destination is Cathomira."

Flinn took this without batting an eye. "We'll never get through."

"You're backing out on me?"

"No!" Flinn straightened up, offended by the suggestion after everything he just said. "I told you I'd fly you there and I will. I just want you to be aware of the danger."

"Danger?"

"You Imperial flyboys don't know anything do you? You guys fly where you're told to and don't ask questions beyond that. The Cathomiran star system has been off limits for two decades. No one is allowed in. I've heard stories about looters who tried to land on the surface years ago and didn't make it out. A few smugglers have tried it and those who made it out, I'll grant you there aren't many, talk of a warship on permanent assignment to the area. It obliterates anything that approaches the system."

Garryn was aware there was a restriction placed on Cathomira because of the virus, but he had never heard of any ship patrolling the area or warding off trespassers with violence and death. Not even the quarantine placed on the system gave anyone the right to use deadly force in such a manner.

Was this what had happened to the *Asmoryll*?

"I'll pay you double. Just get me there."

Flinn stared at him and realised, with Garryn being a New Citizen, this journey home was deeply personal, though he wondered if it was worth the risk the Prime was taking.

"We've agreed on the price. I'm guessing this just a sight-seeing trip for you, so I'm not going to squeeze you for more cash."

"I appreciate that," Garryn was surprised by the honour shown by a supposed mercenary. "Can you get us to Cathomira?"

Flinn considered the question. "It will be tough. I can't vouch for a landing, because I won't have the kind of decontamination equipment or enviro suits needed for that level of radiation. I can probably get you low enough to see the place, if that's enough."

"It will do."

At this point, Garryn had little choice.

XVII

Cathomira

Garryn found the *Wayward Son* very limiting after travelling on large military warships with numerous decks of walking space. After the ship entered hyperspace, there was little to do until it was ready to emerge at its destination. Flinn would occasionally wander into the cockpit to check on things, but once the coordinates were fed into the navcom, the *Wayward Son* could carry out most of the journey on autopilot.

Garryn paced the confines of the ship liked a caged animal, knowing that much of his impatience had to do with his need for answers. For the first few days of their journey, he remained silent about his reasons for going to Cathomira, despite Flinn's gentle probing. Eventually, he found it easier to trust the pilot and he revealed a little bit of his reasons for going to the planet.

As the days progressed, they played cards, drank too much at times, talked about their days in the service, entertaining each other with descriptions of all the places they had been. Sometimes Flinn would ask Garryn about what it was like to be Prime. Garryn, in turn, would ask Flinn what it was like to be so free and untethered to anything or anyone.

Flinn's responses made Garryn feel even more trapped.

* * *

This was new. He opened his eyes and saw something unexpected. He was in a new place. A place in his dreams he had never seen.

She was there again, she with the golden hair and the deep blue eyes. She was staring down at him with a smile. Unlike previous occasions, there was no blood or ash on her skin. Instead, she appeared happy. This time, they weren't out in the golden field, but rather indoors. It took him a moment to realise he was in a room.

The walls surrounding him were painted blue, with cheery pictures of unfamiliar animals adorning them. On the ceiling was a mural of the sky with stars in nonsensical constellations and a crescent moon smiling at the yellow sun. With a flash of insight, he realised it was his room.

She smiled as she reached for him. It was the first time he'd felt her touch.

Her arms around him had the power to make every terrible thing vanish. His head swam at her touch and he wanted to lie there against her breast forever. She was singing some unfamiliar song to him, but the melody made him smile. A tingle of delight ran down his spine as he heard her heart beating in his ears.

He never wanted to leave her.

Suddenly, they were no longer alone. He looked up and saw a man. It was the first time he had seen a face other than hers. In his dreams it was always just the two of them. There were never any intruders. Yet, seeing a stranger walking so casually into his dream unnerved him. But not as much as when he looked into the man's face.

It was his face, or at least he thought it was his face. The man had the same coloured hair, the familiar lines of his jaw and even the eyes. This impostor had his eyes! Yet, as he looked closer, he realised something else: it wasn't his face, even though there were similarities. He even bore some similarities to the Imperator, his father.

It became too much for him.

Suddenly, he was back in that charred field again, with the large, black birds circling the darkened sky, raining death across the golden stalks of unharvested wheat. Around him, the flames burned higher until the smoke began to scald his lungs and the heat did more than prickle at his skin. He was staring at her dead body again, tears of grief running down his cheeks as he brushed aside the blood-matted hair from her face.

Then he was being swept into the air once more, being lifted farther and farther away from the burning field below him. He struggled to break free, but what force had him in its power was not about to let him go. Below him, the field was a burning plain of cinder and ash, with a tiny speck amidst the conflagration that might have been a house. The land beneath him continued to shrink until only the blue planet and the yellow sun remained, held against a canvas of stars.

A single yellow sun.

"Gar, wake up!"

Flinn's sharp demand forced him awake. Garryn blinked wildly at the pilot as he began to register his surroundings. Beads of sweat ran down his forehead and his stomach felt so queasy he thought he might vomit. Tumbling out of bed, he pushed past Flinn and staggered away from the bunk, still shaking a little.

"Are you okay?" The worry in Flinn's voice was obvious.

"I'm fine." The words escaped his dry throat in a hoarse whisper.

"Really?" Flinn retorted sceptically. "You were screaming."

Screaming? Garryn didn't remember screaming, but there were parts in the dream that felt emotionally unbearable. He could have cried and been unaware of it. His throat certainly felt raw enough to prove it. Wiping the sweat from his brow, he tried to hide how shaken he was, but suspected it was too late for that.

Leaving the cabin to escape Flinn's concerned gaze, he was embarrassed at the outburst, but at the same time fighting the disorientation resulting from the nightmare. He was disoriented by a flood of memories from the dream that was no longer fading away.

Why was he suddenly able to remember?

In the past, the dreams faded when he woke up. It had taken Jonen's neural analyser to make him remember the details, but now as he stood here drenched in his own sweat, he remembered everything. He could see the lines on her face, the way she lit up when she smiled and her soft voice as she sang to him.

"Want to talk about it?" Flinn asked. He was uncomfortable with prying, but over the past few days of the charter, Flinn had realised there was more to the Prime's story than he let on.

Garryn was touched by the sentiment and wondered if an impartial opinion might have value.

"I have bad dreams," Garryn confessed after making his way to the main cabin. A compartment against the wall held Flinn's liquor collection. Garryn wasted no time in pouring himself a drink. He needed one badly.

"Is that why you're going to Cathomira?" Flinn joined him for the drink.

Garryn nodded.

"I remember. I never remembered before. The dreams used to be vague and I never knew what they were about until I went to Jonen."

A wave of grief swept over him in memory of his friend.

"Jonen showed me what I was dreaming about. I sent him with a scientific expedition to Cathomira, but their ship suffered a catastrophic core breach. They're all dead. Now, for the first time, I can remember the dreams without him and what I remember scares the hell out of me!"

Flinn did not meet his gaze, but stared instead into his glass for a few moments. In the past few days, Garryn had learned that there was a great deal of substance beneath the thin facade of the cocky star pilot. When he spoke it was almost revelation.

"You don't think you and the New Citizens are really from Cathomira, do you?"

Hearing suspicions he himself harboured spoken out loud was jarring. Garryn met Flinn's gaze and nodded.

"I have to go to Cathomira myself to know for sure," he finally admitted, staring vacantly at the bulkhead. "Only then am I going to be able to accept it."

"And then what?"

Garryn looked up at him directly. "Then I start looking for the truth."

* * *

The *Wayward Son* emerged from hyperspace as close as possible to the Cathomiran star system. After learning of the *Asmoryll*'s destruction shortly after arriving in the system, Flinn decided to take no chances. Despite having difficulty believing any warship could take on Admiral Vyndeka and win, the pilot held no such illusions about his own ship.

Flinn and Garryn watched the blur of stars around the canopy of the cockpit settle gradually after the ship entered normal space, once the hyperspacial eddies dwindled around them. Flinn immediately set the ship for cruising speed as the cockpit glowed with the amber light of Cathomira's lone star. The red giant seemed to fill the cockpit window and immediately automated alarms began to warn the occupants of the Wayward Son of the increasing radiation levels.

"I'm going to have to divert extra power to give us more shielding," Flinn explained as his hands flew over the controls.

Garryn averted his eyes from the massive star, but it was difficult to keep it from view for very long. The size of it filled every corner of the cockpit window. Blast shields began to lower across the outer window, shutting out the harmful rays. Prolonged exposure to the powerful radiance would cause permanent damage to their eyes. Once the thick plates slid into place, it took a few seconds of adjustment for Garryn to see clearly again.

From this point on, their only view of the star would be through the cockpit's holographic viewer.

"I'd keep the long range scanners running," Garryn suggested, remembering most acutely how the *Asmoryll* had met its end. How far had the *Asmoryll* travelled into the system before she was destroyed? How had Vyn been bested?

"I've set the sensors to give us a perimeter alert," Flinn replied, not looking up at him from the controls. Flinn was just as wary as Garryn about an attack. He had no wish to tangle with a warship if it could be avoided.

"Good." Garryn eased back into the co-pilot's seat, trying to dispel the tension he was feeling. "How long until we reach Cathomira?"

"About twenty minutes, but we're in scanner range now if you want to take a look."

He did and leaned in and, within seconds, the holographic image of Cathomira appeared before them both.

Garryn held his breath as he saw, for the first time, the planet of his birth. Not even the visual enhancement to the feed could hide the fact that Cathomira was a bleak and desolate world. The hot, acidic gases of the planet's atmosphere had given it a yellowish glow. Garryn could see continents riddled with large craters and expanding patches of charred earth where the planet was lashed by massive solar flares. Its proximity from the sun destroyed any remaining doubts as to the existence of life.

Cathomira was a dead planet.

"Can your scanners run some numbers for me?"

Flinn's boast of upgrading the Wayward *Son's* equipment included sophisticated multiphasic sensors from Jynes. Despite his dislike of piloting fleet ships, it was obvious Flinn found some elements of a starship useful. Legion ships possessed the most sophisticated scanning equipment in the galaxy. They took pride in the ability of their equipment to home in on a single strand of DNA from a planet of millions.

"Sure. What are we looking for?"

"How long has the climate been like this?"

Flinn glanced over his shoulder at Garryn, aware of the implications of the answer. "Let me check it out."

It took a few minutes for the computer to calculate the answer and, during those minutes, Garryn's thoughts were racing. Earlier on, Garryn had told Flinn that until he saw Cathomira for himself, he could not rest. Now that he was here, his gut told him his worst fears were about to be confirmed. Perhaps he'd always known it and the dreams were his way of confirming it.

When Flinn looked up at Garryn again, his face was grim and Garryn knew the answer before he even spoke.

"Fifty thousand years according to the computer."

Fifty thousand years. The sun had been baking the planet for *fifty thousand years*.

Flinn saw his distress and tried to reassure him that all was not lost, even if the pilot knew better. "Look, for all we know, the Cathomirans could have lived underground. They might not have been as highly advanced as Brysdyn, but they could have found a way."

"No," Garryn discounted the possibility immediately. "The official reports say that the children from Cathomira were taken from cities. Above ground cities! Can you find evidence of any?"

It took a few more minutes for Flinn to give him that answer, but by now the truth was undeniable.

"No cities," Finn's guilt oozed at every word confirming Garryn's worst fears. "Just because none were left standing doesn't mean there weren't any. This planet has been bombarded with radiation, massive solar flares and energy discharge for decades. It there was anything on the surface, it would have been obliterated by now."

Flinn's efforts were admirable, but futile.

"I think we both know why they're not there, Flinn."

The captain was truly sorry for Garryn. He tried to imagine what it must be like to realise everything you believed about your life was a lie.

"I'm sorry, Gar. I don't know what to say."

"There is nothing to say." Garryn rose from his seat. "All of us, every New Citizen in the empire, has been lied to. We never came from Cathomira."

Once that fallacy was done away with, another, more sinister theory began to stir in his head. Words were tumbling out of his mouth with the momentum of his anger to carry it along.

"Cathomira was convenient, just a name to give us when we were old enough to ask questions about where we came from. They concocted a story about a biological war so no one would try to land on the planet and discover the lie. After the Scourge, they knew no Brysdynian would take that kind of risk."

"The 'they' you're talking about. Are we talking about the Empire?" Flinn asked. He found it impossible to believe that a conspiracy like this could exist without the highest levels of power manipulating it.

Still, the Brysdynians of that time were very much a warrior culture and would find such treachery beneath them.

"I have to consider it."

The thought that his father might have lied to him all these years made him sick to his stomach. He refused to believe the Imperator could have orchestrated such a monumental deception. His father was a good man. If Garryn did not believe that, then everything he'd endured to become Prime was for nothing.

"It must have come from pretty high up, Gar. If what you say is true, if Cathomira is just a smoke screen, then some pretty powerful people in the Empire must be behind this."

"No," he shook his head. "Not some. Just one."

"He must be pretty connected to have this kind of power."

It fell into place perfectly, once Garryn discounted his father's part in this. He knew he would have to re-examine the Imperator's involvement at some point but, for now, he chose to live with the illusion. If it wasn't the Imperator, then it could only be one other person.

General Edwen.

Anything else Flinn was going to say in response was forgotten as a loud klaxon screamed angrily in their ears seconds before the ship shuddered violently.

XVIII

Nova

"What the hell was that!"

This and a string of obscenities escaped Garryn's lips as he picked himself off the floor after the ship was struck. The deck continued to shudder as the bombardment continued, making it difficult for him to regain his balance.

Flinn was already on his feet and studying the sensor readings. Instruments were screaming out in protest with erratic readings and flashing red lights wherever they was capable. The holographic screen was flashing with colour, indicating the full extent of their troubles.

"It's a solar flare!" Flinn barked, even though Garryn was capable of interpreting the same data.

"I've never seen one this big."

Flinn did not answer as he reclaimed the captain's seat. The ship was being swept backwards, trapped in a wave of solar fire. Despite his ship's superior shielding, he knew they could not withstand the intense radiation for very long. Disengaging the emergency klaxons, he attempted to regain helm control. They had to free themselves of this nuclear wave or else die by radiation poisoning, long before the shields buckled and incinerated them.

Flinn's fingers flew effortlessly across the panel as he regained control to steer them out of the wave. After a few seconds, the dangerous rocking eased to a gradual shudder as the ship reached the edge of the solar current. The holographic screen began to clear and the image of Cathomira's sun returned when the ship was considerably steadier.

Garryn was impressed by Flinn's efficiency. Now, more than ever, he felt glad that he'd chosen the former Fleet officer to take him to Cathomira. He must have been a great pilot in his Fleet days, Garryn thought. Even though Garryn was a good pilot, he had little experience in dealing with anything larger than a one-man craft.

"Are we clear?"

"Yeah, we're clear," Flinn replied distractedly. He was running a quick diagnostic over ship's functions to ensure they had not sustained any permanent damage they would be sorry for later. As it was, the sensor readings emanating from the Cathomiran sun gave him reason to be concerned. After viewing the sensor data, he realised how lucky they were to have survived that initial blast.

"How bad?"

Flinn's grim mood was telling. They may have escaped the wave, but they were not out of trouble.

"Bad enough." Flinn glanced at him. "Radiation levels have just jumped up 2000 percent. The temperature outside has quadrupled. My shields are barely keeping the heat out as it is."

Garryn could believe that. While the temperature in the cabin was not uncomfortable, it was warmer than before.

"We were lucky we didn't get vaporised. That sun is about to go nova. According to the sensors, she'll go anywhere within the next 22 hours." He gestured to the holographic image showing a cross-sectional view of the sun. The pressure was mounting under the surface and the temperature of the sun's core was rising rapidly. "I give it less time than that." He turned to Garryn and took a deep breath. "With all due respect to you and your charter, I'm getting my ship out of here."

"No arguments from me."

Garryn was a pilot too and knew what this space would be like if the red giant went nova. As it was, the erupting solar flares were steadily turning the area into a hellish mix of superheated gases and intense radiation. The planets, already radioactive, would start to disintegrate. Smaller spacial bodies would actually explode, sending their debris into space as flaming asteroids. It was no place for any ship, no matter how well equipped.

Most of his passengers rarely showed any good sense, so Flinn was grateful for Garryn's attitude.

He turned back towards the cockpit controls and the ship jolted violently again. This time, Flinn managed to remain seated, but once again klaxons across the ship began screaming.

"That was not a solar flare! Something hit us!"

"I know!" Flinn shouted back in turn. "The radiation is interfering with the sensors! I'm going to have to lower the blast shields!"

Another blast rocked the ship and Flinn swore angrily. The *Wayward Son* reeled from the impact. As the shields began to lower, the strong crimson light illuminated the cockpit. Garryn looked up to see in what form this new attack had come.

"It's a warship!" Garryn exclaimed, Finn's claims confirmed when he identified its origins. "A Brysdynian warship."

"Great! I'm diverting all auxiliary power to my targeting scanners. I need another hand in my port gunnery turret!"

"I'm there." Garryn jumped from his chair immediately and headed out of the cockpit. He had not taken more than a few steps when another blast impacted against the hull, throwing him against the wall. A sharp pain cut through him as his elbow slammed into the metal wall, making Garryn wince.

"You okay?" Flinn cried out.

"I'm fine!" Garryn retorted before going for the door again. "What are they doing? They could just grab us with a tractor beam or disable us. Why are they dragging this out?"

"They're driving us," the captain said grimly. "They're forcing us into the sun's gravitational field."

Of course. Why soil their hands when they could let Cathomira do their work for them? Driving the *Wayward Son* in the sun made things considerably easier to explain. When Iran went searching for his son, there would be nothing to find.

"How close are we to that happening?"

"Too close, now get going!" Flinn snapped impatiently. He did not look up to know that Garryn had gone and, at the moment, there were other concerns on his mind. The warship commander had timed his attack perfectly, using the sensor interference to remain hidden until the distraction by the solar flares.

Flinn poured more power into the engines, causing the *Wayward Son* to fly out of range of the warship's tractor beam, if that was even their intention. The fact the enemy made no demand for surrender while in a position of advantage did not bode well.

The warship meant to destroy them.

Another blast impacted against the ship. Flinn could see the rapidly extinguishing plasma explosion in the corner of his eye as the flare lit up the cockpit momentarily. Ahead of him, the star was continuing to expand and Flinn brought the ship about sharply to get as far away from it as possible. The warship's larger size forced it to continue onward for a few seconds before making the course correction to match the *Son's* trajectory.

Very soon, it was firing on them again.

"Are you ready?" Flinn yelled into his headset. A blast detonated alongside the ship, closer than before.

"I'm primed." Garryn shouted, finding the return to the gunnery turret almost comforting.

"Good, I'm going to stay ahead of them while I'm plotting the jump into hyperspace. We need to confuse her scanners as much as possible so she can't track us in normal space. If she can't chart us, she can't keep up with us."

It was not an optimum strategy, but Flinn did not want to engage the warship in a fight. Brysdynian warships were well armoured, carrying heavy artillery capable of a sustained fight. All Flinn Ester wanted to do at this moment was to get out alive with his skin and his ship intact.

"I'll get it done, make the computations!"

Inside the gunnery turret, Garryn could see the ship clearer than Flinn. All that lay between him and the cold vacuum of space was a thick sheet of plexiglass. The vessel, a Brysdynian Slicer class, was currently firing its own thrusters to keep up with Flinn's manic manoeuvres. A less experienced pilot would have felt some alarm at the tight swerves and spins Flinn was forcing the *Wayward Son* to do.

The controls differed a little from the one-man fighters Garryn was accustomed to piloting, but he was able to adapt easily enough. The targeting scanners, the control throttle and instruments were generally configured the same, so adjusting was a matter of a quick study. There was little time to waste in familiarising himself before Garryn placed his hands on the controls and returned fire on the warship.

A volley of fire strafed the front bow of the warship. Plasma impacted the hull with a white hot flare before turning into ribbons of energy cackling against the greyish dish of the scanner array. The ship faltered for an instant as it attempted to recalibrate from the sudden disruption. The moment was brief. Within seconds, the warship's engines flared to life and continued the pursuit.

"That's it!" Garryn heard Flinn through his headset. "You had them for a few seconds. Keep doing that! I need a few more minutes!"

A few more minutes seemed like an eternity. The warship commander was not a fool. It wouldn't be long before the warship commander recognised the tactic and took counter measures to protect his ship's scanning equipment. Still, evasive manoeuvres were easier to perform on a small freighter than a large, military ship of the line.

More plasma bolts escaped the dual barrel of the gunnery turret. Garryn maintained a continuous barrage of fire until the sound of escaping plasma boomed in the small cubicle. The warship shrugged off the assault with ease, but each volley widened the *Son's* lead.

In a desperate attempt to prevent their impending escape, the warship fired an equally deadly barrage of fire at the smaller ship. But by this time, the *Wayward Son's* lead on the warship was significant enough to blunt the assault. Without warning, another flare of light filled in the corner of Garryn's eye but this was far more intense, making him flinch away.

"Close the turret shields!" Flinn was shouting in his ear. "Close it now!"

Without thinking, Garryn did as he was told. The low hum of the duranium plates enclosed the plexiglass around him. The darkness caused bursts of colour in front of his eyes and the hull shook with a violent tremor. The ship lurched forward and Garryn was thrown against the wall of the turret. His skull slapped against the hard metal surface and he felt a mixture of dizziness and pain as he tried to regain his balance.

"Gar!" Finn was again shouting at him through the ringing pain in his head.

Flinn's voice came through a stutter of static, making his words hard to decipher. Garryn tried to adjust his headset to compensate but the static still remained.

"Are you okay?"

"I'm fine," his voice sounded muffled in his ears. "What happened?"

"Cathomira."

"Cathomira?" Garryn asked and then became conscious of a dull, thumping noise against the hull.

"Lower your canopy shields," Flinn instructed.

The shields lowered to reveal the space beyond the plexiglass filled with floating debris. As the *Wayward Son* sped away from the destruction, Garryn saw huge blocks of rock swirling around the ship, smashing into smaller fragments as they slammed against one another. Some fragments were as big as the ship itself, while others were no bigger than pebbles. The sight of it was both horrifying and fascinating. They couldn't even see the warship through the veil of dust and rock.

Cathomira had just gone nova.

* * *

For a minute, Garryn did not know what to feel.

All his life, he'd known Cathomira as the place of his birth. When he had made this trip, it was in the hopes of proving it once and for all. While it was all too clear he was never from the planet, Garryn still felt some bond to it. With its demise, Garryn was faced with the stark reality of not knowing where he came from. By coming to Cathomira, he had only created new and more perplexing questions.

Where had he really come from?

"We can't jump in this," Garryn stated. The bombardment of the debris against the hull was slowing them down considerably. As it was, Finn was manoeuvring through the debris field at dangerous speed, trying to avoid one hurling fragment of rock after another.

"Not until we clear this debris field and that's not going to be easy," Flinn agreed grimly.

The warship appeared through the storm of dirt and debris, resuming its pursuit since it was not as disadvantaged as the *Wayward Son* in the debris field. Moments ago, its size hindered the chase, but it was now giving them the advantage. Their lead was dwindling rapidly as the warship's armour and shielding allowed it to move through the deadly fragments without fear of catastrophic hull breaches.

"We got to get moving now!"

"I'm doing the best I can!" Flinn barked back.

The *Wayward Son* accelerated again, but was severely impeded by the asteroids flying at them from all directions. The ship swung from side to side, avoiding the larger blocks of rocks as it made its way out of the system. Behind them, the warship continued its relentless pursuit. Garryn remained in the gunnery turret, firing on any asteroid that came too close, turning it into rubble, leaving Flinn to concentrate on manoeuvring through the debris field.

Despite the circumstances, Garryn admired the skill by which Flinn Ester flew his ship. Garryn considered himself a good pilot, but Flinn made him feel outclassed. Under the captain's expert hands, the ship seemed to weave through the hail of rock and earth effortlessly.

After an eternity, the concentration of asteroids thinned out and Garryn let out a sigh of relief. Even though he could still see the warship dangerously close behind them, they would clear the field and be able to jump to hyperspace without much difficulty.

"We made it. How soon can we make the jump into hyperspace?"

"I'm doing the calculations right now. I'm keeping the ship on full throttle so we'll stay ahead of them long enough to jump."

Flinn's confidence reassured Garryn they would still be alive tomorrow.

Garryn relaxed a little at hearing the news. He wondered if this was just another day for Flinn, living the life he did. The captain did not sound perturbed at having a large Brysdynian warship in pursuit, because the ship had less reason to be in Cathomiran space than they did. Garryn doubted they would be likely to maintain the chase once the *Wayward Son* returned to core space.

For the first time, Garryn was able to study the ship closer. He zoomed in on it using the targeting scanners and magnified the image. Nothing about the warship seemed out of the ordinary. It was, in every sense of the word, a standard Brysdynian warship. It was one of the newer Slicer class ships deployed to protect the main space lanes and distant colonies' worlds.

If anything stood out, it was the lack of markings on its hull. Garryn could see no traces of its wing designation or anything indicating to which part of the Imperial Navy it was attached.

"Strap yourself in, Gar," Flinn's voice commanded.

Garryn was still studying the ship, but he made sure he was firmly buckled into his seat.

The Security Elite have ships, Garryn thought.

They have their own ships and their own commanders. Security Elite officers were trained killers and fanatical to the last. Their devotion to the cause and their master was legendary. More and more, he was convinced that if anyone was responsible for this it was the master of Security Elite.

The last thing he thought before the brilliant burst of stars filled his world was whether or not Edwen would allow him to live with what he had just learned.

XIX

Audience

The Imperator stood before the Enclave.

It had been years since he had made a personal visit to the domain of the Security Elite. Very little about the place had changed since that visit. The building still bore close resemblance to a fortress stabbing at the heart of Paralyte. Its great height and black marble construction cast a shadow over the city more symbolic than any other structure in the city.

Iran felt a cool shiver as he stared at the tall monolith of a building.

He had always disliked the design, but understood the reasoning behind it. The master of Security Elite wanted a monument to intimidate and strike fear into the hearts of the masses. The high stone walls and citadel-like proportions of the building served its purpose. It was the bastion from which Edwen ruled his private army of disciples.

The Enclave was the antithesis to the Domicile. Both buildings sat on either end of Quorum Hill, facing each other like titans on a battlefield, each representing its own set of values and beliefs. The Domicile's construction was almost as ancient as Paralyte itself. It stood as the symbol of endurance for White Star survivors and a monument to all they had built since arriving here.

When Garryn becomes Imperator, Security Elite will cease to exist. I know it and, to be sure, Edwen knows it as well.

Thinking of Garryn reminded Iran why he had come to the Enclave. In truth, being here was awkward. Since the speech revealing his anti-alliance stance at the Quorum, the battle lines between both men had been drawn. Right now, it was surprising for the Imperator to come to the Enclave like a supplicant. Iran knew he would always feel this way with the General.

By the time Iran's father had passed away, Edwen was already the undisputed leader of Security Elite. Still, he'd had none of the power he now possessed. To most, the organisation had been little more than a splinter group of the Central Police. Its resources had been few and it had little of the jurisdictional powers that now inspired so much fear among the masses.

To gain the kind of influence he wanted for his ambitions, Edwen needed powerful friends. At the time, there was none more powerful than the newly ascended Imperator. Iran was eager to prove himself to the pompous Imperial Guard who felt him too young for the position. Their mutual needs were realised during their first meeting and neither had looked back since.

Together they had gone on a campaign of conquest unparalleled in Brysdynian history. Who knows where they might have ended up, if not for the Jynes? Initially, the Imperial Guard followed the Imperator reluctantly on his first military expedition. They were unashamed in admitting their doubts about his ability to command. Iran remembered the sniggers, the snide remarks and the condescension in their voices.

Edwen followed him unconditionally, with no demands or doubts about his decisions. All Edwen required were ships to carry his Security Elite troops and the right to command them. Iran, who wanted to show his gratitude, gave Edwen everything he wanted. Edwen was smart enough to stop short of asking for complete autonomy, because Iran would never grant it.

Nevertheless, Security Elite was given the same unlimited resources as the Imperial Fleet. Before the Scourge, this was quite considerable. Edwen was an institution all by himself and, while he lived, so would Security Elite. In the years passed, Iran had ignored the occasional whisper reaching his ears about how the Elite conducted itself.

Most of these were about how the Elite maintained its power base. It was an institution built on secrets and threats, increasing its influence beyond the wildest imaginings of its commander. Iran turned a blind eye to everything he heard, because in his heart he knew the General was a patriot. Edwen would never consciously harm Brysdyn and he served a purpose. Great empires always needed men like Edwen.

* * *

As expected, his sudden arrival at the Enclave caused a state of mild panic to run through the establishment. His personal guard secured the area long before Iran disembarked the skimmer. Running his gaze across the courtyard, he couldn't see any of them. By now, his personal guards were firmly entrenched in strategic locations across the complex, dissolving into the sea of faces with complete obscurity.

In the meantime, Security Elite officers were running through the main doors, warning the higher echelons of the Imperator's arrival. Others were frozen where they stood, unable to do more than offer the customary salute as he passed by. Iran ignored all these distractions. His only concern was reaching Edwen.

Garryn was gone and Iran wanted to know why.

Since the announcement regarding the destruction of Vyndeka's ship, nothing in the Imperator's world made sense. In the past twenty-three years of Garryn's life, the Imperator had come to know one thing about his son. The lad was never impulsive. Garryn had always been a quiet and deliberate child and

grew up into a likewise adult. Now, for some unknown reason, Garryn had abandoned all his responsibilities to disappear without a word.

Until yesterday.

Last evening, Iran received a communication from
Garryn transmitted from the civilian spaceport in
Paralyte. The message was brief and little more than
obligatory. It spoke of Garryn's intention to take
some time for himself without the pomp of a royal
trip. Garryn sent his regards to Elisha and Kalistar
with apologies to Iran for his sudden departure. He
would be home soon enough. The message was more
enigmatic than it was explanatory.

Iran's attempt to track down his son was met with
little success and increased his frustration. He was
able to trace Garryn as far as the space station, but
no farther. If he'd left Brysdyn, he'd done so without using any conventional means of travel. Further
investigation revealed the boy had emptied out his
private accounts and was travelling with a great deal
of currency.

Summoning Ashner to him, Iran demanded answers. The aide did not stand on ceremony when he
stood before the Imperator. He was just as concerned
about Garryn. Ashner hid nothing and revealed everything he knew about why Garryn might have left.
Though he could not say for certain where Garryn
had gone, Ashner was able to venture a guess.

Cathomira.

Iran was astonished by the story Ashner wove for
him. It went a long way toward explaining his son's

behaviour the past months. He'd wondered about Garryn's sudden patronage of a scientific expedition to Cathomira, but had attributed it to a young man's natural curiosity about his heritage. It never occurred to Iran that Garryn might have ulterior motives.

Why didn't Garryn just come to him? Before Iran finished thinking the thought, he already knew the answer. Investigating his past might be perceived as an insult to his adoptive father, even though Iran would never have begrudged Garryn the need to know. Still, Garryn was a good son who would never intentionally hurt him.

When Iran finally arrived at the General's office, the man's surprise was evident, even if he was warned about Iran's presence at the Enclave. He recognised the other officer in the room as Major Danten, Edwen's second in command.

"Get out," Iran said without looking at the man.

Danten left without saying a word.

By now, the General had emerged from behind his desk to greet the Imperator. While his expression revealed some concern regarding Iran's hostile manner, Edwen did not appear terribly disturbed. As always, the master of Security Elite was always in control.

"This is an unexpected surprise, Imperator…"

"Spare me." Iran was in no mood for false civility. "Where is my son?"

"Garryn? don't know what you mean. I assumed he was in the Domicile."

"He is gone! He disappeared almost a week ago. No one has seen him anywhere in the system. He was traced as far as Home Base, where he must have caught a private freighter off world, since there is no record of him taking a commercial liner. As for Kalistar, Garryn asked her to remain at the Domicile because he was afraid for her safety. He seems to believe she might be in danger."

"She is my daughter. No one would dare touch her."

"Garryn believes that there is a conspiracy involving the New Citizens," the Imperator continued, scrutinizing Edwen's reaction. "I've known you for longer than either of us would like to admit it and I know you well. This has your stink all over it!"

The General did not show any anger at the accusation. As always, he was maddeningly calm. "I have no idea what you are talking about."

Iran looked away so he could regain his composure. He had to remain calm if he was to get to the bottom of this. After a moment, he turned back to Edwen.

"Ashner told me about the mentalist, Edwen. He told me my son has been dreaming about a planet bearing no resemblance to Cathomira. Did you know that Garryn is not the only one? Even Kalistar is dreaming about this place. There are New Citizens all across Brysdyn, waking up screaming from nightmares about being torn away from their homes!"

So that is how it began, Edwen thought to himself.

"Nightmares? This is what it is all about? Nightmares? You accuse of a secret conspiracy on the basis of a few bad dreams?"

"After I spoke to Ashner, I checked the records myself. Fortunately, being Imperator, I was able to declassify the records. Do you know what I found? There are no records! All those older children sent off world to the rest of the Empire, where are they? I found no record of their existence, no documentation, no current histories, not even adoption information! Did they ever exist, or was that a part of the lie too?"

For a few seconds, the General said nothing. He took all the news with little reaction.

Yet, behind his eyes, Iran saw the turmoil, turmoil and resignation.

"Well what did you expect?" Edwen dropped all pretext. Iran wanted the truth. "Did you think it would be that easy? I am a patriot, Iran, no matter what you choose to believe. I have always been a patriot."

"WHAT DID YOU DO?"

"What I had to," the man replied, unperturbed by Iran's outburst. "The Empire was weeping over their lost children. Did you forget the sons I buried? I wept too, Iran. I wept with the rest of Brysdyn and when the crying was over, I stood up and chose to go on. Look outside and tell me I did no good. The Empire will live because of what I did."

"Lords," Iran managed to whisper. His disgust was so overwhelming it felt like bile forcing its way up his throat, ready to choke him. The horror of it was beyond his comprehension, but no more than his own complicity. When Security Elite brought news of the

Cathomiran children to Brysdyn, Iran had suspected something and *ignored* it.

Even with Aisha's recovery from the Scourge after the Cure was administered, his world was shattered. The absence of children made it difficult to care about the future. He'd tried to be supportive and accept the reality of it but, like the rest of his people, Iran had been in a state of shock.

When Edwen brought them the news of Cathomira, a part of him, unclouded by such feelings, questioned the legitimacy of it all. Yet he ignored the nagging doubts and the secret fears, because he wanted a future. He wanted it badly enough to force away his concerns into a place where they would never surface.

Except now they had.

"Where did they come from, Edwen?" Iran found himself asking the question he should have asked years ago. "Where did the children really come from?"

"Is that important? What are you going to do about it? Announce it over the Transband to Brysdyn? Arrest me? Are you willing to tell the people of Brysdyn about their children? Are you willing to tell Garryn the truth about himself, about how he came to be Prime?"

Iran recoiled at the words, but said nothing.

Finding the correct pressure point, Edwen pressed on.

"The only thing that connects him to Brysdyn is you, Imperator. The boy's love for you will force him to endure *anything*. Tell him the truth and you will lose him as surely as I will lose my daughter. Are you ready to condemn yourself as you will the rest of Brysdyn?"

Despite his outrage, Iran was forced to confront the possibility of losing Garryn, but such a compromise would come at price.

"It may be too late already, Edwen. If he hasn't found the truth already, he soon will. You underestimated how determined my son can be. Where will he go to find it, Edwen? Where will the answer take him?"

Edwen did not reply.

* * *

After the jump into hyperspace, leaving Cathomira forever, Garryn found himself at a loss at what to do.

He sat in the cockpit of the *Wayward Son*, manning the controls while Flinn affected repairs on the ship. After its confrontation with the Brysdynian warship and their flight through the debris field left behind by Cathomira's nova, the ship was in need of maintenance. Flinn put them on course for the nearest commercial star base, so that he could conduct the more urgent work.

Garryn stared through the canopy at the stars streaking past him, trying to decide what he would do now. He could admit to himself, finally, how much he had been deluding himself. He did not come from

Cathomira. He did not know where he came from. Garryn's intended course of action, since leaving Brysdyn, had never extended beyond reaching Cathomira. What he'd learned here had only created more riddles.

If he was smart, he would go home to be Prime and forget all this.

Only there was something inside him incapable of allowing him to give up. This wasn't finished! The demons plaguing him now would plague him forever if he returned home like a defeated animal. He couldn't face Edwen knowing the man had won!

Garryn shook such thoughts out of his head, because they did little except to torment him further. Instead, he turned his attention to the archive crystal Jonen had given him. As he studied the piece of crystal, Garryn felt a pang of grief for the thoughtful man who had been his confidante through most of this. He wondered if Jonen had lived long enough to learn the truth about Cathomira, or had he died in ignorance like so many others?

I will never know.

Garryn inserted the crystal into the reader slot on the cockpit panel and waited for a few minutes while the computer deciphered the information into a viewable context. Jonen's face appeared on the console screen a moment later. It was good to see Jonen again, even if it was like this. It served to remind Garryn again just how much he missed the man.

"Case Study 102, Garryn, Son of Iran." Jonen never felt the need to linger on his title, Garryn remembered. It was one of the things that Garryn liked so much about him.

The next few minutes of the recording outlined Garryn's sessions with Jonen and the general impressions the mentalist gained from those sessions. Nothing said surprised Garryn, because Jonen had been up front with him from the very start. It went a long way to explaining Jonen's success as a mentalist.

Included in the crystal was a record of his neural analyser results and Garryn found himself viewing his dreams for the first time while he was awake. It was strange watching the images unfold before him on holographic viewer and even more surprising when it affected him no less potently than it did when he was asleep. Accompanying the images was commentary by Jonen as he explained symbolism in clinical brutality.

"This last image sets Garryn's dreams apart from the others."

A blue planet appeared. He didn't remember this. Garryn leaned closer forward, staring at the blue planet in fascination. It was breathtakingly beautiful, with iridescent colours and swirling white clouds covering parts of the surface. It seemed to be frozen on its axis and Garryn found himself staring at a continent on the southern end, just before the polar ice caps. He knew this world.

Somehow, he knew this world.

* * *

They were making the world spin.

The world spun faster and faster until the continents were a blur of blue and green colours. A child's laughter rang in his ears. A man's hand caught the world and made it slow. The child stopped laughing and there was silence as the man's finger pointed to one particular place...

"This is h..."

* * *

Garryn blinked. It was as if the visual information was too much for his mind to take all at once. He looked back at the screen and saw Jonen's image on the screen again. He quickly found the retrace button to review the part of the archive he wanted. Once the blue planet appeared on the screen again, Garryn froze the image.

The world he had remembered moments ago was like this one, with subtle differences. The continents were more clearly marked when he dreamed. Here, they were obscured by the swirling white clouds, with faint outlines of continents and landmasses. The world in his dreams seemed less real than this one on the screen, but he knew with certainty they were one and the same.

He set the archive in motion again to hear Jonen's opinion on this image.

"It is the first time we are presented with a visual image of a planet. Initially, I believed this to be the home planet of the New Citizens, but this is a very young planet and we know the Cathomiran star is billions of years old and is a red star. Very clearly, the sun in Garryn's dreams is a yellow star. At present, Garryn is the only Dreamer who has seen it."

He was a fool. Garryn had always assumed that the other Dreamers saw the same star in the dreams, because Jonen had never told him otherwise. During the Dreamer session at Jonen's home, Garryn remembered listening to the stories told by the other Dreamers, but realised now that he never actually heard them mention the yellow star. Why was he so different?

Yellow stars were not uncommon. It was only temperature and the view from a planet's atmosphere determining its colour. When Garryn was serving at Erebo, the sun of that system was yellow. It occurred to Garryn that perhaps that was why he dreamed of a yellow star. Was it because he saw the star at Erebo and it awakened the memory inside of him?

Erebo Station had been built on a moon orbiting the fifth planet of the Theran star system.

Garryn leaned back into his chair, absorbing the information he'd inadvertently stumbled upon. The nightmares had begun two days after he arrived at Erebor. He remembered how his bunkmate Shyle had shaken him awake. After a week of similar awakenings, he'd asked for his own private quarters. No one refused him the request.

If being in Erebor was the key, then what about the others? The other Dreamers had never been to Theran. Except the Transband's relentless coverage of the uprising ensured they would have seen the media footage at home. How many times had he and his fellow pilots warded media ships away from the fighting? How many images of Erebor were transmitted all across the Empire, along with its native star?

Garryn could imagine the future Dreamers sitting down with their beverages in the morning to watch the broadcast everyday before they went to work or got on with their lives. How many of them were able to escape the images for very long?

It all made perfect sense now that he was in possession of a big piece of the puzzle. Garryn rose to his feet and hurried out of the cockpit. Running up the length of the *Wayward Son*, he made it to the other end of the ship in a matter of seconds. Garryn paused at the edge of the maintenance hatch and stared into the guts of the ship. Flinn was working diligently on a pressure valve, surrounded by steam and heat.

"Flinn!" Garryn called out over the sounds of engines working.

Flinn looked up at him and put down the tool he was holding. Wiping the sweat off his brow he yelled back at Garryn. "Who's flying the ship?"

"Relax. She's on autopilot. Look, we need to make a course correction."

"A course correction? For where?"

"Theran," Garryn replied intently. "We have to go to Theran."

XX

Theran

There was not much on record about Theran.

As the ship sped towards its new destination, Garryn tried to learn all he could about the star system. Some of what Garryn knew came from his memories of being stationed there, but most of his information came from the star tapes Flinn Ester kept on board the *Wayward Son*. Flinn's collection was impressive, but there was little information regarding Theran.

Theran was a standard G-type star, young by galactic standards, with nine planetary bodies in orbit around it. As star systems went, it was not very dissimilar to a hundred such systems throughout the galaxy. Prior to colonisation, only one of those planets was capable of supporting life. If Theran sparked his dreams, then it was a good place to start.

Little was known about the species inhabiting the third planet, except that they'd accumulated a sizeable nuclear arsenal which ultimately destroyed them. Since they had not colonised the neighbouring planets, the entire race was annihilated in that final confrontation. Little else was known about the species and no exploration could be made of the planet since it was now a radioactive wasteland.

The Empire had charted Theran a year after the children of Cathomira became New Citizens. Exploration expeditions resumed, to bolster public confidence in the belief life was at last returning to normal. During these missions, Theran was charted and science teams found a star system thriving with commercial possibilities. Even though none of the planets were capable of supporting life, it was still a veritable fortune of mineral deposits.

The fifth planet, a large gas giant, yielded high-grade ore in its dozen moons. It was not long before the first mining colonists arrived to exploit these new resources. Building large, life-sustaining complexes on the surface of the moons, they carved out a new existence for themselves in the farthest corner of the Empire.

For the next twenty years, colonies spread across the star system. In response to this expansion, the Empire began the construction of Erebo Station. From Erebo, a permanently assigned warship and a garrison of troops ensured the protection of the star system from smugglers. It was one of the best-equipped star bases in that sector of the galaxy and no expense had been spared for its personnel.

Garryn remembered the place well. He'd spent almost a year at Erebo during the Uprising. It came

equipped with state-of-the-art docking facilities, luxurious living quarters with indoors parks, malls and
restaurants. These were operated by the civilian sector and gave Erebo Station the feel of an Imperial star
base.

While he was on Erebo, far away from Brysdyn
and the Imperator, Garryn had never felt more comfortable. His military service on Erebo made him feel
closer to being normal than he'd ever felt in his entire
life. As they now journeyed to Erebo, he wondered if
his contentment had had to do with more than just
being accepted.

Was it because Theran seemed familiar to him?

* * *

"I don't care how much money you paid, I ought to
have let you off at the first star base after Cathomira,"
Flinn Ester grumbled.

"Stop complaining," Garryn said good-naturedly as
they entered the last leg of their journey through hyperspace. "We'll be there soon."

True enough. It would only be a matter of minutes before they would emerge from hyperspace into
the Theran star system. The trip here had taken three
days and Flinn had spent most of the time keeping a
vigil on the *Wayward Son* engines to ensure she could
make the trip.

Theran sat on the edge of Brysdynian territory. In
recent years, it had been expanded to officially in-
clude the system as part of the Empire. Flinn was

unimpressed at having to make the long journey, mindful of damage to his ship following the encounter with the warship at Cathomira. To appease him, Garryn promised the freighter captain full access to the lavish space dock facilities at Erebo Station once they arrived there.

"Easy for you to say," Flinn continued to grumble. "This is more than just a ship to me, you know. It's my livelihood."

Garryn rolled his eyes, having listened to the nagging for most of the trip here. "So you keep saying. Don't worry, I promised you the best techs in the galaxy to look after your baby and that's what you'll get."

"I'll be happy if no one shoots at us."

"Did you turn into an old woman on the way here? I swear you haven't stopped nagging."

"Get fragged," Flinn said sweetly, completing the response by flashing Garryn an obscene gesture with his fingers.

Garryn laughed, enjoying their banter. He would miss the pilot when he had to return to Brysdyn. Despite the reason for the trip, he couldn't deny he had enjoyed the freedom of the past few weeks more than he cared to admit. Once he went home, his life would return to its regimen of tradition and rule.

"Are you sure Theran is the place, Gar?" Flinn asked, once the playful banter had died down. "There are a lot of yellow stars out there and Theran is pretty ordinary."

"It's where the dreams started. It could be coincidence or it could be something more. I have a strong feeling Theran is the place to start."

Flinn, who was accustomed to relying on his gut instincts to make his decisions, could understand the sentiment. "Fair enough. Theran it is, then."

Garryn was grateful for the Captain's understanding. Ever since he'd made the connection through Jonen's crystal, it seemed as if everything was falling into place. There was more to this mystery than just reaching Theran. Garryn was realistic about that. Yet, for the first time, Garryn was confident, because he was dealing in real facts and not just on his dreams. Whatever came next, he would work it out as he went along.

Right now, he just wanted to get there.

* * *

Days after his meeting with the Imperator, Edwen was still in a state of mild panic.

Despite projecting a façade of complete control in the Imperator's presence after the man came storming into his office, Edwen was still affected. After the meeting, Edwen left his offices at the Enclave and returned home. The crushing weight of impending doom has settled over him and it was no longer a matter of if it would break him but, rather, when.

The end had come, not only for him, but for all of Brysdyn.

Edwen wandered through the rooms of his house and realised how close he was to losing his daughter for good. For the first time in his life, Edwen appreciated the place she held in his life. She filled in the emptiness following the death of his sons and his wife with warmth. For most of her life, he had made her believe she was something he had to tolerate. Only in the last few years did he realise how much she mattered.

How much did she know?

Did she know the extent of his complicity? Somehow Kalistar knowing the full, ugly truth struck real fear into Edwen's soul. Real fear was something he had rarely felt. All his life, he had been the one who made people afraid. His power over their fear made him the master of Security Elite. It kept the Empire in the palm of his hand and allowed him to act in its best interest, even if his methods were questionable. How could a slip of a girl understand the true importance of that?

Edwen wanted her home. After the meeting with the Imperator, he needed her home. A part of Edwen wished Kalistar had never met the Prime, so her voice could still warm this empty mansion when he returned from the Enclave. Yet the part of him clinging to power knew Kalistar's association and possible marriage to Garryn would be a powerful advantage. Kalistar would never allow Garryn to hurt him by dismantling Security Elite.

Thus Edwen spent the evening sitting alone in his study, allowing no one to bother him as he tried to escape the fire awaiting him. Perhaps his actions were doomed to failure from the very beginning. Yet even as he thought that, he regretted nothing. Brysdyn had life now! Twenty-three years ago, there was nothing. They were devoid of hope. Iran could rage at him with self-righteous fury, but the truth was undeniable. He'd saved Brysdyn!

What right did the Imperator have to judge him?

When the next day came, Edwen was still in his study, refusing to see anybody. For the first time in years, he did not prepare to go to the Enclave. He watched the sun rise in his window and his household staff readying themselves for the working day. Edwen allowed them to do so without making a move himself. He was content to remain in his chair and drain the contents of his decanter, while watching the world pass by.

Around noon, a knock was heard on the door.

"Go away."

"General, it's Danten. I'm afraid it's urgent."

"I do not wish to see anyone today, Danten."

"General," Danten tried again. "General, Garryn has arrived at Erebo Station. General, he is in Theran."

Strangely enough, Edwen was not surprised. When Iran had asked the question the day before, the General had a premonition that Garryn would eventually arrive there. Still, hearing it now as a reality gave Edwen the push he needed to rise above his self-pity. He had one more chance at this and it was a gamble. It was not easy to make the decision, knowing how desperate it was, but there was no avoiding it.

"Come in."

Danten did not waste any time on ceremony and hurried into the room. He looked across the floor at the General seated behind his desk and did his best to hide his shock. Edwen was wearing a day's growth on his face, showing how long he'd been sitting behind his desk. Edwen had always seemed in complete control of himself, but right now the General appeared haggard and withdrawn. Like a feeble old man.

"Where is the *Warhammer*?" Edwen asked, aware of how he looked as he ran his fingers through his greying hair.

"She will be arriving in Theran within the next ten hours."

"Good." The General nodded and took a deep breath. "Tell Commander Barin he is to maintain strict radio silence. He is not to contact Erebo Station at all. When the *Wayward Son* approaches the third planet, he is to deploy all fighters and use every available effort to destroy her."

"But Garryn will be on that ship…"

"I am aware of that!" Edwen cut him off savagely. "However, it has gone beyond the point where his safety can be considered. We cannot allow him to land on the third planet. Is that understood, Danten?"

"Yes Sir." The major nodded in understanding. The response was extreme, but there was no other way out of their predicament. Still, killing the Prime to save the Empire made the line between treason and patriotism increasingly difficult to distinguish. He hoped after the deed was done history would judge them kindly.

"What will we tell the Imperator?" Danten asked quietly.

Edwen took a deep breath and met the major's gaze. "When the time comes, I will tell him the truth. For the loss of a son, I owe him that much."

Danten left the room at that moment and Edwen watched him leave. When he was gone, Edwen returned to his chair and poured himself the last drops of liquor from his decanter. He took a big gulp of it, emptying the glass as he stared out the window. The scene outside, depicting serene domesticity, did as much to calm his nerves as the contents of his glass.

Despite everything, he'd never imagined it would come to this.

XXI

Discovery

TWENTY-THREE YEARS AGO

Life goes on, Edwen. Keep saying that to yourself until it makes a difference.

The master of Security Elite stared out the window at the city of Paralyte beyond. Paralyte was calm this morning, with little activity visible on the streets. The morning mist snaked through the laneways to and into the main roads, creating a veil of gloom over a city still trapped beneath a cloud of grief.

Opening the window, Edwen allowed a wave of fresh air to sweep into the room. He took a deep breath of it, allowing it to cool his lungs and strengthen his resolve to face the day. The air was the only thing unchanged by the Scourge, bracing and clean. It invigorated his body if not his mind.

The Scourge was only months behind them and it was still difficult to imagine the carnage was over. With bonfires no longer lighting up the night sky and polluting the air with ash and smoke, it was re-assuring to open a window and know you wouldn't be breathing in the residue of human incineration. Edwen was just grateful to avoid being sickened by the stench of burning corpses.

The Scourge might be gone, but it was certainly not forgotten. Its scars still covered his city in a blanket of doom. It hovered above them, serving as a constant reminder of the futility of their future.

He sat on his chair again, trying to force away the depression threatening to overtake him if he allowed himself to linger too long on dark thoughts. His two boys were dead and his wife might as well be. She spent her days walking around their house half drunk, because it was the only way she could cope with their loss. He doubted she registered anything he had to say, reacting only when she was reminded of her sons, with a fresh wave of tears and a new bottle of brandy.

Edwen could have handled the loss stoically if he still had his work, but not even the Security Elite was unaffected by the Scourge. Its ranks had been decimated during the epidemic and now there was not much of an organisation left to command. At least he'd been wise enough to send Elite ships into space when the disease flared up. The crews of those ships would at least be safe.

He stared into the Enclave's compound and saw a handful of officers walking across the grass. Inside the building, it was no different. When the Elite troops had been called in to quell the riots and looting, many had contracted the disease, even through their protective clothing. The resulting outbreak among the Elite cut their numbers savagely and left the Enclave resembling a ghost ship.

Life goes on, Edwen.

He chanted the words to himself like a mantra, even though it did little to improve his mood. Nothing could do that. Not for him and not for Brysdyn. The Empire was going to perish in a childless future and so would the Security Elite. Why did he even come here today? Certainly, there were better places for him to drown his sorrows, rather than at the one place symbolising the decay of his life's work. What was the point of being reminded of what he was going to lose?

Because desperation can force a man to find a solution! I do not want to lose it all! I want it back, I want my boys and the Elite back! Someone knocked at that point, snapping him out of him out of this self-destructive train of thought.

"Enter," he said wearily, surprised by his anger. Control of himself and his emotions was something he sought all his life to maintain. Failure to do so further fuelled his outrage. Was this slipping away too?

The footsteps behind him came to a halt at his desk and Edwen swivelled around in his chair to face his visitor. Lieutenant Danten, his new aide stood before him. The young man had been fortunate enough to be stationed well away from Brysdyn during the Scourge years and never caught the disease. There was no need for him to be vaccinated with the Cure and he was even capable of having children. Edwen didn't even have the strength to be envious.

Since Danten's return to Brysdyn, he'd established himself as one of the rising stars of Security Elite. While this was hardly a distinction these days, when there were so few others to offer proper challenge, the Lieutenant's ability was genuine and his ambition just as voracious. With sadness, Edwen realised this fair-haired youth was the future of his Elite and would only inherit a crumbling institution.

"I am sorry to bother you, Sir. I've received a report that might be of some interest to you."

"I seriously doubt that," Edwen remarked sarcastically.

Danten did not react to Edwen's black mood and continued, "One of our ships from the northern perimeter has intercepted a probe of unknown origin."

Motivated by some premonition of the devastation to come, Edwen had sent numerous Security Elite ships out of the system during the initial outbreak. These dozen or so ships headed for deep space, searching for a cure from the best minds in the galaxy. They travelled the Empire, consulting every notable physician about the disease, with little success. When the search at home was exhausted, they continued on beyond Imperial boundaries. In the end, their lack of success ensured they were safely away from Brysdyn and the Scourge.

"Unknown origin? Tell me more."

"Very primitive," Danten was glad to see the General's interest. "They homed in on the signal it was generating. It was using a binary carrier wave signal."

"Carrier wave? That's beyond primitive."

"Agreed, but I think you should have a look at this." Danten inserted a data crystal in Edwen's com system. "This was compiled by the science officer of the *Starlight*. They brought the probe on board after finding it travelling through space propelled by its forward inertia. When they were working, the engines utilised a nuclear fuel source, a primitive method, but there is some sophistication in the engineering."

"So it was blind luck that we happened upon it," Edwen remarked as they waited for the disk to reveal its contents. After a moment, the console screen flared with life and Edwen saw the face of an officer belonging to the ship in question. The Science Officer of the *Starlight* appeared to be offering a narrative to the visual record.

"Greetings, General Edwen, I have prepared this report regarding the probe we have come to call *Voyager*."

The focus shifted from the science officer to the probe itself. As Danten had remarked earlier, it was primitive. However, there was also a certain amount of skill applied to its construction. Judging by the engineering refinement of its parts, Edwen did not doubt that this was built with the highest level of technology available to its creators.

It resembled an uneven box with tripod legs. A large dish was attached to the top of it, with a long panelled boom extending outwards. Most likely, this was its main transmitting device. The once shiny surface of the probe was greatly tarnished after so many years in space, but Edwen could make out the markings etched against its metal body.

The science officer continued his report.

"We know the probe was called *Voyager*. Our translators were able to decipher the message left by its recording device. *Voyager* is an exploration probe, programmed specifically to seek out extraterrestrial life, although we suspect the race from which it originates is incapable of interstellar travel. I believe the purpose of this probe is to seek out life and offer an invitation to visit its home planet."

Foolish, Edwen thought. Didn't these people know the galaxy was a dangerous place? Sending out an invitation like this was akin to courting disaster.

"Thanks to the detailed information they provided of their position, including star charts, we were able to extrapolate their coordinates. The location of this world sits beyond the galactic perimeter, almost on the edge of the spiral arm. It is a system we previously classified as LC21JUN. It contains one yellow star and nine orbiting planets. *Voyager* originates from the third planet."

"This is all very interesting, Danten. We intercept numerous probes like this all the time. Galactic law is clear on this. If they are not capable of spaceflight, we do not initiate contact. Why am I watching this?" He glared at the Lieutenant with a hard stare.

Almost on cue, the science officer on the screen responded to Edwen's query. "Under Section 49.5 of the Imperial Mandate dealing with alien life forms, we must ignore this probe and return it to space. We are dealing with an obviously undeveloped culture, clearly incapable of intergalactic spaceflight and therefore restricted, but certain elements have been brought to light that might be an exception to the rule."

The image of the *Voyager* probe was magnified, enhancing the inscriptions on the hull until pristine clarity was achieved. A metal plaque was welded to the hull, scorched by the years of cosmic travel. Fortunately, most of the etched information still remained.

The intelligence responsible for the construction of this probe sought life beyond their planet, but they also had another purpose. *Voyager* was a monument to who they were, a symbol of their existence in the universe. It was a declaration of their first infant steps out of isolation. As Edwen stared at the plaque, at the infant's image of itself, he knew more about them than they themselves ever did.

The infant was human.

Edwen was on a transport within the hour.

* * *

It took him approximately two weeks to reach the *Starlight*.

Officially, he accounted for his absence by inform-
ing the Imperator he needed some leave to recover
from his personal tragedies. In the light of his losses,
Iran didn't question it. His wife, Perdu, showed little
interest in where he was going and Edwen did not
feel obliged to tell her even if she asked.

A strict veil of secrecy was attached to the General's departure. All personnel with any knowledge
of the probe were immediately debriefed and bound
to the same secrecy. Danten had no idea what the
general intended when he relayed the directive, but
he believed sincerely in the man's genius. By the time
they left Brysdyn, all existence of the crystal was
erased and the voices who knew of it silenced.

"Greetings, General Edwen," Science Officer Aaran
found himself facing the General in their first meeting shortly after Edwen and Danten boarded the
Starlight.

Edwen demanded to see the probe as soon as he
boarded the ship. Commander Delea, unsure of its
importance, led them immediately to the cargo bay.
Science Officer Aaran was hunched over the alien
probe, working diligently on what he considered his
greatest discovery.

"Greetings Lieutenant," Edwen greeted the
younger man as he entered the bay, empty except
for the probe and the technicians performing a
regimen of tests under Aaran's direction. Walking
past Aaran, the General studied the probe for the
first time while the others waited patiently for him
to satisfy his curiosity. The impact of what brought

him to the edge of the Empire did not lessen now he was staring at the probe face to face. If anything, it only strengthened his resolve.

"How many have seen this probe?" Edwen inquired, not looking up.

"Just the technicians in the room and the bridge crew who brought it on board," Commander Delea replied crisply.

"Excellent. This cargo bay will be restricted for the duration of my stay here. When I leave, it will come with me."

Aaran opened his mouth to protest at the thought of his prize being whisked away to fuel another man's glory, but Danten silence him with a look.

"What are you orders, General?" Delea inquired, recognising the opportunity for advancement and not about to waste it. After being in the wilderness of space for almost five years, the possibility of returning to Brysdyn, even after the Scourge, was not something he was going to squander. "My ship and I are at your disposal."

"You will lay in a course for LC19UN immediately. Maximum speed."

"Yes Sir, immediately."

"You're dismissed." The general did not want to waste any more time, especially when the success of this depended on the timing. If there was one thing Edwen had learned after being in charge of Security Elite for two decades, it was that secrets were harder to keep the more time that passed.

Delea spun on his heels and marched out of the room, leaving Aaran to the ministrations of the General and his aide. Once they were alone, Edwen studied the young officer, making a few deductions about the man quickly. Aaran was a scientist first, a Security Elite officer second. His treatment of the probe was almost paternal, giving Edwen serious reservations about the man's part in what was to come. Still, he needed Aaran right now and sensed honesty would probably be the best tact to take with the science officer.

"Danten, I need a moment alone with the Lieutenant."

Danten was surprised by the dismissal, but obeyed without question, "Of course, General."

Danten left the room, ushering all the other technicians out at the same time. Only, Aaran remained rooted to the spot, unable to keep the fear from showing in his face. Like everyone else in the Elite, Aaran viewed the General with a mixture of awe and terror. One could not be in Security Elite and be oblivious to the legend behind General Edwen.

"Don't look so frightened. I don't mean to gobble you up," Edwen spoke once they were alone.

Despite those words, Aaran remained nervous. "I know that, Sir."

"Do you believe in fate, Aaran?"

The question threw the Lieutenant off balance. "I don't know sir. Sometimes, I guess."

"I believe in fate." Edwen threw a glimpse at the probe. "Fate has led me to where I am. I trust in it, believe in it, and I worship the morsels it throws me."

Aaran did not respond, wondering where the General was going with this. He was perceptive enough to remain silent and allow the man to continue.

"How long have you been Science Officer on this ship?"

"I was an Ensign when I signed on, Sir. I became Science Officer in the last two years," Aaran said promptly, grateful for a question he could answer.

"So, you have not been home since the outbreak of the Scourge?"

"No Sir."

"Brysdyn is not what it was. Her heart is torn and her back is broken. It wasn't that long ago I looked out the window and saw the night alive with bonfires across Paralyte. Do you know it was like that for almost four years? It was as if the sun never set on the city. Daylight went on forever. May you never know a time where a simple bonfire frightens you more than any enemy of Brysdyn."

Edwen looked up at Aaran again and the Lieutenant saw the mark of untold grief in the man's eyes for a brief instant. "It must have been terrible, Sir."

"It was terrible. I think it was more frightening knowing that these fires weren't just in Paralyte. They were in Tesalone, Rainab and every city in the Empire. I lost two sons to those fires, Aaran, but my grief is not unique. My loss is shared by everyone in the Empire and it is worse now because of the damned Cure. We face extinction, Aaran. As a scientist, you must know the current gene pool cannot support replenishing our society to what it was."

Aaran nodded. He did know that. Out here, so far away from the Empire and Brysdyn, it was easy to forget what they were enduring on the home world. He knew of the Cure and the side effect following its implementation. Like those in deep space, he was spared the mutilation and still capable of having children someday. Aaran felt ashamed to be so fortunate.

"I am sorry, Sir, about your sons," he answered, unable to think of anything else to say. He was more than a little confused by the tête-à-tête with the General, but said nothing to that effect. Instead, he listened patiently, certain the General would speak his mind when the time came.

"Thank you, Aaran. Now, you must tell me what you have done since your report to me."

Thankful that they were at last returning to a subject he was qualified to respond to, Aaran was quick to impart everything he knew. "Well Sir, after we received your instructions, we deployed one of our G8 probes to LC19UN. It remained in orbit around the planet for approximately two of its rotations before returning to us."

"Was it detected?"

"We don't believe so. Their communications and sensor technology is limited. Our surveillance probes are capable of emitting a cloaking field to prevent detection."

"And the inhabitants?"

"The inhabitants, as we believed, are definitely human, Sir," Aaran said proudly. "There can be no doubt about that. Differing environmental factors have split the species into five genetic groups, the differences of which are slight. Mostly related to eye, skin and hair colour. Their genetic material is almost identical to ours. Incidentally, they call the planet Earth."

"Earth." Simple and not at all ostentatious. Edwen liked it. "Do we have any idea as to how humans could be located so far out of the galactic centre?"

"I have a theory, but it's very circumstantial."

"Go ahead," Edwen urged. For some reason, he rather liked this studious young man. It was unfortunate he would not fit into Edwen's plans. He was far too compassionate. These young had that luxury. There was also an idealism about Aaran that Edwen found refreshing. He wondered why Aaran chose to serve Security Elite when it was obvious he was more suited to normal civilian research.

"You realise I'm just theorising," Aaran added nervously. Obviously, his conclusions were dramatic to warrant this much hesitation.

"Go ahead," Edwen prompted him good-naturedly.

Aaran took a deep breath and began. "The probe captured a great deal of information about the inhabitants. The Earthers are capable of remarkably sophisticated computer networking across the globe, so we were able to access quite a bit of information. They also have similar transmission bands linked through satellite relays, which provide visual information. The planet is not unified and still operates under the tribe mentality. These tribes are completely separate in language and culture, so there are more than a hundred different spoken languages. One of the ancient languages of these 'countries' as they are called, bears striking resemblance to one of our White Star houses."

Edwen stared at Aaran in astonishment. "Are you saying this Earth's inhabitants could be descendants of the White Star?"

"House Terralys," Aaran replied immediately. "In the history of this country, there was an unprecedented explosion of civilisation. Very contemporary ideas emerged during this period: abolishment of slavery, elected representatives for government, even similar gender sexual relations. These are ideas only now gaining acceptance in the last century of Earth's development."

"That doesn't prove anything. Ideas have been submerged before."

"True, but these people had an understanding of stars and stellar navigation, but no means by which to prove any of it. We know from our own history during the Exodus, House Terralys also deployed a Worldship and she was destroyed during the journey. What if she wasn't destroyed? What if she crashed onto this planet and was marooned there?"

"But their technology is so limited," Edwen protested, even though it made a great deal of sense. "How could that be?"

"Sir, imagine if you will. You've spent an entire lifetime relying on your machines to do your work.

One day, you've awakened on a planet. Your ship is destroyed. You have none of the aids for colonisation you intended. What would you do? Could you honestly say you are capable of sitting down and completely rebuilding a sophisticated tool using your bare hands? How does one smelt iron for the first time? How does one find it without sensors?"

Yes, Edwen could see it. Technology did have a tendency to render man complacent and weak. Who would need to know how all those things worked, when there were machines doing the work already? Certainly, there were engineers who had the information, but what if they had no resources? "I see what you mean."

"Their own histories are littered with signs of Terralys influence. The culture to which I referred? Its word for Earth is Terra." Aaran's passion for his discovery forced away his previous inhibitions and he was excited at the interest he was getting from the General.

"Sir, I truly believe this planet is the final resting place of House Terralys, and in so being is a part of the White Star. To think Sir, Brysdyn, Jyne and now Terralys. The White Star is finding its children again."

Edwen sighed. This news did not make things any simpler. If anything, it had just become more complicated. It did not matter what the Earth's origins were. Certainly, the rest of the Empire would never know, because Aaran would never be able to tell anyone. Edwen would see to that.

It was a pity, because he really did like the boy.

XXII

The Third Planet

The *Warhammer* moved soundlessly through space.

Its commander, a severe woman approaching her fiftieth year, stood against the plexiglassed view screen. Despite the spectacular vista beyond the glass, she saw nothing. The blue planet twinkled in iridescent splendour and the moon in the distance glowed with silvery light. Over the past three days, during which the *Warhammer* had maintained a steady orbit around the blue planet, the beauty of the scenery below had become routine to most of the crew, herself especially.

She kept thinking how indifferent space could be. The planet had changed little since her last visit here decades ago. It wore the years better than she.

Behind her, the bridge crew went about their business. They were oblivious to everything except their assignments and were perfect examples of the Security Elite. Forcing herself out of her growing melan-

choly, she turned to face them, envying their ignorance. She wondered what they would have thought
it they knew the truth behind their three year assignment around Cathomira. The mission they'd been
forced to abandon only recently.

If only they knew.

She sighed out loud, knowing this self-
examination was not productive. Nothing could be
changed now, no repentance large enough to wipe
out the deception or the stain on the memories of all
those who knew this planet. This planet Earth, she
reminded herself. All that remained was to contain
the lie and limit the destruction the truth could
cause. Soon the *Wayward Son* would arrive and the
Warhammer would destroy her. The integrity of the
lie would be maintained and Brysdyn would be safe.

"Commander Neela," her first officer spoke, approaching her purposefully. "We have just picked up
the *Wayward Son* on our short range scanner. She is
coming up fast into Terran airspace."

"Has she detected us yet?"

"Not that it has been indicated."

"We'll take no chances. Bring the ship behind the
planet's moon. That should give us a little more
cover. Let's get this duty over and done with."

"Yes Sir," he nodded before adding further. "The
General was right."

Other than herself, only Ristan knew who was on
board the *Wayward Son*. As far as they rest of the
crew were concerned, the leader of a terrorist faction
was on board the ship. Edwen's fiction of a secret

underground faction undermining the core of Brys-dynian Imperial sovereignty kept the junior officers satisfied. It would be enough to prevent them from guessing the truth until it was too late.

"The General is seldom wrong."

First Officer Ristan could hardly disagree. All Security Elite officers were trained to believe General Edwen was a god. Those who were unable to grasp the belief were soon buried in a bureaucratic dungeon in the Enclave or discarded from the service altogether. "Our fighter crews are already on standby. Shall we give the order for launch?"

"Not yet. We don't want to spring the trap too soon. They eluded us once already. I'd rather not give them a second chance. Let them get ahead of us and then we'll launch. I want all squadrons in the air."

Rista showed no reaction to the instructions, because he knew the importance of what was taking place here. If the crew knew the passenger manifest on the *Wayward Son*, Security Elite or not, there would be mutiny. Not to mention the ramifications if the ship were actually allowed to land on Earth. Some of her crew were New Citizens.

"Yes, Sir." He strode away to carry out the order. Neela watched him go and felt grateful he at least understood their situation.

The rest of the crew were in high spirits of the destruction of Cathomira. With its sun gone nova, there was no longer any reason to protect the star system from trespassers. She did not doubt that some of her officers harboured ambitions that *Warhammer*'s next tour of duty would be more glamorous.

Neela had no such hopes. She was nowhere near retirement age, but she no longer wished to command the *Warhammer*. In her recent discussions with the General, Neela had requested a new assignment on the home planet and, if such a position was unavailable, would be content to leave the Elite altogether. There would be enough blood on her hands after this day. She did not want the rest of her career, if it meant staining them even more.

The murder of a Prime was a lifetime's worth.

* * *

Once Erebo Station conducted repairs on the Wayward Son, the ship departed quickly. Neither Garryn nor Flinn wanted to remain there. After their encounter with the warship, Garryn was convinced if they remained at the station long enough Edwen would find them. Flinn, on the other hand, simply felt uncomfortable receiving the hospitality of the Brysdynian Empire. He was too much of a loner skirting the wrong side of the law to be comfortable around so many soldiers.

Once they'd left, Garryn decided to begin the search for a habitable world with a yellow sun. He remembered Theran had one such world and it couldn't be a coincidence the dreams started when he was in this system. Besides, after confirming the official record of Cathomira being habitable was an outright lie, Garryn wondered if the same could be said about the third planet of Theran being a nuclear wasteland.

The trip took only a matter of hours and Garryn questioned why he never made the journey during his military service. There was a general caution warning travellers away from Theran 3 due to the nuclear destruction wrought by its inhabitants. It was a common tale. Usually the make-or-break of any civilisation was their ability to manage their weapons of mass-destruction. Overcoming the desire to use such weapons to reach a peaceful solution was usually the first step to more enlightened thinking.

Unfortunately, Theran 3 did not make that leap.

"There she is."

At Flinn's announcement, Garryn saw for the first time the third planet of Theran.

At first, he could only see the outline of the planet, the rays of the distant yellow sun bouncing off the horizon. His breath caught at the tinge of blue against the amber and he made out the wispy tufts of cloud cover of brilliant white. Next to the blue world, a smaller body orbited like an infant lagging behind its parent. The moon's silvery light was a stark contrast to the warm heat of the sun.

"It's real," Garryn whispered as the planet and its moon came into full view. "It's really there. That's the world I saw in my dreams."

"Are you sure?" Flinn shot him a look, finding it hard to believe they were lucky first time out.

"It's exactly the same as in Jonen's crystal. A blue planet with a single moon."

Seeing it there before him, filling his world with its resplendent beauty, was like cool water being poured on the spinning thoughts in his head. Garryn took it all in, the swirling white clouds against the brilliant blue oceans and deep green continents. It resembled a jewelled orb suspended against a blanket of glitter. Finally, he had proof everything he was dreaming wasn't just some fantasy. This planet existed and, if this existed, then so had everything else in his dreams.

A shrill sound tore through the cockpit and shattered the peace that was settling over his mind.

Garryn snapped to attention, his eyes darting towards the readings on the communications panel of the cockpit controls. The ship was reacting to the emergency signal that had forced its way into the ship's communication frequencies. Garryn recognised the type.

"It's a slicer signal," Garryn declared, recognising it from his military service. "We use these to carry transmissions from warning buoys."

"Warning buoys?" Flinn shot him a look, scanning for signs of any other ship. He saw none, though he pinpointed the origins of the transmission. It was being generated from orbiting satellites in a geosynchronous trajectory. A visual image of one appeared in the holographic viewer.

Garryn recognised it. "It's a Brysdynian quarantine buoy. It's harmless."

The devices were mostly placed around planets that had suffered serious environmental damage, where it would be dangerous for off-worlders to attempt a landing. Though mostly used for planetary disasters, it also warded off potential visitors from biological diseases or, in this case, nuclear or similar radioactive devastation.

"It's probably the standard warning to keep away from the planet because of radiation levels. The locals got into a turf war using nuclear weapons."

"Nice way to keep visitors away," Flinn remarked, and then added, "if it's true."

"Yeah, if it's true." After Cathomira, he took nothing for granted. "Just in case, though, I hope you have radiation suits in this ship."

The *Wayward Son* zoomed past the moon quickly, allowing Garryn a closer look at it as they moved towards the blue planet. They did not see any of the warning buoys, although Garryn did not doubt they were orbiting the planet somewhere in the darkness beyond the ship. The moon was as Garryn expected as well. The thin atmosphere had left it incapable of habitation, unless sophisticated technology was available.

"It's a pretty planet," Flinn commented as they approached it.

Garryn had to agree. The holo disks did it little justice. A tiny voice started echoing in his head, softly at first, but growing louder as they drew closer.

Welcome home.

The homecoming was abruptly interrupted as Flinn's excited cry invaded his thoughts again.

"We're in trouble!"

Garryn turned away from the planet and followed Flinn's gaze, now firmly fixed on the scanner. His expression was grim. A swarm of holographic small attack fighters corresponding with the real life view appeared before them. They emerged from behind the moon, on apparent intercept course after waiting for the *Wayward Son* to pass by them.

"I can count three squadrons," Flinn said grimly.

"There has to be a warship around here. Those are short range fighters. If I'm right, we're up against four squadrons, most likely the entire complement of a warship."

Garryn did not need to see the sensors to know that, behind the planet's moon, a Brysdynian warship was waiting for them. Probably the same warship that had attacked them at Cathomira.

"Nice," Flinn muttered, barely listening as he turned his attention to getting himself and his ship out of this situation. His fingers flew over the ship controls, firing thrusters to send the ship surging ahead. The burst of acceleration took them towards the planet even faster.

"They're fanning out." Garryn watched the flight patterns taken by the fighters and quickly assessed their attack plan. He'd been a fighter pilot once and recognised the strategy. "They're trying to drive us into the moon."

"I know," Flinn agreed. "If we don't do something about it, we're going to fly straight into it and it's not going to be a soft landing."

Without further prompting, he jumped out of the chair and returned to the gunnery turret. Climbing into the cubicle, he fastened himself into place before the controls of the massive guns. The starboard side of the *Wayward Son* jerk violently to one side before he could even lay his hands on the controls. His head smacked against the cushioned headrest of his seat as he fumbled for the headset attached to the side of the control panel.

Slipping the device over his ears, he saw a flurry of shapes zoom past him through the windows. Although in space the vacuum made it impossible to hear them, the *Wayward Son* shuddered in the wake of their passing. The hull vibrated loudly as powerful engines moved past it in large numbers.

"I'm all set," he announced into the head set after the brief pause.

"Alright, I'm going to get us out of here if it's still possible. Anything gets in our way, shoot it down. You think you can keep up with me?"

"You just do the flying," Garryn shot back.

The *Wayward Son* continued towards the planet at top speed, still managing to keep ahead of the fighters. This could not last for long, Garryn thought. The angle of descent into the planet was all wrong. It was coming in too steep. At this vector, the ship would bounce right out of the atmosphere, if it didn't overload the engines or burn up in the ozone.

As a trio of fighters converged on them, Garryn fired, unleashing a barrage striking one of the ships while scattering the others. They broke off at a tangent, trying to keep formation before regrouping to continue their pursuit. One of the ships lagged behind the others with obvious scorching on its hull.

In the meantime, Flinn continued towards the planet. The squadron of ships flew around the *Wayward Son* like mites attacking a large beast. There were so many fighters in the air, making it difficult to manoeuvre. He knew the tactic and felt a wave of anger at being penned like some stray animal.

As the blue planet rapidly expanded in his cockpit window, Flinn put more power into his acceleration. Across the cockpit console, various emergency lights and warnings were flashing in protest. He did notice one thing about their strategy: they were determined to keep the *Wayward Son* from landing on Theran 3. Gambling on their determination to keep his ship from getting there, Flinn flew his ship at full throttle. He wanted them to alter their blockage strategy and give him an opening he could use to his advantage.

A trio of ships swooped past him, flying across his bow to disrupt his forward trajectory. Flinn ignored them, manoeuvring hazardously past them. Hull temperature jumped up another fifty degrees and the ship was starting to superheat. A dozen ships were in pursuit now, firing at him and doing everything possible to keep the *Wayward Son* from entering the planet's airspace.

"Flinn, what are you doing?" Garryn demanded over the headset. "Pull up! You're coming in too fast!"

"I know what I'm doing!" Flinn barked, not accustomed to having his actions questioned on his own ship. "You just keep them off our backs."

Just a little more, baby. Just a little more.

He could start to feel the heat inside the cockpit now. The illumination from the planet lit up the cockpit until it felt like daylight inside the ship. Ignoring his instrumentation, Flinn diverted power to the front shields and adjusted his vector just a few degrees. Once done, he released the plasma valves, allowing it through the engines and fired his ship's boosters.

The sudden burst of power threw the ship forward in an explosion of light just as the hull began to glow with crimson heat. As expected, the fighters did the same, accelerating to keep up. Beads of sweat ran down his brow as the temperature rose steadily inside the cockpit. Finally when they reached the point where the dark canvas of space started to diminish, Flinn pulled up the control throttle.

In the gunnery turret, Garryn was slammed back in this chair as he saw the world banking hard in a neat arc. There was an instance of disorientation with space, ships and the beautiful blue world spinning in perfect disarray where Garryn thought he saw multiple explosions erupting in quick succession. Then as suddenly as it began, the *Wayward Son* started climbing away from the planet back towards the stratosphere.

The ships that had been in pursuit were no longer there. Garryn realised Flinn had pulled up just before he entered the atmosphere and bounced right back off it into space. The fighters in pursuit, unprepared to escape the gravitational pull of the planet, were unable to compensate, resulting in their ships tearing apart.

"You're a crazy bastard!"

"Yeah, my mother used to say that all the time. We're not out of this yet though. Pick up your forward scanner."

Garryn glanced at small digital screen next to the gunnery controls. The image of the moon almost eclipsed the entire display, but what Flinn wanted him to see was painfully obvious.

Sliding almost languorously from the dark side of the moon, the Brysdynian warship *Warhammer* emerged from its hiding place and accelerated into intercept position.

XXIII

Distress Signal

Garryn stared at the ship and immediately recognised it as the one encountered at Cathomira.

Despite its lack of markings, there were only two places a ship of this design could have originated, either from the Imperial Navy or the Security Elite. Garryn discounted the ship belonging to the navy immediately. He'd served as one of its officers for years. He knew their first reaction to an incursion into restricted space would not be the overwhelming response the Wayward Son had just escaped. They would have, at the very least, made an attempt at communication.

No, this ship was Security Elite.

In determining this, Garryn also knew the commander of the ship probably knew who was on board the Wayward Son and cared little if he murdered a Prime to complete his mission.

"Got any ideas?" Garryn asked Flinn. "We can't outrun them forever."

"I've got a plan. Its risky, but right now we don't have a lot of choices."

"Let's hear it, then." At this point, Garryn was prepared to entertain any insane idea Flinn had. The remaining fighters were now regrouping, coming up with a new strategy.

"No time. Just stay calm and keep those guys off my tail."

"I had every intention of that anyway."

A dozen more ships appeared behind them in pursuit. This time, the fighters were trying to drive them towards the warship. Their blaster cannons erupted with more ferocity, bombarding the hull of *Wayward Son* with a relentless barrage. Their savagery of their attack fuelled Garryn's own aggression and he returned fire with equal vehemence. He tried not to think some of them might be pilots he'd flown with.

Unlikely, he told himself. They were Security Elite.

Releasing another succession of blasts, the energy bolts found their targets promptly, despite the best efforts of those in pursuit to evade them. He destroyed two fighters simultaneously, a flight leader and his wingman. Their ships flared with cackling energy before the explosions consumed them.

Don't think about them, he told himself. *Don't think about who they were.*

The warship was coming up fast on them and Garryn realised that Flinn was speeding to meet it. Why was he playing into their hands? The action confused the fighters in pursuit, who were trying to determine what the pilot was doing. They began flying at the *Wayward Son*, attempting to throw it off its current trajectory, since shooting at the craft might result in the warship taking fire.

The ship veered from side to side, barely avoiding a collision in some places while weaving through the large number of fighters as nimbly as a ship of that size was capable of doing. In the cockpit of his ship, Flinn was working furiously to counter anything they could throw in his path. Once again, he was relying on their inability to predict what he was doing. If they guessed what he was up to, then they would really be in trouble.

Like before, Flinn kept the warship in his cockpit window, just as he kept the planet. Emergency systems on board his ship were sounding collision alerts as he poured more power into propulsion. Flinn ignored the alarms he could hear ringing in his ears. He ignored fighters firing at him and the bombardment against his front shield. As he closed in on the warship, Flinn began calibrating his targeting scanner.

It has to be a precise hit, he told himself. Nothing less than a precise hit would save them.

What he intended to do was drastic, not to mention extreme. He doubted any other pilot would dare to make the attempt, but Flinn Ester was never one to play it safe. This was their only way out, short of surrender. Even if Garryn was an excellent gunner, there was no way he could sustain a prolonged defence against all those ships. As it was, Flinn was amazed they hadn't taken a direct hit already.

With the warship looming closer now, the ship went into a barrel roll, tumbling through two fighters while trying to shake off the others in pursuit. Within seconds, he was flying over the hull of the enormous ship. The warship's artillery batteries began firing at the underside of the *Wayward Son* as she flew over it. The fighters continued their head-on assault and Flinn reacted, pouring all power to his front shields and smashing through their formation. The fighters spun out of control as they were swatted aside, crashing into the hull of the large ship.

The *Wayward Son* returned to the warship in a tight loop before launching a strafing run across its front bow. Flinn did not know how much damage he was doing, but it did give him a great deal of satisfaction to see the hull igniting under the bombardment. He was realistic about the extent of the damage because the reputation of Brysdynian shields was well known, but he was approaching his primary target with little interference.

The plasma torpedoes in his ship's armoury were a luxury item Flinn had purchased through an illegal arms' supplier in the wake of a very successful charter. Although the weaponry he'd installed on the *Wayward Son* was already an adequate defence against enemy ships, he'd purchased the torpedoes on a whim.

Rogan, a fat, sluggish man who was very happy with his charter, offered the torpedoes to Flinn at half their normal rate. He was not fool enough to refuse. In space, it was more common for a ship to be destroyed by a spacial anomaly than a marauding warship. During his days in the fleet, he'd encountered spacial phenomena like cosmic strings and gravity wells capable of destroying starships and often it was their plasma torpedoes saving them.

As much as he disliked wasting his torpedoes now, Flinn saw little choice. The fighters were bad enough, but trying to fight them and a warship was playing too much against the odds, even if his luck had been extraordinary so far. He needed to even things out before it was too late.

"Garryn, I want you to raise your canopy shields."

"What?" Garryn's astonished reply resonated through the room. "How am I supposed to shoot if I can't see?"

"Just use your computer. I don't have time to debate this with you. Do it now!"

Flinn took another pass at the warship as Garryn's compliance was reflected on his instrument panel. Fixing his concentration on the targeting computer, he noted that the ships in pursuit abandoned their strategy of interception and were outright firing at him. He suspected they'd guessed at the last moment what he was planning. Multiple blasts rocked the *Wayward Son* precariously and Flinn knew his ship could not take much more of this assault.

Again, emergency klaxons signalled the impending danger of a complete shipboard systems failure. Once that happened, *Wayward Son* would short out and be dead in space. They had one chance at survival and he had to take it now.

"Hold together baby, this is it," he whispered to himself and his ship, convinced she understood him.

The second he saw the target area slip into the cross hairs of his firing scanner, Flinn acted without hesitation. Multiple plasma torpedoes escaped from the main guns, sailing towards the bridge of the warship with singular purpose. Unlike the clumsy randomness of normal ship's blasters, the purity of plasma moved through the dark sky with a streak of comet-like grace.

The bridge of the *Warhammer* flared up in a burst of white hot brilliance as the plasma torpedoes met their mark. The burst contracted, replaced by the thickening spread of amber, deepening swiftly into crimson. The bridge of the warship exploded in an eruption of metal, fire and plexiglass. Debris could be seen leaking out into space as Flinn pulled the *Wayward Son* away from the destruction.

Widening the distance between his ship and the crippled vessel, Flinn knew the warship was by no means done. At least the blow delivered would be potent enough to occupy its attention until they could escape. The warship, having lost all navigation control, was caught in an erratic trajectory towards the moon. Like terrified children, the fighters returned to the mother ship as she fought for survival.

"Were those plasma torpedoes?"

"Yeah, and trust me, you're paying me back for them," Flinn quipped, only half-joking. "Now, let's land my baby before anything else happens."

"No arguments from me," Garryn replied.

* * *

As the *Wayward Son* descended into the planet's atmosphere, the cockpit began to fill with daylight from the blue sky outside. Garryn stared through the cockpit window for a few seconds, letting the vista sink into his mind. The blue sky, so vivid in his dreams, actually existed. Once again, Garryn felt relief surging into him at being neither mad nor delusional. None of the Dreamers were, he thought with some satisfaction.

"Any ideas where you want to land?"

This was still Garryn's charter, even if Flinn received more than he bargained for when they first negotiated the charter. Right now, his only condition for a landing site was that it be peaceful, so he could conduct some much needed repairs to his ship. In any case, the information discovered while he ran a routine scan of the planet was disturbing, to say the least.

"The continent on the southern hemisphere, the one closest to the southern polar ice cap."

It was the location on the globe Garryn had seen in his dreams.

"Okay," Flinn nodded and paused a moment before speaking again. "Garryn, I've just run a sensor scan on this planet. There is no nuclear holocaust."

Garryn didn't look at him, because nothing surprised him anymore.

"No, I don't suppose there would be."

Flinn continued to speak. "No holocaust, no natural disasters, nothing. Perhaps a little pollution content in the upper atmosphere and a slight depletion of ozone levels, but that's consistent with a nuclear age civilisation."

Garryn finally understood the reason for the warning buoys, the Security Elite warship and the lie about Cathomira. All of it was designed to keep anyone from landing on this planet. Its entire existence was always a maze of misinformation to obscure any path to the truth. Even hiding it in plain sight. A lie about nuclear holocaust made sense. In a twisted sort of way, it was almost logical.

"Any life readings?" Garryn asked, although he already knew the answer.

"Massive life readings. Almost on every continent except for the polar caps."

Garryn blinked. Another lie disproven. What would he find on the surface?

He was about to answer Flinn when he saw something on the communications panel that made him sit up. At first, he had no idea what he was looking at as he studied the colourful assortment of sensor lights.

"I'm picking up a signal."

"You got through to Erebo?"

Since encountering the warship, Garryn had been trying to raise Erebo Station without much success. As crippled as the enemy craft was, it was still capable of jamming them and preventing any signal for help to escape into space.

"No. This is coming from the planet."

"You're joking. Are you sure?"

"I'm sure," Garryn proceeded to triangulate the location of the weak transmission. "It's being transmitted by carrier wave signal. Binary, I think."

"I didn't find any complex communication network across the planet during my scan, but carrier wave transmitters are very primitive. It would be easy to miss. The orbital satellites we saw on our way in weren't too sophisticated. They could have been used for carrier wave transmissions."

Garryn had remembered seeing them when they entered the planet's atmosphere. The majority of these satellites were drifting aimlessly in space, trapped in perpetual orbit around the planet. Still, the transmission he was trying to locate did not come from the air. It didn't take long before he was able to pinpoint exactly where it originated.

"Change trajectory, we're going to the source."

"You sure about this?" Flinn asked, sceptical of it being anything of value. It could be a leftover automated signal for all they knew.

"Yeah, I'm sure," Garryn replied. "The signal's Brysdynian."

* * *

Yellow sun.
Blue sky.

Garryn stared into the sky above and saw these things, knowing he was neither asleep nor dreaming. If there were any doubt left in his mind about this world, it disappeared the moment he set foot on the ground and gazed up into the sky.

Around him were the decaying remnants of what would have been an impressive metropolis in its day. Tall buildings, even if somewhat unimaginative in architecture, rode the skyline as far as he could see. There were bridges and roads, houses and shop fronts, street signs and transportation vehicles. It almost reminded him of Paralyte.

Somewhere in the midst of all this, the transmission device bringing them here to begin with was waiting.

The signal led the *Wayward Son* to a city in the northern hemisphere. Of the continents on the planet, this one seemed to have the most cities. The city was abandoned, although remnants of its masters still remained. Their monuments of glass and stone remained behind to mark their existence and their civilisation. Even though scans revealed there was life teeming on this planet, the litter and debris-covered streets revealed all evidence to the contrary.

They are hiding.

Why shouldn't they be afraid of us? Garryn thought. If he were a part of this primitive world, with no contact with the spacefaring races of the galaxy, the sight of a space ship landing in their city would be quite alarming. This was a civilisation with no knowledge of intelligent life beyond their own.

The inhabitants of this world were probably watching them now, from behind broken windows of the houses and the tall skyscrapers, trying to determine what he was.

Flinn was dubious about the authenticity of the transmission, believing it might be a trap set by those who'd tried to keep them from landing. Garryn discounted this, since the fighters and the warship seemed reluctant to approach the planet. After entering the planet's atmosphere, the fighters gave up their pursuit as if warded off.

The presence of the signal only served to deepen the mystery. How had a Brysdynian come to be on this world that was declared restricted to the rest of the galaxy? More importantly, why use such an obscure code? If it had not been for his time in the service, he doubted he would have recognised the signal for what it was.

"Are you ready?" he inquired as Flinn walked up alongside him.

"Yeah, the ship's secured. Let's go."

Garryn glanced at the portable signal tracer leading them to the source of the transmission.

"This way," he started walking.

"Here." Flinn handed him a blaster. "You never know what's around the corner."

Garryn could not argue with that. They proceeded walking up the street, taking note of the terrain as they progressed. One thing became apparent very quickly as they made their way through the upturned vehicles, the garbage-filled streets and their first glimpse of the city's inhabitants: whatever happened here was sudden and quick.

Skeletons began to appear sporadically, some lying on the sidewalk, some in their vehicles, others hanging from open windows, all left to rot where they fell. There were other signs of the world's violent end. Dark scorch marks blackening the sides of crumpled buildings struck Garryn as oddly familiar. He tried to recall why, but the answer was still trapped behind a wall in his mind.

"What the hell happened here?" Flinn asked, not one to keep anything to himself.

"I don't know."

"Those blast marks," Flinn stared hard at another scorch mark. "They almost seem…" His voice trailed off.

"Like what?"

Flinn did not answer, but Garryn suspected he knew the answer.

* * *

Less than an hour later, Garryn and Flinn found themselves standing before a tall skyscraper. Surprisingly enough, most of the windows on this glass edifice remained intact. The sunlight bounced off the reflective surface, making it difficult to look at for very long. At the top of the building was a pointed metallic spire. Even though the construct was primitive, it was obvious to the two men what it was.

"A transmitter." Flinn glanced at Garryn.

"I'm amazed its still functions," Garryn replied.

"Someone has been taking care of it."

Flinn pointed to the main entrance of the building. A wire mesh was haphazardly strung across the front, held in place by metal twine. Now he was closer, Garryn saw angry red letters painted across the glass in an unknown language. He guessed it to be a warning of some kind to the locals. The mesh protecting the building from intruders was jagged and sharp. Anyone trying to cross it would find themselves severely lacerated.

"Someone has," a new voice spoke.

Both Garryn and Flinn turned simultaneously, going for their weapons. The stranger had crept up on them without making the slightest noise. The man made no effort to hide himself as he emerged from behind an overturned vehicle. He was aiming at them with a dark metal object with a long barrel that both men knew immediately was a weapon.

"What did he say?" Flinn glanced at Garryn. The man spoke in Brysdynian, not Standard Galactic.

"What are you saying?" the man demanded to know, the barrel of the weapon moving in Flinn's direction.

"It's alright!" Garryn called out, speaking Brysdynian. "He didn't understand what you said! He's a Jyne!"

The man stared at him with wide eyes. It was difficult to guess his approximate age, because his faced was lined from too many years outdoors and his hair was sun-bleached. If Garryn had to take an educated guess, he would estimate the man to be in his early fifties. He was just a little younger than his father, if not slightly worse for wear. There was also something about his clothes that struck a chord with the Prime, but Garryn couldn't put his finger on it.

"Who are you?"

"We picked up a distress beacon," Garryn answered quickly, not trusting the wild look in his eyes. Who knew how long he had been trapped here and what it had done to his sanity?

"That distress beacon has been there fore twenty-three years! Are you telling me you just happened upon it?"

Garryn slid his weapon back into his holster as a show of faith and gestured at Flinn to do the same. The pilot frowned unhappily at the idea of leaving himself so vulnerable, but he followed suit, trusting that Garryn knew what he was doing.

The stranger relaxed a little after their blasters were put away and Garryn decided he might now be ready to listen to what Garryn had to say.

"We mean you no harm. We were told that this planet was devastated in a nuclear holocaust. There are warning buoys mining the area. I believe they might have interfered with your signal. It was too weak to overcome the interference."

He took this rather well and Garryn wondered if he had really spent the last twenty-three years here, keeping a vigil for a rescue. There were so many questions that Garryn wanted to ask him, but the

Prime restrained himself while the stranger was still so unnerved about seeing them.

Instead of plying them with questions, the stranger lowered his weapon and started to laugh. His laugh was deep and throaty, without any trace of humour, only bitterness. Garryn and Flinn exchanged puzzled glances, but said nothing for fear of provoking the man further.

After a moment, he composed himself and spoke, "I thought they would come up with something more original."

"Who's 'they'?" Garryn asked.

"The Security Elite."

Garryn's expression darkened. Now, he realised why the mishmash of clothing the man wore seemed familiar to him. Under the wear and tear and the patches of foreign fabric was the same dark uniform of a Security Elite officer. "You're one of them, aren't you? You're Elite?"

"I was."

"My name is Garryn. He is Flinn. I came here looking for answers, friend. I think we can help each other." Garryn approached him cautiously, his hand extended for the man to accept in friendship or agreement. Garryn wasn't selective on which.

The man's face softened, lapsing into a kind of contentment when he placed his weathered palm against Garryn's to return the handshake. "It was so good to hear our language again. I never thought I'd ever hear it spoken from another Brysdynian. I am pleased to meet you, Garryn, and you too, Flinn."

This time, he spoke in Standard Galactic.

"My name is Aaran."

XXIV

The Greater Good

Twenty-three Years Ago

Within an hour of Edwen coming on board, the *Starlight* was underway. Only the bridge crew were aware of the ship's destination, but Aaran knew they were headed for Earth. The meeting with the General unnerved him, though he did not understand why. Nevertheless, he felt the excitement of discovering another White Star colony.

Three ships would meet them on route, the *Fury*, *Vigilance* and the *Nimbus*.

Each were ships of the Elite, pulled away from their current assignments far away from Brysdyn and the Scourge. As the fleet converged, Aaran's anxiety continued to grow. Greeting a culture unaccustomed to extraterrestrial life with an armada of warships seemed like overkill to the science officer, but his protests were ignored. It only heightened his concern about the General's plans for this world.

The day before the rendezvous with the other ships, Aaran returned to the cargo hold where the *Voyager* probe was kept. If they were going to meet the people of Earth, then it was prudent to conduct more studies into the culture. Upon entering the hold, he expected to see his science staff continuing the analysis of the probe as instructed. What he found was an empty room. The equipment, his staff and even the probe were gone.

Bewilderment gave way to anger before he spun around on his heels and stomped out of the room to demand answers.

As Commander Delea's science officer, the two men had come to an understanding early in their relationship. Delea appreciated Aaran's ability to get results when time was crucial, in exchange for a pure research environment when Aaron needed to solve a difficult problem. Delea always afforded him the courtesy of not interfering with his examinations until he was ready to present a conclusion.

He was barely thinking as he made his way up to the bridge. Full of indignant rage, Aaran arrived on the bridge completely forgetting it was no longer Delea's ship. As he stepped onto the imposing centre of the *Starlight*, he saw the General taking up position in the command chair. The anger he felt was extinguished in a single moment of clarity like ice water splashed across his face.

Delea was not responsible for the removal of *Voyager*. It was Edwen.

Reason returned to him rapidly when he saw De-lea standing beside the command chair, taking up right flank to Lieutenant Danten's left. Perhaps there was some logical reason to Edwen's actions. As the thought crossed his mind, he felt a wave of shame at his cowardice. It was obvious the General had usurped his research, probably assigning a team of his own personnel to head the project. Aaran was af-fronted by the insult. He was good enough to conduct any research the General needed. He had five years experience in the field!

Stop it!

The effort of his inner mind to save him from him-self was almost as ferocious as a physical blow. He forced himself to calm down before he said or did anything to endanger not only his career, but quite possibly his life. Edwen had the power to erase him from existence and was reputed to have done just that to better men than he. Prudently, Aaran decided against confronting the General and went instead to his workstation.

"Lieutenant Aaran." He heard Edwen's voice and froze.

"Yes, Sir?" He turned to the General, showing none of the outrage he felt about the probe's removal. He noticed Commander Delea seemed unable to meet his gaze, while Lieutenant Danten's face revealed nothing but cocky arrogance.

"I think you should be aware that you are no longer to be associated with the *Voyager* probe. From this moment, you are to conduct yourself to the regular duties of your position as science officer."

He knew he should have let it go, but the finality of those words made him throw caution to the wind. "Permission to speak, Sir?"

"That's enough," Delea spoke up quickly, trying to save the boy from himself. "You have duties to perform."

"Let the man speak, Commander. I'm curious to hear what is on his mind."

Aaran saw Delea wince and his inner voice cautioned him from acting irrationally, but he couldn't help himself.

"With all due respect, Sir, if there is some question regarding my competency in regards to analysing the probe, I would like to know what it is. There is still much to learn about the Earther culture. We should not abandon research prematurely, especially since we are going there."

Suddenly, Edwen's face darkened. "Who said we were going there?"

"Aren't we?" Aaran asked, and felt a surge of fear running through him when he realised it was meant to be a secret.

Edwen glared at him through narrowed eyes and Aaran wondered if he had crossed a line speaking so frankly with the General.

"You are not to have anything further to do with the probe. Am I understood?"

This time Aaran did not mistake the threat in his voice.

"All data regarding the probe has also been erased, so there will be no continuation of the work, by you or by anyone else."

Aaran's outrage exploded without him even realising. "Why? That was valuable scientific research belonging to Brysdyn! How dare you destroy it!"

"You will not take that tone with the General, Lieutenant!" Danten snapped angrily to the defence of his master.

Delea merely sighed and Aaran realised he was now beyond helping. Edwen rose to his feet and stared at Aaran with little mercy.

"How dare you presume to question me, you arrogant upstart? Do you even comprehend what it is happening on the home planet? Do you have any idea the things we have seen these past five years? You, with your world of books and numbers and facts, so completely out of touch with what is happening at home. I do not require your opinion on what must be done regarding the probe. As far as you are concerned, it no longer exists." Edwen's head snapped towards Delea. "This man is to be confined to his quarters for the duration of my stay on this ship. If I see him any time before I leave, you may consider yourself relieved of command."

Too stunned to speak, Aaran did not even noticed when he was escorted off the bridge.

* * *

Days later, he was escorted to the same cargo hold where the *Voyager* probe had been analysed, only to find it occupied by five long missiles, outdated for almost a century. Somewhere in the back of his mind, Aaran wondered where Edwen had managed to obtain these in such pristine condition. He did not doubt their mechanics were in similarly good state.

A hundred years ago, the Empire had banned the use of biological warfare in its campaigns. The missiles used to deliver toxic payload were decommissioned and placed in storage. As Aaran stood next to them now, he could see the compression unit that would turn liquid into a gaseous mass. Although these projectiles were in no way beautiful as *Voyager* was beautiful to him, Aaran admired the elegance of their construction.

"I felt I owe you an explanation."

Startled, Aaran turned around to see the General in the corner of the room with a contingent of Security Elite officers and Lt. Danten. For a moment, he was almost afraid to meet the General's gaze. The man stood before him, with his aide close by, wearing an expression Aaran could only describe as resignation.

"What is this?" He gestured to the projectiles.

Edwen ignored his question, turning instead to the others in the room, including the guards who'd escorted Aaran to the cargo hold. "Leave us."

The leader of the security team stared at the General with question.

"Now," Edwen repeated icily.

Within seconds, they marched out of the room, leaving Edwen, Danten and Aaran alone.

"You are an exceptional scientist, but shockingly naïve. I question why you joined us in the Elite."

He had joined because he wanted to help Brysdyn, had wanted to belong to something greater than himself. There were so many reasons, but none of it mattered anymore.

"You said you were going to explain. What is this?"

"Survival," Edwen answered walking towards the closest projectile. "What it is, my boy, is the survival of the Empire."

"I don't understand." Aaran looked at him, puzzled.

"I think you do." The General stared back.

Perhaps he did at that. Aaran sucked in his breath, trying to control the horror sweeping through him like the rising stench of foul water from a dank sewer. Yes, he did understand what Edwen meant, but Aaran had to hear it from the General himself to know it was real.

"What are they armed with?"

Edwen nodded in Danten's direction, giving his aide permission to take up the explanation he was so graciously giving Aaran.

"Prothos B34," Danten answered.

"I've never heard of it."

"Of course. You wouldn't have," the aide retorted with similar contempt. "Prothos B34 was manufactured on the Halos Research Station approximately a year ago. At this time, all research on the project has been destroyed and its creator is indisposed."

"You mean *dead*," Aaran spoke before thinking better of it.

Neither Edwen nor Danten denied the allegation, but the aide kept speaking, ignoring the interruption. "Prothos B34 was developed as a possible vaccine for the Scourge. Unfortunately, as we found with many of the possible vaccines presented to us over the years, it had a small drawback. It could only protect children from the age of infancy to those prior to the onset of puberty."

"Was it ever deployed?"

"No," Danten replied. "It was in the process of undergoing trials when the Cure was announced. With a vaccine supposedly capable of curing the entire population, Prothos became obsolete."

"And now?"

"Now," Edwen took up the narration again. "Now Prothos will save Brysdyn. All it needed was a few modifications to the original vaccine and the properties of the drug took on an entirely different nature. Instead of a vaccine, Prothos B34 is now a powerful nerve gas. With five projectiles, we can effectively wipe out the entire population of a planet."

"Why don't we just drop the charade? Don't insult my intelligence by saying you have no target in mind. You mean to use these monstrosities on Earth!"

Aaran was horrified by what they intended, and even more confused by their reasoning. What could possibly justify all this?

"You are correct," Edwen answered, unperturbed by his outburst. "We do plan to use it on Earth."

So now he knew and the words spilled out of him like the dying request of a condemned man.

"How does this save Brysdyn, General? How can genocide save the home world? The Empire is almost a thousand years ahead of them in technology. We are a unification of more than hundred star systems. How can one planet with practically no spacefaring capabilities, relying on carrier wave transmissions, be a threat to us?"

"Genocide? Is that what you think? I'm afraid you are mistaken. Perhaps I did not explain clearly enough." He glanced at Danten and gestured for him to speak.

"Prothos B32 is a nerve gas and it will kill two thirds of the population. However, we will be taking survivors home with us from those remaining."

Aaron's mind reeled back to the conversation he'd shared with Edwen during the man's initial arrival on board the *Starlight*. he recalled the stories Edwen had told him about Brysdyn, about the deaths and the end they faced because the Scourge.

May you never know a time where a simple bonfire frightens you more deeply than any enemy of Brysdyn.

At the time, Aaran had viewed the admission with sympathy, being unable to imagine what it must have been like for Edwen to bury two sons in the midst of some much desolation. Now, he realised Edwen's intentions were far more sinister than anything of which Aaran might have thought him capable. What was it the General had said?

We face extinction, Aaran.

"Lords," he whispered staring at both men, his mouth agape with shock. "You're going to take their children, aren't you? You're going to murder the adults and take their children!"

Edwen's face revealed no emotion, but his eyes seemed darker now someone finally said it.

"The Empire must *live*, Aaran," he said softly, almost believing the words himself. "To survive, we must be beyond petty concepts of good and evil. The slar in the forest does not weigh right or wrong when it needs to feed. It just does. This is no different. If we are to survive, we must consider ourselves above remorse or guilt. We must think of ourselves first."

"That is a lie!" Aaran shouted, leaning against the nearest projectile for support. His lungs felt heavy, as if all breath was forced from them. "The slar does not eat its own and it does not shed the blood of another pack or steal its young! You may justify it as much as you like, but if you do this thing you intend, if you butcher all those people, then whatever decency in being Brysdynian dies along with them!"

"Perhaps you are right, but I swore my life to the service of the Empire. If there is an afterlife to which I must be held accountable, I shall accept my punishment. But, for Brysdyn, no sacrifice is too much."

Aaran closed his eyes and turned away from the two men, unable to look at them anymore. In his heart, he knew the die was cast. Earth was going to be sacrificed.

Her invitation to visit was going to be her doom.

They returned him to his quarters and kept him confined. His spirit was shattered and, in the midst of its destruction, he descended into despair. Trapped in his quarters, he imagined what was happening beyond the hull of the ship and his dreams were filled with a world dying. He thought about how eager he'd been to reveal his findings about the probe, to glory in the discovery of the century.

The price of his ambition was the death of a world and the price of his conscience was equally high.

Aaran did not know how long he remained in his quarters. He saw no one other than his guard and had no visitors except the guilt-ridden conscience whispering accusations at him during his waking moments. When the guilt became more than he could bear, he consoled himself with thoughts about the *Voyager* probe, wondering where it was now. Was it destroyed or sent hurtling into space to continue its lonely journey?

When Delea came to see him, he'd lost track of how much time he'd spent confined.

Deprived of anything to help him distinguish night and day, Aaron could not really say just how much time had passed when Delea visited him at last. He thought it must have been weeks or more, because the stubble on his chin was thick and his skin had taken on a decidedly pasty pallor.

The man who entered the cell was a considerably different person than the one Aaran served with the past five years. Delea looked as if he'd aged a decade in a matter of days, but then so had Aaran. They faced each other like the last sane men in a world gone mad. Finally, they were equals.

"How are you, Sir?" he asked, sitting across the commander at the table in his quarters. His voice was almost a croak. It had been so long since he'd spoken to anyone.

"Better than you, it seems."

He chuckled slightly, even though it was gallows humour. "I've let myself go in here. So little to do."

"I'm sorry this happened to you, Lieutenant. I tried to warn you..."

"It's alright, Sir," Aaran stopped him before he could continue. "I didn't help myself. How long have I been in here?"

"Three weeks. I cannot help you, Lieutenant. I don't even think I can help myself."

Aaran realised being trapped in here saved him from having front row seats to what was happening to the Earth. Delea's eyes showed just how much of his soul was lost to save Brysdyn from extinction.

"It is done, isn't it?" he finally asked.

"Yes," Delea nodded grimly. "It was done well and thoroughly."

"The rest of the crew went along with it?"

"Of course they did. Why wouldn't they?" Delea snorted bitterly. "It's only the bridge crew who are aware of where we are. We are at radiation alert with all external canopies lowered. The rest of the crew can't see outside to know they're not where they are supposed to be. As far as they're concerned, we are in the outer perimeter of a star system called Cathomira."

"Cathomira?" Aaran searched his memory to recall the place and failed to do. "I've never heard of it."

"It sits on the other side of the spiral arm. Jut beyond charted space, on our northern frontier," Delea explained dully. "It has a giant red star meant to go nova in the next few decades or so. The rest of the crew believes we are performing a rescue mission. The story being told is we've received a distress call from Cathomira."

"What about the missiles?" The audacity of the lie shocked Aaron, because it would be believed.

"No one other than the bridge crew and a handful of Security staff know about them," Delea explained. "The crew thinks we've launched probes with duranium shielding to withstand the high radiation content of the Cathomiran star system."

"And the *Fury*, the *Vigilance* and the *Nimbus*?"

"Like us, only the bridge crew is aware of what is really happening. As far as they are concerned, they've taken on the last survivors of the planet Cathomira. We should be on our way home to Brysdyn within the day."

"What about the bridge officers who know?" It was inconceivable anyone should remain silent about what had taken place on Earth. How could anyone ignore planetary genocide? Promotion or not? "How can Edwen guarantee that no one will talk?"

"It is easier than you think. Everyone wants to save the Empire. Thanks to us, there will a new generation of children borne of a White Star world, populating Brysdyn and the Empire. How can anyone see the crime in that? Self preservation is the constant of all civilisations."

"No doubt there'll also be bribes to ease their conscience?" Aaran's tone was full of accusation. "What did you get?"

"Retirement," Delea answered without hesitation. "I am finished with this. I asked him to let me go and the General has agreed."

"Commander, we can't be silent about this!" Aaran cried out, unable to believe this atrocity was going to go unpunished. "People are dead and we have stolen their children! You can't allow this to go unanswered!"

"It is over, Aaran! I saw the gas kill that planet by the billions! I watched the Earth come to a stop. The very absurdity of it all is that we didn't get everybody! Some of them survived the nerve toxin. So what did we do? We sent in our pilots to rain artillery on any adults left. If we killed a few children in the process? What was the harm? They were roughly several million, so we would not miss much."

Aaran was beyond horror and managed to ask, "how many children did we get?"

"Approximately two million. Seventy percent of the children taken on board are barely three years old."

Delea did not elaborate on the reports from the men and women chosen to retrieve the children. They knew what they'd done was for the good of the Empire, but the duty would haunt them for the rest of their lives. They tore screaming babies from the bosoms of dead parents and subdued older children fighting feebly to keep their younger siblings from being taken. These were scars that would last forever.

"I came to say goodbye, Lieutenant."

"Goodbye? You're leaving?"

"No," the Commander of the *Starlight* shook his head. "You are."

The door to Aaran's quarters slid open to reveal Edwen and Danten at the cell door. With them was a contingent of security officers and they invaded the room like a swarm.

"I'm sorry, Lieutenant," Delea said finally before stepping out. He had no wish to see this. "If you'll excuse me, General."

"Dismissed, Commander," Edwen permitted him to leave, understanding the man's conflict.

Aaran's heart clenched. Was he going to be executed in this room?

"What's going on?" he demanded when he saw Delea leave. The sight of his departing commander sent a stab of fear through his heart.

The General's response was an order barked at the guards in the room. "Bring him."

Panic struck Aaran without warning as he saw those security officers moving towards him. He tried to bolt past them and felt a dozen hands slamming him into the wall, restraining him. Once he was properly subdued, he was dragged out of his quarters, for the last time.

* * *

Aaran was taken to the main flight deck of the *Starlight* and bundled into the cargo hold of a small shuttle. Once the hatch shut behind him, he heard the sounds of boarding in the main passenger centre of the craft. For a terrible moment, he thought the shuttle was going to take off into space and jettison him to the vacuum. Seized with fear, he pounded on the steel hatch, but no one paid attention to his hysterics.

As Aaran feared, the shuttle did launch. The journey took a few hours and Aaran spent the time curled into a ball, because even though the cargo hold was oxygenated, it was not temperature controlled. Except for himself, there was nothing else in the hold with him. Aaran wondered if this was intentional. Perhaps Edwen was hoping the temperature drop would kill him and spare his security team the trouble.

Defiantly, he refused to allow himself to succumb to the cold. Several hours later, he felt the temperature rise sharply in one burst of rapid heat. Without even needing to see it, Aaran realised the sudden warmth had come from an entry burn. The shuttle was landing on a planet. Within minutes of penetrating the atmospheric layer, the small craft touched down on its surface.

When the hatch opened again, his eyes were bombarded with the brightness of daylight. He squinted hard and tried to focus. The security team dragged him out of the cargo hold and led him away from the ship. When they released their grip on him, he sank to his knees, still feeling the effects of the cold and the sudden illumination after hours of total darkness.

"Welcome to Earth," Danten said, with Edwen standing beside him.

Aaran gazed into the sky and saw it was the crispest colour of blue he'd ever seen. A brilliant yellow star shone brightly through tufts of white clouds. He did know much about Earth, but Aaran knew immediately this was a beautiful day on the planet. The beauty stopped when his gaze reached the landscape.

They were standing on the outskirts of a ruined city. In the distance, he could see buildings still burning, with charred marks across the paved roads. Vehicles had smashed into each other and buildings, their owners slumped across the front of the controls, dead. There were so many bodies. The carnage was worse than he had ever imagined in his worst nightmares.

"You murderers!" he screamed, rushing at the General.

Edwen stepped back and allowed Aaran to be properly restrained by his men. The butt of a rifle slammed into the back of Aaran's head and the pain flared across his skull, driving him to his knees. Someone yanked his head back and forced him to look at the General.

"I never wanted this for you, Lieutenant," Edwin said sincerely. "We have so little talent left in Brysdyn now. I hate to waste it. I hoped you would be able to understand what we are trying to do. I hoped you would possess more vision."

"More vision?" Aaran stared at him incredulously. He gestured in the direction of the burning buildings, the gutted homes, the twisted wreck of metal and stone, with everything reeking with death. "You call this vision?"

"You really don't see, do you? You see this as murder! I see it as salvation. You yourself furnished me with what I needed to make my decision. You showed me their wars, their utter disregard for life, towards themselves and the other species inhabiting the world. You showed me widespread famine, global pollution and plunder of every natural resource! If we had not come along, they would have destroyed themselves long before we did. This way, at least, their children have a future in a society of enlightenment and benevolence."

"Enlightenment? This is supposed to show how much better we are than they?"

"You still don't understand. It is the constant in the universe that the weak are devoured by the strong. We are the strong and what we do for the survivors on the *Starlight*, and the other ships, is more kindness than any predator shows a fallen prey. We saved them so they can save us. The Empire will live, as will the Earth when its children become our own."

Aaran stood up and faced Edwen. "Murder is what you have done, General Edwen of the Security Elite. No ideal is worth that. You may lie to yourselves and create every justification under the universe for what you have done, but that's the truth no amount of debate is ever going to change."

"Sir, must we listen to this anymore? The *Starlight* and the convoy are waiting our return," Danten asked impatiently.

"Go ahead! Kill me! What is one more dead body on this planet?"

Edwen looked at him. "I am not going to kill you. There has been enough Brysdynian blood shed in my lifetime."

At that, he saw one of Edwen's men raise their weapons to fire. In a flash of brilliant light, he felt his body drained of all consciousness when the blast hit him squarely in the chest.

* * *

When he woke up an hour later, they were gone and so was the shuttle. There was no sign of either anywhere on the ruined landscape and, with an awful realisation, he realised what they had done to him. They'd marooned him here on the planet Earth.

Forever.

XXV

Young

"I think I'm going to be sick."

It was the only thing he could say when Aaran's story reach its inevitable conclusion.

When Garryn had embarked on this search, he'd expected to find a conspiracy regarding the true origins of the New Citizens. Never in his wildest imaginings did he suspect the truth could be this horrific. Of course there was no doubt in his mind that Aaran's tale was anything but the truth. The pieces fit too neatly with what he already knew about Cathomira and the Dreamers. The nightmares so full of violence made perfect sense and made Garryn wish he'd never learned the truth.

"I'm sorry," Flinn didn't now what else to say. Sorry didn't seem like enough.

"Come on," Aaran started walking. "We shouldn't stay out here."

He led them through the barricade protecting the building with his transmitter. It was also his home and he protected it from intruders by constructing an access way through the barricade reinforced by mesh and razor wire. By Brysdynian standards, the measures were primitive, but still quite effective.

The city was once called San Francisco. Even though it appeared dead, Aaran assured them it was nothing of the sort. As Garryn suspected, the population had gone to ground the instant they had seen the *Wayward Son's* landing. For many, there was little difference between the freighter and the Imperial fighters assaulting their world twenty-three years ago.

Aaran had built his home within the transmitting tower to ensure he was near the signal in case a rescue ever came. He occupied a suite of rooms, several floors from the lobby. Occasionally, he ventured beyond the city limits to explore the rest of the planet. He found there were survivors everywhere and most of them were children approaching their early teens. As his language skills improved, Aaran convinced them he was one of the few adults who survived the invasion.

Leaving Garryn to regain his composure after what he was told, Flinn questioned the man further.

"So you have been here on your own for all this time?"

"No. Although, in the beginning, I kept to myself because I still had hopes someone would come for me. I really believed I wouldn't be left here forever.

When I realised no one was ever coming, I tried to do what I could for the survivors. There were so many of them and I did what I could, but most of them were children, deeply traumatised by what had happened."

Taking a deep breath, he continued speaking. "Some survived by scavenging and creating a society of their own, but others are savage and violent. It's why I fenced off this building from the rest of the city. I have a life here, as well as a wife and child. When I saw your ship, I sent them to a safe place to wait for me."

After what Aaran had told them, Flinn could understand why.

"We'll find them and bring them to Brysdyn with us," he offered.

"Home," Aaran said with a deep sigh, his emotions overcoming him for a moment. "I never thought I would ever see it again."

Turning to Garryn, who was still staring out the window," he asked quietly. "You are one of them, aren't you? One of the children who were taken?"

The expression on Garryn's face was answer enough. "I have no memory before I was three years old. They told us we came from Cathomira."

Edwen's speech about the Empire's survival flashed in Aaran's mind. The master of Security Elite had given the Empire a new generation of Brysdynians who had no idea everything they knew about themselves was a lie. For the past twenty-three years, he had lived with the consequences of Edwen's atrocities and prayed the General's crime would be revealed. Now his outrage at being stranded paled in comparison to the wrong done to the children spirited away from everything they knew.

Children like Garryn.

"I'm sorry," Aaran said softly, "but how did you find your way here?"

"It was a hunch," Garryn admitted and then proceeded to tell the former science officer about the nightmares plaguing him for months, the nightmares that had led him to Jonen and the rest of the Dreamers.

"After the *Asmoryll* was destroyed, I decided to find out the truth for myself. I chartered Flinn's services as a commercial pilot and got him to take me to Cathomira. Once I realised everything about the New Citizens being from Cathomira was a lie, I took a chance that this planet might be the one I was seeing in my dreams. It's the only system I ever visited with a yellow star and it was here the dreams started."

Reaching behind him, Garryn took the gold chain and medallion hanging from his neck. After removing it, he handed it to Aaran.

"Can you read this? My mother tells me I was wearing this when I came to them."

Aaran took the round, gold object and studied it closely. After a moment, he answered. "This is English."

"English? Is that what they speak here?"

"It's the native dialect of this continent. As I explained, this was not a unified planet. They were divided into countries with their own individual dialect."

"So you can read it?" Flinn asked, aware of how important this was to Garryn.

"Yes, it's an inscription. J. Alexander. Young. NSW."

The words sounded odd to hear and were meaningless to him.

"Could that be my name?" Garryn asked, thinking it was too long to be a name unless it was the custom on this world.

"If I understand the naming conventions, Alexander would be the family name. Earther names are like the Jynes," Aaran glanced at Flinn. "Personal name first followed by family names in order. The initial J is probably your first name."

"Alexander." Garryn mouthed softly. The word sounded alien to him. "What about the rest of it?"

"I'm not sure." Aaran continued to study the medallion, "I think if might be a place."

"Maybe on that continent we were going to land on before we picked up the signal. The one you recognised," Flinn reminded Garryn.

"Which continent is this?"

"One located near the southern polar cap," Garryn answered.

Aaran stood up and disappeared into an adjoining room. This room was the man's study and surrounding their leather chairs were an impressive collection of old paper books, maps and parchments. Garryn was not surprised Aaran had used his exile to learn everything he could about this planet.

A moment later, the former science officer returned with a larger leather book requiring both hands to handle it. He motioned them to a nearby desk and splayed it open. The size of the book covered most of the desktop. Aaran turned the yellow pages as Garryn and Flinn took up position on either side of him. It didn't take long for Garryn to realise that Aaran was thumbing through a book of maps. Finally, Aaran splayed out the book and showed the continents of the planet spread across two full pages.

"Which one is it?"

"That one," Garry recognised it immediately.

He pointed to the continent located almost at the edge of the page. On the glossy paper, it resembled the image in his memory much more closely than his flash of memory upon approaching the planet.

"You know this continent?" Flinn asked the older man.

"Yes. They call it Australia."

* * *

Aaran had met his wife Rachel two years after his exile on Earth. She was one of the few adults immune to the Prothos virus. Over the years he'd come across others with a natural immunity to the nerve gas, but Rachel was the first. It was the first time he had seen another adult since his exile. He had found her amongst the ruins, fending for herself and the growing number of children over whom she had assumed guardianship.

After Rachel taught him to speak English, Aaran learned some of the surviving adults had led the remaining children into parts unknown. There were rumours they left the city for the country, where the main food growing areas were located. Rachel had been a schoolteacher and she was in her classroom with her pre-adolescent students when the missiles hit.

In the years after their meeting, these children became his responsibility as well and Aaran was happy to watch them grow up to find lives of their own under his and Rachel's tutelage. He saw no reason to hide his past with Rachel, because she was an intelligent woman who would learn the truth anyway. By the time he was able to communicate with her fully, Aaran knew he could hide nothing from her.

Aaran convinced Garryn Rachel would be better able to find the place inscribed in his medallion. Garryn conceded the point, because this 'Australia' was a big continent and, despite the years Aaran had spent on this world, there were limits to his knowledge. They needed the expertise of a native.

Once they returned to the *Wayward Son*, it did not take them long to find Aaran's family.

The safe house was a dwelling located in the green hills of the city overlooking the ocean. Flinn set the ship down some distance away so Aaran's family wouldn't be frightened by it. Although it would be impossible to hide the roar of the ship's engines, Flinn was sensitive to Aaran's need to protect his family. While Aaran and Garryn went off to find Rachel, Flinn remained in the *Wayward Son*.

As they approached the house, Garryn held back and allowed Aaran to continue ahead alone. He stood in the cover of the shadows and shrubbery surrounding the brick dwelling as Aaran hurried up the front steps, calling out to his wife loudly. No sooner than she heard her name, a petite woman with shiny dark hair and deep brown eyes hurried out into her husband's waiting arms.

Garryn allowed them a few moments of privacy before he stepped out into the open. Rachel reacted to his sudden appearance, but Aaran quickly assured her there was no danger.

"Rachel, this is Garryn," Aaran said, speaking in English, introducing the new arrival to his startled wife. "He is Brysdynian."

Despite the harsh existence she shared with Aaran, she wore the years well and was a handsome woman, Garryn thought. Her jet black hair was held together with a cord of colourful material and she observed him with dark brown eyes.

"Hello," she greeted him cautiously, still uncertain about him despite Aaran's claims. "You Brysdyn?"

She spoke with the skill of a child, but Garryn was impressed by the effort nonetheless.

"Yes, you speak our language."

He ignored the nagging voice reminding him Brysdynian wasn't *his* language either.

It took her a moment to fully grasp what he had said in return, but when she did, Rachel smiled back graciously despite her fear. "Thank you. Aaran good teacher."

"As are you, madam," Aaran winked at his wife.

The young lady who stood in the doorway watching the exchange between her parents and the stranger said nothing until she was remembered. Motioning her forward, Garryn saw a tall, lithe figure walk down the stairway with exceptional grace. As she neared them, Aaran introduced his daughter with typical paternal pride. "Garryn, this is my daughter, Hannah."

As with her mother, Garryn regarded her presence with a nod. Despite the illumination of the full moon, it was difficult to see her very clearly. What he did see told him she was a striking beauty. Since her mother's genes were most dominant, her hair was the same jet black, while her eyes were her father's green and her skin was light like her mother's but bore a more ivory complexion. She was exceedingly pretty.

"Are you really from another planet?" She spoke better Brysdynian than her mother, although the words did sound odd coming from her mouth. While she could speak the language, her pronunciation and accent made it sound more exotic than authentic.

Garryn liked how it sounded.

"I am," he said with a smile and averted his gaze before her parents found this inappropriate. This was not the time for distractions, Garryn chided himself silently.

"What's happening, Ari?" Rachel asked her husband, now that it was obvious that they were not in any danger.

"We are going home to Brysdyn," he declared happily.

Although he could not be certain of what they were saying, Rachel seemed ambivalent at the thought of returning home. Garryn couldn't blame her for her hesitation. Aaran had hardly been treated fairly by Security Elite and his reappearance would cause ripples through the Quorum, especially after revealing his story. At the moment, however, Garryn was more concerned with reaching Australia.

"We can talk about this once we're on the ship," he told the family.

"The ship?" Rachel understood enough to look sharply at Aaran with uncertainty.

"It's alright," Aaran assured her, taking her hand in his. In that moment, Garryn saw how deep the bond between them was and hoped Aaran would be able to allay her fears. To Aaran, Brysdyn was home, but to Rachel it was the world whose inhabitants destroyed her people.

* * *

Australia.

He said the name several times during the short journey across the planet. Garryn kept repeating the word, hoping it would trigger some hidden memory. He clung wildly to the hope that something would rise out of the fog in his mind and give him all the answers he craved and, yet, the word still sounded unfamiliar. It sounded almost as strange as knowing that his family name might well be Alexander.

J Alexander.

Was J his name? Rachel had told him J was part of the English language alphabet. It was the abbreviation for something else. What was it? The answer was maddeningly close and he walked around the ship for the duration of the journey ignoring the others, focused only upon reaching his destination. Fortunately, Flinn was conversant enough to keep them occupied until their arrival and Garryn was grateful for that. At this stage, Aaran had no idea who his rescuer was – the Prime of Brysdyn. Such revelations could wait until they reached home.

Home.

Like everything else, nothing felt the same anymore. Brysdyn least of all. This ruined blue world was the planet of his birth. His heritage and his past were here, decaying from an act of horrific callousness. This world was his home, even when he was fighting the urge to tell Flinn to take him home to Brysdyn, to the world he had always known. Anywhere would have done, as long as it was far away from the truth.

Garryn isolated himself in the gunnery turret for some privacy while he wrestled with these thoughts. As the ship sped over the planet at sub-light speed, he was treated to a spectacular view of his home planet through the plexiglassed window. Earth was a world teeming with life, of large magnificent mountain ranges, expansive blue oceans and white snow-capped peaks. It was a world of numerous extremes, a melting pot for so many different climates thrown into the mix. Ice covered plains on one continent, while the next was warm and dry, with dense jungle belts.

Armed with the map book from Aaran's library, Rachel pinpointed the exact location of where they needed to go. Aaran had been correct when he said Young was a place. Rachel had found it in the map book or 'Atlas' as she called it. It was the name of a small town in the east coast of the continent. NSW was a province as near as he could understand it. What had she called it? New South Wales?

The continent was like the rest of the planet, a place of extremes. The coasts were covered with thick jungles. Swirling hot clouds above them indicated the density of the humidity level. As they moved further into the continent, the jungle thinned into farming land. However, as they reached the centre of the continent, the greenery was replaced by harsh red desert terrain. As they moved closer to the surface, Garryn saw great herds of animals bouncing across the landscape with an unusual kind of grace, trailing clouds of dust as they moved.

His stomach clenched when he recognised them. It was the same creatures he had seen in his dreams and he knew with utter certainty this was where he needed to be.

Thanks to the Atlas, Flinn knew exactly where he was going once he fed the coordinates into his ship's computer. With usual expertise, he was able to fly straight into the town.

The *Wayward Son* began its descent some hundred kilometres from the coast. The land in which they would shortly set down was decidedly rural. Beyond the town limits, the settlements were sparse. It was strange how farming communities always looked the same, even in a distant world such at this. From above, there seemed to be very little evidence of the invasion. Natural vegetation had overtaken most of the buildings, reclaiming it for the land.

The ship set down in the centre of town. Flinn conducted a sensor sweep prior to their descent and found no evidence of any life. This was hardly surprising. Farming communities were harsh environments at the best of times. With the loss of the adult population, Garryn could not see the children surviving any longer on their own. They would have left or perished.

When it was time to leave the ship, Flinn elected to remain in the ship and Garryn saw no reason to convince him otherwise. He allowed Aaran to take the lead when they left the ship and entered the small settlement.

Hannah fell in step with him as they moved into the main road through the town. In its day, it could have been considered a growing population, Garryn thought. There certainly seemed to be enough evidence of it. The local merchants had sold everything, from vehicle components to textiles and food. There were restaurants and bookstores. It would have been a nice place to live, Garryn thought.

On the morning of the attack, it had been shaping up to be a busy day. Most of the population had been out and about, as evidenced by the bodies on the street. Skeletal remains lay across sidewalks and behind glass shop fronts. A number of vehicles had crashed into buildings. The bones of the dead were covered in cobwebs and dust, exposed to the ravages of weather.

"Are you alright?" Hannah asked as she came up alongside him. It was still jarring to hear her speak with that unusual accent.

"I thought you would be more disturbed at seeing this than I would."

She looked down the dark paved road, with a hint of sadness in her face. "I've grown up with all this."

"Of course you have." Garryn felt embarrassed he'd forgotten that. "I'm trying to imagine living in a world that feels like a graveyard."

"You become accustomed to it." Her tone indicated that she did not like speaking of it, so he did not push. Instead, he called out to her parents. "None of this seems familiar to me."

"That is hardly surprising, Garryn," the scientist looked back at him. "You were barely three years old the last time you were here."

"If I was here. Everyone is dead. There is no way to know for sure."

"There might be a way," Rachel declared and broke away from them and entered the first shop she encountered.

They followed her in as she moved past the doorway, ignoring the dead bodies on the floor gathering dust. Garryn winced at the musty smell in the confined space and wondered what it was she was doing.

Cautiously, Rachel walked around the store's dusty counter and found another dead body. The skeleton was lying across the counter and was most likely the proprietor of this establishment. They'd be conducting business when the end had come. Moth eaten reels of material lay strewn across the table, with scissors and marking chalk looking equally worn.

This was some kind of dress shop, Garryn thought.

"What are you looking for?" he asked.

"Well," Rachel rummaged behind the counter, "if you are from this town, then your family could be listed in the phone book." She explained in English to her husband so he could translate.

"What did she say?" Garryn looked at Aaran but even the older man appeared similarly puzzled.

A few seconds later, Rachel straightened up again. In her hand was a thick yellow book with soft covers. It was covered in cobwebs and dust like everything in the place. It unsettled the dust on the counter when she placed it on the surface and spread the thin pages open. Flipping through the pages one after another, it was a few more minutes before she found what she was looking for and faced her husband with a smile of triumph.

"Translate for me," she told Aaran and started speaking.

Aaran translated as required. "Garryn. This records the name of everyone who has a telephone. It's an Earther communication device. Almost everyone possesses one and, if they do, their names are listed in this book. Rachel has found five listings of Alexanders in this book."

Aaran paused and looked up at him. "One of these could be your family."

XXVI

Justin

The first three names in the 'telephone book', as Rachel called it, were residents who lived within the town limits. Proving herself to be an adept guide, she led them to the town square and found a map of the area for the tourists, behind the smashed glass of a display board. With it, Rachel was able to pinpoint approximately where these people lived. Despite his initial reservations about involving Aaran's family in this private search, Garryn was grateful for Rachel's help.

With Aaran translating, Rachel explained the principle behind the telephone register. Like the census records of Paralyte, it was kept as up to date as possible. As they moved through the town, he noticed the telephone devices were almost always accompanied by the yellow books. Perhaps this planet was not quite as advanced as Brysdyn, but it appeared to Garryn Earth had potential. If left untouched, she would have been able to take her place as the third member of the White Star Alliance.

The hot, dry weather had kept everything intact. Houses remained standing, although some succumbed to fire and other natural calamities following the deployment of the missiles. Walking through the streets overgrown with weeds and other vegetation, he could feel the warm waves of arid air scraping against his skin. There was no sound except the wind and the soft chirps of birds in the distance.

After half an hour of walking through the home of the third Alexander on their list, Garryn found nothing useful. He paused in the middle of the living room and sighed deeply before instantly regretting it. The stale and musty air made him sneeze and the odour in the room made his stomach lurch. Striding out of the place, he emerged into the sunlight, grateful for the warmth after feeling the chill in that haunted place.

"Are you alright?" Hannah asked, concerned.

Garryn nodded.

"This isn't it," he told Aaran.

"How do you know?"

Garryn stared at the house, seeing nothing that seemed familiar to him. Nothing that looked like that place in his dreams. "I just know."

"According to the map," Rachel spoke in English, relying on Aaran to translate for Garryn, "the other two Alexanders lived out of town. I think we should try and find those before it gets dark." She knew if it was her family she was trying to trace, waiting another day would be too much.

"I agree." Garryn nodded once her words had been translated to him. "Although we ought to go back to the ship. Flinn has a skimmer on board the *Wayward Son*."

"A skimmer?" Hannah inquired. "What's a skimmer?"

"It's a land transport," Aaran answered before he could.

"Like a car?"

Garryn had no idea to what they were referring, but gathered they must have been speaking of the vehicles he saw earlier.

"Close enough."

* * *

"I don't normally use the skimmer," Flinn explained as he drove the terrestrial transport out of one of his cargo holds. "But you never know when these things will come in handy."

Despite what he said, Garryn noticed that the skimmer was kept in prime condition. It was an older model, but it seemed maintained with a great deal of care. The paintwork remained unblemished and there was a surprising lack of dust on a vehicle spending most of its time locked away in a cargo hold. Garryn suspected Flinn spent considerable effort in the upkeep of the skimmer and his affection for it was more than the pilot led them to believe.

Normally the skimmer took only four but with a bit of effort, they were all able to fit into the vehicle. Rachel sat up front with Flinn and, with Aaran's aid, navigated the skimmer through the maze of roads that ran throughout the town limits. The fourth Alexander lived out of town and Garryn noticed a strange thing once they had moved out of the tree-lined avenues and quiet suburban streets.

I have been this way before.

It came to him in a flash of memory so potent that, for a moment, he could visualise travelling along the road now taking them out of town. For a moment, he wondered if it was real or just wishful thinking. He could almost see the people in their lawns, hosing their gardens, washing their cars in the driveway and children playing ball on the roads, getting reprimanded by their parents for doing it.

He said nothing to the others as they left the houses behind and the journey ahead revealed field after field of long grass slowly turning into a dark gold. Staring at the passing scene, he saw a fence line disappearing into the distance. The livestock it was meant to keep penned in were nowhere in sight. Tall trees with grey trunks waved at them with bare branches. Their leaves lay at the base of their trunks, flying in all directions as the skimmer drove past.

Garryn closed his eyes and tried to fight the images flashing through his mind like a storm of white birds in his head. His mouth and throat felt dry and Garryn swallowed hard, trying to quell the hollowness in his stomach.

"Garryn, are you all right?" Hannah noticed his pallor.

It took him a moment to realise that she had spoken before he was able to respond. "I'm sorry. My mind was elsewhere."

"Do you remember something?"

Flinn and her parents, who were discussing the quickest route to their destination, were oblivious to their exchange.

"A little," he replied, feeling a little distressed by what he was seeing. "I keep seeing things. There is this wall in my head that's letting me see cracks but not the whole picture."

"Then we must be going in the right direction," she said firmly, taking his hand in hers. "You must be strong. Your mind at least remembers this place and is trying to tell you slowly."

Her insight reminded him for a moment of Jonen. A wave of grief rose within him for the man, but he quashed it quickly. "You could be right. I think the wall is starting to crumble the nearer I come to the end."

"This is it!" Aaran announced.

The skimmer turned down a dirt track off the main road. As they left the tarred surface, the engines of the skimmer blew dust in the air as they drove up the rise of a small hill. Once it reached the crest and started moving downhill, they were treated to the view of the fields below.

Garryn saw waves and waves of rolling gold hills. The tall stalks of deep yellow were almost too dazzling to look at directly. Standing over the sea of gold were tall trees with grey bark and big open branches.

In the air, he saw birds flying. They were moving too fast to see them clearly, but he could see they were white.

A dirt track was flanked by thin wire fences running along the length of the road. As they continued around a bend, they could see it emptying into the grounds of a modest sized house. The roof of the house was made from corrugated steel and standing next to the house was a windmill. At least, that's what it looked like to him. Its iron blades were rusted, but it still stood proudly over the house in silent vigil.

A wave of dizziness overtook him as the skimmer came to a halt. As they others emerged from the vehicle, Garryn remained seated, trying to fight the swirling images in his head. This place, with its rusted iron roof, its overgrown garden and derelict appearance, opened something in his mind. As his eyes swept over the dwelling, he saw flashes of memory before his eyes.

Garryn wasn't even aware of it when he staggered out of the skimmer and started running.

"Gar!" He heard Flinn calling in the background but ignored him.

As he ran past the house, he saw the faded paint and knew it hadn't always been in this dilapidated condition.

Yellow! It was a yellow house with white eaves and gutters. Sunny colours. I called them sunny colours!

By now, he was in a heightened state of panic. He ran past something resembling a child's swing, tipped over and almost engulfed in tall grass. Another flash of memory stopped him for a second before he was running again. An animal with short brown and black fur was wagging its tail as it chased after a small, luminous coloured ball.

Einy! Einy! Bring ball, Einy!

Garryn was moving again. This time, he ran through the gap in the fence where a gate had once hung. He could see the corroded lines of its frame resting against the ground and concealed by vegetation. Beyond the gate, he entered the field of tall golden stalks and saw the hills in the distance. Driven by instincts he could not control, Garryn only knew he had to keep going.

He heard the loud chirping of birds on a nearby tree and looked up at them. They stared at him in question, unafraid of him from their high perch. Garryn saw their white feathers and the yellow crowns on their heads. One of these creatures stirred and took flight, sailing across the blue sky and the sun that was beginning to make its descent into the night.

Inside the mind of Garryn, Prime of Brysdyn, the wall finally came down.

* * *

"Don't go too far, Jus."

The boy stopped running and glanced over his shoulder. He paused at the command given, even though his desire to keep going was still strong. He bit his lip as he saw the man a short distance away. Although the adult's concentration seemed no longer centred on him and had returned to the large bovine whose foot he was tending, the boy knew better.

He watched the man working deftly on the bovine's cracked hoof, taking usual care to clean the infected flesh. The man stopped a moment and wiped the pregnant drops of sweat rolling into the lines of his skin. His face was a myriad of creases, lined from hard work under the sun. His hands were similarly marked, with palms just as cracked and hardened after a lifetime working the land.

Once the child was certain he was not being watched, he faced front again, staring longingly into the brilliant afternoon sky. He could smell the faint scent of the wheat fields nearby, tickling his nose with its dry pollen. The hot glare of the sun made him squint. In the back of his mind, he remembered being told he should never look straight at it. The conditioning to obey that voice was too strong and he gazed into the horizon instead.

Beside him, the dog waited impatiently. The animal circled him repeatedly, waiting to see where he would go next so it could follow. It wagged its tail furiously, as if to convey its displeasure at the interruption in their walk. The boy smiled at the sight of the long tail moving back and forth in rapid succession, finding the whole thing rather amusing.

"I'm here daddy," he replied, placating the man as he started moving again.

At the response, the man looked up again. He adjusted the brim of his hide-skinned hat to keep the sunlight out of his eyes. "Justin, you and Einy stay where I can see you!"

"Yes, daddy!" the small singsong voice responded as the child ran a short distance away and the man continued working, glancing up periodically to keep an eye on the boy's whereabouts. At the moment, the child was not so far away the man considered calling him back.

The boy was throwing a ball in the air. The yellow felt-covered orb sailed through the air as the dog ran after it in pursuit. It scampered through the long blades of grass and found the ball quickly before running back to its young master. It was a simplistic game, but neither child nor dog seemed to tire of it.

"Catch it, Einy!" The child giggled as he threw the ball forward again, sending the animal running. It retrieved the toy and padded faithfully back to him.

Einy the dog disappeared into the foliage as the ball flew into the air again. Its movement through the tall grass was signalled by crisp rustling as it searched for the ball. While the dog searched for the toy, the boy cast his eyes into the sky again, squinting as the sun shone on his face and eyes. For a moment, he was unsure he was seeing anything out of the ordinary, if he could be certain of what ordinary meant in his limited experience.

They looked like birds, the dark shapes moving across the sky at lightning speed. He knew what airplanes were, but these moved without the linearity of conventional flight. There was fluidity to their movements, a grace belonging only to denizens of the sky. The shapes looked like the biggest birds he had ever seen! They flew fast and made a loud sound as they approached. Only when they flew overhead did he realise that they were not birds at all. They did not look like airplanes either. If the truth be known, they looked like more like something he had seen on television. Suddenly, he felt a spark of recognition. They looked like one of his toys.

"Buzz Lightyear," he muttered. It looked like a toy at home!

"Buzz Lightyear!" He shouted this time, pointing at them.

The adult looked up at this point, following the direction of the child's pointing finger. Even if neither ship were making any hostile moves, it was enough to make the adult stand up abruptly. The child was still mesmerised by the two fast moving ships and did not associate them with danger, not yet. The power in those engines ripped through the serene quiet of the air and hastened the farmer's approach.

The man kept his eyes trained on the two alien vessels and saw when they split formation to fly in two opposite directions. One moved into a classic loop and began descending to the ground at rapid speed, the other headed straight for them. With his inner senses tingling, the man forgot the two ships and looked around for his child.

The ship was less than a thousand metres from him when it started firing. Deadly bolts of plasma energy struck the raw earth, sending soil and debris into the air with each blast. The shots ignited the dry grass and quickly set the ground ablaze. The man simply stared in disbelief for a moment, trying to grapple with what was happening. Yet the smoke and fire motivated him to move.

"Justin! Stay where you are!"

"DADDY!"

His vocabulary did not extend beyond a dozen words, but his terror was articulated in that one scream. Frozen to the spot, the child began to cry harder as he saw the man approaching. He remained where he was, crouched low in the grass, frightened by the loud noises and the rising smoke. The dog was tugging at the child's shirt, trying to prompt him into leaving this dangerous place, its tail no longer wagging.

The man was running harder now, unconcerned with his own safety. All he cared about was reaching his son before the fire or the deadly blasts of energy. Only a few meters away from his child, he was oblivious to the fact it was not the child who was in mortal danger. Suddenly there was an explosion of sound and the man thought for a brief instance he had fallen. Only when he felt exquisite agony did he suspect the worst, but he had no more time to ponder that question before he died.

"DADDY!"

The child scrambled forwards, still on his knees, towards the dead form of his father. The ships in the clouds had moved away and the boy did not notice where they went. The dog followed sedately and whimpered, recognising the stench of death in the air. It understood better than the boy did.

"Daddy, wake up!" he wailed, kneeling against his dead parent and shaking him with his tiny hands. The blood that stained his hands made him recoil a little, but the boy was beyond caring.

"Justin!"

The child reacted instantly to his name being called. The voice carried above the roar of the fire and the shrieking animals fleeing the blazing field. Behind him, the dog had started barking, torn between his natural instincts to run and its loyalty to its young charge.

"Justin! Where are you, baby?"

The woman was running up the hill, coming from the direction of the house. She ran over the hill, fighting her way through the rising smoke and heat. By now, thick clouds of smoke had fogged away most of the landscape, but she kept coming, ignoring the noxious fumes. The dog's barking became more frantic, allowing her to pinpoint the child's location. Where the dog was, the child would not be far away.

"Justin!" she shouted again.

Her voice was becoming more desperate, more edged with fear than ever before. She glanced up in the air and she saw one of the ships returning. The other had already landed somewhere close to the house. The ship still in the air was closing in on her, making the woman run faster, trying to stay ahead of it.

She would keep running. She would run until the very last moment. She would never find the child, because her vision was too obscured by smoke and tears. In her last few paces, she would start to cough because her lungs required fresh oxygen and could find none because of the billowing smoke.

The ship swooped in for a final pass firing a blast of energy from its guns. In that last second, when it dawned on her that she would not escape, that she would not see her son ever again, she let out an anguished cry of desperation.

"RUN AWAY JUSTIN! RUN AWAY!"

The child saw her coming, just as he'd seen his father running towards him a short time before. He saw hope disappear with a blast of plasma and screamed when he saw her body hit the ground. The force of the bolt had flipped her onto her back and he heard the sickening squelch of bone snapping as she hit the ground.

"Mummy! Mummy!" He began to wail... "Mummy!"

XXVII

Home

When he opened his eyes, he found himself on his hands and knees.

It was odd, because he did not remember falling. What he did remember was a vision of pain he wished he'd never unlocked. In the cold light of consciousness, Garryn felt tears running down his face. At last, he remembered. He knew who he was.

Staring at the grass beneath him, the raging fire in his head diminished and Garryn began to sob quietly. The truth had always been inside him. His mind kept the memories, despite his years away. In his dreams, he was capable of accessing them, even though he understood little of what he had seen. All it required for those memories to surface was one simple act.

Coming home.

In doing so, he now remembered both of them. His mother and his father. He remembered sitting in the sun, watching his mother feed the animals, her golden hair bouncing off her shoulders. The memories he had were few, but some, like this one, were vivid. He'd had a dog whose name he could never get right, so he'd ended up calling it Einy. Its fur was brown and black in patches and she was his constant companion. When it came time to remember his father, his sobs became more anguished.

He remembered a big desk. He remembered sitting on it while his father worked on papers. The globe sat on the edge of the table and he kept spinning it around. He liked watching the colours blur as it moved like a spinning top. His father looked up and smiled at him before placing a hand on the globe to stop it moving.

"This is where we are," his father explained, pointing to the continent on the globe.

Garryn blinked the memory away. He did not want to look in the face of all that pain. At this moment, it was enough for him that he remembered. He would deal with his grief when he was alone.

Hannah stood behind him and Garryn saw things clearly there as well. She cared for him. He did not know why, but she cared for him, this stranger who had just entered her life a few hours ago. That, too, would have to be dealt with later. He rose to his feet. Despite his anguish, he knew what to do.

"Gar," Flinn spoke first. "Are you okay?"

Garryn wiped the tears from his face and nodded slowly. "I'll live."

He turned away from them and looked into the horizon of the setting sun.

"This was my home. Somewhere out there," he gestured to the swaying stalks of long grass, "are my parents." He swallowed thickly, not realising how hard those words were to say. "They died out here. They were attacked by Brysdynian fighters. One landed to get me and the other killed them both from the air."

"Lords," Flinn whispered, but Aaran and his family said nothing. They knew this story already.

"We're leaving," Garryn said abruptly. "I've got what I came for. Its time to go. Aaran, you and your family are welcome to join us."

He heard the man's hesitation and paused. Garryn turned around to see Aaran conferring with his wife. Hannah was also included in the conversation and for a few minutes they engaged in native speak. Garryn allowed them the time to decide, knowing this was not as obvious a decision as it seemed. Harsh as this world was to Aaran, it had been his home for the past twenty-three years. For what Garryn was about to embark upon when he returned to Brysdyn, he would need the former science officer.

"I always thought, given the choice, I would leave immediately," Aaran replied. "Now the moment comes, I don't know what to do."

"Aaran," Garryn said with a sigh. "I need you to come back to Paralyte with me. I need you to provide testimony to the Imperator."

"I don't know..." Aaran started to say.

"Aaran, I am the Prime."

Aaran's eyes widened in shock. "You are Iran's son?"

"My mother, the Lady Aisha, contracted the Scourge. She could not have children either. I was adopted when I was three years old and have been, for the past twenty-three years, the heir apparent to the throne of Brysdyn. Since I saw that yellow star in the sky, I have dreamt of nothing but *this* place." He let his gaze sweep across the plain before looking at Aaran again. "I require your presence on Brysdyn, Aaran, but this is not a command. I'm asking you."

Aaran took a deep breath in realisation of what Garryn was attempting to do. "Edwen is still alive, isn't he?"

Garryn did not have to answer. The look he returned Aaran was more than enough.

"You're going after him."

Garryn nodded slowly. "I have no idea what I am going to do, yet, but what happened to this world has to be answered for."

He thought of all the other Dreamers whose nightmares were likely interpretations of what happened to them when they were taken. He remembered Nikela, the youngest of the Dreamers, who had visions of being born. How would she take it knowing that she was taken from her mother's body after it was slit open like a ripe fruit? How could any of the New Citizens bear to know what he did?

Nightmares were one thing, but did he want them to suffer this terrible knowledge as well?

Garryn had no answer to that, but Edwen needed to pay for what was done to the Earth.

"I need your testimony, Aaran. I need you to stand before the Quorum and tell the Empire what you know. This world deserves justice and it needs help. I do not know much about Earth, but I do know that maybe Earth could have helped Brysdyn. There was no need for what he did. There was no need for people to die."

He saw the look of concern on Rachel's face and quickly added. "Once we do what we have to, I'll bring you home to Earth or any other place you wish to go."

Aaran turned to his wife and related Garryn's words. Her face lit up immediately and she addressed him with her limited vocabulary. "We will try to help you."

While there was hesitation in Rachel's face, Hannah's showed eagerness. Garryn supposed that, having grown up on this ravaged planet, the chance to leave it was an exciting prospect. For some reason, he wanted to show her Brysdyn.

"I made some repairs to the ship after our run-in with the warship," Flinn announced. "She's ready to leave when you are ready."

"I want to go soon," Garryn answered, before his gaze shifted to the house beyond the gate. "There's just one thing I need to do first."

* * *

Despite the fire to the surrounding fields, the house was unscathed.

The garden and lawn within the enclosed fence around the house was now covered in overgrown weeds and grass. Garryn knew it was once just dirt. There were two main entrances to the house, but it was the back door that was wide open. The screen door swayed back and forth in the wind as Garryn brushed aside the cobwebs and stepped through.

There was plenty of light inside the house, because the curtains were frayed and many of the windows were broken. He entered what appeared to be the kitchen. Dishes remained in the dry and rusted sink. There were still plates on the dining table, coated in traces of food, long since decayed. Flashes of memory came to him as he took in the room. He could visualise sitting at this table with the two people he now knew were his parents.

It was not a terribly ostentatious house. There were no fine silks or expensive tapestries. There was no lavish lifestyle here, just the simplicity of a rural existence for people born to work the land. He heard noises in the ceiling and guessed it was likely the native wildlife taking up residence in the crawlspace above. The furnishings were eclectic and put together by people who wanted more than just a place to live. They had wanted to make a home.

He paused at the mantle place and felt his boot crack something underfoot. Garryn looked down and saw a wooden frame surrounded by broken glass. Lifting his foot off the crushed fragments, he saw the corner of something peering over the edge of the frame. Garryn bent down to investigate. As he turned over the frame, his breath caught. Garryn found himself staring at a squarish piece of paper. It was a picture.

A couple was seated on a large divan, but not the same one he saw in the house. He briefly wondered where it had been taken. They were smiling happily and displaying, with great pride, their son, who was seated on his father's lap. The child was looking up at both parents, wearing a delighted expression on his face.

Garryn did not realise he was crying until he saw the first tear splatter on the paper. It rolled quickly off the edge and was followed by another. Garryn wiped away the tear, angered by his lack of control over his emotions. He was the Prime. He ought to have more restraint than this.

Not here. You're not the Prime here. You're Justin Alexander and you've come home.

Garryn bit down on his lip, letting the sharp pain centre him. He tore his gaze away from the picture, but did not discard it. Instead, he replaced it on the mantle piece where it had stood for many years. This house was his now and, someday soon, he would reclaim it. But first, he had business on Brysdyn. Those two dead souls lying in the undergrowth beyond the house demanded justice.

He had to give them that. He had to do it for them and for the billions who died to save Brysdyn.

* * *

By the time they returned to the ship, the sun was well and truly fading from the sky. The temperature had dropped considerably and Garryn was grateful to be indoors again. There were too many ghosts here. Even though they remained unseen, their presence could be felt. Their voices could be imagined in the eerie silence of the deserted cities and the cold wind moving through their exposed bones.

They were airborne within the hour. Even though it had been years since he had embarked on any kind of space travel, Aaran had no difficulty becoming accustomed to it again. His wife viewed the journey with trepidation, considering she was from a species yet to experience specialised space travel. Hannah, on the other hand, was full of excitement at her first trip off world.

Garryn remained in the gunnery turret. He needed the solitude. He was coming to grips with much and wanted some time to think about what came next. As much as he wanted to tell the Dreamers what he'd found, he was also afraid of shattering their lives, as his was now in ruin. He was torn between the world below and the life he had left behind on Brysdyn. How could the two ever be reconciled again?

"Garryn, get up here!" Finn shouted through the communicator.

As the *Wayward Son* entered the space above the planet, Garryn jumped out of his chair and hurried to the bridge, fearing why Flinn was calling out so anxiously for him. As he entered the cockpit, he saw what the rest of the *Wayward Son's* passengers were gaping at. The holographic screen revealed the image, not only of the warship they'd crippled, but also the dreadnought class battleship with it.

Brysdynian Dreadnoughts were fully armoured, with reinforced tritium shielding, able to withstand multiple detonations from torpedoes. Their fighter complement was larger than a standard warship and they were able to punch a hole through a planet if so inclined. While they lacked the speed of newer class ships, their fuel capacity allowed them to wear the enemy down in pursuit. Since Brysdyn no longer embarked on expansionist campaigns, the dreadnoughts were now obsolete.

Obsolete perhaps, Garryn thought, but still more than capable of obliterating this ship from the sky.

"It's the *Dragon's Eye*," Garryn explained, recognising this particular battleship. "It's Edwen's ship."

"Edwen?" Aaran declared, staring instinctively out of the cockpit window, trying to see the ship, even though it was hidden behind the planet's moon at the moment.

"I guess he decided this required his personal attention," Garryn said grimly.

No sooner than he had uttered those words, he saw a multitude of electronic bleeps appear on the screen. They were so many of them approaching them rapidly, it was impossible to count their numbers. Flinn estimated more than twenty-five of them. Twenty-five to one odds. Garryn was good, but he did not know if he was *that* good. Taking a deep breath, he tried to think of options. Unfortunately, none seemed to come to mind.

"Can we outrun them?" Aaran asked first.

Garryn and Flinn exchanged glances.

"Not a chance," Flinn replied grimly. "Not for long, anyway. I can't afford to burn up my fuel before we go to hyperspace."

"I'd start anyway," Garryn retorted, making his way out of the cockpit. "I'll try and hold them off as much as I can. Try and keep ahead of them."

"You don't have to tell me twice," Flinn retorted and glanced at his other passengers. "Strap yourselves in, it's about to get bumpy. Here they come!"

Garryn saw the flotilla of ships emerging from behind the thin crescent shape moon, heading towards them. There were so many, Garryn thought. There numbers filled up the space between the planet and the moon. Despite themselves, neither man could deny the shudder of fear felt as they saw those ships approaching them at top speed.

"They're breaking formation!" Garryn declared as he clung to Hannah's seat to keep from falling over.

The tight pattern of ships began to break apart, splitting into groups of three as they fell into pursuit from all directions. A small group was heading towards the planet and both Garryn and Flinn recognised the tactic for what it was. "They're cutting us off. They're not going to let us back into the atmosphere!"

"Get to the turret! I'll take care of the flying!"

Garryn needed no further prompting, running out of the room.

Suddenly the hull shuddered with the first blast of enemy fire. The ship heaved in protest and the two women cried out in fright. Recovering in an instant, Flinn increased thruster power to the main engines. They had to stay ahead of this group because it would take time for him to plot the course to hyperspace and they were still too close to a planetary body to make the attempt.

"There are no warships behind the moon," Aaran stated as he stared into the scanner. It had been a long time, for certain, and while he was nowhere near as adept with technology as he once was, Aaran knew how to interpret a scanner readout.

"What do you mean? They're right there!" Flinn retorted and turned back to the screen. However, as he turned to look, he realised that Aaran was right. Both ships were gone. This meant...

He looked ahead just in time to see the *Dragon's Eye* emerge from behind the planet to cut them off. The sheer immensity of the ship nearly blocked out the sky from the canopy window. The *Wayward Son,* borne on the force of its own speed, was quickly heading straight for the large ship and the docking would be anything but smooth.

"Pull up!" he heard Aaran scream in the background. "Pull up!"

XXVIII

Dreadnought

Garryn slammed into the side of his seat. His shoulder stung in pain despite the cushioned seats. Below him, he felt the *Wayward Son* veer sharply to starboard. Steadying himself, his chair pivoted with the motion of his body as he placed his hands on the firing controls and sought out his target. There were more than enough ships in pursuit to make the selection easy.

Garryn fired into the thickest part of the air wing group, trying to send their formation into disarray. The sky flared up when one of his energy bolts met its mark. Yet for every one he destroyed, there seemed to be another getting closer and closer. Realistically, he knew they would eventually overrun Flinn's beloved ship, unless they could make the jump to hyperspace.

When the ship banked abruptly, Garryn was able to see what caused Flinn to change direction so drastically. The *Dragon's Eye* glided into view of his window. Flinn took the ship into a tight loop, trying to put some distance between the *Wayward Son* and the dreadnought. In the process, the ship flew head on into a fighter contingent. The freighter scattered the formation more effectively than Garryn's earlier effort.

Garryn used the momentary disruption Flinn had given him to fire at the enemy ships in rapid succession. The sky lit up with ship after ship exploding until his eyes began to blur from all the brilliant flares. The space surrounding them filled with debris and flaming pieces of metal quickly extinguished by the vacuum.

Suddenly the *Wayward Son* made a sharp turn upwards and began climbing in a steep ascent. Garryn was thrown back against his chair, his fingers snatched away from the controls.

"What the hel..." he started to shout in this headset when he glanced through the window and saw the *Warhammer*.

Despite the damage to its bridge, it was still firing its main guns and direct hits would have vaporised the small freighter. With a sinking feeling, he began to understand what Flinn must have already deduced.

They'd fallen into a trap.

The dreadnought and the warship had outflanked them. They were caught in the middle, unable to reach enough velocity to make the jump into hyperspace, not with fighters dogging their every move. The fighters matched Flinn's speed because they were able to refuel and knew he would not. Soon, they were all around the *Wayward Son* and it was a credit to Flinn that they were still alive. But they wouldn't be able to hold out for long.

"Flinn," he said quietly into his headset.

"I'm kind of busy right now, Gar."

"Send a distress signal," Garryn replied.

He heard a sudden pause.

"We're not done yet!" the Jyne insisted, refusing to give up.

"I know. Do it anyway."

"It's impossible. They're jamming us! We'd never get a message to Erebo Station. Not in time to help us! Wait a minute..." Flinn's voice drifted offline for a moment. There were seconds of undecipherable whispering in the headset before Flinn spoke again.

"All right, Gar, I'm going to send a message to Erebo because the old guy's got a good suggestion. I'm going to do it through carrier wave signal."

It was a stroke of genius. There were so many orbiting satellites around the Earth the signal could come from any one of them. Even then, he was sure no one would think to look for a transmission coming from such a frequency. They had to send a message distinctly Brysdynian, capable of sparking Erebo's interest enough to decipher it.

"Do it," he answered. "Do it before it's too late."

It did not take long for Flinn to send the message. The dispatch went smoothly, being undetected by the dreadnought or the warship. In either case, the pursuit was coming to a close and they all knew it.

The *Wayward Son* manoeuvred through the sea of smaller ships in its attempt to escape, only to come face to face with the two larger warships keeping them penned in.

As Flinn banked the *Wayward Son* to sweep past the dreadnought, the freighter suddenly jerked violently and began losing speed. Anything not bolted down in the ship went flying through the air. Garryn was jostled violently in his seat as the ship shuddered around him. According to his sensors, the ship was still at maximum thrust but, as he looked outside the canopy window, it was evident the *Wayward Son* was no longer moving forward.

It was moving backwards, towards the *Dragon's Eye*.

Unfastening himself from his seat, Garryn ran out of the cubicle. The ship was shaking hard and Garryn wondered how much longer Flinn would try to break free. The tractor beam ensnaring them had far more power than the *Wayward Son*. Flinn could not keep firing the thrusters like this, or else the ship would tear itself apart. He could feel the ship groaning as the stress mounted in its superstructure.

"Flinn, shut it down!" he shouted, entering into the cockpit.

"They'll kill us!"

"You'll kill us if you don't shut the engine down. You know as well as I do, the ship can't take this kind of stress for long. She'll break up!"

Garryn saw the defiance in Flinn's eyes evaporate to resignation. No matter how much he hated to admit defeat, he could not deny Garryn's words. If he kept trying to break free, the only thing that would come undone was his beloved ship. He could hear the incessant rattling throughout the structure indicating how close it was to the breaking point. The hull would begin to buckle in places if he did not act now.

"Listen to him!" Aaran shouted.

"All right! I'm powering down." Reluctantly, he began shutting down the engines, easing the stress on the ship as it decelerated down with a low whine. Inside the cockpit, the lights dimmed to near darkness. The mood within the room was grim and no one spoke as the ship continued its journey towards the *Dragon's Eye*. Very soon, the space around them was replaced with the hangar doors of the dreadnought.

"Why don't they destroy us? Rachel demanded. Her composure was shattered and she buried her head in her husband's shoulder, weeping. Garryn wished he'd never coaxed them from their safe and anonymous existence on Earth.

"They want us alive," Garryn answered, although the truth might be closer to them wanting *him* alive.

"Are you sure?"

Garryn took a deep breath and met Flinn's gaze. "I don't know. I just don't know."

* * *

It was hard not feel overwhelmed by the sheer size of the Dragon's Eye as it swallowed them whole.

At present, the only thing that Garryn was able to take comfort in was the fact Edwen wanted them alive for a reason. If Edwen wanted them dead, he could have blown them out of the sky easily.

The freighter was pulled in through the main doors of the *Dragon's Eye*'s docking station. Once the ship had passed through the opening, the doors slid to a close behind them with a loud thud reverberating throughout the *Wayward Son*. Rachel and Aaran were huddled close, while Hannah's arm had somehow found its way around Garryn's waist. Flinn stared stonily ahead, still in denial at being taken by the enemy.

Not for the first time, Garryn wished he had never allowed any of them to become involved in this. Was the truth really worth paying the price of all these lives?

"We could try blasting off again," Flinn suggested as the ship descended onto the landing bay. Outside, pressurisation had begun to take place. It would not be long before life support systems would allow troops to enter the area.

"We'd never get far enough to escape. The tractor beam will just catch up," Garryn replied wearily. "Right now, we'll just have to play it by ear. Edwen has something up his sleeve."

"For you, maybe," Flinn answered, meeting his gaze. "The rest of us are expendable."

Garryn was aware of that too. "Let's hope not."

Aaran was holding Rachel close, but he looked up and added. "Surely the rest of the crew would not

350

stand by and watch him kill the Prime. Things on Brysdyn could not have changed *that* much to allow it to happen."

Garryn had to admit it was an interesting point. Edwen might be the master of Security Elite, but in the absence of the Imperator even Garryn superseded him in authority, even in Security Elite. Those in Elite were a fanatical bunch, but they were also wildly patriotic. It was difficult to believe they would stand by and watch him commit treason.

"Maybe they don't know," Flinn suggested, voicing Garryn's unspoken thoughts.

"Can't you just tell them?" Hannah asked.

"I don't know that'd do any good," Garryn said sceptically. "Most of them have no idea what I look like. I'm afraid my public career only began recently at my Ascension. Besides, who would believe it? The Prime travelling on a freighter firing on Brysdynian ships? If I weren't living it, I wouldn't believe it myself."

"True," Flinn nodded in agreement.

"There is a way I could confirm my identity," Garryn considered his options, wanting to give Aaran and his family some hope. "But to do it, I need to get to the bridge, and I doubt Edwen will allow that."

"We may get lucky," Flinn replied.

The way things were going, Garryn didn't think luck was on their side at all.

* * *

"Passengers of the freighter *Wayward Son*, Registration No. 33432, you are in violation of the Imperial Code S152-A relating to planetary travel. You have failed to lodge a correct flight plan and have also violated the restriction placed on the planet Theran 3. You have also been charged with the death of Imperial citizens. Please disembark your vessel immediately or be prepared to be removed by force."

"They're trying to justify all this because I don't have a damn travel permit!" Flinn exclaimed in a mixture of surprise and disgust.

"Why not? As far as they're concerned, it's true. We did violate restricted space by going to Cathomira and then here. We did resist their attempts to stop us and we did fire on them. What else is Edwen going to tell them?"

"This guy is oilier than a Sekerun slug," Flinn retorted.

"You'll never know how much," Aaran whispered softly.

After a short discussion, they came to the decision that it was probably better if they emerged from the ship of their own volition. Security Elite troops were not known for their good manners and, at this point, Garryn did not want to give them a reason to hurt anyone. To some extent, he could be assured of his own safety, but he could not say the same for Flinn or Aaran and his family. Flinn was a commercial pilot who barely operated within the law. In Edwen's eyes, he would never be missed. The same could be said for Aaran and his family, whose existence was even more tenuous.

Garryn emerged first. He walked down the extended ramp of the *Wayward Son's* main hatch with his hands up, showing he was disarmed. Even though he wanted badly to carry a weapon, he knew it could be interpreted as a hostile gesture and Garryn did not want to provoke the troops into doing anything rash. Convincing Flinn took a great deal of effort, but eventually the pilot had to concede to the sensibility of the act.

Once they were on the floor of the deck, the officer in charge motioned the troops to take them into custody. As the Elite troops swarmed around them, the officer approaching Garryn recognising him as the leader. The officer looked into Garryn's face. His brow knitted in momentary confusion as he saw something he might have seen before but was unable to place it. Shaking the thought from his mind, he waited patiently as binders were placed around all their hands.

"Take the others to the brig," he said to one of the troops. "The General wants to see this one personally." His eyes met Garryn.

"I trust that my companions will remain alive while I am in audience with the General?"

"You may trust nothing," the man said derisively. "You are not in the position to demand anything." He turned sharply on his heels and began moving. "Bring him."

Garryn felt a sharp jab in his shoulder and was prompted to move by the trooper standing behind him. Garryn began walking towards the door, reluctant to leave the others. But knew he had little choice in the matter. He threw a glance over his shoulder at Flinn and the others.

"Flinn, stay calm."

"No speaking!" The trooper behind him snapped.

Garryn said nothing further, but saw Flinn nod slowly at the request. Next to Flinn, Hannah clung to her mother, offering her what support she could. Both stared after him with a mixture of fear and longing. Aaran's expression was simply unreadable. As Garryn was led out of the room, he prayed this would not be his last view of them ever.

* * *

They led him through the length of the ship. If the *Dragon's Eye* had seemed enormous from the outside, it seemed endless inside it. The ship was a collection of twisting and turning corridors, leading to a dozen decks, several lounges and a vast series of rooms and compartments. Strangely enough, Garryn did not see many crew members. Somehow it was difficult to believe that a ship this size could operate on anything less than a full crew complement, unless dreadnought class ships had recently undergone refit for partial automation.

It suddenly occurred to Garryn with a flash of clarity that he was being intentionally kept out of sight.

His route to Edwen was through the engineering and maintenance decks, where crew traffic would be minimal. Perhaps Edwen was aware of what a gamble he was taking by doing this. If it was realised he had taken Garryn prisoner, he would be guilty of high treason.

Edwen's quarters were located in the starboard section of the ship. The entrance to the General's suite was marked by two Security Elite sentries flanking the doorway. His escort was promptly dismissed and Garryn was ushered through the doors by the guards who abandoned him once he'd entered the room.

The room was larger than the normal commanding officer's cabin. Even for a dreadnought, the space within the room was luxurious in comparison to others he had seen before. Garryn guessed this was once a conference room or something similar before Edwen had gutted it to make it his own. Despite its size, its furnishings were nothing out of the ordinary and looked like standard military issue. The decor seemed draconian, like Edwen himself.

"Greetings, Prime."

Behind the glass top desk, he saw Edwen sitting in wait. The adjutant, Danten, if Garryn remembered correctly, was standing next to the General.

Garryn maintained his calm, even though there was a part of him that wanted to tear Edwen's heart out in the light of what he had learned on Earth. He chose instead to walk casually to the nearby sofa and sit down. This was not the time for allowing his emotions to overwhelm him. Edwen wanted information and Garryn needed to bargain for the lives of his companions.

"Greetings, General."

Edwen rose to his feet and looked up at Danten. "Get the Prime some refreshment."

Without question, the Major walked to the sideboard at the corner of the room and began pouring Garryn a drink from a crystal decanter. Garryn could not help feel the absurdity of the situation with all its forced civility. Only after he was served did Edwen finally speak.

"It has been a merry chase hasn't it?" He took a seat on the chair across from the sofa.

"Yes, it has. I have to admit, even for you this is beyond belief."

"I take it that Aaran has apprised you of the situation. Frankly, I had hoped he was dead, but then he was always so determined."

Garryn did not ask Edwen how he knew about Aaran. The man had probably viewed their entire arrival on board the ship. "He told me enough and I found out a few things myself."

"You must understand, Garryn," Edwen explained, impressed by the restraint shown by the young man and wondering how long it would last. "Twenty three years ago, the home world was on the brink of extinction. There is no Empire if Brysdyn itself is no more. Almost ninety percent of our population was sterilised by the Cure. We had no future. I could not allow that to happen. The Empire had to endure.

"I don't question your motivations," Garryn answered, surprised by his own understanding of Edwen's intentions. He had not meant to see his enemy's side of it, but he was Brysdynian too, no matter where he was born. "I love Brysdyn as much as you do, but you cannot believe our people would have stood for this. We are a warrior people and there is no honour in a war waged this way. No one on Brysdyn, no matter how desperate the need, would have justified what you've done."

"I agree." Edwen nodded with maddening calm. "A true patriot must do things for their world no matter how painful it is. I did what was necessary to keep Brysdyn from bleeding to death. The fruits of what I achieved are all around us. The New Citizens gave the Empire much needed life again. We, in turn, gave them the universe. They have known lives that were centuries beyond their primitive beginnings. You of all people should understand that."

"You mean being Prime?" Garryn said sharply. "You think it gives me comfort knowing I am going to be Imperator some day? I can't even close my eyes without seeing my parents blown apart in front of me." His feelings began to show between the cracks of his icy demeanour, but Garryn did not care at this point. "You'll forgive me I am not more gracious."

"Yes, your father told me of your problem," Edwen replied, unaffected by Garryn's outburst. "He explained your association with the mentalist."

His attitude infuriated Garryn. "You didn't have to kill him! You tried to destroy all evidence of what you did on Earth and you still have no idea why, do you? You can't comprehend how much of it is out of your control already!"

Edwen blinked, perhaps feeling a little more than he should have. "Brysdyn is not ready for such truth. The people are happy and content. The Empire is stronger now than it ever was. Security Elite was created to protect the sovereignty of Brysdynian rule and its survival depended on the infusion of new blood. Believe me, I do not take what I did lightly, Prime, but I understood that it needed to be done for all our sakes. Warriors must be born to defend the Empire."

"Warriors?" Garryn looked at him incredulously. "You really believe you lived up to some ancient warrior code? Poisoning an entire world to steal their children is not the way of warriors. I don't care how much the Empire needed defending! I am not alone, Edwen. Your daughter dreams as well. The mentalist you so casually refer to was treating dozens of us. They are emerging from their sleep across Brysdyn. What are you doing to do? Murder them too?"

"Enough," Edwen said icily, glaring at Garryn with similar venom. "I had hoped you would understand. Even if you did go to the planet. You know as well as I do that, in war, sacrifices are necessary. I made a decision, saving our Empire at the cost of one insignificant planet."

"Except it was my planet!"

"Perhaps it was once," Edwen countered, "but no more. You are as much Brysdynian as I am and you have a responsibility to the people who have chosen you to be their Imperator! Will you destroy them with what you know?"

"I will do what is right," Garryn replied, but inwardly he wasn't so sure. Despite his outrage, the general's words hit home.

"Then I will do what I must. I will not allow you to tear Brysdyn apart. Even if it means sacrificing our next Imperator."

XXIX

Escape

Once the sentries were ordered to remove the Prime from his presence, Edwen downed the entire contents of his untouched drink with one stiff gulp. The fine taste of cognac did little to improve his mood. No matter how much he justified in the name of Brysdyn, nothing could ever make him feel comfortable about assassinating the future head of state. Then again, what was one more death after all the others?

Edwen wondered at what point life had become so cheap to him.

"Speak."

Danten was present throughout the exchange but had remained silent, as always, in the background. In fact, now that he thought of it, Danten had been silent a great deal lately.

"Are you really going to have him killed?"

"Having an attack of conscience, Major?"

Edwen avoided Danten's gaze by staring into the bottom of his glass, as if the remaining contents could offer him comfort.

"No Sir, I just hoped we could have convinced him."

"He is angry and full of self righteous rage, not to mention he absolutely despises me. I never really believed we could convince him, but who could foresee going back to the planet would actually awaken all his memories of it?"

Edwen thought about Kalistar. Garryn claimed she dreamed as well. What were her nights plagued with? To his shame, he'd never thought to ask her if there was a problem when she had come home to Brysdyn. Then again, she knew his views on mentalists and probably thought it better to remain silent.

"How..." Danten tried to speak, but the words caught in his throat. When he found his voice, he tried again. "How will it be done?"

"We will place him and his companions inside his ship." It was as if a stranger was speaking with his voice and committing treason with each word. "Their ship will launch from the *Dragon's Eye* and, once it is in orbit around the planet, we will blow it out of the sky."

"May I speak candidly, Sir?"

Edwen turned to him in mild surprise. It was not a request Danten often made. Despite their years of service together, Edwen had very little idea on how the man felt about most things. Danten obeyed without question and kept his own counsel.

"Go ahead."

The general's appearance unnerved his loyal servant. The master of Security Elite, always supremely in control, now looked worn and tired. More than ever, Edwen now resembled a greying old man, unable to cope with the burdens of his position. Seeing him this way made Danten hesitate, but it was too late to withdraw the request.

"How will we explain this to the Imperator? You said he knows everything. If Garryn should suddenly turn up dead, surely the Imperator will know that we are responsible."

"Of course he will," Edwen nodded. "Fortunately, during our last meeting, I clarified our position. If he retaliates because I took his son's life, then he risks exposing Brysdyn to the truth about the New Citizens. Iran is not strong enough to survive the chaos this will cause in the Empire. He barely survived the anarchy during the Scourge. I think the Imperator knows not even a child is too great a sacrifice for Brysdyn."

Danten said nothing. When he was the young ambitious aide, their path was clear. They were saving Brysdyn from a slow death. In those days, he seldom lay awake at night, thinking about the choices of his life. Youth made one feel invincible. Now that youth was gone, and experience had given him a greater understanding of what they'd done. The more he pondered what lay beyond death, the more convinced he became a higher power would hold him accountable for his actions.

Garryn was correct. Control over this dark secret was beyond them now. The Dreamers were awakening across the Empire and, sooner or later, they would remember. As much as the General needed to believe what they were doing was for the greater good of Brysdyn, Danten knew better. This had stopped being about Brysdyn a long time ago. This was now about saving their skins and about saving the Security Elite.

For the first time in his life, Major Danten started to wonder if it was really worth saving.

* * *

"Are you really the Prime?"

The question startled him. As Garryn glanced over his shoulder at the guard asking the question, he wondered if his other escort was just as surprised. There were two of them, wearing the dark uniform of Edwen's private guard, with faces hidden behind the faceplate of their helmets, marching him back to the others.

"I am."

Except for them, the corridor was deserted, maintaining the secrecy of his presence on board the ship. He wondered how Edwen planned to get rid of him and the others.

"Shut up!" The other guard barked angrily.

"Come on, Yarn. You heard the General call him Prime."

His voice betrayed his uncertainty. He had to be a relatively new recruit to the Security Elite, Garryn decided. An experienced Elite trooper would never think to question his superiors, most of all the General.

"Maybe we should think about this…"

"I SAID SHUT UP!" Yarn cut him off before he could say anything else.

"Yarn! If this is really the Prime, we're committing high treason!"

"We are Security Elite! If the Prime threatens Brysdyn, then he is an enemy! You took the Oath! You know that! Now stop this!"

The guard fell silent and it appeared the temporary rebellion was over as they continued a little further along the corridor. Then, without warning, he stopped abruptly and swung around to face his comrade. The other man had barely a second to register what was happening before he pulled the trigger. The blast struck the older Security Elite officer dead centre, flinging him back against the wall. He slumped to the floor in a heap, his armour smouldering with heat.

Pulling his helmet off his face, he showed Garryn just how young he was. He couldn't be more than twenty years old, with olive skin and brown eyes.

"How can I help you, Prime?" he asked quietly, his voice indicating how overwhelmed he was by his own actions.

"What's your name?" Garryn wasted no time with the opportunity presented and quickly retrieved dead Yarn's weapons.

"Nyall," he replied, hesitating adding his rank after what he'd just done.

"Nyall, thank you for what you've done. I know it can't have been easy."

Nyall shrugged. "You're the Prime. I didn't sign up to stand by and let you be killed, whatever oath I took. But what now, Sir?" This impulsive step didn't come with any idea on how to proceed next.

Garryn considered their options before turning to Yarn. "We need to hide him. I don't want a general alert sounded until I get to the brig. Is there anywhere we can put him for the moment?"

"There are maintenance compartments along all corridors in this deck. It will be a tight squeeze, but I think we can fit him in there."

"Good. Let's do it," Garryn replied impatiently, eager to get moving. As it was, it was a small miracle no one had happened along yet. As big as this ship was, Garryn did not think much time would pass before someone discovered what they had done. He had an idea how they might escape, but he needed to reach Flinn and the others first.

They carried Yarn down the corridor quickly before shoving him into one of the compartments Nyall spoke about. It was a tight squeeze with all the cleaning equipment already in storage, but the door slid closed without issue.

"Would you know where the people who came on board with me were taken?" Garryn asked as they hurried away from the compartment.

"Unless the General requested otherwise, I would assume they would be taken to the brig."

Garryn had thought as much. "Okay, then that's where we're going."

* * *

Next time, Flinn, just walk away.

Flinn told himself this repeatedly over the duration of time he spent sitting in the cellblock with his companions, on the verge of execution. Even though he knew he would never have abandoned Garryn if he had to do it all over again, it still made him feel better thinking it. It was better than driving himself crazy thinking of a way to escape their cage.

His companions were in similar torment. Aaran and Rachel were huddled together in one of the bunks. They had remained in that same position since they were placed inside this cell and Flinn saw no reason to disturb them. While Aaran wore a look of resignation, Rachel's terror was plain. For an instant, Flinn forgot his own troubles long enough to feel for the poor woman who, until today, had never even left her home, let alone her planet. Now it seemed the journey would cost Rachel her life.

Hannah was in a better state. She didn't show her fear, but occupied her mind by studying everything closely, even though there wasn't much to see in their cell. He noticed they were the only prisoners in the brig. All other cells were empty.

They were sealed in by a wall of energy facing the corridor. At the end of it was a central hub where three guards and one communications officer kept a vigilant eye on them. With frustration, Flinn realised there was no possibility of escaping without being seen.

"How are you holding up?" Flinn asked, walking next to Hannah. He thanked the maker that the guards had let him keep his translator so he could at least speak to her.

"Alright," she said, trying to smile but not quite managing it. At that point, Flinn realised she was afraid but was hiding it better than her distraught mother. "Do you think Garryn is still alive?"

"I think so," Flinn replied with a sigh. Truth was, he had no idea if the Prime was dead or not.

"They will kill us, won't they?"

The acceptance of this fact made Flinn wish he could lie, but wouldn't insult her by doing so. "I think so."

"My father told me stories of Brysdyn all my life," she said, glancing at the elderly man holding her mother. "I always wanted to see it. It sounded so pretty. I made sure when he taught me to speak Brysdynian I learnt everything I could, so if I went there I wouldn't sound strange. I got part of the way, I suppose."

Flinn did not know what to say to her. The translator made everything said intelligible, so he could not say for certain if her fluency with Brysdynian was genuine or not. Fortunately, he did not have to answer, as their attention was taken up by the opening of the main doors to the cellblock. Garryn appeared, much their relief. The Prime seemed unhurt as he was escorted into the room by another guard.

Garryn scanned the room quickly, searching the cells until he found his companions. Once he met Flinn's gaze, the pilot saw the relief in the Prime's eyes.

"I thought there were two of you," Flinn heard one of the guards say.

"Officer Yarn was called away."

Something was up, Flinn thought.

It was very bad practice to pull a guard off a prisoner as important as Garryn, especially while escorting him to the brig. Flinn knew it and he was sure the other guards knew it as well. Before anything else could be said, Garryn suddenly dropped to his knees as his escort opened fire. To Flinn's amazement, Garryn reached behind his back and produced a weapon as well, shooting the other guards taken by surprise.

Bolts of energy were ricocheting off the walls and flying in all directions. One impacted on the outside wall of their cell, barely missing the door panel.

"Get cover!" he ordered. As Flinn retreated to the far wall of the cell, he grabbed Hannah and both of them scrambled under a table as the firefight continued outside.

Nyall's aim was deadly accurate and he killed two guards with one shot each. Garryn was impressed, but had little time to comment as he leapt out of the way of a stray bolt. He reacted quickly, shooting the communications officer who scrambled for the com terminal to call for help. The man jerked spasmodically after Garryn's shot struck him in the chest. He fell across the communication panel, quite dead.

"Prime!" He heard Nyall shout.

Garryn looked up to see the last guard standing taking aim at him. Instinctively, Garryn rolled out of the way as the bolt streaked past his ear, impacting on the steel floor inches from him. Wasting no time, Garryn fired his blaster again and send him flying backwards from the force of his fire. The man hit the ground hard and Garryn heard bone snapping against the plating of the steel deck.

"Are you all right?" Nyall asked, hurrying to him.

Garryn waved him away and got to his feet. "I'm fine. Go secure the door. I'll get the others."

The sentry nodded and turned to the door as Garryn made his way down the corridor. Flinn and Hannah emerged from their hiding place behind an overturned table as Garryn approached the cell.

"Good to see you in one piece," Flinn said with a smile as Garryn deactivated the door.

"Likewise," Garryn said, grateful they were all unharmed.

Hannah was not so restrained and threw her arms around him in a happy embrace. "We were worried about you," she gushed before pulling away, her cheeks reddening.

"I had some unexpected help," Garryn gestured to Nyall. "Is everyone alright here?"

"Yes," Aaran nodded, his arm around Rachel. "Did you see Edwen?"

"I did, but I'll tell you about it later. Right now, we need to get out of here."

Flinn was already heading towards one of the guards to get a weapon. He would have preferred his own blaster, but that had been confiscated shortly after they were taken. Realising their escape was far from secured, Flinn also took the dead man's rifle and slung it over his shoulder.

"What's next?" he asked Garryn, once the Prime introduced the group to Nyall. Flinn hoped Garryn had some plan on how to escape, because he sure as hell didn't.

"Well," Garryn said, catching his breath. "I have an idea…"

* * *

This situation was rapidly deteriorating.

After the General's meeting with the Prime, Danten had the impression Edwen was no longer in any mood for company. The major retreated to the bridge of the *Dragon's Eye*. Not only did he have a chance to get a breath taking view of space from the bridge, it also allowed him to keep an eye on rising talent. The reputation of *Dragon's Eye*'s bridge crew preceded them.

Today the ship was functioning on a skeleton crew. A few of its officers had transported to the *Warhammer* to assist after the destruction to its bridge. He felt a pang of loss knowing that Commander Neela was among the casualties listed.

Although Commander Jemyn had offered him the command chair while he was on the bridge, Danten declined the offer. He wanted to see the Earth in quiet contemplation. The third planet had changed little, appearing just as iridescently beautiful as it had twenty-three years ago.

"Major Danten," Jemyn suddenly came up behind him.

"Something I can do for you, Commander?"

"We seem to have lost contact with the brig."

Danten turned around sharply. "What do you mean?"

Jemyn, who was almost his age but showed it more, fidgeted uncomfortably. "We are unable to raise any of the guards on duty."

The Prime. Suspicion sprang instantly to mind. "Send a detachment there immediately."

"Already done."

Danten understood why Jemyn had approached him. The coward did not wish to be the one to tell the General there was a possibility of trouble with his prisoners. Jemyn had no idea who was incarcerated in his brig, other than the fact the prisoners had violated restricted space. Giving the man a disapproving frown, Danten brushed past him and went to the nearest com panel.

"What is it?"

"General," Danten said, taking a deep breath. "We may have a problem."

XXX

Firefight

The ship moved silently through space.

Her quarry lay in the distance, orbiting the blue world around which so many secrets were buried. While not as large as the dreadnought she was preparing to confront, she was certainly more manoeuvrable than her larger counterpart. Her builders wanted to design a ship possessing the strength and presence of a dreadnought, coupled with the manoeuvrability of a frigate.

She was called the *White Star* and was the first of the Ravager Class Destroyers.

These days the *White Star* bore the prestige of being the ship of choice for the Imperator when he travelled. While her duties were mostly limited to diplomatic missions, she was nevertheless required to be at combat readiness at all times. For this journey, the *White Star* could be called on to do both.

She had departed Brysdynian space less than an hour after the *Dragon's Eye* made its own hasty departure. Being the ship of the Imperator, the *White Star* was always on standby to depart at a moment's notice in the event of some crisis. Shortly before the *Dragon's Eye* left the home world, the Imperator had boarded the ship without warning and issued orders for pursuit.

Throughout the journey, she kept her anonymity by maintaining a discreet distance behind the dreadnought. The crew was suitably intrigued by the clandestine mission, but no one dared to ask the Imperator what it was about.

* * *

"Keep going! Keep going!" Flinn shouted over the sound of blaster fire.

A dozen Security Elite troops were behind him in pursuit with their guns blazing. The corridor was a kill zone of criss-crossing bolts of energy, ricocheting off the walls. Further along, shielded by the corner hooking to the right, Nyall was covering Flinn's approach, shooting into the thickest part of the approaching group. Keeping his head down, Flinn rounded the corner quickly, giving Nyall respite so he could provide similar cover for the former soldier and the others to escape.

Despite the tactic, the sheer number of pursuers told the space captain he couldn't remain here for long.

As it stood, his skin still stung from the embers he could feel through his clothes when the energy blasts struck the hull and produced sparks that bounced across the deck. Smoke from so many discharging blasters drifted down the passageway, making it increasingly difficult to see how many troops were in pursuit.

"Go!" Flinn snapped and continued to fire back now that he'd taken Nyall's place at the corner.

Aaran and his family were waiting for them around the corner. With Nyall joining them, they could now find an alternate route to the flight deck where the *Wayward Son* was kept. The trooper ran ahead and made sure the corridor they would be taking to reach the deck was clear, ushering the family along before he hurried back to Flinn. Surprisingly enough, Nyall found the pilot to be quite adept in cutting down the numbers of the latest group of troops trying to recapture them. He could see only two of his former comrades firing back at Flinn.

"Let's go!" he said, tugging on Flinn's arm.

Flinn ignored him and took careful aim. There were two troopers left standing. While the logical thing would be to wait until reinforcements came before resuming pursuit, it was possible they might ignore good sense and maintain the chase. Either way, Flinn was not to let anyone get shot in the back. He fired a few more times, driving them back the way they'd come. After a few seconds, the corridor fell silent and all that remained were bodies killed in the firefight.

"You're good," Nyall said, looking at them.

"Too good," he grumbled, wiping the sweat from his brow. "Which way next?"

"This way," Nyall gestured to the intersection of corridors up ahead. "We make a left turn at that junction and head down until we reach the maintenance deck. According to the schematics I saw at the last access terminal, it runs directly under the flight deck. At the end of the deck, there ought to be a maintenance stairway leading directly into the landing bay."

"Sounds good to me," Flinn replied before he looked up at Aaran and his family. "Everyone alright here?"

"As well as we can be," Aaran answered, glancing at his wife and daughter. He should never have allowed them to leave Earth with him. At least there they were safe from Edwen. Rachel was doing her best to hide her fear, but he knew she was terrified by their situation. After spending years on a savage planet, she was accustomed to concealment.

Around them, klaxons were screaming news of their escape all across the ship. Red beacons were flashing across the ship, indicating the urgency of the situation. The ship would be in full alert now and Flinn had no illusions that their approach to the *Wayward Son* would be at all easy or unexpected. Edwen knew they had nowhere else to go.

Don't think about it, Flinn told himself. He had thrown his lot in with the Prime and prayed this played out the way...

The discharge of a blaster halted the thought in his head abruptly.

Glancing over his shoulder, he turned just in time to see a bolt of energy strike Nyall in the back. The soldier stumbled forward, an expression of surprise on his face before his knees buckled beneath him. He landed on his face, his back smouldering from the shot that had burned through his clothes and then into his flesh.

Hannah uttered a short scream and buried her face in her father's arms at the sight of the dead man, while Rachel simply turned away. Flinn cursed under his breath, knowing he did not have to examine their fallen ally to know he was dead. Blaster wounds were ruthlessly efficient and the smell of burning flesh told Flinn that Nyall did not survive his.

The shot had come from the first of three guards rounding the corner and Flinn reacted instinctively, opening fire on them with enough shots to drive them back for a second.

"We have to move now!" he barked at Aaran and his family, prompting them to break into a run to get away. There was no time to mourn the soldier, not when they had perhaps a few seconds head start and no more.

Less than that, Flinn realised, when he barely had enough time to shoot before the troopers charged around the corner firing again. This time, he didn't take up position, he just turned and ran, hoping the maze of corridors would protect them. He fired as he raced forward, his eyes fixed on the troopers behind him. He wasn't sure which one of them had killed Nyall, but at this point he didn't really care.

Years of dealing with killers and scum in the seediest parts of the galaxy had made Flinn Ester very capable of staying alive. Since his Fleet days, he'd been a deadly shot with a blaster. It took him a matter of minutes to dispatch all three troopers even as he evaded their return fire. Shooting with more accuracy than his attackers, he kept blasting away until they stopped following.

Somewhere in the distance, Flinn heard Hannah scream.

When the ringing in his ears from the cacophony of exploding ceased, he saw the pursuing soldiers lying dead behind him. The wounds in various parts of their anatomy were still smouldering. Returning his attention to his companions, he realised then, to his dismay, why Hannah had cried out.

Hannah was kneeling down next to her mother. Aaran held the woman in his arms.

Flinn could not see the wound, but didn't have to. Blood was seeping onto the floor, creating an ever-darkening pool of crimson, staining Aaran's hands as he wept. Hannah was holding her mother's lifeless hand to her breast in similar anguish. Flinn blinked, unable to believe that he'd failed them so miserably. Just like Nyall: another life he was unable to save.

Flinn took a deep breath and approached them slowly.

"I'm so sorry," Flinn said softly, knowing words meant nothing in the face of such a loss. He wished he could allow them time to grieve, but it was impossible. Those three he just killed would be followed by others. At the thought, he glanced up to make sure no one else was approaching. He saw no one yet, but it would only be a matter of time.

"Aaran," Flinn placed a hand on the man's shoulder in sympathy.

Neither father nor daughter looked up at him.

"We have to keep moving. Believe me, I would like nothing more than to allow your grief, but we don't have the time. Very soon, reinforcements will be coming and we don't want to be here when that happens. I don't think Rachel would want you to die here as well."

After a long pause, Aaran replied, "I won't leave her." His voice was a monotone and his spirit seemed greatly diminished without Rachel's presence.

"I know you want to bring her with us, but we have to move fast," Flinn explained, and once again glanced at the corridor before regarding the man again. "Aaran, you still have a daughter to think about. We need to get her to safety."

Aaran shot him a look as if he were going to bite back in response, but then Flinn saw the man's grimace as he realised Flinn was right.

Reluctantly, Aaran released his grip on his wife's body. Laying her gently on the floor, he wiped the tears from his face and got to his feet, taking Hannah's hand. The young woman buried her face in her father's shoulder as she wept.

"You are right," he said, holding his child, "I still have Hannah to think about. Above all else, she must be safe."

* * *

The bridge of the *Dragon's Eye* was nothing less than chaotic.

Edwen made his arrival on the bridge after Danten notified him about the situation in the brig. Reports were coming in about a running firefight across the ship, originating at the brig and heading steadily towards the landing bay. The team Danten sent to the brig to investigate found the sentries assigned to guard Garryn's companions were dead. There was no sign of the Prime.

Once the General arrived, he assumed control of the bridge and Danten noted that Commander Jemyn was content to let the General take personal charge of the recapture. Danten wondered if the man was truly as complacent as he seemed. No commander liked being usurped on the bridge of his own ship, even if it was by the master of Security Elite.

"Double the guard around their ship," Edwen snapped at an audience of junior officers. "I also want additional security in the landing bay. Their leader is extremely dangerous, so inform your people to expect the unexpected. Shoot to kill."

The major cast his gaze out the observation windows of the bridge, admiring the stars beyond and the blue world he had last seen twenty-three years ago. It was not the only thing he was starting to see clearly. It was hardly the best time for soul searching, but when was it ever? In the last few hours, Danten had been faced with the consequence of his actions two decades ago. He'd spent most of his military career believing the Elite could fix anything. It was a shock to the system to realise this was not the case.

"I want a deck by deck search." He heard Edwen continuing to issue orders, but he was no longer paying any real attention. "Check every compartment and every room, even maintenance shaft and access way. I want a full sensor sweep of all decks leading to the landing bay. I do not want them leaving this ship!"

The only thing Danten could not understand was why the Prime was heading towards such an obvious destination. Surely Garryn knew the minute news of the escape reached the bridge, the ship would be heavily guarded. What possible reason could Garryn be engaged in a gunfight that would alert everyone on the ship to their presence?

* * *

Flinn did not know how much longer they could remain on the run like this.

More and more troops were starting to appear behind every corner. The intervals between the firefights were less frequent. Despite descending into dimly lit maintenance decks in an effort to throw their pursuers off their scent, it did little good. Not only was the entire ship aware of their escape, but also they were on their way to the *Wayward Son*. Every possible route was being systematically sealed off. They time was drawing to a point where they could not run anymore and Garryn's gamble would either work or they would all be dead.

This part of the ship was not designed with aesthetics in mind. Much of it was constructed with the essentials only. There was no steel plating to cover the hydraulic pipes and energy conduits, only rubber insulation where necessary. The dim lighting and the exposed veins running along narrow passages way made it seem more like a dungeon than a corridor for maintenance personnel.

Next to him, Aaran and his daughter were silent. Flinn made no comment on it, aware the family was still raw from their fresh loss. Flinn wished they could have taken Rachel's body with them, but it was impossible in their current circumstances. Carrying the weight would slow them down and they needed to remain one step ahead of Edwen.

They reached another junction of corridors. The heat from the hydraulic pipes against the cold air created a steamy fog that made this place hot and humid. He strained to see through the veil of swirling air. His clothes were stuck to his skin and sweat was running down his cheek. Motioning them to stay back, Flinn took a tentative step forward into the centre of the juncture. Hannah and Aaran remain hidden while he checked to see if it was safe to proceed.

In the background, he heard the slamming of pistons against one another and servos moving amidst the gentle hiss of vapour escaping into the air. He took it all in, even the low drone of the engines in the deck beneath them. Then, without warning, he turned sharply to the left corridor and started firing blindly. No sooner than he pulled the trigger of his blaster, voices cried out in disarray. He didn't wait long enough for them to start firing at him.

"Surprise, surprise," Flinn muttered under his breath. He reached the corner just as a pipe burst, spewing steam after being hit by a blaster bolt.

"Where's your father?" he demanded when he reached Hannah and saw Aaran wasn't with her.

Hannah had been watching Flinn so closely she didn't notice that her father was slipping away. The realisation that he was gone sent her into raw panic.

"I don't know!" she exclaimed in horror and retreated up the passage they had just come down. "He must have gone back to see if there was another way out!"

Flinn overtook her in a number of strides. He rounded the turning corridor just as he was fired upon again, this time from the direction Aaran had gone. Hannah let out a startled cry as she stumbled backwards, scrambling to safety. As Flinn remained on his knees, he saw Aaran firing frantically down the steamy aisle. While he couldn't see who the former science officer was shooting at, it wasn't hard to guess. Worse yet, it meant they were cut off in both direction.

Aaran dropped to his knees, narrowly avoiding the shot that flew above his head and struck a piece of machinery. As the energy burned through the steel, Flinn heard the disturbing sound of metal groaning from the assault. A large jet of plasma spewed down the passage. It created a chain reaction that caused emergency venting from other pressurized systems to erupt in a fiery ball of fire. Aaran had enough time to register what was happening before the flames reached him.

The roar of the fire eclipsed any scream he might have let out. Flinn saw the faint outline of a body encased in fire, struggling momentarily in agony before disintegrating all together. It took place in seconds, before the fireball raced towards him and Hannah. Without thinking, he grabbed her and got clear before the flames could reach them.

"DADDY!" Hannah squirmed free of him when it was all over and the smoke had cleared, trying to reach her father in a futile effort. Flinn pinned her against the wall and she glared at him in almost feral rage. "Let me go! He's still out there!"

"Hannah, he's gone!"

"No he's not!" she protested and started fighting him. This time, Flinn's grip was stronger and he dragged her away from there. He did not want her to smell the stench and know it was the remains of her father's flesh she was breathing.

"It's too late, Hannah!" Flinn tried desperately to convince her again. "I'm sorry."

"No, you're wrong!" she answered defiantly, but her voice wavered and her response felt like a sob.

Flinn shook his head and as it sunk in. She ceased struggling and started to weep. Her entire body shook in anguish and there was little he could do to ease that pain. In the background, he could still hear the cries of troopers caught in the fire and remembered that there were more of them on the other side of the corridor. Once again, he was going to deny her grief.

"We've got to go," he urged, wanting to take her from this place. He did not want her to look down the passageway and see what remained of her father. He wanted to spare her that.

"Not the both of them!" she wailed, "not the both of them!"

He didn't know what to say, so he remained silent and led her away, searching for another way out, even though they were trapped on both sides.

Even as he said that, Flinn was starting to wonder whether it was simpler to just surrender. This was not his fight. It was not even hers. He was here because of some misguided loyalty to a friend. Was any friendship worth what he had seen these past hours?

Did Garryn know what price his plan had cost?

XXXI

One Last Time

Time was running out on him.

As the General stood on the bridge, trying to orchestrate the recapture and murder of the Prime, the master of Security Elite was gripped with a feeling of futility. All his life, he'd controlled his fate like a god. A life lived with such certainty had its disadvantages, of course: the lack of challenge and surprise being the most common. Still, it was a small price to pay.

Twenty-three years ago, all this was so simple.

There was little need to grapple with his conscience at the magnitude of what he had done. He was not an evil man by nature, but he was ruthless, like the slar that kills to protect its cub. Edwen killed to save Brysdyn. The reason seemed so noble then. The world as he knew it was on the brink of extinction and he had to save it.

The decision to sacrifice one world among billions in the universe did not appear so terrible. Yet as he looked down onto that pale blue planet, what he remembered most about it was the voices. The communications centre of the ship had been almost drowned in the frantic energy of multiple broadcasts in every frequency conceivable. Military signals, civilian entertainment, infant attempts at interstellar communication, they had been there.

As a grim reminder of his crime, when the *Dragon's Eye* took orbit around the planet, the communications channels opened found nothing but cold static. There were no noises, no primitive chatter or strange music. It was the silence that drove home to him the magnitude of what he had done.

"General," Jemyn's voice snapped him out of his thoughts. "We have some further news."

"What is it?" Edwen replied wearily.

"We've just found the body of Trooper Nyall."

The name did not sound familiar. "One of the assault teams assigned to recapture the prisoners, I assume." Edwen met his gaze without much interest.

"No Sir, Nyall was one of the prisoner's escorts."

Edwen looked up sharply. "He is dead?"

"Yes Sir," the commander answered. "His body was among the dead involved in the fire fight in Sector G."

"Near the landing bay," Edwen remarked. That would make sense. Garryn and his group were trying to reach their ship. Sector G was in the path of the most direct route. Jemyn looked uncomfortable and Edwen wondered what was it he was finding so difficult to say.

"What else, Jemyn?"

"It was what the trooper was wearing, General."
He met Edwen's gaze.

"Well out with it!"

"General," Jemyn swallowed. "He was wearing the prisoner's clothes."

Edwen's eyes flew wide open.

* * *

Garryn had never thought he would get this far.

While Flinn and the others were causing pandemonium at the other side of the ship, he was moving through the ship unseen. No one was paying much attention to one Security Elite guard working his way towards the bridge. When he first proposed the idea, it was more of a last ditch effort to save their lives rather than a genuine plan capable of success. Even a foolhardy attempt at escape was better than nothing at all.

Judging by the number of troops running down the corridors and the frantic evacuation of non-combat personnel from key areas of the ship, it was working. Flinn was leading the Elite in the opposite direction, while Garryn continued towards the bridge. He prayed Flinn could keep one step ahead of the guards.

Initially, Garryn had hoped it would be a simple matter of getting to the bridge and carrying out the next phase of his risky plan, but the *Dragon's Eye* was not a freighter. She was a dreadnought class warship almost four miles in length, with ten decks and a maze of corridors and passageways that seemed to run on forever. As he neared the bridge, the traffic in the corridors increased and he kept his head down, hoping he was not discovered.

As the two officers walked past him, he picked up snippets of conversation. It was difficult to focus with so many voices chattering around him. Still, Garryn managed to hear some of their words before they moved out of earshot.

"They found another one of the bastards in Sector G," one remarked.

"Really? That makes two, doesn't it? The first one took out half a dozen of our security boys before they killed him."

"Yeah, except this one was a *woman*."

Garryn froze at the statement.

For a moment, he could not move. Only when he saw a few heads looking at him in question, did he force his legs to move. Under the faceplate, he closed his eyes and tried hard to force away the pain threatening to overwhelm his being.

Two of them are dead? Who?

He wanted to scream, kick, and express some of the fury surging inside him. Garryn felt sick to his stomach knowing that, once again, he'd failed to protect his friends. Was he capable of protecting anyone who chose to help him? First it was Mira and then Jonen, followed by Vyndeka and all those on board the *Asmoryll*. Who was it now? Who did he get killed now?

Maybe this was a trick, something to distract him. Perhaps they knew he was coming and they were trying to force him into exposure. During his final approach to the bridge, these were the morsels of hope to which he clung. When he finally reached the bridge, he knew the Weaver was nowhere that kind. Two of his companions were dead and, if he was going to save the others, he needed to focus.

Damn you, Edwen, you're going to pay for this, Garryn swore inwardly.

* * *

His rifle felt hot in his hand. The temperature of the metal had been rising steadily for the last hour, but now it was becoming uncomfortable to hold. As it was, it was becoming increasingly difficult for him to aim with any accuracy, but that was the least of it. Very shortly, he would be unable to keep his grip on it at all.

Flinn knew the signs well. Overheating was only a symptom of a larger problem. The rifle was drawing every particle of energy left within its power coils to fire and there was simply nothing left to tap. Very soon, the weapon would be dead in his hands and he would have nothing but a single hand blaster to fight off the latest batch of troopers.

They made it off the maintenance deck by squeezing into an air vent to avoid the troops closing in on both sides. It took them close to a steel stairway leading to the landing bay.

"This is it," Flinn said to her.

Hannah studied him for a moment and saw the sweat on his brow, the bruises on his skin and redness of his hands where the heat of his rifle blistered his palms. While he didn't appeal to her the way Garryn did, there was nobility in him that countered his swaggering bravado. Looking into his eyes, she realised they were not going to make it off this ship.

After living on a war-ravaged planet since the day she was born, death did not frighten Hannah very much. Her mother told her once that death was a passing to a better place and was something to be looked forward to, nor feared. Losing her parents meant if death took her, they'd be together again all the sooner.

"Thank you for what you've done, Flinn," she said softly, understanding this was the time to make such declarations.

Flinn didn't protest at what was essentially a farewell speech, because the situation warranted it. "I did what I could. I wish I could have helped your family more than I did. They were brave people."

"You did everything that you could," she said softly, wishing that she was as strong as she was trying to sound. "You saved my life."

"For what it's worth," he said with a grim smile.

Hannah returned it. "Shall we?" She looked up towards the stairway and the light that beamed from the powerful illuminators in the landing deck above bathed her face with a determined glow.

"They'll be up there you know?"

"I know. Let's go anyway."

At that, Flinn straightened up and reached for his blaster. He tossed the rifle aside. It would do him little good now. Taking her hand in his, he started up the metal steps, their footsteps clanging against the steel. He emerged head first on the floor of the landing bay. The *Wayward Son* stood patiently a few meters away from the stairway. Even now, she was still the most beautiful thing in the universe to him.

While the first thing he saw was his beloved ship, the next was the garrison of Security Elite troops surrounding him with their weapons drawn. He exhaled loudly at the sight of them, unsurprised by the volume of their numbers. This was the last focal point for an ambush and he had expected them to come well prepared.

"You will drop your weapons!"

The order came from an officer standing directly in front of the *Wayward Son's* main entry hatch with a dozen troops to reinforce his demand.

For a moment, he considered fighting it out, but then looked at Hannah and realised his choice affected more than just his life. The part of him that once was an officer of the Fleet would not allow him to jeopardise her life. Tossing both their lives to the fates, he dropped his gun on the deck.

Wherever you are, Garryn, it's all up to you now.

* * *

The ensign checked the readings on his scanner console once again. This time, he did so just to make certain he was not in error.

Even though he was inexperienced, he knew he was a good officer, not prone to reaching poor conclusions. Despite the fact their mission here was meant to be of the highest security, he was convinced of what he was seeing on his console. Nevertheless, before he made his announcement, it was always wise to double check.

"Commander Jemyn, there is another ship approaching."

The statement captured everyone's attention, particularly Edwen's. Jemyn crossed the floor of the bridge in a number of long strides, while the General maintained his vigil at the command chair. Even though he obviously believed he was in charge, to the crew of the *Dragons* Eye, Jemyn was still their commander.

"Can you identify her?" Jemyn asked as he approached Ensign Lyan and stood over his shoulder. He saw Lyan's fingers flying deftly over the console pad, confirming his readings. Lyan was one of his better officers. The ink on his commission papers was hardly dry, but Jemyn saw a bright future in store for the young man, because he was a meticulous worker.

"Yes, Sir. It's a Ravager Class Destroyer. Identification No. 197403." As more images flashed on his console screen, Lyan's eyes widened in surprise before turning to look Jemyn in the eye. "Sir, it's the White Star."

Jemyn straightened and swung around instinctively to face Edwen. "The White Star is the Imperator's ship."

Somehow Edwen was unsurprised. When he had heard Trooper Nyall was found without his uniform, Edwen understood Garryn's plan.

The Prime exchanged uniforms with the sentry so that he could move about freely. Edwen also knew the only way Garryn could transmit a call for help was on the bridge. What was equally frustrating was the fact that he couldn't tell Jemyn. No terrorist would be foolish enough to make an attempt at infiltrating the bridge. Everything was in Edwen's favour as long as no one knew Garryn was on board.

The arrival of the *White Star* changed everything.

Had Garryn been and gone already while Edwen was sending men all across the ship to find him? Impossible! Even if it were true, there was no way the *White Star* could get here this fast. It took a week for the *Dragon's Eye* to arrive here from Brysdyn. At last report, the *White Star* was orbiting the home world. Whatever brought her here was not because of any message sent by the Prime.

"Is she in communications range?" Edwen inquired, walking towards Jemyn. For now, his concern regarding Garryn's whereabouts would have to wait.

"It is, Sir," Jemyn answered, but his face reflected his puzzlement. He was not alone in this feeling. The mood on the bridge was one of puzzlement. "She's not attempting to communicate. We are certainly in their visual range by now. They cannot be unaware of us."

From where he was standing next to the large windows of the bridge, Danten stared at Edwen and wondered how the General was going to explain this away. A communications blackout like this was the practice adopted by hostile ships approaching each other, certainly not the flag warship of the Imperial Navy.

"She is in visual," Danten declared as the *White Star* appeared off the starboard bow of the *Dragon's Eye*. The warship was growing larger in the window, but had to slow as it approached the dreadnought.

"General," Jemyn spoke up. "Do I have permission to transmit greetings to the *White Star*?"

Edwen frowned, still troubled by the Imperator's appearance. If Garryn had not contacted the *White Star*, then what was she doing here? Aware that Jemyn was waiting for an answer, there was no choice but to agree to the request.

"Go ahead."

Suddenly, from the corner of his eye, he saw movement. Nothing unusual in itself, but Edwen reacted immediately. A guard stepped onto the bridge and was making his way across the floor towards the main computer. Without thinking, Edwen grabbed his sidearm and fired. The bolt sailed across the floor and struck him on the shoulder. The man went down hard amidst the pandemonium on the bridge.

Danten hurried next to the General who holstered his sidearm and was calling for security. A few bridge officers were aiming their guns at both the General and the fallen guard who was scrambling to his feet.

"What the hell is going on?" Jemyn demanded, forgetting the order to communicate with the *White Star* or the fact that Edwen was his superior officer. "General, what is the meaning of this?"

Blood seeped through the guard's uniform and, despite the guns pointed at him, he was still moving towards the main command console. "Tell him, Edwen. Tell him if you dare."

"Silence!" Edwen shouted with uncharacteristic outrage. "Security, take the prisoner to the brig!"

"Or what?" Garryn reached for his helmet.

"Don't try it! You know I won't hesitate to have you killed where you stand!" Edwen warned. Suddenly, it dawned on Edwen what Garryn was intending. He was never after the communications console at all. He was after the main computer. The computer held verification codes, the same codes that gave the Prime command override over every ship in the fleet.

"Commander Jemyn," Garryn spoke knowing this was his last chance. "Do you know who I am?" Garryn had also seen the *White Star* off the starboard bow. His father had come after him. Only the Lords knew how Iran discovered he was here, but it no longer mattered. Edwen would kill him, unless Garryn proved to these officers he was the Prime.

The question took Jemyn off guard. The air of superiority worn by the man shook him slightly. "You are terrorist scum!"

"Let me take off my helmet and I'll give you proof that your General has led all of you to commit *high treason.*"

There was an audible rumble of shock running through the bridge and Edwen started to feel the situation tumble rapidly out of control. "Do nothing that he says! He is a terrorist attempting to cloud your minds!"

Jemyn did not know what to do. He was conditioned to obey the General no matter what. He'd lived a lifetime in service to the Security Elite and the Brysdynian Empire. In all that time, Edwen had never ceased to remind all of them that loyalty to the Security Elite first began with loyalty to him. If he disobeyed Edwen now and he was wrong, the General would utterly destroy him.

"Jemyn," Major Danten spoke for the first time. "Allow the prisoner to remove his helmet."

Edwen spun around and glared at Danten, in disbelief and fury. "What are you doing?"

Danten did not react to the insult, but regarded the General with resignation.

"Edwen, it is time to stop this. We have gone as far as we can go with this subterfuge. If we are going to be judged for what we have done, then let it be because it was for the good of the Empire, not because we committed treason."

It was the first time Danten had ever called the general by name.

"Do nothing that he says!" Edwen warned Jemyn again, refusing to yield.

Across the bridge, Danten could see the other officers starting to become nervous at the possibility they were being led to commit a crime against the Empire. The outcome of this entire affair now rested with the commander of the *Dragon's Eye*.

Jemyn looked at Danten and then at Edwen. The Major had been Edwen's aide for longer than Jemyn could remember. The evidence was certainly there to indicate Danten might be the one to follow. Edwen's reluctance to allow the prisoner to show his face and the sudden arrival of the *White Star* was suspicious, to say the least.

"Take your helmet off," Jemyn ordered Garryn.

Garryn let out a sigh of relief and pulled off his helmet.

His hair stuck to his head in an unruly fashion and salty trickles of sweat ran down his brow. Garryn ran his fingers through his hair, hoping that would make him somewhat recognisable. As he met Jemyn's gaze, he realised there was no need.

The commander's face was ashen.

"What have you done?" Jemyn turned sharply to Edwen and grabbed him by the arm. "What stink have you brought upon my ship?"

"You will not speak to me that way!" Edwen yanked his arm free and returned with just as much venom. "Your oath lies first to the Security Elite, the Imperator second."

"What is it, Sir?" Jemyn's first officer asked with rising fear. Indeed, the entire bridge was quickly disintegrating into a mass of extreme emotions. Some still clung to the hope that their commander could provide an explanation.

"Commander Jemyn," Garryn spoke, ignoring the outburst. "I can prove my identity if you like. Allow me to access the command console and your crew will understand."

Garryn couldn't assume he was recognisable to the rest of the ship the way he was to Jemyn, especially in the uniform of a Security Elite guard. The commander only recognised him because he was likely present at the Ascension ceremony in Paralyte.

"Let him," Jemyn told his first officer.

Garryn stepped forward, entering the code though the keypad. First Officer Sala, who stood over his shoulder, looked up a second later and exclaimed with a gasp, "He's the Prime!"

"Whether he is Prime or not is hardly significant," Edwen quickly spoke up. "Your oath is to the protection of Brysdyn, not its leaders. The Security Elite is above the petty distinctions of rank. This man is attempting to harm the fabric of our society with his lies. Would you allow Brysdyn to be destroyed because of rank?"

"I am your Prime and on the *White Star* your Imperator awaits," Garryn interrupted him before he could go any further. "Your people are understandably confused, but it is your lead they will follow. Only you can decide how this will end."

At that, Garryn looked at Edwen again. Tossing the helmet aside, he walked to the General, still clutching his bleeding arm. The pain was growing and soon he would succumb to it, but not at this moment. Edwen's time had come.

"It's over, General."

"You would destroy Brysdyn with what you intend to do, Garryn! You would tear her heart out!"

Garryn ignored him.

"Contact the *White Star*, Jemyn. Tell them that under the authorisation of Garryn, Prime of Brysdyn, I hereby charge General Edwen of the Security Elite with treason and the attempted assassination of a member of the Royal House."

"Yes Sir," Jemyn answered, still shaken by what was going on. "Why did you do this, General?"

Edwen did not reply and Garryn saw the frightened and confused faces on the bridge waiting for an answer. The truth changed everything he believed about himself. He'd seen many good friends die. What he now knew would never again allow him peace.

Edwen was a genocidal maniac, but he gave Brysdyn a chance of life after the Scourge. The Earth was destroyed and nothing could change that outcome, but Brysdyn still lived. The New Citizens were proud to be Brysdynian. Technology could allow the dreams to be suppressed and forgotten. The Dreamers could be happy again. Brysdyn did not deserve to know something so terrible about its children.

"The General was afraid that I would dismantle Security Elite," Garryn spoke up. "I was aware of an assassination attempt and I laid a trap, not knowing who I would expose. I made it no secret I would be travelling to the third planet. Until I was taken on board this ship, I had no idea it was Edwen was responsible for these attempts."

Edwen stared at Garryn in shock for a moment, but recovered quickly.

"Yes," he said, his voice sounding dazed. "I could not allow you to destroy my life's work. Major Danten and I orchestrated this entire scheme to assassinate the Prime and make it look like he disappeared during his travels. I should not have involved you in this, Major." His eyes touched Danten, pleading for corroboration.

Danten held his gaze and answered, "I have always stood by your side, Sir, and that will never change."

For Brysdyn, he would stand by Edwen one last time.

XXXII

Judgement

He took the floor of the Quorum Hall for the first time as speaker.

Before this, the Prime was only an observer. For months, he sat on the polished wooden seats, hearing the oratories recited and watching the august body of men and women conduct matters of policy. In their presence, he always felt young and inexperienced. Indeed, he was raw in comparison to what they knew about holding an empire together. Garryn hoped he had learned enough from them to make his debut.

Today, the Quorum was closed to the public. A wall of silence trapped them inside the ancient structure, while troops guarded the doors and the security teams monitored airwaves to ensure secrecy. Such extraordinary measures were never required for a meeting of the Quorum, not since the days of war, but those who were expected to appear understood the situation.

The public were kept in the dark, fed only what was necessary. The secrecy was explained away as matters of galactic security not for public consumption. What news they *did* receive left them astonished. The master of Security Elite had attempted to assassinate the Prime and failed. He would stand trial for his crimes on the floor of the Quorum, where his fate would be decided by the members of that body.

Garryn swept his gaze across the room, seeing familiar faces: his father, Ashner, Flinn and Hannah, to name a few. Ellisha was sent to Jyne for a diplomatic mission, keeping her well away from here. Garryn had no wish for his sister to know the truth any more than the rest of the Dreamers.

He avoided looking at Kalistar, though he knew her eyes were boring into him. She was seated next to her father and, though she was not implicated in his crimes, Kalistar chose valiantly to remain at his side. He was her father and she would not abandon him. Despite their friendship, Garryn had not spoken to her since his return home. He knew he would have to face her sooner or later, but right now this needed to be done.

"The Prime has the floor," Garryn heard the voice of the First Speaker bidding him to come forward.

Garryn stepped forward and began speaking.

"My friends, we are gathered here today to address the crimes of General Edwen, Supreme Commander of the Security Elite."

Edwen stared back at him with little emotion. Kalistar's face was another matter entirely. Garryn could not look at her for long.

"You may wonder why I requested an information blackout from the public. When I returned from Theran, I had no intention of revealing what I discovered there. There are some truths that should remain buried forever, but not to the point of ignorance. You need to know what happened there, so it never happens again."

The hall was silent. No one seemed to react and all were captured by his voice resonating throughout the room. "It began shortly after I commenced my military tour on Erebo Station in the Theran star system. Almost from the beginning, my sleep was filled with violent dreams of death and a world with a blue sky. I persevered with this condition for a long time, afraid to admit that there might be something wrong with me.

This situation continued throughout the war and after I returned home it was even worse. There was not a night I could sleep without seeing these terrible images. At this point, I confided in my sister Ellisha, who persuaded me to seek assistance. I followed her advice and sought out a mentalist from the Rura District."

Some of the faces flickered in recognition as he related the story of Jonen's treatment and the discovery that he was one of the many afflicted with the condition called the Dreaming. His narrative was short and concise. He told them about Mira and her death, and the attempt on Jonen's life when the mentalist inquired after the older New Citizens existing off world.

As he progressed deeper into his narrative, he saw little reaction from Edwen and a great deal from the Quorum. Their faces filled with horror and accusation as their eyes darted back from Garryn to Edwen. Edwen's composure was glacial under their scrutiny and seemed only to heighten their belief in his guilt.

"There are elements of this story that can never be fully corroborated until we set down on Earth and see the scorch marks on her cities. Their dead lie where they fell, gassed by Prothos B32. I have the daughter of the science officer on board the *Starlight* who initially discovered the planet." He gestured toward Hannah and allowed the Quorum to take a good look at her before he continued.

"You have a tragic story of not just one world, but two. I am a Brysdynian, but I am also an Earther. I was raised to believe I came from a dead world called Cathomira. Cathomira no longer exists, so no one will ever know the truth about it. The other Dreamers can be cured. Undoubtedly, they will always have questions, but bad dreams are within our technology to eliminate. I propose we leave things as they are. The New Citizens believe they are from Cathomira. I see no reason for that to change."

Even as he concluded that part of his speech, he could see it in their faces that they agreed. When he stepped off the podium and joined his father, he finally met Kalistar's gaze. Her sorrow was indescribable. He wished he could have spared her this, but being Edwen's daughter made it impossible. He saw her tears and understood in one leap of insight the tears were not for her father but for the two of them. Whatever friendship or possible romance they'd had was over.

The Custodian of the Chamber scanned the agenda pad on the podium before addressing the audience. "Before the Quorum Council makes its final deliberations, we will hear from General Edwen."

Edwen rose to his feet, showing the pride and superiority he'd always worn like a cloak during his days as supreme commander of the Elite. Every step was taken with dignity and composure, even though the General now stood under the light of total exposure. His gaze swept across the room and the faces looking back at him showed little mercy, although there was some understanding.

"My Prime has spoken most eloquently. I commend his decision to keep the populace from this hearing." For the first time in his life, Edwen decided to speak from the heart, because he knew his words here would mark how he would be remembered throughout history. If he was to be damned, then he would be damned for what he was.

"I created the Security Elite to protect Brysdyn under any circumstance. True, I am an isolationist, but I will not use this as a platform for my ideas. I am here to face my accusers and to be held accountable for my acts. Before I give you my plea, I will ask that you hear my words for one final time. I lost two grown sons to the Scourge and I know many of you share the same grief. I always thought I could protect Brysdyn from anything. When the Scourge came, I found that I could not save Brysdyn any more than I could save my sons. I watched my children grow sick and die. I still remember the bonfires."

Edwen blinked, allowing, for the first time, real emotion to seep into his eyes. In the darkness of his memories, he saw that blaze in the distance when the bodies of his sons were taken away. He remembered the stench coming from the fire and smoke and how he knew the ashes he was breathing were his children.

"I saw my wife descend into despair she never recovered from. I saw my friend, the Imperator, slip into the same anguish as his world crumbled around him. I saw chaos and destruction wrought by the Scourge because I failed to anticipate something as simple as a micro-organism. We were on the verge of extinction. We, who left the white star and journeyed across ten millennia of space to create this civilisation, were going die because we could not have children. I refused to accept that."

He looked up at them and saw Iran's sympathy. There was no condemnation there, just sorrow.

"When I learnt about Earth, I immediately latched on to the possibility of a new lease on life for the Empire. Perhaps, in my madness, I simply overlooked the utter monstrosity of it. I have told the Prime and even Officer Aaran it was a matter of the strong devouring the weak. I believed that no more than you do, Garryn."

"I buried my feelings and my shame under the notion that what I did was right. I do not lie to you when I say that I see those deaths as potently as Garryn does now. He is fortunate, because he knows he was a victim. I cannot boast the same. I am the murderer and the genocidal madman who destroyed a planet. I require no leniency and I admit my guilt. I do so because I will not make this any harder for Brysdyn than it already is.

I brought the children who have become our sons and daughters. They became the future of our Empire. They are called the New Citizens, but they are more than that, and every man and woman in this room knows it. I do not want them to suffer for my crimes any more than they already have. I stand before you ready to accept your punishment. I only have one plea to make and that is that you honour the request of the Prime."

With that, he was done and he relinquished the podium to return to his daughter.

Kalistar took his hand as he sat next to her and Edwen smiled at her before whispering softly.

"You may never forgive me, but this is a price worth paying just to have you as my daughter."

"I know, father." She smiled despite the tears. "I know."

* * *

408

The Quorum deliberations lasted for no more than an hour.

When everyone was seated, the First Speaker delivered the Quorum's decision to the Imperator. Iran took the podium and looked at his old friend, unable to believe time had brought them to this place. Iran felt just as culpable and knew he would have to pay the price for allowing Edwen to do what he had. A part of him would always wonder if he was really duped by Edwen's tale of Cathomira, or was he deliberately oblivious because he was just as desperate to save the Empire?

"I have something to say before I reveal the Quorum's decision," Iran stared Edwen in the eye. General, we are not barbarians and we have a code of honour even in the most desperate situations. To save our Empire, your crime will remain a secret, but we here will always remember the horror of it. You didn't simply commit genocide on some random alien species. You destroyed a child of the White Star. The people of Earth were our brothers and sisters! They came to that planet on a Worldship!"

Iran paused, reining his emotions.

"We could have helped each other, Edwen. We could have asked them for help. They were young and we could have shown them where they came from. Now it's too late. To the survivors, we'll forever be the people who destroyed their civilisation."

Edwen broke Iran's gaze, remembering the same argument from a young Science Officer, twenty-three years ago. The Imperator was correct. It was too late.

"It is the decision of the Quorum," Iran said, after drawing a deep breath, "that you will be sentenced to permanent exile on the planet Earth."

"What sort of sentence is this?" Edwen exclaimed, taken aback at the decision. He had expected death. This was worse.

"The same sentence you passed on Officer Aaran, I believe. You will remain silent, General. I am not finished."

Edwen fell silent, but Garryn could see the distress on his face. The Quorum was wiser than he gave them credit. He never expected them to produce such an appropriate sentence for Edwen's crimes. It was more than the man deserved.

"The Quorum also agrees our children be spared the knowledge of what we now know. They need not be burdened with such terrible knowledge of their past. As you asked, General, we will think of them, if nothing else."

* * *

That night, after the sentence was given and the hearing concluded, Edwen was escorted home to gather whatever personal effects he might require for his exile. From there he would be taken to the Orbital Station and placed on a prison ship delivering him to Earth. Kalistar, refusing to abandon her father, was prepared to go with him into exile, despite Edwen's efforts to dissuade her.

410

When he realised she could not be deterred, he acquiesced and told his daughter to pack. Requesting privacy when he entered his study, the guards could not refuse him because he still commanded respect, whatever his crimes. There was no way for him to escape the room and it seemed a safe enough request.

When he did not emerge, they broke down the locked door and found the General dead. He was lying face down on his desk, an empty glass of wine next to his unmoving head. The contents smelled suspiciously of Night Rose, a poison made from a flower of the same name.

At his funeral, only the Imperator and Kalistar were present.

XXXIII

Sacrifice

The tale of the blue planet remained a secret.

No one would ever know about the third White Star world and how it paid for Brysdyn's survival with its children. Garryn met with Jonen's colleagues, mentalists Darix of Tesalone and Alwi of Rainab, to reveal what he learned at Cathomira. Due to the high nitrogen content in the planet's depleting ozone, the sky did appear blue from the surface of the planet. This was also the cause of the sun appearing yellow in his dreams. Despite Cathomira's destruction, Garryn was satisfied there was no other cause for suspicion.

The dismantling of Security Elite continued under Garryn's strict supervision. The members of the organisation were absorbed into the Imperial army and the Enclave was left deserted until some other use could be found for the building. Major Danten pleaded guilty for his complicity in the General's crime, but asked for no clemency. Sentenced to a penal colony on the far side of the Empire, he received none, and was given a life sentence.

But the damage was done.

Once the fallout from Security Elite's demise settled, the Imperator was left with an uncomfortable truth. His son could not replace him.

When the truth was revealed to Iran back in the Enclave, he knew there would be a price to be paid for his part in all this. True, he would never have sanctioned what Edwen did to Earth, but how hard had he questioned it when those children were brought to Brysdyn? Wasn't there a part of him wondering how this convenient miracle came to be? If the need was not so desperate, Iran knew he would have been more determined to learn the truth. His desire to save Brysdyn kept him from asking hard questions.

Now Edwen was dead and his precious Security Elite was gone. Iran knew he too had a price to pay and it would be Garryn.

There was no way he could allow Garryn to succeed him when the boy carried the ugly truth inside of him. Could he run the risk that someday Garryn would come to resent the Empire for what it did to his home world? The boy remembered his natural parents, he remembered their deaths. Could such resentment manifest itself and what would the consequences be to Brysdyn because of it?

* * *

"You want me to step down as Prime?" Garryn stared at his father in astonishment.

When Iran asked Garryn into his private study after the evening meal, Garryn assumed he wanted an update on the progress of Security Elite's dismantlement. Edwen had constructed a vast network of informants and resources needing careful redistribution. It never occurred to Garryn the Imperator's agenda was far more astonishing.

"Do you think I want you to?" Iran asked, unable to look at Garryn.

His father, who always seemed so alive and vital, now seemed decades older than his years. Garryn couldn't deny that the truth about Earth created a rift between them. They had always been close, but now there were uncomfortable silences that neither man dared to break. As the weeks had gone by, it had only seemed to worsen and, while father and son loved each other, they were at an impasse neither could overcome.

"Of course not, but that's not why you're asking me to leave, is it?"

When Iran looked at his son, Garryn saw the anguish in eyes. It hurt him to see his father this way. This man was his father. Whatever his origins, that would never change. He had been a good father, a good man Garryn admired and loved. At no point did Garryn blame the Imperator for what Edwen did, but it appeared he did not have to. Iran blamed himself enough as it was.

"Do you really want to stay?" Iran countered, studying his reaction closely.

"I am Prime. I have a responsibility to you, to El-lisha and to Brysdyn."

"That's not the question I asked. Do you want to stay? Do you want to become Prime? With everything you remember about Ther...I mean Earth, can you tell me in all honesty that your heart is still here?"

Garryn opened his mouth to respond, but stopped himself before he could say the words. He fell silent immediately, betrayed by how he almost answered.

"I don't want you to go, Gar," Iran stood and placed a hand on his shoulder. "I wish this never happened and you didn't know where you came from, but you do. With anything else, I would say we would get through it together, as a family, but not with this. You'd have to bury your feelings about Earth and perhaps you might learn to live with it, but you might not and what of your sister? She doesn't know and you'd have to lie to her or tell the truth."

Garryn blinked, unable to imagine shattering El-isha's world by such a revelation. His father was right. He knew, and every day he found himself thinking about what he'd lost on Earth. He thought about the mother and father, murdered in the fields so he could be stolen away. His name wasn't even Garryn.

"I can't simply leave..." he started to say, rallying a last bit of defiance to his father's words. "I couldn't put this on Ellisha."

"Your sister is strong, Gar. I think she would do quite well as Prime. In any case, I am far from retiring. Ellisha could marry and decided to pass over the line of succession to her children. It's not unworkable."

As Garryn stood in front of him, reflecting on his words, Iran could see that he'd thought about leaving before this moment. He was just never able to overcome the obstacle that was his responsibility to his family.

Garryn wanted to protest, but this was about more than just his own conflicted emotions. His father was telling Garryn to go because he had to. Iran was Imperator first and he could not gamble the future on an heir that might end up hating the people he was meant to govern. As much as he wanted things to stay the way they were, what his father proposed was inviting. To be able to walk away from the title of Prime and a life decided for him was more than he dared to dream. His father was giving him a chance to see it realised. Could he really refuse?

"I wish I never went to Cathomira," Garryn whispered, dropping his gaze to the floor. "I wish I never found out any of this."

"I wish that too. You'll always be my son. Nothing will ever change that, but you need to go. You would be an adequate Imperator, perhaps in time even a good one, but Brysdyn deserves better and so do you."

Iran watched as Garryn's shoulder slumped in defeat.

"I've tried so hard, father," Garryn admitted at last. "I've tried to forget I came from Earth, but I can't. You're right. I can't be Prime with this inside me. I can't be Imperator to Brysdyn when I know what Edwen did to save it."

"I know." It was killing Iran inside to do this, but a sacrifice had to be made for Garryn and Brysdyn's sake. "No one could and that is why I am letting you go. Go wherever you must and live. Ellisha and I will always be here if you need us."

* * *

Garryn found Kalistar at her father's estate.

Kalistar was the one person he'd avoided since his return to Brysdyn. Guilt at destroying her father kept Garryn from facing her. Even after Edwen's death, Garryn stayed away because he had no idea what he would say to her. The feeling seemed mutual, because Kalistar made no attempt to see him either. With his intention to leave Brysdyn for good, Garryn decided it was time they talked.

He found her in the gardens surrounding the house. According to the housekeeper, Kalistar spent a great deal of time on the well-manicured grounds, painting.

"Hello, Kal."

She was painting one of the better views of the city from the garden and, when she heard his voice, put the brush down slowly onto the palette to turn around. Her eyes widened at the sight of him, but

417

that was as much emotion that she cared to show. At that moment, she looked very much like Edwen's daughter. Mercurial.

"As I live and breathe, the Prime."

Garryn took a deep breath, telling himself again this was never supposed to be easy. "How are you, Kal?"

She raised a brow at the question. "I do well, Prime. To what do I owe this pleasure?"

"I came to say goodbye."

She raised a brow at that. "Goodbye?"

"I'm leaving Brysdyn for good."

"I see," she took the new with little reaction. "Well, thank you for your time and I wish you well." At that she turned around and resumed her painting.

"Kal," Garryn sighed, realising he would have to press the issue, "don't let us part like this."

She spun around and glared at him savagely. "What in Weaver's name is that supposed to mean to me? Do you think I will weep that you are leaving? You think I care after your reprehensible behaviour! I cared for you, Garryn, even though I never expected anything from you. I just wanted to be in your life. You discarded me like I was nothing. You couldn't even face me! You turned me out of the Domicile like some whore you paid for. I deserved better!"

Her words stung him, but it was the truth. Her anger was all she had left and Garryn would not deny her the chance to vent it. She was owed the opportunity to speak her mind.

"Kalistar," he said once she stopped speaking. "You're right. I behaved unforgivably. I am not going to waste your time or hurt you any more by making excuses. I don't have any. I didn't want to face you because of your father. What I did to him affected you and I didn't know how to say sorry for that. I care for you, Kal. I always will. And you are right, you do deserve better than me. I can only say I'm sorry."

There was no reason to linger and he didn't want to stretch this out longer than necessary. Giving her a nod, he turned around and started walking away.

"Wait! Where will you go?"

Garryn faced her again and answered with a shrug, "I don't know."

Kalistar knew better, "You'll go to Earth."

"What makes you say that?"

"Because I'm smarter than you, remember?" She gave him a said smile.

Her glacial demeanour thawed a little and she took a step towards him. He met her half way. They embraced in mid stride and held onto each other for a long time. For a while, at least, everything else seemed far away. He remembered their first meeting at the Myzyne Ball and how they'd caused a stir when he'd asked her to dance. He heard her breathe and remembered her soft cries the first time they made love. She was the one thing these past few months that was worth anything to him. Perhaps, someday, he might come back for her if she'd have him.

She pulled away first and wiped the tears from her eyes. "Take care of yourself, Garryn."

"Only if you do," he replied, her hand still in his.

"I will be fine, Prime, and I think you will be now."

Strangely enough, Garryn thought so too.

Epilogue

Justin Alexander sat on his porch staring into the parched landscape.

It was a glorious day, ideal for lazing away the afternoon in its golden heat. Although there was still a great deal of work left to do on the old house, it seemed too lovely a day to be wasted on toil. This kind of sunshine was delicious and intoxicating.

For the first time in years, he had all the time in the world and, at the moment, the world seemed very unconcerned with him.

Beyond the porch of the house, tall stalks of dried grass rustled as they swayed in the breeze. The heat carried by the wind left the landscape parched and dry, but this was nothing new. It was summer in this part of the world, as he understood it. Eventually the rains would come and make everything green again. Until then, he enough supplies to be comfortable and could take his time learning to grow things.

After all, it was supposed to be in his blood.

Behind him, he heard the wooden floor of the house creaking as soft footsteps approached. Justin glanced over his shoulder and saw the animal emerging from the flap cut into the doorway.

"Hello, Einstein," he greeted the animal with a smile.

The dog sauntered past his chair and sat down at his feet, its russet pelt shimmering in the sunshine. In the past few weeks, the animal had become a part of his life he simply could not do without. It followed him on long walks, ate with him at meal times and slept at the foot of his bed at night. He also found that it was quite useful as a sentry of sorts.

Justin wished he could say he'd found the dog but, in truth, it was the dog who'd found him. Shortly after he had taken up residence at the house, the animal had appeared out of the scrub, sniffing for food and perhaps a little companionship. Thanks to Hannah being able to translate some of the papers in the house, he was able to learn that the animal he remembered in his dream was named Einstein. It seemed appropriate.

"Maybe we'll go for a little walk later."

Einstein seemed content at this and lowered himself next to Justin's chair, content to laze the day away with his human companion.

It was hard to grasp how radically his life had changed in the past few months. It seemed like only yesterday he'd returned to this house and begun working to make it liveable, with Hannah's aid. He'd arrived here on a small ship he'd bought himself. While not as sophisticated as the *Wayward Son*, it served its purpose by allowing him to bring supplies, including a skimmer, from Brysdyn. It was berthed a short distance from the house, in one of the empty fields and lately Justin had begun using it to go exploring, with Einstein occupying the co-pilot's seat.

Thanks to Hannah, Justin learned the farm was called Makari, belonging to Helen and Cameron Alexander, his parents. Aaran's daughter was of great help to him during his first weeks here. She helped convert his language modulator to understand English and eventually helped him learn to read it. Now he was able to read most of the books scattered around the house.

After he'd settled, Justin had contacted Flinn to make good on his promise to show Hannah the worlds beyond Earth.

Even though she wouldn't be gone for very long, he was surprised by how much he missed her.

* * *

He looked up and saw it was almost dark.

The sun dragged a blanket of twilight over the sky as it prepared to sleep. The air was still warm, but temperatures around these parts plunged drastically at night. He rose to his feet lazily, feeling the stiffness in his joints creak in protest as he stretched his cramped muscles. He could hear the dog in the house and, upon investigation, sighted the animal in the kitchen sniffling at its empty food bowl.

"Okay, I get the hint, time for dinner."

A roar rumbled across the sky, but the sound did not alarm him. Lifting his eyes to the evening sky, he saw a familiar shape descending into the fields beyond the house. The dog ran out of the house at the powerful reverberation and stood on the porch, yapping in short, harsh barks. Justin watched long enough to see the bright glow of landing lights in the distance.

"Looks like we're getting company for dinner, Einstein," Justin commented. Einstein was not so easily appeased and continued his barking.

By the time his visitors approached the house, it was after dark. Einstein resumed his barking again as they were drawn to the lights of the house. He stepped onto the porch and placed a calming hand on the animal for silence as he saw his guests coming through the front gate.

"Nice pet," Flinn Ester complimented, studying the animal with a mixture of curiosity and suspicion.

"You're his first visitors." Justin grinned, pleased to see Flinn and Hannah. "Come on in, I've got dinner cooking."

Flinn made a face. "Brysdynian ration packs. That should be appetising."

Hannah gave the pilot a look and nudged him the ribs. "Thanks Gar...I mean, Justin."

As they walked up the porch steps, the dog's initial caution melted away to curiosity and he inspected the visitors with a gingerly sniff. Hannah bent down to pat it gently on the forehead and the animal began licking her hand to get better knowledge of her scent.

"Well, he likes you," Justin replied.

"I used to have one," she answered, following the two men into the house. "When I was a kid."

"Hey," Flinn remarked, looking around the house with approval. "You've really fixed this place up."

"You've gotten so much done since I last saw it," Hannah complimented as well.

The last time she'd been here, the house was in the dilapidated condition they had found it in when Garryn first arrived on Earth. While it was nowhere near complete, Justin's improvements using Brysdynian technology were obvious. Furniture was repaired, windowpanes were fused into place and the place bore an appealing look of warmth.

"Thanks," Justin gestured at them to sit at the dining table. As they took their places, he went to check on the progress of the food cooking on the stove. "It has been educational trying to get half this stuff to work, but I managed to do it without blowing up too many things."

"I'm not surprised," Flinn answered, studying Einstein who was sniffing at his leg. He ran his hands though the fur on the dog's flank and gave it a little scratch. Einstein panted his approval.

When dinner was finally served, the three friends caught up on old times. It was the second time Flinn had come here to see him. The first time was when Flinn collected Hannah to take her off world. Justin could not deny he was glad for their company. Even with Einstein, it did get a bit lonely at times. While

Justin had a communication device in his own ship, nothing could take the place of human contact.

"How are you finding your sightseeing tour of the galaxy?" Justin asked Hannah.

"I spend a great deal of time trying to keep him out of trouble," she laughed.

"Let me guess, during his card games?" Justin gave Flinn a look.

"I don't get into that much trouble," Flinn protested, but his smirk indicated it was exactly as Justin guessed.

"Enough to keep me busy," she added before all three of them broke out into a short laugh. "I'll be sick of it in a few months and come home."

Justin didn't ask her where home was. He hoped it wasn't a continent away where he'd found her and her parents, but rather nearby so he could see her. Still, her comment implied this return was premature and that made Justin wonder why.

"So what brings you back now? It couldn't just be to eat ration packs. What's happened?" Justin questioned, eyeing Flinn suspiciously.

Flinn tensed, exchanging a glance with Hannah, who looked decidedly uncomfortable and unable to meet Justin's gaze. For a moment, Justin felt a surge of panic, expecting the worst. Was something wrong with his father and sister? Logic prevailed and he told himself if it were anything that bad, Flinn would have told him already.

The news was bad, he concluded, but not tragic.

"All right," Flinn conceded with a loud sigh, "it came over the Transband about two days ago. I thought we'd better tell you before you went home and found out for yourself."

"Tell me what?"

"Your father is getting married again," Hannah declared, sparing Flinn the trouble.

Justin tried to hide his shock, but could not. His father was getting married again? Justin never imagined Iran would want to after Aisha's passing. Then again, why shouldn't he? He was young enough to take another wife. Still, he shouldn't be surprised either. Without even meeting his stepmother, Justin knew she was young and capable of bearing children. There was more than enough time for an heir if Ellisha refused to be Prime.

"I never thought he would," Justin admitted, his shock yet to fully dissipate.

A part of him was affronted at his mother being replaced, but the sentiment did not last. His father was a good man who deserved happiness. It was hard enough being Imperator without having one's family torn apart by death and circumstance. If Iran saw a chance of happiness, then Justin would not begrudge him for it.

That wasn't it, he realised when he looked at Flinn and Hannah again. They were still tense.

"Is that it?" he ventured to ask.

"No, Justin." This time it was Flinn who spoke. "He's marrying Kalistar."

For a moment he thought he'd heard incorrectly and was unable to respond. It took only a glance at both their faces for Justin to realise he hadn't misspoken. The expression on his friend's face left no doubt in his mind. Flinn would not have flown all the way here otherwise.

"How did it happen?" Justin asked and then realised Flinn would not be privy to such information.

"We don't really know. We just heard the announcement, that he'd picked a new consort and it was Kalistar. They're going to be married next year."

He always knew Kalistar could find someone after he'd left her behind, but he never thought it would be his father of all people. Yet the more he thought about it, the more sense it made. As unpalatable as it was to him, it wasn't an outrageous choice.

Kalistar had spent a great deal of time in the Domicile when he left Brysdyn to find out the truth about Earth. Who was he to say her time spent in the Imperator's company did not impress upon Iran her suitability as a mate? If Kalistar reminded Justin of his mother, then wouldn't she have the same effect on his father?

"It makes sense, I suppose. She is young, healthy, beautiful and intelligent. If he was going to pick someone, she's an excellent choice."

Understanding didn't make it easier to bear. In his own way, he cared for Kalistar. He remembered thinking he might go back for her when their wounds were sufficiently healed. Hearing this felt like the door slamming closed on his life on Brysdyn for good. The finality of it left him shaken.

"Are you alright?" Hannah asked, resting a sympathetic hand on his shoulder.

"I'm fine," he assured her, even if it did sting. Justin knew he had no right to complain about how Kalistar conducted herself. He was the one who'd turned his back on her. She deserved the chance to be happy, even if it was with his father. Besides, the person she knew was no more.

Garryn the Prime was gone and in his place was Justin Alexander.

Justin was the person he'd sacrificed everything to be. He knew the price for his freedom and paid it, because his destiny lay here on Earth. It was still a beautiful world, even after Edwen destroyed its people. In his journeys across the planet, Justin had seen unlimited potential, just like the White Star settlers who had claimed this world for their own.

The survivors of Earth were lost and frightened, disconnected from each other because Edwen tore apart their community. Justin didn't know whether or not he was the person to help them find it again, but he knew he was of Earth and his future lay here.

Beyond that, he could only dream.

Dear reader,

We hope you enjoyed reading *Children of the White Star*. Please take a moment to leave a review, even if it's a short one. Your opinion is important to us.

Discover more books by Linda Thackeray at
https://www.nextchapter.pub/authors/linda-thackeray-science-fiction-fantasy-author-australia

Want to know when one of our books is free or discounted? Join the newsletter at
http://eepurl.com/bqqB3H

Best regards,
Linda Thackeray and the Next Chapter Team

You might also like:
Alternate Purpose by Christopher Coates

To read the first chapter for free, please head to:
https://www.nextchapter.pub/books/alternate-purpose

About the Author

Linda Thackeray works at an online educational service a stone's throw from the Sydney Opera House in Australia, but lives on the coast in a suburb called Woy Woy, which apparently means "big lagoon" with her two cats Newt and Humphrey. She has been writing for as long as she can remember and doesn't care if she ever has fame and fortune. She just needs to let the characters out of her head so she can think straight. It's getting pretty busy in there.

Also Published by this Author

The Queen of Carleon

When Arianne is told by her mother that her unborn son will cover the lands of Avalyne in darkness, she sets off on a quest to ensure this terrible future never comes to pass. Accompanied by the warrior Celene of Angarad and Keira of the Green, Arianne is in a race against time, as an ancient evil prepares to supplant her son's soul with a monster.

This is a tale of adventure, romance and frendship, with an epic battle between good and evil for the soul of an innocent.

The Easterling

In her dreams, Melia hears her mother screaming.

When Watch Guard Melia sets out to find her mother, Ninuie, elf Prince Aeron of Eden Halas joins her as her guide across his homeland to find Tor Iolan, the abandoned fortress where the agents of the Aeth Lord tortured and maimed innocents for their master. Within its cruel walls, Melia hopes to find truth about her past while pondering a future with a prince, who has yet to learn that falling for a mortal may cost him more than a broken heart.

This is a tale of darkness, romance and loss where Melia and Aeron are faced with the reality that some-times love may not be enough and sacrifice may be the only course left to them.

Hunter's Haven

After taking revenge on a drug lord and his crew for murdering his sister, John Hunter is a wanted man. It's 2030 and in the aftermath of the great plague, John makes his way to Haven, craving sanctuary and peace but instead runs into a rogue religious group who wants to play God even as they run rife with corruption. But they haven't counted on meeting big bad John who's meaner than they could ever be. And just when they think they've put him out of their misery, he's resurrected from his hospital bed and hell hath no fury like a hunter scorned...who's become a devil with a cause!

HUNTER'S HAVEN is an action packed thriller that grabs you by the throat and won't let go until the end of the book. To miss this incredible adventure would be criminal! Get your copy today and enjoy the read of a lifetime.

Children of the White Star
ISBN: 978-4-86751-208-1 (Mass Market)

Published by
Next Chapter
1-60-20 Minami-Otsuka
170-0005 Toshima-Ku, Tokyo
+818035793528
29th June 2021

Lightning Source UK Ltd.
Milton Keynes UK
UKHW041503150721
387206UK00001B/27